PRIMARY VALOR

(THE FORGING OF LUKE STONE—BOOK 5)

JACK MARS

Jack Mars

Jack Mars is the USA Today bestselling author of the LUKE STONE thriller series, which includes seven books. He is also the author of the new FORGING OF LUKE STONE prequel series, comprising six books; and of the AGENT ZERO spy thriller series, comprising twelve books.

Jack loves to hear from you, so please feel free to visit www.Jackmarsauthor.com to join the email list, receive a free book, receive free giveaways, connect on Facebook and Twitter, and stay in touch!

ISBN: 978-1-0943-7396-6

BOOKS BY JACK MARS

LUKE STONE THRILLER SERIES

ANY MEANS NECESSARY (Book #1)
OATH OF OFFICE (Book #2)
SITUATION ROOM (Book #3)
OPPOSE ANY FOE (Book #4)
PRESIDENT ELECT (Book #5)
OUR SACRED HONOR (Book #6)
HOUSE DIVIDED (Book #7)

FORGING OF LUKE STONE PREQUEL SERIES

PRIMARY TARGET (Book #1)
PRIMARY COMMAND (Book #2)
PRIMARY THREAT (Book #3)
PRIMARY GLORY (Book #4)
PRIMARY VALOR (Book #5)
PRIMARY DUTY (Book #6)

AN AGENT ZERO SPY THRILLER SERIES

AGENT ZERO (Book #1)
TARGET ZERO (Book #2)
HUNTING ZERO (Book #3)
TRAPPING ZERO (Book #4)
FILE ZERO (Book #5)
RECALL ZERO (Book #6)
ASSASSIN ZERO (Book #7)
DECOY ZERO (Book #8)
CHASING ZERO (Book #9)
VENGEANCE ZERO (Book #10)
ZERO ZERO (Book #11)
ABSOLUTE ZERO (Book #12)

CHAPTER ONE

March 24, 2006
12:05 a.m. Eastern Standard Time
Wrightsville Beach
North Carolina

Charlotte was drunk on the beach.

She was sixteen years old, and she had slipped out of her mom's house to come to this party. It was clever, and daring, the way she did it. It went like this:

She had told her mom, and her mom's boyfriend Jeff, that she was tired and was going to bed early. She said she had an exam in the morning. Tomorrow was Friday, a school day. The test was in World History. It was a hard class.

There was no test, of course.

Her mom would be up and off to work early. Jeff was rich, didn't seem to work at all and never got up before noon. When Charlotte left, the two of them were watching a movie in the TV room, like they often did.

Charlotte locked the knob on her bedroom door, then pulled it shut behind her as she entered the hall. She had stashed a bookbag with her party clothes in the garage. She quietly slipped past the TV room, into the laundry room, then out into the silent three-car garage. If they happened to catch her, she was dressed in sweatpants and a Hello Kitty T-shirt—she was going to bed, but had wandered down to the laundry room to look for some socks she was missing. And wouldn't you know it? She had locked herself out of her bedroom!

But it didn't come to that. Instead, she moved through the garage.

Mom's white Volvo was there. Jeff's BMW convertible and his classic old Hudson from the 1940s were there. Jeff went crazy if someone touched that car. He drove it like once a year to show off.

Charlotte picked up her bag and went to the side door of the garage. Her heart skipped a beat. She had pulled this off a few times before, but she was still nervous. There was a stone walkway out there, flanked by bushes and leading around to the front of the house. Her mom never set the house alarm until she was going to bed. A lot of times she forgot to set it at all.

Charlotte took a deep breath, went through the door, closed it carefully behind her, and she was outside the house. Her friend Taylor was waiting for her three blocks away. The party was at Taylor's house on the beach. Taylor was eighteen, and had graduated last year. Taylor's parents were away in the Bahamas.

Taylor would drop Charlotte off at school tomorrow morning like none of this had ever happened. When Charlotte got home in the afternoon, she would tell Jeff she accidentally locked herself out of her room again, and he would open the lock with a screwdriver. Charlotte was a little spacey like that—she locked herself out of her room sometimes.

Now, on the beach, she breathed the cool night air.

Rob was a little bit ahead of her, laughing and shouting about something. The waves were crashing, drowning out what he was saying. There must be a storm at sea, the waves were so big.

Behind them, what seemed like all the lights were on at Taylor's mansion. The pool area was lit up. There were only about ten kids at the party—it was a school night, after all—but Taylor liked to do things big. The music was booming. Charlotte could no longer make out the songs, but she could still hear the rumble of the bass.

Her head was spinning with sensations. Two vodka tonics. Taylor poured them heavy. The cold air—the chill was reaching her now. She had just climbed out of the hot tub, and was wearing only a bikini with a plush towel wrapped around her. The freedom of being out, the freedom of having a friend like Taylor, one of the real super rich.

The surge of fear at the risks she had taken to get here.

The surge of… feelings… maybe… that she had about Rob.

Butterflies in her stomach.

It was a crazy night.

"Rob!" she shouted. "Rob! Where are you going?"

"Come on!" he shouted.

He was tall and blond, a year older than her, on the football team, a lifeguard in the summer. His hair was nice—it flopped down in front of his eyes. He was cute, and had a great body. He was buff. That's what everybody said. Rob was buff. He wasn't wrapped in a towel. He was just wearing red shorts. Wasn't he cold?

It was dark out here. There was no moon tonight. And it was getting way too cold now. She wanted to go back to the house. The sand was cold on her feet. A chill went through her and gooseflesh rose up on her skin.

"Rob!"

Suddenly he was right in front of her, and she bumped into him. He was like a foot taller than her.

"Hey you," he said.

"Hey."

He made a face, eyeing her suspiciously. "You okay, pretty girl?"

"I'm cold. I want to go back to the house."

"Already? Come on. Stay out here with me. I'll keep you warm."

He slipped his big arms around her, and she let him do it.

Now the sensations were stronger than ever. She pressed against him and shivered. But then everything changed.

Suddenly, there was a shadow in the darkness with them. No, it was two shadows. She and Rob were pulled apart somehow. She fell to the sand.

She looked up.

"Rob?"

Rob was still there, on his feet. There were also two men, fully dressed. They were wearing dark hoods, like ski masks.

One pulled Rob back by the hair. The other punched him. Rob struggled with them for a few seconds. But then he was down on the sand, too. The men were punching him, and then kicking him.

Why? Why were they doing that?

"Rob!"

Charlotte jumped up, threw her towel away, and ran back toward the house. It was there in front of her, lights blazing, music thumping, tantalizingly close, but much too far away. She ran and ran.

"Help!" she screamed. "HELP!"

The waves crashed behind her, the ocean roaring.

She gasped for air.

A hand gripped her hair from behind.

An instant later, a strong arm was around her waist. It was the strongest arm she had ever felt—stronger than Rob, and he was a football player.

"Hold on, my friend," a voice growled in her ear. "Wait a moment."

She tried to kick and punch, but now the other man was there. He circled around and stood in front of her. All she could see of his face were his eyes inside the mask. He held a hand out. There was a small towel in his hand. He pushed it against her face. It had a sweet smell.

She tried to turn away, but couldn't. Strong hands shoved her face into the cloth.

In a few seconds, she began to feel dizzy. The lights of the house, looming *right there*, began to fade. It no longer occurred to her to scream, or try to move her head.

Slowly, slowly, everything went black.

CHAPTER TWO

6:01 a.m. Eastern Standard Time
South Ward
Newark, New Jersey

Luke Stone felt the acceleration of the armored car as it turned the final corner and started its run toward the house.

"One minute," the team leader said. He was three people up the bench to Luke's left.

"Rock and roll," someone on the other side of the truck said.

"Move fast," the team leader said. He stood, holding onto the railing above his head. He was helmeted, visor down, making his features hard to see. Luke knew him as a tall guy with a bushy beard and Coke bottle glasses strapped on his face, former 1st Special Forces captain. The guy seemed utterly fearless. This was not his first rodeo.

"Hit hard. No hesitation. It's all bad guys in there. Do not let them give you one second of fight."

Luke couldn't see the house from where he was sitting, but he could recall every detail of it in his mind. He had studied the photographs and the house plans.

It was a low-slung, one-story bungalow in a neighborhood of very similar homes. The front yard, and the property around it, was overgrown and choked with weeds. A couple of small bicycles lay on their sides near the wall.

The place was five blocks from a massive landfill—if it weren't for the dump trucks constantly driving on top of it, and the flocks of seagulls diving from the sky for scraps, the grassy landfill could be mistaken for a small mountain, like a park for people to go walking and hiking.

There were three bedrooms and one bathroom inside, the bedrooms down a narrow hall. The living room was where you entered the front door. A combined kitchen and dining room. In the kitchen was a door leading down to an underground cellar. There was a fenced-in backyard, as weed-choked and overgrown as the front.

A squad of doorbusters from the Drug Enforcement Agency were likely hopping the fence into the yard at this second. A DEA helicopter with a sniper in the doorway was trailing this armored truck by about a quarter of a mile. It would arrive seconds after the truck.

"Thirty seconds," the team leader said.

The engine of the big armored truck increased in pitch. They were really moving now.

Luke glanced across at Ed Newsam. Ed sat on the opposite fiberglass bench, helmeted, visor up, black tactical vest with the letters DEA in white across the front. His shotgun rested across his knees. Ed and Luke were both bunched between other men in black jumpsuits, helmets, tactical vests. The line of men all looked like so many nameless, faceless storm troopers.

Luke's eyes met Ed's. Ed nodded, but Luke couldn't read those eyes. The two of them were on an interagency loan. They were here as guests, to do an outside assessment of a drug house takedown. They'd driven up from Washington, DC, thirty-six hours ago. These were good guys, but Ed and Luke barely knew them.

The team leader swayed with the movement of the truck.

"Here… we… go!"

Luke glanced past him at the front. The truck was wide open and he could look through the windshield, seeing what the driver was seeing.

The house was straight ahead. Pale yellow, long faded; brown shingle roof with a slight overhang. It was coming fast.

The truck burst through the fencing and down the short incline of the driveway to the house. It bumped and bounced over the uneven gravel. The driveway dead-ended at a picture window, blinds drawn. The truck was headed right for it.

"Impact!" the driver shouted.

Luke braced himself without thinking.

BOOOM.

The truck crashed through the window and the wall that held it. Luke caught a glimpse of the glass and the wall—aluminum siding, outer wall, Sheetrock, all of it—exploding inward.

He put his visor down.

Then the back door was open and he was up and moving.

"Go! Go! GO!"

Ed and the man next to him were out the door ahead of Luke. Luke landed on the carpet of the living room with both feet.

"DOWN!" someone shouted. "DOWN!"

Two helmeted figures in black threw a guy in a T-shirt and jeans to the floor. A table was upended, several guns, money, and bags of white powder flying. One beefy man in black wrestled the guy onto his stomach, pulling his arms behind him.

Then Luke was moving down the hall, steps behind Ed and the other man. Their target was the third bedroom. Agents were bursting into rooms right and left. Their chatter came through the speaker inside Luke's helmet. Ed hit a door to his right and blasted through it. The next agent went in. Luke was three steps behind.

"Drop it!" he heard a voice shout. It was Ed.

Luke turned the corner. Ed was there in the room, his huge body crouching forward. His shotgun was in his left hand, pointed upward toward the ceiling. His right hand was extended, fingers splayed out.

Across the room, in front of a narrow twin bed mattress on the floor, was a kid. Luke absorbed everything about him in a split second.

He was a skinny black kid in a white T-shirt and blue shorts. His feet were bare. His thick hair was out in a crazy Afro, a bright green plastic pick protruding from it. He seemed like he was twelve years old but could have been a little older. Regardless, he looked barely strong enough to hold up the rifle he was leveling at Ed.

"Wait," Ed said. "Wait. Don't you do it."

The DEA agent with them was in a two-handed stance just inside the door, his Glock pointed at the kid.

"Drop it!" the agent shouted.

"Wait," Ed said again.

BANG!

The kid fired. The round hit Ed's vest and knocked him backwards against the wall.

BANG! BANG! BANG!

The DEA agent fired three times in fast succession.

The kid bucked and shivered as the rounds ripped through him. He dropped his gun, his head drooping at the top of his neck for a second. His eyes seemed surprised, like the possibility that he might get shot, that he might in fact die, had never occurred to him before this moment. His shoulders dropped and he slid bonelessly to the mattress. The kid's white shirt, and the dingy white sheet on the mattress, instantly began to turn red.

"Man down!" Luke shouted into his microphone. "Man down!"

"Medic!" the DEA agent shouted into his own mic. "We need a medic in here!"

Luke went to Ed. It seemed as if Luke's feet were floating several inches above the ground. Bad memories flooded his mind.

Suddenly, the drug house was gone, and Luke was *back there*. Afghanistan, along the eastern border with Pakistan. A long, bad night in a dust storm. A bad mission, poorly conceived and planned.

He was in a stone house inside a walled compound. A large back room. Luke's team had fought their way through the house to reach this room. The floors were covered in thick, overlapping carpets. The walls were hung with carpets—ornate, richly colored carpets depicting vast landscapes—deserts, mountains, jungles, waterfalls.

Luke glanced around the room. There seemed to be corpses everywhere.

Luke went to one man in particular, a huge lump of a man. It was Hendricks. Wayne.

WAYNE.

He was still moving.

Luke kneeled by him and pulled off his helmet.

Wayne's arms and legs were moving slowly, almost like he was treading water.

"Wayne! Where are you hit?"

Wayne's eyes rolled. They found Luke. He shook his head. He began to cry. He was breathing heavily, almost gasping for air.

"Oh, buddy..." Wayne said.

"Wayne! Talk to me."

Feverishly, Luke began to unfasten Wayne's ballistic vest.

"Medic!" he screamed. "Medic!"

Wayne was hit in the chest. Somehow shrapnel had gotten under his vest. Luke's hands searched him. He was also shot high in the leg. That was worse than the chest, by a lot. His pants were saturated with blood. His femoral artery must be hit. Luke's hand came away dripping red. There was blood everywhere. There was a lake of it under Wayne's body. It was a miracle he was still alive.

"Tell Katie," Wayne said.

"Shut up!" Luke said. "You're going to tell her yourself."

Wayne's voice was barely above a whisper.

"Tell her..."

Wayne seemed to be looking at something far away. He gazed, and then did a double take, as if confused by what he was seeing. An instant later, his eyes became still.

He stared at Luke. His mouth was slack. Nobody was home.

Just like that, Wayne was dead. Luke's blood brother. The godfather of Luke's unborn son. A long, helpless breath went out of Luke.

Luke shook his head to clear it. Now, he kneeled over Ed. For a moment, Ed didn't move at all. His eyes were closed.

"Come on!"

Luke felt for a pulse at Ed's neck. It was strong. Fast. Ed's heart was pounding, probably from all the excitement.

Ed opened his eyes.

"How you feeling?" Luke said.

Ed stared at Luke. For a moment, he didn't say anything. Harsh breaths escaped him. He struggled to speak.

"The kid?" he said finally.

Luke looked across the room. The kid was a bloody wreck on the mattress. The DEA agent was pumping the kid's chest. Another agent came storming in, helmet off, and kneeled next to the first one.

Luke shook his head. "Doesn't look good."

Ed made a sound like a groan.

Luke paused, then started again. "You hurt?"

Ed touched his chest where the round had hit him. He pulled the smashed bullet out of the front mesh of his vest. "Only my feelings."

"He's gone," one of the agents across the room said.

Ed closed his eyes for a long moment, then opened them again. He shook his head. "God," he said. "He was only a child."

* * *

"I thought I lost you there for a second," Luke said.

It was later that day, early afternoon. They drove south on the New Jersey Turnpike in a nondescript government sedan, Luke at the wheel. They were dressed in white shirts and ties. Their sports jackets were draped over the back seat. In a few miles, they would reach the Delaware Memorial Bridge. Ed stared out at the passing woods.

Traffic wasn't bad. It was a sunny day in early spring.

Ed nodded. "Me too."

"I think there's an important point to realize here," Luke said.

Ed shrugged his big shoulders. He seemed noncommittal.

"Do tell."

"You can't control what people do," Luke said. "You can't control if a kid is going to get mixed up in drug dealing at an early age. You can't control if a kid is going to pick up a gun. But given your skills, to a large degree you CAN control whether that kid gets a chance to shoot you or not."

"That kid should have been in school," Ed said. "In a just world, he would have been."

Luke shrugged. "In a perfect world, anyway."

"It doesn't take a perfect world to put sixteen-year-old kids in school," Ed said.

"I joined the Army at seventeen," Luke said.

Ed shook his head. "In any case, whether the kid is in school or is in a drug house with a gun, I don't want to be the man who pulls that trigger. I do not envy that DEA guy. He's got years of thinking ahead of him."

The kid in question was Shavod Michael Holmes. He went by the street nickname Ice Cold. He had turned sixteen two months ago. He had grown up in foster care, had a list of prior arrests as long as his own arm, including crimes that would be felonies if he were an adult, and he had been in and out of juvenile detention facilities since the age of thirteen. He had died at the scene.

The house had about $151,000 in cash inside of it, cocaine with a street value of nearly $2 million, and a dozen guns of various calibers. All of this was left in the custody of three individuals, the eldest of whom turned out to be twenty, not quite old enough to legally buy himself a beer.

Ed had gotten lucky. He was going to be sore for several days. Probably have a funny lump on his chest tomorrow.

"Yeah," Luke said. "He probably has a lot of thinking to do."

You could tell yourself anything you wanted. The kid had a gun. I had to kill him. But at night, lying in bed with his eyes open and staring at the ceiling, that guy was liable to play the scene over in his head ten thousand times. And he was liable to weigh everything that happened against the fact that *it was a kid.*

A kid has his whole life ahead of him. A kid is not set in stone. A kid can change, no matter what has come before. A kid, even a kid in a drug house with a gun in his hands, to some extent is innocent.

Ed hadn't wanted to kill that kid, but the kid was fine with killing Ed. Now Ed was lucky to be alive. And the kid was dead.

Luke drove onto the massive bridge. It rose ahead of them, seemingly straight up, high into the air above the Delaware River. Ed stared out his window, seemingly fascinated by the oil storage tanks along the river banks.

"What are you thinking about?" Luke said.

"Cassandra's pregnant," Ed said.

Luke smiled. "Yes. I'm well aware of that."

Cassandra was now LARGE with child. That baby was going to come bounding out of there any time now. Ed and Cassandra didn't know what sex it was. They had chosen to go old school, get the ultrasounds to ensure the baby's health, but decline to know whether it was a boy or a girl. They were going to find out on the day the baby was born.

Given the sheer size of Cassandra's belly, and the sheer force of Ed's vitality, Luke was willing to bet that it was a boy coming, a very large boy.

"So I'm thinking about my child," Ed said. "And I'm thinking about this world my child is coming into."

CHAPTER THREE

Time Unknown
Place Unknown

Charlotte was tired. Very, very tired.

She could barely open her eyes. At first, she didn't know why she was even awake. After a moment, she understood. A sound was waking her up. And the sound was still happening.

CLAP! CLAP!

She looked up. A woman was standing several feet across the room from her. The woman was pretty, with dark hair. She was older, maybe what they called middle-aged. She wore a green turtleneck sweater and green pants. The clothes were nice, and fit the woman very well. You would say the clothes looked expensive, as if they were designer made. The woman was staring down at Charlotte and clapping her hands.

CLAP! CLAP!

"Wake up, girl. Are you awake?"

Charlotte nodded. She didn't see any point in pretending otherwise. She and the woman had already made eye contact.

"Then sit up, if you're awake."

Slowly, Charlotte pushed herself into a cross-legged sitting position. It took a lot of effort, and she almost lost her balance. She could barely keep her chin up. She looked at the spot where she had just been curled up. There were a couple of pillows there. She looked down at herself, and where she was sitting.

She was on a large, soft cushion, like something a dog would sleep on, only bigger. She was wearing a light blue sweater and dark blue jeans. The sweater said something on it, but she couldn't seem to make out the words. She stared and stared. The word was upside down from her. It was a long word. She remembered it from another time. It had some meaning.

Nantucket.

This was not her sweater. Nantucket was a place, and she had never been there.

She was also wearing soft pink socks. They were very nice, comfortable and warm. Someone had put clothes on her. The last thing she remembered, she had been wearing a bikini on the beach. It was cold out. She had been on the beach with…

"Rob?" she said out loud.

The woman shook her head and came closer.

"Don't worry about that. That's all over now."

The woman stood over her, and for the first time, Charlotte realized there were bars between them. The bars were not thick. They were thin, like the bars of a cage that you would put a large dog in. She looked around again.

She was inside exactly that kind of cage. The top of the cage was just above her head. She couldn't stand up, even if she wasn't so dizzy. She reached out and touched one of the bars with her fingers.

"Yes," the woman said. "You're in a cage, for now. It's for your own safety."

"Where am I?"

The woman crouched down until she was on Charlotte's level. They faced each other through the bars.

"You're on your way to your new home."

The woman had green eyes. They were very green. You might call them emerald eyes. There was no kindness in those eyes. They were hard eyes.

"We're in an airplane, if you hadn't noticed."

Charlotte hadn't noticed. She looked around the room again. It was small, like a storage room. There were no windows. There was nothing to give away the fact that this was an airplane.

But now she realized the room was vibrating. There was that faint vibration, like a plane flying across the sky. Every now and then, there was a lurch as the plane hit a spot of turbulence. And there was that sound, the loud background hum of the engines.

"Have you been on an airplane before?"

Charlotte nodded. "Yes."

Of course she had. She had flown to New York and Boston with her mom. She went to California once, with her dad. They went to San Francisco and also saw giant redwood trees. She had flown down to Disney World three times when she was a kid. She had been on planes a lot.

"And yet, you didn't notice you were on one now, did you?"

Charlotte felt something she didn't remember feeling before. It seemed to take a long time to put a name on it. The name was helpless.

She was inside a cage. Everything had to be pointed out to her. Things that should be obvious, she did not notice. She couldn't remember… anything. She had no idea who this woman was. She had no idea where she was. And that made her sad. She felt like she might start crying at any second.

"I want to see my mother," she said.

The woman shook her head. "I'm your mother now."

Charlotte stared at her.

"It's okay," the woman said. "You'll understand everything in time. Are you hungry?"

Charlotte realized, only after the woman asked, that she was hungry. She had no idea what time it was, or when she last ate. She had no idea if it was night or day. She didn't know anything. Except that she was on a plane, and she was very, very hungry.

She nodded. "Yes."

"My name is Elaine," the woman said. "At first, you will call me Mistress Elaine, or even Mistress. That's my title. You'll never just call me Elaine, not for a while, anyway. Do you understand?"

Charlotte stared at her. She did not understand. It sounded like crazy talk.

"What's your name?" the woman said.

"Charlotte."

"Charlotte what?"

Charlotte thought for a moment. Her brain wasn't working. Then she remembered the strong hand pushing the scented cloth in her face. They had drugged her. That's why she couldn't think.

"Charlotte Richmond."

Now the woman shook her head. It wasn't a sad shake. It was the simple head shake of someone refuting false information.

"That's not your name, not anymore. It was never really your name. They lied to you. The truth is you don't have a name. Maybe one day you will have a name, if you're good and you learn to obey. We may send you out into the world with a name. But if that happens, it will be in the future. Right now, you don't have a name. You're just a number. Not a name. Do you understand? You're number 21."

Charlotte mouthed the number, without saying it aloud. 21.

"Do you see what I have here?" the woman said. She gestured on the floor next to her. It was a plate, covered by a glass top. Steam rose inside of it, obscuring the contents.

"It's a hamburger. It's very good. We only have the best food. Do you like hamburgers?"

Charlotte nodded.

"I will give you this hamburger to eat. But first I need you to answer a question. It's an easy question, and I want you to answer to the best of your ability. Okay?"

"Okay," Charlotte said.

The woman looked at her intently. There were those green eyes again. Charlotte got the sense of a bird of prey, a hawk, circling high above a small rodent skittering on the ground and trying to hide.

"What's your name?"

She had just told this woman her name. Did she not understand it the first time? Did she not believe it?

"Charlotte."

The woman shook her head again.

"It was a trick question. The right answer is you don't have a name. You have a number. It's 21. That's your number. 21. It has always been your number."

Charlotte stared at her.

"Please stick your right hand through the bars," the woman said.

Without thinking, Charlotte did as she was told. She didn't know why. It seemed important right now that she obey. Her hand was just small enough to fit through the bars if she held her fingers tightly together.

The woman grabbed the hand. Charlotte tried to pull it back, but it was too late. The woman's grip was too strong.

"What's your name?"

"Char…"

A long thin reed of some kind had materialized in the woman's other hand. She brought it down hard across the back of Charlotte's hand. It stung.

"Ow!"

"You don't have a name. What's your number?"

"Wait!"

The woman brought the reed down again. Charlotte stared at the spot. Instantly, a red welt appeared there.

"What's your number, girl?"

Charlotte hesitated.

The switch came down again.

"What is it? What's your number?"

"I don't remember!"

The switch came down again. It hurt. It hurt a lot. But Charlotte could not pull her hand away from this woman. Why was she doing this?

"Stop!"

"Your number is 21."

The switch came down again.

"Ow! Stop! Please stop. You're hurting me."

Charlotte's hand was turning bright red. It looked like any second it would start to bleed.

"What's your number?"

"It's 21," Charlotte said. She burst into tears. "Please."

"Tell me. Say, my number is 21."

Charlotte closed her eyes. "My number is 21."

She felt the tears welling under her closed eyelids.

The woman's strong grip released. Charlotte opened her eyes and guided the abused hand back inside her cage. She had to squeeze it tight to get it through the bars. Even doing that much hurt. It hurt as her skin scraped against the metal.

Now the tears began to stream down her face.

"Good girl, 21. Please try to remember that. Your number is 21."

"I want to go home."

The woman stared at her for a long moment. There was no kindness in those eyes at all. It was like looking into the eyes of a shark.

The woman's mouth made a thin line. It was something like a smile. Any second, she could open that mouth wide, and there would be rows of serrated teeth, like a shark, or a monster.

"We decide when you go home," that mouth said. "We even decide where your home is. You see, you belong to us now. You were given away, like a bag of used clothes. Like trash. No one wanted you anymore. So now we decide how much value you have."

They stared across the bars at each other for another long moment.

What could this possibly mean? She wasn't trash. No one wanted to throw her away. Her mother loved her. Her father had loved her.

She hadn't seen her father in a long time. He had died and now he was gone. But that didn't mean… anything.

Charlotte held her sore right hand with her left. As she watched, the woman opened a slot at the bottom of the cage and slid the plate inside. Now the hamburger was inside the cage.

"Enjoy that burger, 21. It really is very good. I had one earlier. Eat it all, if you can. There's something inside it to help you get back to sleep. This is a long trip we're on. We've only just gotten started, and I imagine you would like to escape from this for a little while. The burger will help you, and it won't hurt you a bit."

She stood and looked down at Charlotte again.

"It's been a pleasure to meet you, 21."

* * *

She woke some time later, but it was different this time.

She couldn't make her eyes focus. She had emerged from a deep darkness, and now there was light all around, but none of it made sense. She couldn't force it to *resolve* into anything.

She couldn't feel her senses. She couldn't think. Her life was being decided by strange and scary people. She could not resist anything. She could not say anything. She did not speak at all.

Who are they?

What do they want?

She was out of the cage now, and on her feet.

Was she hallucinating?

A plane. I was on a plane.

Some men stood around her. They were large men, and they all seemed to have the same facial features, which was to say no facial features. They were just blank, scrubbed out, as if they did not have faces at all.

One of the blurry faces spoke to her.

"Don't worry," it said. "Be a good girl. Don't resist."

Suddenly, the dark surrounded her again. But this new darkness was different. It was not sleep. It was the dark of blindness. It was the kind of darkness the condemned man experiences when he is put against the wall to be shot.

They had covered her head with a black hood or sack.

She stood, not moving, as someone cinched the hood tight. She couldn't breathe! For a moment, her heart raced in her chest. But then she felt herself sinking again. She would fall, but someone was holding her up.

One of the men carried her. She felt herself become like some boneless deep sea creature, a jellyfish. Her breathing slowed down, her heart was barely beating, her muscles became limp, and her body was slung over someone's shoulder.

She knew it was the end. The woman who hit her had been lying. They weren't taking her anywhere. There was no new home. It was pointless lying, not for any kind of gain, but because that's what people did. They just lied for no reason.

Soon she would be killed. There would be no explanation of anything—just confusion, this deep darkness, and then death.

CHAPTER FOUR

March 26, 2006
10:15 a.m. Eastern Standard Time
The offices of Richmond, Baker, Hancock and Pearl
K Street, Washington, DC

Politics is war by other means.

Don Morris liked to remind himself of this whenever he found himself in places like this one. He walked side by side down a wide corridor with his old friend, the United States Representative from North Carolina, and current House Minority Leader, William Ryan. The carpet beneath their feet was deep pile and dark blue. There was hardly a sound anywhere.

Bill Ryan was tall and handsome, with graying hair. He carried himself with ruler straight posture, and his large jaw jutted forward as they walked. Even though it was Sunday morning—or perhaps because it was—he wore a sharp blue business suit, black shoes polished and shining.

Don, in contrast, was more casually dressed in khakis and a blue dress shirt with an open collar. He wasn't here to supplicate for the Special Response Team budget today. He was here because Bill had asked him for a favor.

"Here" was the headquarters of a lobbying firm, in the K Street neighborhood that was ground zero for lobbyists and special interests of all kinds. The American Heritage Center. Pro-lifers. The World Bank. If they had an axe to grind, they were around here somewhere.

A late-middle-aged woman with gray hair, wearing a dark red sweater and slacks, moved ahead of them, walking quickly and with purpose. Don knew the type—they were everywhere here in Washington. The long-time executive assistant, a consummate professional, able to juggle dozens of facts, appointments, problems, and issues in her head, while simultaneously riding herd on a mob of young staffers.

A woman like this could run the show herself, of course, but she was born too soon. She had probably started out in life fetching coffee for overconfident young Republicans with slick haircuts and their feet up on the desk. Today, on this disaster of a Sunday morning, she was here at work, the most trusted employee of a very powerful man, on a day when his world was falling apart.

The woman reached a set of wide double doors at the end of the hall, opened them, and turned to wave Don and Bill in.

"Gentlemen," she said, "this is Mr. Richmond's office. Please don't hesitate to alert me if you need anything while you're here."

"Thank you," Don said.

The doors opened into a huge corner office. The ceilings were high and ornate, with crown moldings and an intricate center light fixture. A gleaming oak desk ruled on the far side of the room. Behind it was a long row of windows, giving a panoramic view of Washington Circle at the confluence of K Street and Pennsylvania Avenue, several stories below. Sunday morning traffic, sparse by DC standards, raced silently in each direction. It was springtime, and along the concrete boulevards, the trees were in bloom. The man who occupied this office had arrived, or at one time believed he had.

The man was here. He stood and came out from behind his desk to meet them. He wore an impeccably tailored blue pinstripe suit and a red tie. He had white hair, narrow shoulders, and a bit of a stoop. His nose was the beak of a vulture, redder than the rest of his face. His eyes were sharp, but bloodshot, and his face was lined. He looked like a man who hadn't slept in days. Perhaps he was ten years older than Don. Perhaps he was a thousand years older.

"Don," Bill Ryan said. "I want to introduce you to my good friend Miles Richmond."

The man offered his soft hand, and Don took it, careful not to squeeze it very hard. Men of a certain age often became fragile with arthritis. There was never a way to know until it was too late. Don didn't have that problem. His problem was not crushing such a hand.

"Miles, Don Morris and I were at the Citadel together, many years ago, and we've remained close. Other than that, I suppose he needs no introduction."

Richmond shook his head. He looked Don directly in the eye. "No. No, he doesn't. You're a fine American, Don. And we're very proud of the work you've done. The country needs more men like you."

"Thank you," Don said.

He didn't offer a compliment in return. America didn't need any more lobbyists in fancy offices. America didn't need more vultures tearing the flesh of the body politic. Miles Richmond probably knew what he was without having to be told.

"Won't you sit down?" Richmond said.

He indicated a meeting area with plush high-backed chairs situated on either side of a low, solid block of heavy blond wood. The block made a coffee table of sorts. A thick book, *Atlas Shrugged* by Ayn Rand, sat upon it. On the cover, a muscular man carried the entire world on his shoulders.

The men sat down, three chairs in a rough triangle.

Richmond gestured at the block of wood between them. "A Zen master from Japan gave me this table."

"It's quite something," Don said. He barely glanced at it.

"He told me that the key to life…"

"Miles," Bill Ryan said, cutting him off. He said it gently, but it stopped Richmond's patter like a sudden gunshot. Richmond looked at him. His eyes were furtive, almost afraid.

"This is hard," Bill said. "We all know that. But there's no need for games, or niceties, or ice breakers. Don isn't that kind of man. I don't think any of us here really are. Let's just get to it."

Now Richmond looked at Don. He saw what was in Don's eyes, and nodded.

"Okay. Okay. Don, I want to thank you for taking this meeting."

Don shrugged. "Bill and I go all the way back, Miles. He vouched for you. That's good enough for me."

Richmond took a deep breath. He stared at the table now.

"There was an abduction," he said. "We think it was Thursday night into Friday morning. Did you read the news about it?"

"I only know what Bill told me last night. I didn't want to prejudice my thinking about it. I wanted to hear it from you. The news…"

Don stopped, then started again. "It's not how I get my information, generally speaking."

"I understand," Richmond said. He was still staring down at the table. His mouth hung slack for a moment. He spoke, but it was as if he had forgotten there were others in the room with him.

"Charlotte. Her name is Charlotte. My youngest son's daughter. My… uh… my granddaughter. Charlotte. Has disappeared."

He looked up at Don, his head moving in a convulsive jerk. Tears were already streaming down his face.

"I bounced that child on my knee. When she…"

Richmond's voice cracked. He shook his head emphatically, tears flying off his cheeks. His teeth were gritted together.

"When she was small."

Don nodded. He felt for Richmond, perhaps more than the man could know. Don had gone through the same experience with Margaret, less than six months ago now, when she was taken by the hijackers. He remembered those moments in the San Juan airport, desperate, alone, like his heart had been ripped out through his chest.

No. That wasn't right. There were emotions that could not be explained by words. It was deeper than words, it was an agony from deep in human memory, from a time before language. It was a fire that had burned through Don, burned him away completely, as he tried not to imagine all the terrible things that could be happening to his beloved wife.

He had come through to the other side, and Margaret had been saved. But that was because men like Luke Stone and Ed Newsam had risked their lives to bring her back. Brian Deckers, a man who had never even met Margaret, had given his life to do so. Don Morris had been lucky to have men like these in his life.

Miles Richmond did not know such men. But he did know Bill Ryan, and Bill Ryan knew Don. Don was here for that reason—because Miles Richmond and Bill Ryan lived in a world of rich, well-connected and influential men doing each other favors. Don didn't love that fact, but he did understand, deep in his bones, the terror Richmond was facing.

A shadow had reached into Richmond's life, suddenly and without warning, and now it was breaking him. The darkness, the beast, the pure evil that so often seemed to rule this world. It was ripping him to pieces. He was breaking, and when he finally did break, he was going to come all the way apart.

"We need your help, Don," Bill said. "If there's anything at all..."

"Oh my God," Richmond said. "Oh my God. I don't know what I'm going to do."

His chest began to heave, gasping for air. He covered his mouth with his hand. A low moan began to emanate from behind that hand.

"Miles," Don said. "I promise you that I will do everything I can. I work with people who…"

The moaning became louder.

Then, just like that, the dam, which the man had held in place by an effort of will, broke under the onslaught.

Miles Richmond, one of the most powerful men in Washington, DC, high born, a multimillionaire, a man who had gone to all the right schools and who had made all the right moves, began to scream.

CHAPTER FIVE

1:30 p.m. Eastern Standard Time
Queen Anne's County, Maryland
Eastern Shore of Chesapeake Bay

The telephone on the kitchen wall started ringing.

Luke stared at it. It was an old blue phone, the kind that had hung on kitchen walls for decades. They were disappearing now, gradually being replaced by small black phones that you held in your hand, carried in your pocket, and brought with you wherever you went. The wall phone was a relic from a simpler time.

Luke ignored the phone for a moment, reached into the refrigerator and came out with a cold beer.

The weather was fine. The surroundings here were beautiful. He and Becca were at her family's cabin in Queen Anne's County for the weekend. The house had been in the family for over a hundred years.

The place was an ancient, rustic place sitting on a small bluff above Chesapeake Bay. The house was two floors, wooden everything, with creaks and squeaks everywhere. There was a screened-in porch facing the water, and a newer stone patio down a small hill from the house. The patio sat right on the bluff, with commanding 180-degree views of the water. Some mornings Luke walked out of the house in his bare feet, with his coffee cup in hand, and was staggered all over again by the panorama, as if seeing it for the very first time.

It really was an incredible place. Luke loved it here.

The only problem was sometimes the house came with Becca's mother and father. Luke looked out the picture window, at the group of people down on the patio. Becca was there at the table, Gunner on her lap.

Gunner was ten months old, and zooming toward his first birthday. He was getting big. He wore blue shorts and a yellow pullover fleece today. He was about as cute as humanly possible. His head was huge! Luke liked to think it was because of the brains it held inside there.

Also present were the in-laws, Audrey and Lance. They had a bottle of white wine on the table with them, and they were getting tipsy.

Luke picked up the phone.

"Luke Stone," he said.

"Son, it's Don."

Who else would it be on a sleepy Sunday afternoon? The same man who had given Luke and Ed the day off tomorrow.

"Hi, Don. How are you?"

"Good. Good. Listen, I'm going to keep this short and sweet. I need you to come in tomorrow, bright and early, and I need you to be prepared for a day or two out of town. Sorry about that."

Luke didn't even try to argue. Don wouldn't rescind a day off lightly. At the same time, Luke never knew quite what "a day or two out of town" meant. In the past, it had meant a trip to gun battles on the other side of the world.

"A day or two?" he said.

"Yes. For real. I was asked to look into a missing person case in North Carolina. We're going to keep it quiet. I want you and Ed to drop down there and poke around a little. It's not official SRT business, so we're not going to get our noses dirty on this. I just want to see if we can turn up anything the locals haven't."

"Sounds like you're doing someone a favor," Luke said.

"That's what I saw in you when we first met," Don said. "You catch on quick."

There was a pause between them. Luke understood that part of the game, part of what kept the agency alive, was Don scratching backs, and getting his own back scratched in turn. Luke understood it, but he knew very little about it. It wasn't his department.

"Trudy Wellington is digging up the details on this as we speak. She'll have everything for you tomorrow morning. For now, let's keep this under our hats."

Let's keep this under our hats.

That meant don't tell anyone about it. Of course, anyone could be listening to this conversation, and anyone probably was.

"Sure," Luke said.

"Good. Thanks, Stone. I'll make up the free day for you guys, and I'll double it. In the meantime, I'll see you tomorrow."

Luke put the phone back on its cradle. He walked out the screen door and headed down to the patio. The door slammed behind him. The door had tight springs—it always slammed with enthusiasm.

Everyone at the table looked up and watched him come down the hill. Even Gunner seemed to follow Luke with his eyes. Within reason,

Luke was not the paranoid type. And yet, he often had the feeling that people in his own family were eyeing him with suspicion.

"Did the phone ring?" Becca said.

Becca's brown hair was straight and long. Her bright blue eyes were alive and aware. She was as physically beautiful as ever, possibly even more beautiful as she headed into her thirties and embraced motherhood.

Luke nodded. He took a sip of his beer. It was cold and delicious.

"It was Don. He needs me to come in tomorrow."

"Luke," Becca said. "We just got here yesterday. He promised you a three-day weekend."

"I know it," Luke said.

"How is work?" Audrey said.

Luke gazed at his mother-in-law, taking his time, soaking her in. She had deep-set eyes with irises so dark, they seemed almost black. She had a sharp nose, like a beak. She had tiny bones and a thin frame. She reminded him of a bird—a crow, or maybe a vulture. And yet, in her own way, she was attractive.

Audrey St. John was born wealthy, and as a general rule, she frowned upon work. She didn't understand why someone would do the kind of dangerous, dirty work that occupied Luke Stone. She seemed continually shocked that her own daughter, Rebecca St. John, would marry someone like Luke.

That had changed a bit when Gunner was born. Audrey went for the jugular a little less often now, and Luke would happily take whatever positive interactions he could get from her.

"It's going okay," he said now, still a little wary, like a fighter circling a dangerous opponent. "It's been pretty quiet these last months."

Luke didn't mention that it had been quiet since he and Ed and Kevin Murphy had saved the President of the United States from a hijacking to Somalia. That part was classified information, and anyway, among the people at this table, it was understood.

And quiet didn't begin to describe how these past months had been.

Despite the success of the Somalia operation, the FBI brass had decided that the Special Response Team was a rogue department, and needed to be reined in. Until the raid on Friday, Luke and Ed had largely been on the bench while Don Morris negotiated with the higher-ups what kind of agency the SRT would be, what its expertise was, and how its future would unfold. It seemed that at the moment, the SRT had been sidelined.

Luke had been going a little bit crazy. He'd told Don from the beginning that he wouldn't be the type of agent who wore a shirt and tie to work every day, sat at a desk, made phone calls, and filed reports. But that's what he had been doing.

One day a while back, he got a postcard in the mail. It had been mailed two weeks before, from Cape Town, South Africa. It had a picture of fancy modern houses built onto a mountainside, sloping steeply downward toward the dark blue ocean, just as the sun was setting and night was coming in.

It said, *Cape Town: most beautiful city in the world.*

On the other side, there was a brief note, in a blocky handwritten scrawl. *Beautiful continent. Friendly people. Endless opportunity. YOU should be here.*

It was unsigned, but Luke didn't have to think very hard to guess who had sent it. The mercurial Kevin Murphy, former Delta operator, former SRT agent, hell in a gunfight. He and Murphy had never been friends, but they had a rough sort of respect for one another. It wasn't clear what "endless opportunity" was supposed to mean, but what it certainly didn't mean was boredom. If Luke weren't married, if he didn't have a child, he would be sorely tempted to join Murphy on his adventures.

"Becca said you were in New Jersey on Friday," Audrey said now. "A training with the Drug Enforcement Agency, was it?"

Here came the lies. The lies were bad enough on their own. When Audrey forced them into existence, it was always somehow worse.

"Oh, I was there with Alcohol, Tobacco, and Firearms. Not DEA. It was at an outdoor facility in the woods north and west of Paterson. My partner Ed and I were guests brought in to do an assessment of..."

"Were you at the drug raid on the house in Newark?"

Luke shook his head and looked out at the deep blue of the bay.

"No. We heard about it. People in the ATF were talking. It's a..."

"It's a shame," Lance said. "A young boy like that getting killed by the police."

"We saw it on the TV news," Audrey said. "They said one of the officers was shot as well, though his identity was kept a secret. The secrecy made us think of you. We were wondering if you were there."

She eyed Luke closely.

"No," Luke said. "And I'm glad I wasn't."

"It's always a tragedy when an innocent life is taken," Audrey said.

CHAPTER SIX

March 27, 2006
10:05 a.m. Eastern Standard Time
The Headquarters of the FBI Special Response Team
McLean, Virginia

"I'll admit I don't get this operation," Mark Swann said. "A missing persons case doesn't seem very SRT. Not to be uncouth here, but it is just one girl."

Luke glanced down the conference table at Swann. Luke often didn't know what to make of Swann. The guy was clearly super smart, but sometimes his mouth ran far out ahead of his brain.

Swann looked at Luke. "Usually we're saving the world around here, aren't we?"

Swann was tall and thin, wearing a black T-shirt with the logo of the old punk rock band The Ramones. The logo was made to look like the Seal of the President of the United States. He was wearing a pair of yellow-tinted wraparound aviator sunglasses, and his long hair was pulled back into a ponytail.

There were exactly five people in the conference room. Swann, Luke, Ed Newsam, Trudy Wellington, and the man himself, Don Morris.

"Swann," Don Morris said. Don was dressed in a blue dress shirt, sleeves rolled up to his thick forearms. Don's eyes were like those of a tiger, something that hunted weaker animals for a living. And those eyes were focused on Mark Swann.

"What would you say is your job with the Special Response Team?"

Swann shrugged. "I'd say I'm a tech guy. Communications. Data acquisition, you might say. I've heard some people call it spying."

Don nodded. "That sounds right to me. And you're pretty good at that. Now what would you say is my job?"

Swann smiled and shook his head. "I'd say you're the boss."

Don pointed at him. "Exactly right. And what types of things do you suppose that includes?"

"Hiring and deploying personnel," Swann said. "Setting policy."

Don was grinning now. "Yes, indeed. What else?"

"Uh… choosing missions?"

"Beautiful," Don said. "So let's do this, okay? I will do my job, and you do yours."

Swann nodded. "Good idea."

"The truth is," Don said, "this isn't technically an SRT mission. That's why there's just a few of us here. And for now, what we will discuss is for the eyes and ears of the people in this room only. We are doing a favor for some people I know, very likely a small favor because others are already working on the problem. Consider it a good deed. So if Swann has no more objections…"

He looked Swann's way.

Swann shook his head.

"Then I will ask Trudy to begin again."

Trudy nodded, eyes owlish behind her red glasses.

She began. "As you know, this weekend Don asked me to look into a missing person case in North Carolina. I've spent several hours on it last night and this morning, contacting a few people with knowledge of the situation. I also had the assistance of Swann, who got me some details that haven't exactly been made public yet."

Swann nodded. "Reports filed in a local police database. Information in a high school database. Medical reports at a local hospital. A few other things. Child's play. I was doing stuff like that when I was a kid."

"In any event, here's what we came up with," Trudy said. "This past Thursday night, there appears to have been an abduction of a girl from Wilmington, a small coastal city in the southeast corner of the state. Charlotte Richmond, a sixteen-year-old, appears to have slipped out of her house, apparently while her mother and her mother's boyfriend were asleep. She is an only child, and there is thought to have been no one else in the house at the time.

"The girl attended a party at an oceanfront home in nearby Wrightsville Beach. There were about a dozen people at the party, mostly underage high school kids, and alcohol was served there. Some individuals were also smoking pot. The party was hosted by eighteen-year-old Taylor Seifert, whose parents were out of the country at the time. The family are heirs to the original Seifert Beverage fortune, and continue to have a significant minority stake in SBS Distributors Worldwide."

Don nodded. "Continue."

"Some time during the night, Charlotte Richmond disappeared. Actually, that's not quite accurate. She left the grounds of the house with a seventeen-year-old boy named Robert Haskins, and walked down to the beach. Haskins is both the starting tight end and a linebacker on the Hoggard High School football team in Wilmington. According to his coach, he stands about six foot three, and weighs a little over two hundred pounds. He is handsome, or was until last week. He is apparently very popular with teenage girls."

"Is he a suspect?" Luke said. He found himself lured in by this Peyton Place–style mystery.

Trudy shook her head. "The local police consider him a witness, not a suspect. Also, he's a victim. Haskins was beaten severely and knocked unconscious by what he says were two men. The extent of his injuries suggest a blitz attack by a person or persons well-versed in the use of violence, who wanted to neutralize a large opponent quickly. Five missing teeth. Broken orbital socket around his right eye. Hairline skull fracture. Four broken ribs. Seven broken bones in his right hand, consistent with a crushing injury. Internal bleeding and minor organ injuries, including to the spleen and kidneys. He remains in the hospital as of this morning. Whoever took Charlotte Richmond beat the hell out of this kid."

"Did he get a look at them?" Ed said.

Trudy shook her head again. "The statement he gave suggests he didn't. It was a dark night with only a sliver of moon, he and the Richmond girl were quite far from the house, and there were rip tide and high surf warnings that night. The waves were booming, and Haskins had been drinking beer since early evening. He told the local police he didn't hear anyone coming. He said that he and the Richmond girl had been flirting in recent weeks, exchanging text messages, and he thought that the night of the party might be the night they… consummated, let's say… their relationship. They were together on the beach, talking, and were suddenly attacked by persons unknown."

"And the text messages?" Don said.

Trudy shrugged. "They've been subpoenaed from the telephone carriers. The Richmond girl's phone is gone, and has been disabled or destroyed. Police tried to ping its location, but there's no signal. Haskins appears to have lost his phone in the attack."

"That's convenient," Ed said. "So this girl's been gone since early Friday morning, and now it's Monday. We are way behind."

"To be sure," Trudy said, "a certain amount of time was lost because there was a delay in the reporting of the crime. Haskins was unconscious on the beach until sunrise Friday, when he was found by a local man out walking his dog. Paramedics arrived and took Haskins to the hospital. Police arrived twenty minutes later, questioned the people at the house, but either the kids weren't aware that Charlotte Richmond was no longer in the house, or they simply didn't report it. By all accounts, it was quite a party. The fact that Charlotte was missing didn't become clear until early afternoon, when the high school contacted her mother."

"Keep in mind," Don said, "I didn't even hear about this until yesterday."

"What about the mother's boyfriend?" Luke said. "Does he have any relationship to this? An unrelated man in the house—isn't he the first place to look?"

Trudy glanced at her computer. "Usually, sure. And he has certainly been looked at. His name is Jeff Zorn, Jr., he's forty-three years old, and a self-employed publicist. His father was Jeffrey Zorn, a partner at Goldman Sachs investment firm in New York City. Zorn has been living with Charlotte Richmond's mother, forty-year-old Joy Simms, formerly Joy Richmond, for the past eighteen months. Zorn is cooperating fully. He was questioned by local police, without a lawyer present. He voluntarily surrendered two cars, a laptop computer, a desktop computer, and two cell phones—a private one and one he uses for business purposes. He is a person of interest in the case, but was not arrested.

"Zorn has a conviction for trafficking in controlled substances—he was selling pills at a nightclub in Manhattan—that stems from more than twenty years ago. He got off with two hundred hours of community service. He has no history of violent activity, is five foot nine, weighs one-eighty pounds, and wears glasses. He is unlikely to overpower a teenage football player. Given that the attack took place miles away from the girl's home, at a time when Zorn had a verifiable alibi, and given his level of transparency, I believe the case will move on without him."

"Where's the biological father?" Ed said.

"Deceased," Trudy said. She referred to the computer again. "Thomas Richmond. He and the mother divorced when the child was young. He was diagnosed with a rare form of blood cancer at the age of thirty-two and died at the age of thirty-six, about six years ago. He became severely debilitated in his last couple of years, and Charlotte was shielded from spending much time with him. In a sense, the girl barely knew her father. The paternal grandfather is Miles Richmond, a high-powered DC lobbyist. He apparently took over providing financial support for the child after the death of Thomas Richmond."

Luke glanced at Don. His face didn't change in the slightest at the mention of the lobbyist.

"I've been looking into that angle," Trudy said. "But so far I haven't come up with anything. Richmond is known to play hardball and almost certainly has enemies. But the world of lobbyists isn't the Mafia. They don't kidnap each other's family members. As of this moment, the Richmond connection seems like more of a coincidence than anything."

"And the mom?" Luke said.

"Joy Simms," Trudy said. "She's an attorney with Edgemont Prender, a small firm in Wilmington. Local stuff—real estate closings, estate planning, drunk driving cases. By all accounts, she has utterly collapsed since her daughter was taken. Very little of value was obtained in her police interview. She is not considered a suspect."

"What's your gut?" Don said. "What happened here?"

"There isn't much to go on," Trudy said.

Don shrugged. "Even so."

Trudy nodded. "Okay. I'm out on a limb, but okay. It was a targeted crime, conceived ahead of time. Charlotte Richmond is a pretty, popular teenage girl. She's a cheerleader and on the dance squad at the local high school. She spends her time with other pretty, popular girls. Someone in her circle, or more likely someone close to her circle, was aware there was going to be a party. That person was aware that Charlotte, or other girls like her, were going to be at the party, and would likely be impaired. The ferocity of the attack on the Haskins boy suggests a planned assault. Someone knew that Haskins was large and had to be incapacitated instantly. Someone followed the two of them onto the beach, stalked them, and then attacked."

She looked around the room. "Since there appear to be no leads at the moment, I would suggest widening the search to family members, associates, and most importantly, enemies of the kids at the party. I would look especially closely at men or boys who frequent bodybuilding gyms or are involved in fighting activities like boxing or mixed martial arts. I would look closely at men who have records of violent crime, or have been involved in law enforcement or the military. I don't believe the attack was a coincidence, or a crime of opportunity. Nothing like that. One or more men just happen upon two young lovers on the beach during a pitch-dark night, quickly overwhelm the male, and abduct the female without a trace? That sounds planned."

"It's a kidnapping, in other words?" Ed said.

Ed was looking at Trudy intently. Luke hadn't connected with Ed before the meeting today, but that look in his eyes—the intensity of it—Luke had only seen Ed that way a few times. Generally, when he was angry, and in danger of boiling over. Or right before combat.

Trudy nodded. "Yes, I think so."

"Is she alive or dead?" Don said.

"Alive," Trudy said without hesitating. "That may be because I want her to be alive, but I think there's more here. If she were dead then we'd probably be looking at a serial killer. There are no serial killers thought to be active in that region at this time, and the modus operandi doesn't fit your typical serial killer. Serial killers rarely attack women who are accompanied by large males. Not that it doesn't happen, but it's rare. Usually they go for women who are isolated. In fact, the classic victim of a serial killer is a poor, drug-addicted prostitute, who no one will miss right away. It is definitely not a well-to-do teenage girl who is supposed to be at school in the morning. I think someone wanted Charlotte specifically, and is holding her captive. It may be that they are holding her for their own purposes, or it may be that they took her with the idea of trafficking her. A young, fresh face, fresh body…"

Trudy shrugged again, looking down at her computer screen as if she didn't want to face them. Everyone in the room knew the implications of what she was telling them.

"I'd say there's also an outside chance they're planning to hold her for ransom, considering that she is Miles Richmond's granddaughter. But as of this morning, no one in the family has admitted being contacted by kidnappers. The more time that passes without contact, the less likely a ransom scenario becomes."

Don looked around the room now.

"I want to tell you all something. I think most of us have either been touched by something like this in our lifetimes, or have known someone who has. For the loved ones, it is horrible beyond words. I nearly lost my Margaret some months ago, and got her back by the grace of God, and by the efforts of the people in this room. Because of that experience, I've agreed to look into this situation. I won't get into the details of who asked me to do so. But you know the reason why—because we have a reputation for getting things done. We have an opportunity to do a good thing here. Maybe. And if it's possible, that's what I want to do."

"Have the local police called in the FBI?" Luke said.

Don shook his head. “Not so far. And even if they did, you know the Bureau wouldn’t give it to us. We’re on a short leash. All we’re doing right now is quietly feeling around, with the emphasis on quietly. We have no official capacity.”

“Clandestine,” Swann said.

“Yes. If the basic questions will get this done, the local police will do it. We’re going to ask the questions no one else is asking. We’ll approach the people no one is approaching. If we think all the way outside the box—and I believe that creative thinking is one of the most powerful tools this organization has—we might be able to come at the bad guys from a direction they’re not expecting.”

“Where do we even start, if we’re not supposed to step on the toes of the local police?” Ed said.

“Trudy?” Don said.

She shrugged. “We could work the family, friends, and enemies angle I mentioned earlier. Start close and work outwards. That’s a little bit of snooping, maybe pulling down text and email messages. I imagine Swann could start to put those relationships together in a day or two.”

“I can have some early concentric circles by close of business tomorrow, in all likelihood,” Swann said. “My hunch is we’ll find something pretty close to the middle. If not, as the days go by, we can sweep it all in. Everyone in that city, if need be.”

Don raised a hand like a STOP sign. “That’s enough, Swann. Do what you do, but don’t incriminate your colleagues.”

Swann nodded. “Understood.”

“What about cameras?” Ed said. “You said it’s a rich neighborhood. Would there be security cameras in the community, and would that footage be processed somewhere in particular? A local home security firm, say? Maybe it picked something up, a car, a van…”

“Two guys walking down the street, carrying a girl,” Luke said.

Ed looked at him. Ed’s eyes were still hot, practically on fire.

“I’ll see what I can get,” Swann said. “I’m guessing that if the local cops are doing their jobs, they already have it. If we were officially on this case…”

He looked at Don.

Don shook his head. “We’re not.”

“We can also work the trafficking angle,” Trudy said. “Charlotte is a very specific kind of girl, who would probably appeal to a specific clientele. It was a high-risk move to take her. There are people with histories of committing these kinds of crimes, and such a person may know something about the who, what, and where."

"What are you saying?" Luke said.

"Human traffickers," Trudy said. The tone of her voice said she was surprised he even had to ask. "Talk to them. Ask them what they've heard."

"Not the most forthcoming people," Luke said.

"Lean on them," Don said. "That's part of your skill set, is it not? You and Ed both have that ability. If you work together…" Don trailed off and shrugged.

Luke glanced at Ed. Ed looked like a dog that just had spotted a bone. Luke suppressed a smile. Was Don really sanctioning this? Extralegal interrogations? If so, it couldn't happen to a nicer group of people.

"Let me get this straight," Luke said. He looked at Don. "You would like Ed and I to go out and… ahem… question human traffickers as to what, if anything, they know about this missing girl?"

Don stared at Luke. He didn't smile at all. "I don't have a lot of sympathy for people like that. If one of them knows something about what happened here, I would like him to share that information with us. It's a start, and time is against us, as Ed indicated. The trail is already going cold."

There was silence in the room. When Don spoke again, his voice was low.

"A couple of points, and they're important. I don't want to see a typewritten report about this afterwards, and I don't want to read your names in the newspapers. Otherwise, do what needs to be done. Is that clear enough to you boys?"

"Clear as a bell," Ed said.

Luke looked at Trudy. "Can you find us someone to talk to?"

She shrugged. "I already have. Louis Clare, fifty-four-year-old white male. Also known as Louis Clark, also known as Lew Clark, also known by the nicknames Spark and Sparky. He spent eighteen years of a twenty-six-year sentence in federal penitentiaries for kidnapping and trafficking in underage girls. He was paroled for good behavior four years ago. He's thought to be rehabilitated, and long out of the game. But as far as I can see, he has no visible means of income or support."

"He's doing something for a living," Luke said.

Trudy nodded. "Yes, he is."

"Where is he?"

Trudy glanced at her computer. "He checks in with his parole officer in Myrtle Beach, South Carolina, every month. His official address is a motel there. Myrtle Beach is approximately ninety minutes by car from Wrightsville Beach, where the Richmond girl abduction took place."

Luke looked at Don. "We'll need somewhere to interview him. Private."

Luke almost couldn't believe the words that had come out of his own mouth. Already they were speaking in code. The word *private* carried a great deal of meaning in this kind of work. Private was a place away from other people, a place that few people knew existed, a place where loud noises, like screams, would not reach anyone else's ears. When you took someone to a private place, you owned that person.

Of course Don knew all this.

He nodded. "Consider it done."

CHAPTER SEVEN

1:40 p.m. Eastern Standard Time
Myrtle Beach International Airport
Myrtle Beach, South Carolina

They were never here.

They flew in on a private plane that belonged to a company called Apex Digital Management. The plane left from an unmanned airfield just south of Langley, for a flight that took little more than hour. Ed's name was Luther Sykes. Luke's was Sem Goethals. Apparently, Luke was not from this country.

Not that any of it mattered. No one would hear Luke speak, or see his face. They didn't check in anywhere, and no one in the Myrtle Beach terminal, crowded with beachgoers and golfers dressed in pastel colors, looked at them twice.

Luke glanced at the Arrivals and Departures boards. The "international" in Myrtle Beach International Airport seemed to stem from the fact that a handful of flights came in from Canada. Private flights were not listed.

A car was waiting for them in the parking lot. It was a dark blue Ford sedan stashed in short-term parking. Folded inside the driver's side sun visor was a machine-generated terminal parking stub. The first thirty minutes parking in the terminal were free. This car had arrived here seventeen minutes ago. They left without incurring any fees, so they didn't have to pay anyone anything. The parking lot attendant didn't care. He barely glanced at them. He was more interested in something that was happening on his computer screen.

"Every time you go away, it terrifies me," Becca had said before he left.

"I know," Luke said. "I know that. But this investigation is exactly the kind of thing we've talked about. It's what you've wanted for me. It's here in the United States. It's police work. We're going down to interview one person, and we'll see where that goes. The guy isn't even a suspect, just someone who might have information. Maybe Trudy Wellington will find us more people to talk to. Maybe she won't. We're not supposed to interfere with the local cops, so there's only so much we can do. It's basically a nothing assignment. Easy-peasy. We'll be down there for a day, maybe two. Then we'll be back. Heck, it's an hour away by plane."

The things he told her were not technically lies. They were sins of omission. Everything he said was true. It was the things he left out that made the difference. He did not tell her they were going down under assumed identities. He did not tell her they planned to disappear someone. He did not say a word about alligators.

"Don got us a little shack about half an hour from Myrtle Beach," Ed had told Luke just before Luke spoke to Becca. "It's on a swamp."

Luke thought about that. It only took a few seconds.

South Carolina… Swamp…

"Alligators."

"Yes."

The way Ed said it was long and drawn out, almost as if the word *yes* had several undulating syllables, and very much as if Ed savored each one. *Yyye-ehhhh-esssss.*

"Is he dangerous?" Becca had asked.

"Who?" Luke really didn't understand the question. "Ed?" Of course Ed was dangerous. Ed might well be one of the most dangerous people on Earth.

"No. Not Ed. The man you're going to interview."

"Oh." Luke shook his head. "Nah. He's fifty-four years old. He spent nearly twenty years in prison. I'm sure he doesn't want any trouble. And anyway, most people get one look at Ed, and they're ready to tell us everything that happened since their fifth birthday."

He paused, then he took her in his arms.

"We're not going to have any problems at all."

* * *

"Nice place," Luke said.

"Yeah," Ed said. Ed was sitting low, staring out the passenger side window with a small pair of binoculars. He was uncharacteristically quiet, responding to Luke with one-word answers. Luke didn't relish the role of the talkative guy trying to carry a conversation, so their stakeout kept devolving into total silence.

It was getting to be dusk. The sun was lowering to their left, dropping behind a flat landscape of parking lots and low slung buildings. They were in the lot of an abandoned fireworks store. The showroom windows were boarded over, but a faded sign loomed over the crumbling lot, with the image of a cartoon cat with its back arched, and the words *Black Cat* still visible.

Diagonally across a dead-end street was the Adventurer Motel, a two-story wreck of a place decades past its prime, and quietly going to seed. There were thirty-eight rooms and less than a dozen cars in the lot. One of the cars had four perfectly flat tires.

The motel's sign depicted a cartoon pirate holding a sword, with his foot up on a chest spilling gold coins. People around here apparently viewed the world through the lens of cartoons. A red neon sign advertising VACANCY was on and blinking, but the office was closed, and a piece of paper taped to the inside of the window had a phone number scribbled on it.

According to Trudy, Louis Clare lived in room nineteen. It was a first-floor room, on the end closest to where Luke and Ed were parked. The door was clearly visible from here, maybe fifty yards away.

Clare didn't seem to be home. There were no lights on inside his room. There was no vehicle parked in front of his door.

As they watched, an old blue whale of a car pulled into the spot in front of the door.

"What is it?" Luke said.

"Mercury," Ed said. "Marquis."

"Plate?"

"South Carolina. ESB-435."

Luke glanced at the paper lying on the dashboard. Swann had gotten Clare's car registration hours ago, and Trudy had passed it on to them.

"That's him."

The Mercury's front quarter panel was a darker shade of blue than the rest. The car itself had rolled off the assembly line in 1992, and had four previous owners. If Clare had gotten a big payday recently, he was doing a good job of pretending he hadn't.

He was alone. He was a thick-bodied man, balding with gray around the edges. He was wearing a white T-shirt and workpants. He busied himself getting things out of the car. He pulled out a twelve-pack of beer and some plastic bags filled with various items. It looked like he had just gone grocery shopping.

"See you in a minute," Luke said.

"See you," Ed said.

Luke got out of their car without shutting the door. He was wearing a gray hooded sweatshirt, the hood up, with a black Oakland Raiders baseball cap protruding from it, and pulled down over his face.

As Luke crossed the parking lot toward the Adventurer Motel, Ed came around to the driver's side of the car.

Luke walked fast and light, his feet in black sneakers.

He did not look directly at Clare, and angled toward the motel as though he was not headed in that direction.

Behind him, the car pulled slowly out of the Black Cat parking lot.

Clare was at the door to the room, hands full, finagling with his keys. Luke made a sharp and sudden right turn and moved directly toward him. Clare got the door unlocked, pushed it open with his foot, and then Luke was running.

He reached into the rear waistband of his jeans and came out with the gun. Clare was just inside the room and the door was closing when Luke arrived. He stuck his foot in the crack just before it shut. He shouldered the door open.

Clare was just ahead of him. The man half turned, the beer still under his arm, still holding the bags with the other hand. Luke absorbed the surroundings in an instant. The room was a tiny efficiency, with a small refrigerator, a microwave, and a hotplate. There was one king-sized bed, and a TV bolted to the top of a dresser.

Clare's eyes went wide. His mouth made a big round O of surprise.

Luke punched that mouth with his left hand. He pointed the gun at the man's head with his right.

"Turn around! Don't look at me!"

Clare did exactly as he was told. His voice was gravelly from long years of smoking.

"I don't know what you—"

"Shut up! Drop the food. Hands in the air, where I can see them."

The beer hit the floor with a thunk. The bags did the same. A can of soup rolled out of one of the bags. Clare raised his hands. He'd played this game before.

"Is anyone else here?" Luke said.

"No."

"So help me, if you're lying…"

"There's no one here."

Luke pushed him. "Face down on the bed. NOW."

Clare lay on the bed. Luke pulled a pair of zip-cuffs out of the front pocket of his sweatshirt. He yanked Clare's arms backwards and cuffed his wrists tightly.

"You a cop?" Clare said.

"You wish," Luke said.

He reached into the pocket of his sweatshirt a second time. He pulled out a black canvas mask. It zipped in the back. It had air holes that were located roughly where a person's nostrils would be. One size fits all. He pulled it down over Clare's head and zipped it closed. Clare gasped.

Luke glanced in the grocery bags and spotted something he might need—a pack of American Indian cigarettes. He went to the drawers in the kitchenette, opened a couple, and found Clare's lighter.

"Listen, man," Clare's muffled voice said. "I didn't…"

The damping effect of the mask made it sound like so much mumbo jumbo.

"Up," Luke said.

He pulled Clare to a standing position, then walked him to the door. He opened it and glanced outside. Ed was here with the car. The trunk was already open, Ed standing beside it. Ed was also wearing a hoodie and a baseball cap.

Luke walked Clare outside into the gathering darkness of evening. The room door slammed shut behind them.

Ed grabbed the man by the back of his T-shirt and the waistband of his workpants. Ed lifted him like a bag of rice and dumped him into the trunk of the car. Clare's legs hit the side as he went in. He was a poor fit for the trunk, but Ed managed to stuff him in there. Clare rolled over onto his side, groaning in pain and surprise.

Luke slammed the trunk shut and looked at Ed. Even this close, Luke could barely see Ed's face under the hat.

"Let's go," Ed said.

CHAPTER EIGHT

6:15 p.m. Central Standard Time (7:15 p.m. Eastern Standard Time)
La Sierra de San Simon (St. Simon's Saw)
Near Honduras
The Caribbean Sea

The heat was like an oven.

When the door opened, Darwin King stepped from the sleek private jet to the top of the stairway. The sun was far to the west, but it didn't matter. He wore a handmade suit of summer linen, and the air conditioning on the plane had let him forget how hot it could get here on the island. He climbed down the narrow steps to the airstrip's tarmac.

He held a satellite phone to his ear, listening to information that annoyed him. As soon as the plane's wheels had touched the ground, he was on the phone. He had an empire to run, and empires didn't like to wait. The information annoyed him because he didn't understand it yet. The man on the other end was talking too fast.

Darwin was a large man. He stood about six foot two, and he weighed 220 pounds. His shoulders were broad, and his hands, his feet, all of his extremities, were huge. His head was big. His jaw protruded. Everything about him was big.

He liked to say that he inherited his father's size and his mother's good looks.

He was one of three passengers disembarking from what had probably been designed as an eight- or ten-seater, but was now laid out like someone's living room. The other two passengers were big men like himself. One had dark hair and a goatee. One had a blond crewcut. Their faces were blank and impassive. They had hard eyes, devoid of things that Darwin didn't like—things like hesitancy, nuance, empathy. These men were here to remain alert, and when the time came to act, to act without thought, or remorse, or judgment.

Darwin was fond of the Eastern concept of non-action. It didn't mean not acting. It meant acting completely, naturally, without the emotional baggage humans liked to carry around. Think of a lioness chasing down, killing, and eating a wounded gazelle.

The men were obviously younger than he was, and slightly larger, but those weren't the only differences. Hidden under their sports jackets were shoulder holsters and handguns with high-capacity magazines.

Bodyguards. Darwin King did not like surprises, unless he was the one springing them. And on the rare occasions when he was surprised, he liked the surprise to be neutralized quickly.

"Tell me again," he said into the telephone. "But more slowly, and strip out all the nonsense this time."

"The deal fell through," a man's voice said. "Our guys were there with the product. We were on time, in the appointed place, everything we promised."

Darwin pictured the product in question. Soviet-era mortars, anti-tank rounds, heat-seeking missiles. It was good stuff, still functional, and kept all these years in climate-controlled conditions. It was not up to date in the sense of being "smart," of course. These were not weapons with tiny high-tech brains, weapons that could think for themselves. But the people who wanted them could barely think for themselves, either.

Darwin's clients—Third World despots, ragtag rebel militias, Central African security firms guarding precious metal deposits in dense jungles—tended to live in the past. Their worlds reminded Darwin of photographs he used to see in magazines during his childhood in the late 1950s. The United States was surging into the space age future, while much of the human race stayed right where it had always been.

It was still there now. And it needed weapons.

"And the client?" Darwin said.

"The bag man disappeared," the voice said. "Just gone. Never made it to the meeting place."

"Any idea where he is?"

"No one seems to know," the man's voice said.

Darwin sighed. "He'd better be dead."

"That's what I told them."

Darwin looked at the pale blue sky and sighed. The veins stuck out on his thick neck, and on his forehead. For a moment, it seemed like he could feel the blood pulsing through them. He took a deep breath. It could be stressful, running an empire. But so what? An empire required an effective, confident emperor, and he was that.

"What else?" he said.

"They think we did it."

Darwin's free hand balled into a fist.

"They think..."

"Yes, that we disappeared their bag man before he reached the meet."

"And the money?"

"Yes."

Darwin thought about it. Something unspoken began to dawn on him. A smile broke out on his face. He gave certain of his field lieutenants a great deal of latitude to seize opportunities. It depended on the client, and what the potential pushback was. In this case, the client was weak, a disloyal politician with a long history of corruption, who was trying to stockpile weapons for a run at the throne. The man's position was precarious, to put it mildly. Who was he going to complain to, the United Nations?

"Did we?" Darwin said. "Did we do that?"

There was no answer.

"Feel free to speak plainly," he said.

Darwin had graduated from the place where you had to be careful about what you said on the telephone. Let *them* listen in all they wanted. He was above that station in life. He owned people, people who would do him favors, people who would protect him.

"Yes," the voice said. "We did."

Darwin almost laughed in delight. A long, quiet moment stretched out between him and the voice on the line. Darwin could almost hear the other man smiling as he delivered this news.

"Is the product safe?" Darwin said.

"We moved it to a secure location."

"Terrific. Then do this. Get in touch with the client. Tell him we're very upset. He wasted our time, and put our people in a difficult position. But we understand that these things happen, and we still want to deal. We'll meet him partway. If he can raise seventy-five percent of the original purchase price, we can close with him. Tell him no funny stuff this time. If we smell any trouble at all, we walk, and he can try to take the capital with pea shooters and slingshots."

"Will do."

Darwin nodded. "Good job."

He hung up the phone.

A silver Rolls-Royce had pulled up and was waiting for him. A black SUV was parked in front of it, and another black SUV brought up the rear. The bodyguards rode in the SUVs. Darwin walked over and slid into air-conditioned comfort in the back seat of the Rolls.

Elaine sat in the car, waiting for him.

She was thin and very pretty, almost as beautiful as she ever was. They were great friends, associates, former lovers, allies in a cold, cold world. Her green eyes sparkled. Her thick eyelashes and her makeup gave her the effect of having cat's eyes. She wore a dark green dress, as though she had prepared herself for his arrival.

"Hello, darling," she said.

"Hello, gorgeous."

He leaned in and they shared a long kiss. He smiled at her, and she smiled back. They had a history together. They understood each other. Love was one thing, and they probably did love each other. But the hardest part was finding someone who could understand. They were both monsters in their own way. They both understood this, and they accepted it. That was rare. That was gold.

"It's good to see you," she said.

As Darwin settled in, the little convoy rolled out. The three cars drove right down the middle of the runway toward a high chain-link fence at the far end—the exit. The fence was topped with razor wire.

The driver of the Rolls was a dark shadow on the far side of a smoked glass partition.

"How was your flight?"

"Fine," Darwin said. "No complaints. How is everything here?"

"Things are good. Do you mind if I smoke?"

Darwin smiled. "Go right ahead. I like smoke."

Elaine took a cigarette out of a small black case, along with a gold cigarette holder. She lit up, folded her legs, and exhaled, filling the compartment with smoke. For a moment, she looked like some sort of strange marionette.

"We brought in a new girl. I happened to be in the States, and I met her for the first time on the flight home. You'll like her. She's perfect. I'm taking charge of her personally."

Darwin nodded. "Excellent. Where did she come from?"

Elaine waved a hand. "Oh, you know. There was a certain individual, a chronic problem with finances. The repayment schedule didn't work out. We've been patient, but it became clear that the options were dwindling. A little research turned up a tasty little morsel very close to his orbit. So he agreed to this arrangement instead. Reluctantly, I suppose, but I don't anticipate any trouble. I think he knows his place in the pecking order."

"Terrific," Darwin said. "If he forgets his place, we'll be sure to remind him."

Elaine took another drag on the long cigarette. "Yes, we will."

"In the meantime, I'll look forward to meeting the young lady."

Elaine nodded. "You will be very pleased."

He reached for her cigarette and she handed it to him. He took a deep drag. He let the smoke settle deep into his lungs. Technically, he had quit smoking thirty years ago. But sometimes he just couldn't resist. Even now, after all these years, there was still nothing like it. It filled some hunger that he had. All real smokers were that way—they had a hunger, a need, that ordinary life simply couldn't meet.

He released the smoke back into the car and handed her the cigarette.

"And the man?" he said.

She arched her eyebrows. "Yes. The one who owed? You know exactly who it is."

Darwin nodded. "Yes, I do. No one has a memory like me. I know all my business. And the man still owes. Whatever he thought the agreement was, that wasn't the agreement. The girl bought him half off the principal, but no more. We've been waiting too long, and it's not as if the transfer of ownership is free. It costs quite a lot of money, as you know. So half off. That's it. The rest is still payable, and the interest is the same as before."

Elaine barked laughter. "You're so wicked. I love it."

Darwin smiled. "Evil."

"The devil," she said.

He winked at her. "God had better watch out. I'm coming for Him next."

The car motored along a narrow, winding concrete roadway lined with palm trees and dense undergrowth. On the right, across more undergrowth, steep green hillsides rose above them. On the left, through the foliage, Darwin caught a glimpse of the turquoise water, and further out, the white foam of waves crashing.

They were the only cars on the road. Of course they were. St. Simon's Saw was a private island, and Darwin King owned it. The only people here were Darwin, the people close to him, and the people who worked for him.

The car and its SUV escorts exited the main road and followed a narrow, well-paved lane uphill through the thick greenery. The ascent was steep for a moment, and then very steep. Darwin sat back in his seat, almost like an astronaut waiting for takeoff. He felt the heavy Rolls working to manage the hill.

The entrance to the estate was at the top. The procession waited while the main gate slid open, then each car passed through in line. The fence itself was a typical metal chain-link fence. Darwin glanced upward and spotted bands of circular razor wire at the top. Beat that outer fence and you faced about twenty feet to an identical one, with identical razor wire on top. The gap between fences was a dog run.

Darwin spotted a couple of Dobermans roaming free in there. This place was paradise, but even paradise had to be fortified against your enemies.

Up ahead, the main house came into view. It was a palace. When the car pulled to the top of the circular driveway, Darwin did a quick calculation. Old quarried stone house, more than a century old, fully restored, probably thirty rooms. He wasn't even quite sure himself how many rooms there were. But it was a beautiful home, he knew that. It was a perfect thing. There were more expensive homes in this world, but none were better.

Darwin exited the car and immediately felt the breeze—the air wasn't nearly as hot up here. Ahead of him, Elaine stepped up the stone front steps. Darwin carried his own bag and followed her.

At the top of the stairs, Darwin turned around for a moment. The front of the house faced inland—a sweeping panorama downhill across the brown and green island, and in the far distance, the ocean. Here and there, wisps of cloud clung to the high treetops—there might be a few drops of rain in those clouds, but not much. It was just hanging moisture, feeding the plant life. This was where Heaven and Earth met.

"I own this," he said in a low voice. "This is mine."

It was amazing, the things he owned. He really did walk like a god among mortals. Everything came to him. No one could resist him.

They crossed the threshold of the house, into the foyer, up the master stairs to the second floor, and down a wide, cool hallway. Their feet echoed on polished stone. They passed through a doorway and here was what might have once been a ballroom—a vast, high-ceilinged room, with large windows, white curtains billowing in the breeze.

Darwin could almost hear the strains of music and laughter from those long ago times—the good old days.

But these were the good old days. Not then, now.

They passed into his apartment, a completely private living space within the much larger house. The apartment was big. Sumptuous, open concept, with two-story ceilings. Stone tiles everywhere, ceiling fans gently turning.

There was a living room with a large white sectional couch. A modern art piece hung behind it, the canvas four feet wide and ten feet long, the painting a crazy horizontal blood-red scrape, like a person scratching at the walls of their prison cell with the last of their fingernails. He loved that painting. Elaine had given it to him. It was a living artist, someone she was collecting. He didn't remember the man's name.

To the left, sliding glass doors opened to a wide terrace. The doors were open. With the doors open, Darwin could listen to the call of the gulls, and smell the sea breeze. The deck faced southwest across the cliffs and over the Caribbean Sea. When you stood out there, the ocean stretched from left to right, a 180-degree panoramic view. The last of the sun was fading now, the light playing on the stonework in the apartment.

"I love this place," he said.

"I brought a couple of girls up," Elaine said. "If you want."

Darwin thought about that for a second. Then he nodded and smiled. "That will be fine. It was a long trip, and I could use a little help relaxing."

"They're in your room, waiting."

He gave Elaine a mischievous sideways glance.

"Is the new one here?"

Elaine smiled, but shook her head. "She's not ready."

He shrugged. "Okay."

Darwin paced into the bedroom. It was very large, with a gigantic, double-king-sized bed. Cool stone floors and windows faced the ocean. Peach-colored curtains billowed in the light breeze. Wide French doors gave out onto a private balcony. Night was coming in, and he was ready for it.

The girls were on the bed, wearing blue robes. They were nice, a blonde and a brunette. They looked up as he came in. Their eyes met his. Their eyes were so big, so beautiful. They were so young, and shy. He knew these girls. He knew their numbers. He knew their skills. And he knew, more than anything, that they belonged to him.

Again, he reveled in the things he owned. It was magic.

It was truly paradise.

CHAPTER NINE

8:45 p.m. Eastern Standard Time
A Safe House
Annieville, South Carolina

"Are those really alligators out there?" Ed Newsam said.

"What do you think?" Louis Clare said. His hands were zip-tied behind his back, his ankles zip-tied to the legs of the metal folding chair he was sitting on. His head was out of the bag, but his eyes were blindfolded.

"I think they are," Luke said. "And they sure look hungry."

Ed and Luke had just come in from the porch with a small flashlight. The light was a very bright LED, and Ed had been sweeping it across the stream that ran past the back of the tiny shack, out to the wide marshlands that opened to a large bay. Luke didn't like the thought of ending up in that water. There were at least a dozen gators out there. The light flashed across their faces in the deep dark of a South Carolina backwoods night, illuminating their eyes.

"I wonder what we could feed them," Luke said.

"I don't know," Ed said. "I guess we'll think of something."

Clare shook his head. He seemed calm for a helpless man in the custody of two strangers musing out loud about feeding him to alligators. He was smoking a cigarette, maybe that's what calmed him. Luke had given him one to get him talking. Like all true long-term smokers, Clare didn't need his hands to smoke. The cigarette just dangled from his mouth.

"Give it a rest," he said. "I've heard all these jokes before. You think I haven't? Feed me to alligators? You guys are cops. You're not going to do anything to me."

"What makes you think we're cops?" Ed said.

"Simple," Clare said. "If you weren't cops, I'd probably already be dead."

"Have you been doing things someone might want to kill you for?" Luke said.

Clare shrugged. "You tell me."

"Well, you've done things in the past that someone might want to kill you for," Ed said. "I'm sure some of your old victims might like to kill you, or their families."

"But you're talking about the past," Clare said. "That's the key phrase. *In the past.* I was young, misguided. I did my time. I paid my debt to society. I'm rehabilitated. If I wasn't, they wouldn't have let me out. I'm better now."

Ed seemed perfectly calm, too. "You'll be better when I say you're better."

"Yeah?" Clare said. "And who are you supposed to be?"

"Nobody."

Clare nodded. "That's right. You're nobody."

Luke was standing in a corner of the empty room. The place was just an old tumbledown shack with three rooms, at the end of a dirt road. The kitchen had been left to deteriorate on its own. There was a microwave oven, and a stove with one electric burner that still worked. There was a small refrigerator that came to about waist height. It wasn't plugged in, and there was black mildew growing inside of it. The sink worked, but when Luke turned on the tap, it had spit and sputtered for about thirty seconds. There was an aluminum pot and some old instant coffee bags in a sealed Mason jar. You could make stale black coffee, if you wanted.

Luke had no idea where Don had gotten this place from. FBI, CIA, DOD. Just a place where you could disappear people for a little while. It seemed like no one had been here in years.

"You're a chump," Clare said. "That's all you are."

It occurred to Luke now that Clare had never actually seen Ed. Luke had already bagged Clare before he brought him out of the motel. They switched from the hood to the blindfold while standing behind him.

He watched as Ed approached Clare. Ed still didn't seem the slightest bit angry. He seemed almost lost in thought, wandering around inside his own head. He put one strong hand on Clare's forehead, and gently pushed the man's head backwards. The chair tipped up on its hind legs.

"Wait!" Clare said. "Wait!"

The chair rolled over backwards. Ed made no attempt to slow the man's fall. Clare's head made a heavy THUNK against the peeling linoleum. Gravity just took him, all impact. His cigarette flew away and rolled across the floor. His teeth clacked together as he hit. He was lucky he didn't bite off the tip of his tongue.

"Ow! What is wrong with you? You can't do this anymore. I have rights. I'm going to have your badge, you know that?"

"You lost your cigarette, Louis," Luke said.

Ed studied the man on the floor. "And you won't have my badge because I'm not a cop. Is this how you did your time, mouthing off and complaining like a punk? I don't believe it. You never would have made eighteen minutes, never mind eighteen years."

There was a long moment of silence.

"You need to understand your situation. Think. If your brain works at all, now is the time to use it."

Clare didn't say a word. Apparently, he was doing as he was told. He was in an odd position, the back of his head against the floor, the back of the chair against the floor, his legs up in the air, tied to the legs of the chair. He was still in a sitting position, but he had been rotated ninety degrees.

"I don't like people like you," Ed said. "You understand that part, right?"

"Yes."

"Does anyone care about you?" Ed said. "Will anyone miss you?"

Clare thought about it, but not for very long. Luke already knew the answer. This guy had a mother once, but she died while he was locked up. He had a couple of siblings somewhere, but Trudy said there was no evidence that he saw them.

Other than that…

"No. There's a hooker that I see sometimes, but you know how that goes. Money."

Ed nodded, though Clare couldn't see it. "I do know. Why would anyone see a man like you for free? So listen. I will feed you to the alligators. I mean that. I don't like you. You know that already. But here's something you don't know. I've killed men before, quite a few, and for less than what you've done. It's really that simple. You will cooperate with me, or I will kill you. No one will find your body. No one will even care. You'll just be a bad guy who disappeared one night."

Clare's Adam's apple bobbed. "What do you want?" he said.

"A girl went missing late last week, up in Wilmington."

Clare's chest heaved. He took a deep breath and let out a long exhale. Luke recognized the movement. It was a sigh of relief.

"Saw it on the news," Clare said. "That's all. I had nothing to do with it. Don't even know anything about it. I don't involve myself in that kind of thing anymore. I'm out on parole. If I get busted again, they will send me away for the rest of my life. I don't want that. I like my freedom, such as it is."

"You know something about it," Luke said from where he was standing.

Clare shook his head. "I don't. I really don't."

"Think," Ed said again.

"I knew you guys were cops. Sorry. I can't help you. And I'm going to talk to my parole officer about this, I promise you. You had me going there for a minute. It's against the law, what you're doing. Habeas corpus, all that. You can't just take people away. You have to arrest me or let me go. And if you arrest me, I have the right to remain silent. So am I under arrest?"

"We're not cops," Luke said. "We're interested parties. We can do whatever we want. We were brought in because some people want this problem fixed, and they're worried the cops can't or won't do it."

Clare was still shaking his head. "Like I said… sorry."

"If you can't help us, that means you're useless to us," Ed said. "You know what we call things that are useless?"

Clare didn't answer, so Luke answered for him.

"Trash," he said.

"And you know what we do with trash, right?"

There was a long pause before Luke spoke this time.

"We take it out."

Louis Clare shook his head. "I don't believe you."

* * *

Clare screamed into the deep darkness. It echoed among the trees and swamps, and came back to them. The sound was haunting.

"Shout all you want," Ed said. "There's nobody else here."

There was a long moment of quiet.

"What do you see out there?" Luke said.

He swept his flashlight across the water. Eyes sparkled in the inky darkness, twenty or thirty pairs of eyes. They were low, at water level, along the embankments of the creek. As Luke watched, a couple of pairs seemed to creep closer. There was a splash as something heavy went into the water.

"Eyes!" Clare said. "I see eyes!"

He was standing now, his blindfold off, at the edge of the deck that looked over the water. The railing had collapsed at some point in the past. Ed had looped a length of thin rope that they'd found in a drawer through the zip ties on Clare's wrists.

Clare leaned way out over the water, his feet on the deck, his body in space. His arms were pulled behind his back at nearly a right angle. His shoulders were bunched, and his neck was sticking out like some strange bird. The position looked uncomfortable.

The only thing keeping him here was Ed, who was holding him up by the rope. The rope was taut, each end of it wrapped around one of Ed's hands. Ed leaned back a touch, the muscles in his shoulders, biceps, and forearms working.

The zip ties were tight on Clare's wrists. His hands had turned red, then purple from the loss of blood flow.

"You want to meet those eyes? In the drink, hands tied. You know what the gators do, right? They hold you down and drown you. Then they save your body to snack on later. They like it when you start to rot and fall apart."

"The meat falls right off the bone," Luke said. For a second, he sounded like a waiter in a nice restaurant.

Ed giggled at that. He must have thought the same thing.

Clare was smoking another cigarette. Even in this moment of extremis, he was putting another nail in the coffin. He would go to the gates of hell with a smoke dangling from his mouth.

"I'll tell you what I know. Okay?"

"I thought you didn't know anything?"

"I don't," Clare said. "But I can guess."

"So guess."

"Someone sold the girl out. It was too easy to take her. Whoever did it knew where she was going to be. That's inside information. They knew everything she was doing. You can't anticipate a kid like that unless you're close to her, real close. They had her texts, they had her emails. They knew what she was up to."

"Who are they?"

He shook his head. "I don't know."

Ed let his grip on the rope slip the tiniest amount. Clare's body lurched forward over the water. He made an animal sound, like a grunt. It was the sound of fear.

"Guess."

Clare was speaking quickly, his words a torrent.

"I don't know. Hired hands. Probably freelancers. Someone wanted a kid like that one. People have their preferences. Sixteen-year-old girl, that's pretty vanilla. Maybe they wanted that specific kid for some reason. I don't know. Anyway, they brought people in, professionals. They did the job, passed the kid along the line, and moved on. In and out in a few hours. Some guys like to work that way."

"Where did they take her? Where does the line go?"

"I have no idea."

Ed nearly let him go again. This time, Clare made something closer to a squeal.

"Last chance, Lou. You're going in. We're out of patience."

"Wait! Wait. I know of a building. I can give you that much. It's a safe place. People temporarily park kids there sometimes, or they used to. I don't know if it's still in operation. It's a couple hours from here. It's all I know. I'm out of that life. Okay? You're talking to the wrong guy."

"Where is it?"

Clare shrugged, but didn't say anything.

"Lou…"

He breathed deeply. "You don't know the kind of trouble I could get in."

Luke shook his head. A memory flashed in his mind of Big Daddy Bill Cronin. This was Bill's domain, making people talk. Luke thought of all the times he had winced inwardly while watching Big Daddy work. Big Daddy would get angry with the interview subjects sometimes, treat them badly, hurt them.

"They're weasels," Bill had told Luke one time. "And they will always try to weasel out if you let them."

Luke hardened. He felt it coming over him suddenly, almost as if someone had dipped him in quick-set concrete. This man, who had been a very bad man and might still be one, was going to try to weasel out. But they weren't going to let him do that.

"I'd say you're in the biggest trouble of your life right now."

He took his gun out of its shoulder holster. He slipped a long sound suppressor from the pocket of his pants, fit it to the grooves of the barrel, and began to mount it. He felt cold now, outside of himself.

"The alligators will eat your body. They just won't have to drown you first."

Clare was looking back at Luke. He eyed the gun warily. He seemed to go limp. He knew what a silencer looked like. He knew what it was for.

"All right. Look. It's up in Florence. Not that far. I don't know the address, but I can tell you how to get there."

With a sudden burst of violent effort, Ed yanked Clare back in. Clare collapsed to the porch, his body trembling.

"We're going there tonight," Ed said. "Right now, in fact. You live here until we come back. If we get there, and it isn't real, I swear…"

"It's real," Clare said from the floor. "It's more real than you could ever want."

"Good."

"I hate you guys," Clare said. "You know that?"

Ed squatted down next to him on the deck.

"I hate you, too."

CHAPTER TEN

March 28, 2006
12:25 a.m. Eastern Standard Time
Florence, South Carolina

"We got a van earlier today," Swann said.

He was still awake, and on the job. He had guided them to this spot, locating it from satellite images, based on the information Clare had given.

Now he was murmuring into Luke's ear. Luke held the phone close. In his other hand, he held a large pair of bolt cutters. On the way here, he had stopped at a twenty-four-hour Walmart and bought the cutters for cash.

Swann droned on. "Your typical Ford van, white, unmarked, the kind of thing people carry junk around in all the time. It was spotted on a private security camera in the Wrightsville Beach neighborhood where the party was held the night of the abduction. It was also on camera footage taken from inside a restaurant on the main drag of the town. The camera was pointed out the window of the place, at the street. The van was at a red light for a couple minutes, a little before two in the morning. Careful driver, didn't risk running the yellow, had his left turn indicator on. No sense getting pulled over for something minor."

"Yeah," Luke said, walking with Ed down a back street in a deserted industrial zone just a few miles from the famous Darlington Motor Speedway. Swann said that when looking at the area from the sky, the race track was easily the biggest man-made thing for a hundred miles in any direction.

Luke would like to go there. He had loved auto racing when he was a kid. But he filed that thought away. Not tonight.

"Here's the kicker," Swann said. "The van was parked outside the girl's high school for half an hour in the afternoon earlier that day, right around the time school let out. Video cameras caught them there, too. There are video cameras everywhere nowadays. These guys were stalking their prey."

"Where's the van now?" Luke said.

"It's a rental van. Not a U-Haul or anything like that. A small business, local to the area. I'm going to give you the details of the place once you finish up there. Maybe in the morning you guys can stop in and have a chat with whoever's on duty."

"All right," Luke said. "That's sounds good." And it did. The van sounded promising, but he was focused on where they were at this moment. "We're almost at the building. I'm going to hang up now."

"Good luck," Swann said.

Luke hung up and put the phone back in his pocket.

They had left the car a few parking lots away. The road here was closed, blocked by a weather-beaten, crazily leaning wooden fence. The fence was easy to walk around, but to bring the car in, they would have had to ram the thing down.

The whole area here seemed closed, a wasteland. There were beer cans strewn all over the unused road. They passed an old sofa, the stuffing ripped up and exploding out of it like some weird volcano. The warehouse building was just up ahead, small, nondescript, and gone to seed.

It was two stories high. Broken windows were covered by wooden boards. Grass grew through cracks in the blacktop of the parking lot. Overhead sodium arcs gave off bleak yellow light. Most of the lights were out.

"Doesn't look like they're using it anymore," Ed said.

Luke shook his head. "No, it sure doesn't."

There was an old box truck in the parking lot, but no cars. The truck had no obvious markings on it, other than a faded serial number at the rear. The lot was fenced in, the fence topped with barbed wire, and the gate had a thick chain looped through it, with a heavy padlock.

Swann had alerted them to the locked gate ahead of time.

"Nobody home," Ed said.

"No."

"Guess we should let ourselves in."

Luke clipped the chain on the gate. The gate was on rollers and was rusty. With a little effort, they pushed it aside.

Now they were trespassing. They had driven up here on the say-so of a former human trafficker who had given them the information because they kidnapped him and threatened to kill him. They had flown here under assumed identities. They were well outside the rules of the game.

When they did black operations, they were usually in some other country. That didn't make this right or wrong, just different.

As they crossed the parking lot, a motion detector light came on. It was very bright, glaring. Luke shielded his eyes. He knew that motion detector lights were meant to keep the amateurs honest. Kids, graffiti artists, vandals—a sudden bright light to the face kept these types out. It did nothing to Luke and Ed but annoy them.

Luke glanced at the truck as they passed it. The door to the box was also secured with a heavy chain and a padlock. That caught his eye. He thought of truck rental places, many trucks in a row, the back doors open, the box swept broom clean.

The box of an empty truck usually wasn't locked. Why lock it when there's nothing inside?

"Let's check the truck before we go in the building," Luke said.

Ed shrugged his big shoulders.

"All right."

They went to the back of the truck and Luke clipped that chain with the bolt cutters as well. He let the heavy chain snake to the ground. Ed turned the handle and yanked the door up.

The smell hit them both right away. It was subtle, no longer overpowering because it was from a long time ago. Even so, they both recognized it instantly. The fact of it was like a punch in the face. The smell of rot. The smell of dead things.

Ed groaned.

"Oh no," Luke said.

They climbed into the truck. It was dark inside, and they flashed their lights around. The inside of the box had been lined with foam egg crate material, the kind used for soundproofing music studios.

Against one wall was an oversized chest, four or five feet long, like something people would put ice in for a family gathering at the beach. Two strong men would carry it, one on each end, and it would be filled with beer and soda, and hot dogs and hamburgers for grilling.

The chest had a lock on it. This was the smallest and easiest of the locks to clip.

Luke felt a rush of dread as he cut the lock.

Ed lifted the lid.

"Dammit," he said, his voice low.

The remains of a person were inside the chest, submerged in filthy water that had probably once been ice. The body was badly decayed, dressed in a skirt and what Luke thought must have been a tube top. The skin of the corpse was sunken and dark, and rotting away. Chunks of it were floating free in the water. It had a full head of long hair, fanned out in the water like seaweed. It was impossible to say much about it, other than it was the body of a child.

"I'm going to kill somebody," Ed said.

Luke stared at it, the horror sinking in. He had spent a lot of time in war. People were killed in war. Children were killed in war. This wasn't war. This was something else… premeditated, thought out. This place was abandoned, and no one came here anymore. The child had been left behind, like an afterthought.

Like garbage.

Someone got what they wanted, a voice told him, *and left this here.*

Without warning, Ed lurched and jumped out the back. The sudden movement of his massive frame made the entire truck shudder.

Luke watched him go.

Ed stumbled a few steps away, then sank to his knees. He was in shadow, outside the range of the motion detectors, but Luke could see him raise his fists to the sky and shout something. The sound was unintelligible. There were words in it, but all Luke heard was the shriek. Then Ed vomited.

He was on all fours now, his body spasming as he wretched up the Taco Bell they had picked up on the way here. Ed had eaten a lot of it. It all came out.

Luke closed the lid of the chest.

He reminded himself that the child was already gone. Whatever fear and loneliness that child had known was over. The real child was not in that chest.

He climbed down and walked toward Ed.

Ed had been to war, done the things Luke had done, seen what Luke had seen. He had never seen Ed react like this. But Ed had a child on the way, and he had been acting out of character for weeks.

An image of Gunner flashed in Luke's mind. A big, fat, happy baby.

He shook his head to clear it. Gunner had nothing to do with this. Nothing like this was ever going to happen to Gunner.

"Are you okay?" he said.

Ed was on his knees now, wiping his mouth. "Do I look okay?"

"No. That's why I ask."

Ed looked up at him. His eyes were red. Not only had he puked, but big Ed was crying. It wasn't a lot, he could speak through it, but it was there.

"You and I don't talk much, do we?"

Luke considered that.

"Like, in a real way," Ed said. "Real shit."

Luke supposed they didn't. That was true. They had been on some heavy metal operations together, and Luke thought of Ed as a good friend. He had trusted Ed with his life many times, and never regretted it. But in their personal lives, they tended to keep it jokey and light. It was easier that way.

"No. I guess we don't."

Ed looked at the ground. "I knew a girl when I was a kid. Cynthia. Just a girl from the neighborhood, but with a fancy name. Not Cindy. Cynthia. She insisted on that, even when she was ten years old. I don't know why."

"Ed..."

Ed raised a hand. "Wait. Let me finish. Cynthia was a good girl. But as we got older, teenagers, she fell through the cracks. Some kids do. Rough home life, problems in school, I don't know. In her case, it was drugs, then prostitution. I felt bad about it, but we had drifted apart in high school, and I was a kid myself. I joined the Army, and then I was out of the neighborhood. I went on a long deployment one time, and after that I had some extended leave, so I went back to the old stomping grounds."

He was quiet for a long moment.

"I was nineteen. Still a kid, but more like a man now. I had been to war. I stood tall. I had filled out."

Luke suppressed a smile at the idea of Ed "filling out."

"When I got back, I looked people up. Cynthia was gone, snatched. Somewhere in my head, I had imagined her getting clean and turning it around. People do that. But it wasn't the case. I had just missed her, as it turned out. She had only been gone a couple of weeks."

He paused for a long moment.

"*They* had taken her. Those people, man."

He gestured with his head at the truck.

"*These people.* You know. These people who think that it doesn't matter. Other people ain't nothing to them. Hopes, dreams. It doesn't mean a thing. They'll do what they want."

Luke had a sinking feeling. He did not want to hear the rest of this story.

"I found them," Ed said. "There are no real secrets. This child here wasn't a secret. People know about these things. People are sitting on information. The trick is to find those people and get them to speak. Which I did. I did not take no for an answer. When I got to the apartment, when I got there, Cynthia was already dead, but they still had the body with them. They had put it in the bathtub. The things they had done to her…"

His voice trailed off and he gritted his teeth.

"There were two of them. I'll never forget them as long as I live. I don't want to forget them. I always want to remember them. The first guy resisted me and he died quick. Too quick. I was sorry about that. So the second guy…"

He looked up at Luke again. Tears were streaming down his face. Luke didn't know whether to hug him or arrest him.

"I kept that man alive for a week while I killed him."

Luke took his cell phone out. He speed-dialed Swann. He found himself suddenly angry at Ed. If Ed wanted to know why they never talked about serious things, this was why. *This.*

This. Was. Why.

"You didn't tell me that," Luke said. "Okay? This conversation never happened."

Ed nodded. "All right."

"We need to call this in, and technically, we aren't even here."

Swann's voice came on the line. There was hard rock music playing in the background.

"Mike's Pizza," he said.

CHAPTER ELEVEN

5:05 a.m. Eastern Standard Time
A Safe House
Annieville, South Carolina

"Wake up."

Clare had fallen asleep in the chair. His chin was on his chest. He opened his eyes a crack, and looked up at Luke and Ed.

Ed slapped him across the face.

"I said wake up."

That got him. His head snapped sideways with the force of the slap, and his eyes popped open wide.

Luke went to the sink and ran some water into the metal pot. It was time for stale instant coffee. It was that darkest point of night, in the hours right before dawn. Soon the sky would begin to lighten. They had another day ahead of them.

He was going to let Ed do the interrogating.

They had barely spoken the entire ride back down here. Ed was such a simmering volcano of rage that Luke almost overlooked his own anger. There was going to be hell to pay. Swann had called them while they were driving. The local cops had found two more decayed bodies inside the warehouse. The South Carolina Bureau of Investigation was already on the scene.

Clare knew more than he was letting on. Of course he did. He had given them the warehouse, maybe hoping there'd be nothing to find—just an old warehouse that criminals once used in the deep, dark past. And maybe that's all it was, but they were going to find out. Luke wouldn't allow Ed to kill Clare, but he was going to step aside and let Ed get the information out of him.

"Why did you hit me?" Clare said.

Ed squatted down close to him. Ed had the crazy eyes now. The scariest thing about Ed was not his size. It was his eyes.

"You're an accessory to murder, Lou."

Clare took a deep breath. “I didn’t do it. Whatever you found there, I didn’t do it. It’s just a place that I knew about. I don’t know anything about…”

Ed slapped him again. And again. Ed’s hands were huge. The slaps were hard, bone rattling.

Luke put the water on the burner and turned it to high.

“Shut up,” Ed said. He spoke very quietly, really just a little above a whisper. “Whether you know anything about those bodies doesn’t matter. Three bodies, by the way. Children. Two in the warehouse, one in a truck parked outside. Okay?”

Clare blinked. He said nothing.

“Whether murder, or conspiracy, or jaywalking would stick to you doesn’t matter. You know why?”

Ed leaned in very close to Clare’s face now. They were almost close enough to kiss. Or maybe Ed would bite him and tear the flesh from his cheek.

“Because I’m going to kill you, Lou. And I’m going to do it slow, right here in this house, starting now. And it’s going to take a long time, and you’re going to cry and beg me to stop. Then you’re going to beg me to kill you. But I’m not going to do it like that. I’m going to do it nice and slow. You and I are going to get to know each other. I’m going to know everything about you, everything you know, and each step of the way you’re going to tell me something more. Every dirty little thing you’ve ever done. The name of every filthy bastard you’ve ever worked with. You’re going to tell me everything, all because you want to make it stop. But it’s not going to stop. Not until I think it’s enough.”

Clare was silently weeping.

“You can start with some names.”

“Don’t you understand?” Clare said. “If I give you anything else, they’ll kill me.”

Ed uttered a short bark of laughter. He spoke as if to an imbecile, someone who could not understand plain English unless you gave it to them slowly and simply.

“You’re already dead.”

The water was boiling. Luke looked at Ed.

“You want coffee?”

CHAPTER TWELVE

Time Unknown
Place Unknown

She woke with a start.

Until a moment ago, she had been wandering in some other world—a world without pain or thoughts, without feelings or experiences. She drifted along in that dream world. She felt like an abandoned ship, floating with the tides and blown by the wind.

Just before she opened her eyes, a thought flashed in her brain, like lightning. For a fraction of a second, it seemed like she had the answer. None of this was real. None of it had happened. There were no kidnappers.

She had fallen asleep and it was all just a nightmare. In another second she would open her eyes and find herself right where she belonged—in her own bed in the house she shared with her mom and Jeff.

She was wrong. Her eyes popped open and confirmed the truth. Everything she hoped was a nightmare was real. Surprisingly, her mind was clear. The drugs they had given her had worn off.

She was in a small room. They had been keeping her here for days, or maybe weeks. It was impossible to tell any more.

"Charlotte," she said, barely even a whisper. The voice sounded to her like the croak of a frog.

No one called her by that name now.

The room was in twilight. On one dark wall, she could make out the slightly lighter square where there was a window. The window's glass had been blacked out. But even through the gloom she could make out its shape, because of a small amount of daylight penetrating along the edges. In here, it was night. It was always night. Outside, wherever that was, the sun was rising and daytime was coming.

She was on a wooden bed, and the bed was pushed up against the wall. Under the only light spot—the window—there was a bedside table. That was the room—bed, window, table. And across from her, a black door. There was no doorknob on this side of the door. You could not open this room from the inside.

Memories began to flood her brain. A lump formed in her throat, and each memory that came back to her caused that lump to swell. Soon the lump was so fat, so thick, it would not let her breathe.

She remembered sneaking out of the house that night, so clever, so smart, so daring, like a teenage James Bond. Like Angelina Jolie in *Tomb Raider*.

She remembered the party at Taylor's house. She had two drinks there, vodka and tonic. Taylor was rich, and her house was incredible, of course. Jeff never tired of telling her that he and her mom were rich, too, and so was she, by the standards of normal people. But Taylor was really rich, filthy rich, crazy rich, and you could tell the difference.

The drinks had gone straight to her head. Lights were flashing, music was pumping. She was in the heated pool, and then the hot tub with a bunch of people. It was a chilly night, but the water was hot and the water jets were pounding. It was so loud!

Everybody was laughing. It was just that amazing feeling like life was totally ahead of you and the sky was the limit. They were all going to be rich and fabulous like Taylor one day. They would make it on their own, or Taylor would bring them with her. It didn't matter.

Then she was on the beach with Rob. Of course it was Rob. Big, beautiful Rob. Rob Haskins, how many girls had ended up down on the beach with him?

Who cares? The feelings were there, so…

Then everything was gone. It happened so suddenly. Rob was gone. She was gone. Misery, sickness, confusion. Waking up in a cage. The woman hitting her hand with a stick. Then giving her food.

And then she was gone again.

She remembered first waking up here. She had been bothered by that window, a window that no light came through. It made everything in the room seem dark and hostile. The first thing she did was take a look to see what was wrong with it. She walked right up to it.

The glass was painted black.

Black. A black window? The paint was solid, caked on in several layers. And it was not painted on the inside—only the outside was painted, or maybe between the panes. A person on the inside, locked in this room, could not scratch the paint off.

What kind of torture room is this? Who paints the windows with black paint?

She remembered staring at the door after that. It was almost as bad as the window. It was just an ordinary wooden door, also painted black. But what was behind it? Who would come through that door?

She watched it carefully. She did not want it to open. But her body was waking up. She was thirsty and she was hungry.

When was the last time I ate? On the plane?

The plane to where?

Where am I? Why am I here?

After a little while, she realized she needed to go pee. She looked around the room. There was nowhere to go in here. Time passed, and the feeling became worse. Now she couldn't hold her bladder much longer. She was nauseated from hunger, and from thirst, and she needed to use the bathroom—all at the same time.

She knew what she had to do. She had to stand up, step toward the door, and knock on it. But she couldn't do it. She was too scared. Her heart started thumping in her chest at the thought of it. Who would open the door? What would she say to that person?

What if the door never opened?

She couldn't bear it much longer—she needed to go to the bathroom!

She got up and moved toward the door. Her heartbeat was so loud that it seemed to fill the whole empty room. If there was someone on the other side of that door, he could probably hear her heart, too.

There were no sounds outside this room. She tapped on the door, three times. Suddenly, someone behind the door was moving toward it. A shadow was there, on the other side. Some sort of bolts, one near the top and one near the bottom, were pulled back. The door opened.

The first thing she saw was a rifle that hung across a man's chest, with the barrel up high and the gun's strap around the man's neck. After a moment of shock, she saw the man himself. He was small and dark, with deep-set eyes. He had dark hair. He wore a green uniform. His arm rested on the barrel of his rifle, which was strapped on so high, it was almost to his chin. The gun seemed so natural on him it was almost as if he was born with it attached.

The man looked at her without emotion.

"I need to go to the bathroom," she said.

The man said nothing. His eyes were flat. She knew he understood her, because he jerked his head to the side, indicating the way. He took a step back and let her come out, then positioned himself in front of her. She followed him.

They moved down a narrow stone hallway. It seemed like they were underground, or in a submarine deep beneath the ocean. The trip took no more than a dozen steps. There was an unpainted wooden door at the end of the hall with the initials WC carved into it. The man pointed at the door.

"Bathroom?" she said.

The man nodded and said nothing.

She pushed the door open and rushed in. The tiny room afforded her a small sense of privacy. It was tiny, maybe three or four feet across. The walls were painted dark green. The toilet itself was gross, disgusting. There was a dark circle of rust inside the bowl.

She suddenly realized that she hadn't showered in a long time. She wanted to wash her hands very badly. She wanted to wash her entire body. But it wasn't to be. There was no sink in this room. There was no shower.

She came out. The guard was leaning against the wall like a statue. He was like some tool that had been left behind, a mop maybe, or a vacuum cleaner. When he saw her, he nodded his head, directing her back to the room where she woke up. She was supposed to go back to the room. She was going to be a prisoner inside there.

He put her inside the small and dark room again. She heard him on the other side, fiddling with the bolts, sliding them back into place. Then she was locked in and silence fell. No sounds. No sunlight. No people. Nothing at all. She was just utterly alone.

She drifted, dozed, and fell asleep.

Only to wake up again, now, in the same horrible place. She stared across at the black door, realizing what had awakened her this time. Someone had pulled back the bolts. Maybe the man with the gun had returned. Maybe he was going to hurt her. Maybe he was going to kill her.

The door creaked open, light from the outside hallway flooding in. She blocked her eyes with her hand. A silhouette stood there.

"Good morning, 21," a woman's voice said.

It was the woman from the airplane. "I'm Mistress Elaine," she said. "You may have forgotten. You should call me Mistress."

The woman was dressed in a bright green wrap, over what appeared to be a yellow-green one-piece bathing suit. She had a sun hat on her head, with sunglasses perched on top. She wore sandals on her feet. In one hand, she held a rod or switch like the one she had wielded on the airplane.

"It's time for you to get out of bed," the woman said. "Today is your big day, and we need to get you prepped and looking your best."

"What is the big day?" Charlotte said. Her voice still sounded like a croak. Her vocal cords were out of use. Her lips were chapped. Her throat felt dry. She could use a glass of water. Or a gallon.

"Today's the day you meet him," the woman said. "I hope you brought your appetite, because we're going to have a nice breakfast on the patio, then get you all cleaned up and beautiful for him. You'll want to make a good first impression."

"Who is he?"

The woman's stark emerald eyes seemed to show surprise. "Don't you know by now? He's the man who owns you."

CHAPTER THIRTEEN

8:05 a.m. Eastern Standard Time
Pistol Pete's Van & Truck Rental
Wilmington, North Carolina

"This was supposed to be an easy job."

Luke was tired. Usually by now, twenty-four hours into an operation without sleep, he would have reached for a Dexedrine. Probably more than one. But he hadn't brought any, and neither had Ed.

They were sitting in the car across a busy road from the truck rental lot, Pistol Pete's Van & Truck Rental. Morning traffic zipped by in each direction. A tall, heavyset guy had arrived half an hour ago. He had turned the sign in the office window around from CLOSED to OPEN just a few minutes ago.

Luke was on the phone with Trudy. They had passed her all of the names and places Louis Clare had given them. It was a long list. When he broke, he broke like a wave. They had left him tied up at the safe house. A couple of agents from the South Carolina Bureau of Investigation were on their way there. They were going to take him into custody, a little more official this time.

Clare was going to be answering a lot of questions in the days ahead. Or he could choose to remain silent instead. He did have that right.

"Swann just came in," Trudy said. "We're going to feed this stuff into intelligence and police databases all day, see what turns up. Mug shots, aliases, who's alive and who's dead, who's in jail, who might be in that area. It's a lot."

"Good," Luke said. "Can you do me one more favor?"

"Sure," she said. "Name it."

"Can you send a prescription of Dexedrine pills for Sem Goethals to a pharmacy around here? I'm beat."

"Luke!"

"Just let me know," he said.

"Okay. I'll see what I can do. In the meantime, drink some coffee."

"I'm long past coffee, darling."

She hung up.

Luke looked at Ed. Ed was in the driver's seat. Ed's eyes were bloodshot. The lids were heavy. His jaw was lined with dark stubble.

"You look worse than I feel," Luke said.

Ed shook his head. "You ready?"

Luke nodded. "Let's do it."

They climbed out of the car and crossed the street. Luke held a slip of paper with half the license plate number of the van in question. That was the best the cameras could do—white Ford van, with a South Carolina commercial vehicle plate starting with LPJ. That was a lot. A van fitting that description was available for rent from this location.

They entered the lot. Before going to the office, they walked slowly down the line of rental vehicles, inspecting the plates. There were only about twenty vans on the whole lot. This was going to take all of five minutes.

"Can I help you gentlemen?"

Luke looked up. Now he knew he was tired.

The man who had arrived stood there, twenty feet away, with a pump action shotgun. He wore work coveralls, and a denim baseball cap. A large belly, like a beach ball, protruded from his coveralls. He held the gun cradled in his thick arms, pointed at the sky. The man had simply appeared there, as if out of nowhere.

Instantly Luke and Ed had their guns out, pointed at the man.

"Drop it!" Ed said.

"FBI," Luke said.

The man raised one meaty hand, but still held the shotgun with the other.

"Drop it!" Ed said again. "Now. FBI."

A long, dangerous second passed.

"It's an expensive gun," the man said. "I ain't about to drop it."

"Then put it down slowly."

The man placed the shotgun on the ground, moving as though he was underwater. He raised both hands.

"Pistol Pete?" Luke said, still targeting the man's center mass.

The man nodded. "The very same."

Luke indicated the shotgun. "What happened to the pistol?"

Pistol Pete shrugged. "Times have changed. A pistol won't do anymore."

Luke and Ed did not lower their weapons.

"Do you know why we're here?" Luke said.

Pistol Pete nodded. "I suppose. The white van."

"Yes."

Pistol Pete shook his head. He spoke as though he wasn't being held at gunpoint. "I knew it was a mistake when I saw him. Man came in here the day before the girl got taken. Wanted to rent a van for cash. Anonymous, no questions asked. Willing to pay three times the price."

"Is that your business?" Ed said. "Anonymous rentals?"

Pistol Pete stared at Ed for a long second. "Part of. The rest is just the same as anybody else, but the big companies don't make it easy, do they? They'll gladly lose money for years to put a man like me out of business. When I go under, they'll raise their prices up the very next day."

"Is that why you didn't report it?"

Pistol Pete shook his head. "I didn't put two and two together until late last night. Woke up and knew what happened. I must be psychic. I had no reason to suspect him. The man brought that van in clean."

"That's your story, and you're sticking to it, right?" Ed said.

"I figured the girl ran off with a boyfriend," Pistol Pete said. He gave Ed another long look. "Maybe some black boy, something along those lines. That kind of thing is frowned upon around these parts, or used to be. Anyway, last I heard, anonymous cash rentals are against the law. Something to do with tax evasion, terrorism, things of that nature. You can see why a man might hesitate to…"

"Can you describe the man who rented the van?" Luke said.

Pistol Pete shrugged again. "Don't need to. Everybody walks in that door gets videotaped twice, once as they come in, once as they stand at the register. I don't advertise that fact, but they do."

Luke looked at Ed. Slowly, they holstered their guns.

"We're going to need to send that video to Washington," Luke said. "And we're also going to impound the vehicle in—"

As he spoke, three cars, all dark late-model sedans, roared into the parking lot. One came in the entryway, and two came in the exit. Instantly, half a dozen men leapt from the cars, guns drawn, and moved toward Ed, Luke, and Pistol Pete.

"Down!" one of the men screamed.

"Get DOWN!"

"FBI!"

Luke did as he was told. Beside him, Ed did the same. It took Pistol Pete a moment longer. He was heavy, and perhaps not accustomed to falling to the ground. So the FBI agents helped him with it. Two men tackled him and pressed him, epic stomach and fleshy face, to the pavement.

Luke lay face down on blacktop. He held his badge in the air behind him.

"FBI!" he shouted.

A hand slapped his badge away, and then two more pulled his wrists behind his back. He went limp. The worst thing you could do was resist. Resistance got people killed. Mistakes were made, and people died. This would all get sorted out eventually.

"I'm Agent Luke Stone," he said to the man handcuffing him. "FBI Special Response Team. DC office." He added DC office as if that would clarify things. Most FBI agents had no idea what the SRT even was.

They lifted him to his feet.

"What are you doing here?" one of the men said.

"Working a case, how about you?"

They walked him over to Pistol Pete, who was still on the ground in front of the office. Pete's nose was bleeding from where it had met the cement. He looked up balefully at Luke. Luke was still handcuffed—the agents didn't seem to be in a big hurry to believe him.

"If these are the FBI," Pistol Pete said from the ground, "then who the hell are you?"

CHAPTER FOURTEEN

12:10 p.m. Central Standard Time (1:10 p.m. Eastern Standard Time)
La Sierra de San Simon (St. Simon's Saw)
Near Honduras
The Caribbean Sea

They brought the girl up to him like room service.

"Yes," he said. "Beautiful. Do come in."

He was sitting in a wicker rattan chair in his living room, admiring the painting over the sofa, and the views through the open doorway to the balcony. Elaine had paid just under a hundred thousand dollars for that painting. Only the good Lord knew what the humidity in this place was doing to it. But it didn't matter.

Darwin King chose to surround himself with beautiful things. If they were destroyed by their proximity to him… well, nothing was meant to last forever.

On a small table next to him was an old-style telephone. Beside that was a glass with vodka, tonic, and ice. Darwin liked to open the bar right after lunch, really any day, but especially when ugliness was bound to arise. A certain person had indicated a desire to speak with him today. Darwin did not like dealing with this person, but he also didn't see much choice in the matter. A little alcohol would put some pleasant distance between him and the information the person chose to share.

And in the meantime…

The girl came in through the wide double doors from the hallway. Beyond those doors lay the house proper, and everything that took place outside of his private inner sanctum. Dozens of rooms, a giant modern kitchen that could run a large and popular restaurant, dining halls small and large—one for the normal pace of activities and one for when celebrations and gatherings were held, the inground pool and hot tub, a small gym, wraparound porches, fruit trees, and staggering views from just about everywhere.

This house must be a whole new world for the girl.

Ah, but she was still living down in the Tombs, so she couldn't enjoy her stay here yet. Well, they would see about that.

Two young men entered with her, flanking her. They each carried Uzi submachine guns. They were on loan from the Honduran army, and wore olive green uniforms. Darwin had friends in the Honduran government. Although this island was not part of Honduras, he was their guest, and under their protection. Darwin had many friends who protected him.

The girl and her escorts moved into the apartment. She was wearing a full white robe and hood, just as he preferred them to do when first meeting him. Her eyes were downcast. He was immediately struck by her. Her eyes, her face, her hair. Just gorgeous. He wanted to know everything about her. He wanted to own her completely. And that would come in time.

He waved the gunmen back to the doorway, and then through it. They were a necessary evil, and they made quite a first impression, but personally, he didn't like to look at them. Their presence ruined the aesthetics of the girl. They were not tall, for one thing. Honduran people, God love 'em, were short.

Darwin King was tall. He preferred tall people. These Hondurans were squat, and if he dared say so, they were not handsome. If he could have his own private army of towering, handsome Germans and Dutchmen, now wouldn't that be something?

The girl was standing there, in the middle of the room.

"21?" he said. "21, come here."

The girl in the robe walked timidly toward him. She did not look at him. She did not look side to side. She didn't look anywhere but at her own bare feet.

"Come on," Darwin said. "Don't be afraid. It's me, Darwin. That's my name. You're going to come to know me very well. I'm going to be your friend."

She stood in front of him. She was guarded and wary. She would not meet his eyes.

"Did they tell you about me?" he said.

She nodded. "Yes."

"Very good. What did they tell you?"

"They said you own this place."

Darwin nodded. "Yes. I do. And I own everything in it. And everyone here works for me. Do you like it here?"

She stared at the stone floor. Tears began to flow. They streamed down her face and dropped onto her robe. It was very sad. Darwin frowned.

"No," she said in a small voice. "I want to go home. Can I please go home?"

Darwin shook his head, and now he was sad, too. "I'm afraid not. You see, this is your home now. Your parents didn't want you anymore, and they gave you to me. Sold you, actually. They gave me what I consider a good price. A fair price, let's say."

The girl looked up and stared at him with round, red eyes. The tears streamed down as if someone had turned a faucet on low.

Darwin nodded. "It happens this way sometimes. It doesn't mean you're a bad person. It just means that they didn't want you, and I did. I knew you, and was watching you the whole time. Because I love you."

She seemed to have gotten stuck on one particular word. They always did.

"Sold me…"

"Yes. It's true. They sold you and I bought you. I own you now."

The girl just stared and stared.

"How is your stay so far?" Darwin said. He felt that he put just the right note of concern in his voice.

The girl shook her head. She wept softly, her body shaking. Such pain! Such sadness! She had no idea what delight it gave him.

"It's horrible," she said. Her mouth turned down and trembled, like a clown's grimace. Her voice was high-pitched, almost a squeak. "I don't understand what's happening here. No one will call me by my name. My name is Charlotte, but no one calls me that."

He watched her.

"It's okay," he said. He spoke softly, like a loving father. "Your name isn't Charlotte."

"It is! It's Charlotte."

He shook his head. "No. I'm sorry. That's false. They lied to you. That name was never you. It belongs to someone who died. You have a number, not a name. Your number is 21. I need you to understand that. People here want the best for you, and they will never call you by a name that isn't yours."

It was an old CIA mind control trick. Darwin had learned it from an aging master, a friend, now deceased, who had been involved in MK-ULTRA back in the Wild West days of the 1950s and 1960s. People had names, and over time they associated traits with those names. Life experiences, memories, loved ones, habits, boundaries. Over time, those traits became cemented in place. Say the name, and all these associations arise. People, quite literally, become their names.

I am Charlotte. Charlotte does these things, but doesn't do these other things. Charlotte loves her mom. Charlotte has dreams. Charlotte has preferences. Young Charlotte has beliefs, maybe even the beginning of a belief system.

But strip the name away. Once the name is gone, you control what comes next. Replace it with a number. A number has no associations. It's completely neutral. Robots have numbers. Robots do what they're programmed to do. Do this long enough (but not even *that* long), and the original personality begins to fade. After a while, the associations are gone, and so is the person.

Replace those associations with new ones, the ones you want the person to have. Number 21 is a slave. Number 21 does what master tells her to do. Number 21 loves her master, and wants to please him. Number 21 has no other purpose.

Darwin was an avid student of many topics, including human psychology. He had used this technique again and again. It was fascinating to him how well it worked.

"They keep me in a dark room," the girl said now.

See? She had already hit a brick wall with the name, so now she moved on. Look how quickly it happened! Textbook. That was a good sign.

"The window is blacked out. There's no light. I have to knock when I want to use the bathroom. Then these men come with guns and walk me to the bathroom. I'm so afraid, the way they look at me. I've seen some other girls, but they aren't friendly. They don't even speak to me. The woman, Elaine, hits me with a stick for no reason."

Darwin ignored her new complaints. It was important not to validate complaints, or even acknowledge them. She had no right to complain. She had no right to her own being. Anyway, what the girl thought of as unpleasant was actually for her own good. It was the start of her training.

That was life in the Tombs. The Tombs were on the first floor, in a part of the house shaded by dense overhanging trees. It was down near the laundry room. That area hadn't been renovated, by design. The windows in the rooms were blacked out. The one bathroom was a disgrace. The girls down there had no freedom of movement. It softened them up quickly, living in the Tombs.

Instead of fielding complaints, Darwin got right to the most important question.

"Have the men touched you at all?"

His orders were that no one touched the goods. Of course no one ever would, unless he said so. The thought of disobeying Darwin's orders… Ha! A breath of air, almost like a laugh, escaped him at the thought of it. He lent the girls to some of his important visitors, at times, but the help? It would never happen. If he heard of such a thing, everyone involved would die.

"No," she said. "None of them have touched me."

Darwin nodded. "That's good. Unfortunately, we are in a high-security situation, and we need the gunmen here to keep us all safe. But you say your stay hasn't been that great so far?"

"It's been awful. I want to go home."

"Well, you might as well get over the idea of going anywhere else. You're already home."

She closed her eyes and began to weep again. She was silent, her body shaking.

"I want you to be happy here, 21. Let me ask you a question. Do you want to get out of your dark room and move to a better one? Maybe even one up here on this floor, with an ocean view? Plenty of sunlight, fresh air. Look around. It's lovely up here. It's perfect."

She opened her eyes. She gave him a sideways look. She didn't trust him, of course. But he was dangling something desirable in front of her, and she was already learning how to navigate her new world. He liked fast learners.

"Look around," he said again.

She glanced around the room. Her movements were furtive, like a mouse would make. In her emotional state, she probably couldn't soak in the extent of the opulence, the totality of it. But she could compare it to the room she stayed in now.

"Is it better?"

She nodded. "Yes."

"Do you want to live up here?"

She hesitated.

"What do I have to do?"

He shrugged. "Simple enough. You take a vow to me. You become my consort, my servant, and in a sense, you become my slave."

He raised a hand. "Don't get stuck on that word. It doesn't mean what you might think. It's a good thing. The girls here, all of them are my slaves. And they enjoy it. You'll see. It comes with benefits. The first of which is you live in paradise. After a little while, when we build trust with each other, you become free to roam the grounds. The pool, the gym, the library, everything is open to you. It is unbelievable here, and I want you to enjoy it all. But the choice is up to you. No one has to become my slave."

"And if I don't?"

Darwin shrugged. He sighed. "Well, if you don't want to, then you can go back to your room. But I can't guarantee your protection down there. Some of these guards…"

He shook his head. "You know, these men are Hondurans, and there has been a lot of unrest in Honduras. A long civil war, rebels, drug cartels, massacres, you name it. It's turned some of these men we hire into savages. Nothing can be done about that, I'm afraid. It's just all the murder and death. People lose their sense of humanity. They're liable to do anything. They see a pretty young girl, living in the dark, all alone, unprotected…"

He shook his head again. He watched the calculations going on behind the girl's eyes. He had presented her with a new problem. Not only was it dark and dreary in the Tombs, it was also dangerous. It was a basic math problem, very simple, and he didn't have to wait long for the answer.

"I want to stay up here," she said.

He paused. "Okay. Good. For now, you're going to stay where you are downstairs. You have to earn your way up here. But in the days ahead, you'll get the chance to do just that. Just focus on it. Focus on the opportunities that come your way."

Her disappointment was written all over her face. Disappointment was a mild word for it. It was heartbreak. It was despair. It was terror. All of those words and more, wrapped into one. Already, she would do almost anything not to go back to the darkness. But she had to wait.

"Can you do that for me? Can you focus on the opportunities that come your way, and grab them when you get the chance?"

She nodded. "Yes."

"I demand complete obedience," he said. "That's what will get you out of your dark room. Can you give me that gift? The gift of obedience? Doing what I say, when I say it, without question?"

"Yes," she said, barely more than a whisper.

"That makes me very happy."

Darwin felt his grin go nearly ear to ear. The promise of complete obedience—it was music, sweet music. Of course, it was a hard promise to keep, but he would help her. He would light the stones along her path.

"21, I want to tell you something. Right now, this moment, is the most beautiful you've ever been. And the longer you stay with me, and the better you obey me, the more beautiful you'll become."

He paused, just for a moment. "Do you believe me?"

He gazed into her doe eyes.

"Yes," she said.

"Then do something for me, 21."

She nodded, but said nothing.

"Remove your robe."

She froze for a long moment. Darwin didn't touch the moment, or try to control it. He let it unfold by itself. After a while, she undid the belt of the robe, but didn't open the robe itself.

Darwin gestured with his hands. "Just open it, and let it fall to the floor. Remember the promise you made. Total obedience, without question."

She did as she was told. The robe dropped. Underneath it, she wore a small blue bikini that Elaine must have provided to her. It fit her small body perfectly. The sight took his breath away.

"Turn around," he said. "All the way around, so I can see all of you."

She did.

"My God, 21. What an angel you are. Only God could have made you."

Someone cleared his throat. Darwin looked up and a man was standing there at the doorway. The effect of 21, the dream of her, was suddenly shattered. The man was one of Darwin's private bodyguards, not one of the Hondurans. He was a big man, an American, wearing dress slacks and a sports jacket despite the heat. The jacket was to conceal his gun, of course. He looked a little sheepish for a hired killer.

"Yes?" Darwin said.

"Sir, that call you were expecting? I'm told he's on the line and ready."

CHAPTER FIFTEEN

1:15 p.m. Eastern Standard Time
Cape Fear Hyatt Regency Hotel
Wilmington, North Carolina

"It's okay here," Luke said. "Kind of pretty. I mean, it's not the Grand Canyon or anything."

Luke stood on the balcony of the hotel room, sipping a paper cup of room coffee, and talking to Becca on the telephone. From where he stood, he could look across the Cape Fear River at the historic brick buildings of downtown Wilmington. The river was dark brown and the buildings were three and four stories high.

Up the river from here was an old naval destroyer they had turned into a museum, and further upriver were the massive dock cranes of the Port of Wilmington.

Luke had slept a bit, and had strange, vivid dreams.

Ed wasn't the only one who had lost a girl when he was young. Luke never spoke of it, and could go years without even remembering it, but there had been an incident when he was a child. It was not his life. It took place entirely on the TV.

He had grown up in Northern California. When he was seven or eight, a pretty blonde-haired girl about his age had disappeared from a town near his. Her name was Megan. Megan Rose Abbott. God, he could see her so clearly, even now. There was a photograph of her, smiling in a pink dress and a sun hat. The light around her seemed to shimmer.

She was gone, just gone, her family distraught and crying on the TV news every night. The days turned to weeks. Her father was detained, but then released. A local auto mechanic was detained, but released. Hundreds of people were searching for her in woods and grasslands. Time passed, and the story faded from the news. Then only a handful of people were still looking.

One day, they found her body at the bottom of an old boarded up well twenty miles from where she lived. How did she get there? Did she fall in?

No. She had been taken. She had been viciously assaulted. Then she had been thrown away, discarded. The man who had taken her was an animal. He was not fit to live. A man like Ed Newsam, if he could find this animal, would pull him apart, like taffy, like a Thanksgiving turkey. Maybe Luke would even do the same. He wasn't sure, and he didn't want to find out.

But the animal was never found. DNA evidence did not exist in those days. There were suspects, but they all had alibis. A drifter, a beast, someone unknown, a darkness in human form, had stolen Megan, and he had done this.

Luke used to dream of her, off and on, for years. And he did again, today.

She was still a child. They were sitting together, cross-legged on the wooden floor of a cabin, like children would do. It was similar to the cabin where he and Ed had brought Louis Clare, but it was not that cabin.

Luke and Megan faced each other. She was his mentor. She knew more than he did. Her suffering had made her wise, not beyond her years, but beyond all time and space.

"What is this nightmare world?" he asked her.

She looked into his eyes. She was a very serious little girl now.

"It's a vale of tears," she said.

She nodded to herself. "It's a valley of shadow."

"'Yea,'" Luke quoted, "'though I walk through the valley of the shadow of death, I will fear no evil.'"

She shrugged. "If that helps you."

He nodded. "I think it does."

"Okay," she said softly.

"Is there anything I can do for you?" he said.

She shook her head. "No. What's done is done. There is no going back. All you can do is your best."

Luke was crying then, tears streaming down his face. Megan stared at him, her face blank. She said nothing.

Later, he dreamed of a sturdy oak door. He was on one side of the door, trying to keep it shut. On the other side were at least a dozen men trying to push their way in. With a giant effort, he was able to slam the door closed, but then found out that the lock was broken. As he stared at the broken lock, it changed. Not only was the lock broken, there was no lock. In fact, there wasn't even a doorknob. There was just a hole in the door where the doorknob would be.

A hand came through the hole. It wasn't attached to a wrist. It was just a hand. It reached Luke's side of the door and crawled up the door toward his arms like a crab.

That's when he woke up.

He imagined that this was the life of a real FBI agent. Hotel rooms in semi-picturesque places, waking up with a start from strange dreams, nightmares about the victims of horrible crimes. Spending the days following up on leads, chasing the nightmare, closing in on it, then chatting pleasantly with the spouse on the phone during downtime. This had never been his life before now. He didn't know what to make of it.

Becca, for her part, seemed to like it. It was what she had been hoping for when he joined the SRT.

"How did the interview go?" she said now.

"It went all right," Luke said. "We might have gotten some things we can use. Not sure yet. We passed it up the line. Trudy Wellington and Mark Swann and some other people are digging into it."

The lies were still part of this. That hadn't changed. He made no mention of traveling here under assumed identities, of how they extracted the information from Louis Clare, or of the three dead children they'd found as a result of that information. He would never, if they lived to be 100, tell her about the child they found in the ice chest.

He also made no mention of driving through the night, or the rental van owner appearing with a shotgun this morning. He made no mention of being arrested by the FBI, the same agency he ostensibly worked for, or of the fact that he and Ed were probably off the case now.

All he and Ed had done so far, according to this conversation, was interview one man. It had run late, so he hadn't called her to say goodnight. They were at the hotel now, would probably spend one more night, and come home in the morning. They were just waiting for instructions.

Police work. Following up leads. Sending in the information. Waiting for further instructions.

"That's good," Becca said. "It sounds like you've done your part."

"Yeah," Luke said. "Maybe so."

"Well, Gunner and I miss you. We can't wait to see you."

"I miss you, too," Luke said. And he meant it. One some level, he would just as soon walk away from this life, from career criminals and alligators and nasty surprises lurking in the back of abandoned trucks parked in the middle of nowhere.

He could easily imagine a life of just him, Becca, and Gunner spending the vast majority of their time out at the cabin, time passing, the seasons changing, Gunner slowly growing to manhood.

It was so idyllic, in fact, that…

A knock came at his door. The hand that made the knock was heavy enough that Luke knew right away who it was.

"Hold on one second, honey," he said. "Yeah?" he called.

"Stone. It's Ed. We're doing a conference call with SRT in five minutes. My room. They tried to reach you, but you're not answering your phone."

"Hon, I have to go," he said to Becca. "I have a meeting."

"Okay, sweetie. Call me later."

Luke hung up and went to the door. He opened it and Ed stood there in a dark blue SRT T-shirt and athletic shorts. Everything Ed wore clung tightly to his body.

"Going for a jog?" Luke said.

Ed didn't smile. "I was sleeping. I just woke up. But I talked to Trudy briefly. We're back on the case. No more sneaking around. No more fake names. The Special Response Team has been brought on board. They're making it official now."

He gave Luke a funny look.

"But we're on a short leash this time."

* * *

"It was a long night," Ed said. "But we've had longer."

Ed's cell phone was on the desk in his room. He had the speakerphone feature on, which made this something like a conference call. Luke could picture the rest of them in the conference room at SRT headquarters, talking into the black plastic octopus on the long table.

"You boys were busy," Don said. "Good work."

"Thanks," Luke said.

He glanced at Ed. Ed was not his normal self. He had exactly zero sense of humor left. He had stopped smiling entirely. Luke wasn't the staff psychologist, but it wasn't hard to put a finger on it. Ed had a baby on the way, and he was worried. Luke knew that feeling very well.

Also, Ed had a traumatic experience when he was younger, an experience with a girl he knew being abducted. Now they were on the trail of another girl who had been abducted, and they had no idea what they were going to find at the end of it, or if they would even find the end.

In the course of it, they had found a dead child, thrown away like trash. And there were two more at that site. They'd had to deal with a man whose specialty had once been trafficking people, including children. If Luke hadn't been there, Ed would have killed that man. But he would have tortured him first.

Ed was nearing some kind of breaking point. Luke had seen it before, in combat. And this had all started as some kind of favor. You scratch my back, I'll scratch yours.

"Wellington will bring us all up to date about the developments since this morning," Don said. "Some have been significant. Trudy?"

"Hi, guys," she said. She spoke mechanically, as if to keep her emotions walled off from the situation.

"First off, the warehouse in Florence. The children are two Jane Does and a John Doe. There is very little in the way of fingerprints or identifying features left to go on. Their DNA is being matched to a database of missing children, in an attempt to get some closure. In terms of who the perpetrators may be, the South Carolina Bureau of Investigation is sweeping the truck and the warehouse for fingerprints, hair samples, DNA. The place has not been used in a while, but at one time, there had been a fair amount of activity. There is a working kitchen, with food left behind in the cupboards. Much of it was consumed by rats or mice. There are also several rooms sectioned off with drywall. The best guess is they were used as cells in which to keep prisoners."

Luke let that sink in. He realized this case was affecting him, too. The changes coming over him were not as stark as the ones coming over Ed, but it was clear to him they were happening. The people they were dealing with were not combatants. They were predators. And their behavior was premeditated. They didn't fight for any cause. No religious dogma or nationalistic glory. They just defiled the innocent for some sick, twisted pleasure that was impossible to understand.

Luke didn't want to understand it. He wanted to kill it.

"Who owns the building?" Ed said.

Trudy paused. "Richard Davis Spence, a forty-nine-year-old who lives in Atlanta, appears to be the owner. He hides that ownership behind multiple shell companies based in Bermuda and Aruba. The building is three years behind on its property tax payments. Spence has a long history of court cases and criminal charges for wire fraud, impersonating various people, credit card fraud, and the like. He has never done significant jail time. He was brought into custody by the Atlanta PD this morning. His house was raided, and his phones, computers, and cars were seized. He was taken by surprise and offered no resistance. He was questioned with a lawyer present. So far, he claims to know nothing about the warehouse or what went on there. He was booked on suspicion of kidnapping, capital murder, and accessory to capital murder. That's for starters. He'll see the judge tomorrow morning."

"I hope they give him bail and he gets out," Ed said. "Keep me posted about that."

"Next," Don said, quashing that kind of talk instantly.

Trudy went on. "We've been following up on the names and aliases that Louis Clare gave you. So far we've got exactly one hit, but it's a good one. The Bureau shared with us the videotape taken from Pistol Pete's. The man he rented the van to appears to resemble a certain Felix Ramirez Cienfuegos. He is thirty-eight years old. He has a long list of aliases, and his nickname is a Hundred Fires, which is what the last name means in Spanish. He's originally a Honduran national from the ruling class, but has kept an address in Miami for at least ten years. His great-grandparents on his mother's side were Spanish nobility. He was educated at private schools in Spain, then joined the Honduran Special Forces, a unit notorious for human rights violations against civilians."

"What else?" Luke said.

"If it's him, then we might have a better idea what the deal is here. Cienfuegos is an international high flyer, a border crosser. The intelligence suggests he has moved contraband of all kinds. Freelance cocaine trafficking until the cartels shut him down. Suspected kidnapping and human trafficking. Suspected trafficking in stolen antiquities, as well as illegal traffic in poached animal products, like the horns of rhinos and ivory from elephants. It's thought to be more his thing to capture women moving across borders, immigrants from Central America headed north for example, than to abduct young American girls. But you never know."

"Whatever pays the bills," Mark Swann said. It was the first indication that he was even on the call.

"Not random in any event," Luke said.

"No," Trudy said. "If it is Cienfuegos, it was definitely not random. He didn't accidentally turn up in Wilmington, North Carolina, the day of a kidnapping, case a certain girl's high school, then coincidentally snatch her during a party later that night. He was sent there to get that specific girl, and he had inside information about her plans ahead of time."

"Why would a man like Cienfuegos walk into a rental place, knowing that he might be videotaped?" Ed said. "Especially if two men were involved in the kidnapping?"

"One guess is he was the less conspicuous of the two. Cienfuegos is thought to associate and partner with a man named Camilo Ortiz. Ortiz is a shadowy figure who keeps a low profile. CIA documentation suggests he is a Panamanian national with a prominent vertical scar on the left side of his face."

"Hence the need to stay out of sight."

"Yes," Trudy said. "And while Cienfuegos is fluent in Spanish, English, and Portuguese, Ortiz might be a native Spanish speaker with only limited English."

"Which one is the boss?" Luke said.

"Not enough is known about Ortiz to even say. We don't know how old he is. He's never been arrested and doesn't seem to have a passport, at least not under that name. We don't know how he gets in and out of the country. He may have protection at high levels that keeps his identity in the dark."

"Protection by whom?" Ed said.

"We don't know that, either."

"He's a ghost," Luke said.

"We don't know if he even really exists. This is all theory. If he does exist, he may go by the nickname El Tigre. It's Spanish for The Tiger."

There was a long moment of quiet.

"How did the FBI turn up at that rental place this morning?" Ed said. He said FBI as if it were the sinister intelligence agency of a foreign country, and not the organization he himself worked for.

"The Bureau proper appears to have started looking into this case around the same time we did."

"Why?" Ed said. "Who called them in? They seem to have been tracking us."

"They say it's a coincidence."

"There is no such thing as coincidence, not when intelligence agencies are involved."

"Okay," Don said. "This is where I step in. The Bureau in its infinite wisdom has decided to take on this case. It has all the markings of an interstate human trafficking operation, and they say that's what pricked up their ears on it. Personally, I don't believe that. We are sweeping the entire building for bugs, right now, as we speak. In the meantime, after a great deal of string pulling, and a certain amount of negotiating, and you can read that as begging, we are partnering with the greater Bureau on this case, and they are giving you a field agent to work with."

"Terrific," Luke said. "A real G man from Dragnet?"

"A minder," Ed said.

"Listen," Don said. "The Bureau would like to pull down our shingle and scatter us to the winds. We have friends in high places ourselves, and we're being protected for the time being. But don't kid yourselves. The FBI knows everything. They know you guys were down there under assumed identities. They know you bent the arm of Louis Clare, and found the bodies in Florence. They're not even hiding the fact that they're monitoring us. This room was clean as of noon, but that doesn't mean diddly. They could be listening in some other way. One of us could be feeding them information. It doesn't matter. All that matters is they knew what we were doing. It's possible that they let us run because they knew we would turn up leads in a… what would you call it?"

"Informal manner," Swann said.

"Yes. An informal manner. You bring a man like Louis Clare into a police precinct, and he dummies up. He wants to see his public defender. You bring him to a cabin near a swamp…"

"Understood," Luke said.

"I want to be very clear with you. I want to bring this young lady home, if we can. But you men don't have to continue on the case. You've done enough, and you've already faced some disturbing—"

"You can call me off or someone can kill me," Ed said. "Otherwise I will be staying on the case. It has become important to me to solve this."

"Good," Don said. "I am very glad to hear that. Stone?"

"You know where I am on this, Don."

"I want to hear you say it."

"I'm in."

How could he be anything but in? These people were sharks, and they were operating with something close to impunity. For an instant, Luke remembered the moment he was falling asleep this morning. He had closed his eyes, and as he drifted off, he saw the body in the ice chest. You don't just walk away from something like that.

"Good," Don said again. "Trudy, tell us about our new guardian angel from the Bureau, who will look after our men and keep them on the straight and narrow path."

"At first glance, he looks okay," Trudy said. "Henry Bowles. Thirty-five years old. Yale graduate, Army ROTC, with honors. Did his military obligation with 1st Special Forces, joined 1993. Four years, in and out, then went straight to Quantico. He's been with the Bureau nine years. He's had a handful of high-profile busts, a couple of commendations. He looks like a guy on the way up."

"Then why is he babysitting us?" Ed said. "Seems like he'd have something better to do with his time."

"Good question," Trudy said. "You'll have to ask him that yourself."

"Where do we meet Henry?" Luke said. "Is he going to come here to the hotel?"

"No, you're going to meet him tonight in Florida."

"Florida?"

"A house in Fort Lauderdale is the last known residence of Felix Cienfuegos. Real estate records suggest it's an eighteen-hundred-square-foot one-story bungalow. An old Florida house from the days before air conditioning. It's owned by a company called Gold Coast Property Management, who rent about a thousand homes on the east coast of Florida. Nothing much there. Cienfuegos probably rents from them for the anonymity of it. Just another guy in a rented house in Florida. Swann checked satellite imagery of the place. There's recent activity at the house. Swann?"

"Yeah," Swann said. "Actually, I borrowed a drone for a brief flyover earlier today. There were two cars parked there. It's a place on a canal. Swimming pool in the backyard, fresh clean water in the pool. There's also a boat tied up in the back. The boat is nothing special."

"The place looks lived in is what Swann's trying to tell you," Trudy said.

"Yes," Swann said. "Someone is home."

"The two of you and your new friend Special Agent Bowles," Don said, "are going to stop by there for a little chat."

CHAPTER SIXTEEN

12:45 p.m. Central Standard Time (1:45 p.m. Eastern Standard Time)
La Sierra de San Simon (St. Simon's Saw)
Near Honduras
The Caribbean Sea

"I'm afraid you've stepped in it this time, Darwin."

Darwin sighed. He was already aggravated. It had taken the operator half an hour to connect, and reconnect, and then re-reconnect this call from the United States. While waiting, Darwin had poured himself another vodka tonic.

The call itself, apparently connected for good now, just made everything worse. The caller spoke with a quaint Southern accent that was supposed to remind the listener of genteel plantation times gone by. Just sitting on the porch, sipping mint juleps on a hot day, and watching the slaves pick cotton.

"Do tell," Darwin said.

"Is this line secure?"

Darwin shook his head. "Who cares?"

"I do," the voice said.

"In that case, it's secure as can be."

It grew tiresome, dealing with these people. Politicians, always conniving, maneuvering, self-dealing. They thought they were smart, and they were, in a sense. They were about as smart as chimpanzees. Chimps were our close cousins, and they spent their time screeching, fighting, and plotting against each other. Darwin King had studied chimpanzee society. People would be surprised to learn how similar it was to human society. The United States Congress could easily take place in the forests of Africa.

"The girl. The newest one."

Darwin shook his head. "I have no idea what you're talking about."

And this man, this Southern fried cracker, was prone to making phone calls like this. Bill Ryan, Minority Leader of the House of Representatives. An ambitious man. A man with plans.

He was not Darwin King's friend. He was no one's friend, but especially not Darwin's. He had never been a guest at one of Darwin's homes. Unlike so many of his peers, he had never partaken of Darwin's… gifts. He scrupulously avoided entanglements like that.

But other sorts of entanglements were not a problem for Bill Ryan. In other ways, the man was an entanglement factory.

"You know exactly what I'm talking about, my friend. You steal young girls to feed your warped, perverse desires. You're a sick man, Darwin."

"Judge not," Darwin said, "lest ye be judged."

"I don't judge you. Time and the Lord will take care of that. As ye sow, so shall ye reap. In the meantime, I will use you as I see fit."

Darwin felt the rage rise within him. No one talked to him in this way, no one on the entire Earth.

"How dare you?" he said. "You and your Lord. Save your moral judgments. Do you know what I could do to you? Do you know the things I know about you? Sir, I keep you in my back pocket, all your little dirty deals, all the bad actors you've been to bed with. In the unlikely case I ever find myself in an awkward position, do you know how I'll get out of it? I'll give them you."

"Darwin, be careful what you say to me. I may take you seriously."

Darwin took a long, slow sip of his drink.

"Why are we talking right now, Bill?"

"You made a mistake," Ryan said. "You overstepped."

"I don't overstep. It is not possible for me to overstep."

"All right," Ryan said. "But something happened, something that has your fingerprints all over it, and a powerful but desperate man asked me for a favor. Do you know who the man is?"

Darwin shook his head. The guessing game. The question game. "Of course I know. He and I go all the way back. But this wasn't personal between us. It was just the repayment of a debt, and not his debt. He had nothing to do with it. Tell him so, if you think that will help him any."

It was a kind thing to say, Darwin thought. It made him seem like a reasonable man. But the truth was this little move was doing double duty. It was absolutely delicious that the theft of 21 hurt Miles Richmond. Delicious wasn't even the right word. Euphoria-inducing… was that a word?

God, when he was finished with her… When he was finished…

"It's too late," Ryan said. "I granted him the favor he asked of me, and now people are coming for you. They are people you do not want to meet. I have no idea how long it will take them to find you, but I imagine not terribly long. In a very real sense, they are already on their way. I did this to you. Yes. It was me. I want you to know that."

…he would leave her somewhere for Richmond to find her.

Darwin took a deep breath. "You have no idea how many times I've been threatened like this."

"You have *never* been threatened like this."

"What do you want, Bill? Please. I'm about to hang up."

"Well," Ryan said. "The way I see it, there are only two ways you can get out of this. One is to give the girl back, immediately and unharmed. Just drop her off somewhere. In front of a police precinct somewhere anonymous, in Florida or Texas, say, and direct her to walk inside and introduce herself. Easy enough."

"Impossible," Darwin said. He caught an image in his mind of the girl he had just sent back to her dungeon. She was too perfect to ever surrender to anyone. If it came down to it, if it ever happened that he couldn't have her, he would see to it that no one could have her.

"I've already grown attached to her. She's quite precious to me. Like a diamond."

"I imagined you would say that. So here's your second option. You give me two people that I want. You probably know who they are without my having to say their names. One is a senator from my home state, a good friend of yours, but not one of mine."

"You have no friends," Darwin said.

Ryan ignored the comment. "This man is the wrong party, of course, but everything about him is wrong, and I'm trying to cleanse my state of vermin like this. His weaknesses are a disgrace. A scandal would clear the way for someone better, younger, more in touch with the constituents."

"Someone you control," Darwin said.

This was Bill Ryan in a nutshell. He wanted power. It was all he seemed to want. Power for power's sake, as an end in itself. His lust for it was single-minded and all-encompassing. Darwin supposed he could respect that. Himself, he wanted more than that, much more, but Darwin King was well-rounded, much more so than your typical politician. Strip away the veneer, the pomp and circumstance, and Congress was a long line of one-trick ponies.

"The second person I want is the erstwhile former governor of Pennsylvania," Ryan said. "Another good friend of yours, and a frequent party guest at your apartment up in Manhattan, as I understand it."

Darwin smiled, in spite of himself. The vodka had settled into his system, and he was finally beginning to enjoy this conversation. Bill Ryan wanted dirt on Thomas Hayes, the Vice President of the United States.

"Not that frequent a guest," Darwin said. "It was quite some time ago, and it happened less than you probably think. I suspect he was just tasting the forbidden fruit, as so many do. He moved on pretty quickly."

There was silence over the line.

"He has higher ambitions, doesn't he?" Darwin said. The governor of Pennsylvania had stumbled into the vice presidency. There were only a handful of offices higher than the ones he had already held, and only one that the man in question would even want.

"Most people do," Bill Ryan said.

Darwin nearly clapped his hands. "That's it, isn't it? My, my, my. I told him that would be a terrible mistake. I told him the best thing for him was to stay in his lane."

Hayes should have declined the vice presidency, not because of the office itself, but because being that close to the throne would be such an irresistible temptation. Clement Dixon was old. He had just survived the hijacking of Air Force One. He probably wouldn't run for a second term. Hayes could probably just walk in the door, especially if the crusty, popular, straight-talking and tough-minded outgoing President endorsed him.

"I'm not the only skeleton in his closet," Darwin said. "But you must know that already."

"You have the goods on him though, don't you?"

Darwin's shoulders slumped a bit. "The goods?"

If photo and video evidence, as well as sensual love letters the man had exchanged with underage girls, were the so-called goods, then he did indeed have them.

"Yes," Ryan said. "The goods."

"Of course I have them. But I don't sell my friends out quite that easily. What am I supposed to get out of this arrangement?"

"Well, it's too late to call the dogs off," Ryan said. "If you won't give the girl back, then they're coming for you. Even I can't stop that now. Too many forces are in motion. But I can let you know when and how they're coming, so you can be ready."

Darwin didn't like this. He didn't like Bill Ryan. Who were these fearsome dogs that supposedly couldn't be called off?

It wasn't as if Darwin King didn't have resources he could draw on. It wasn't as if Darwin didn't have friends in high places. Darwin King had his own attack dogs. He had his own spies, and they were everywhere.

In the end, a dog was just a dog. The help was the help. And a hired killer was a hired killer. In Darwin's experience, they were all more or less the same. They canceled each other out. Ten elite killers on each side was a wash. They'd be lucky if any of them survived.

"I'll look into the situation and get back to you," he said.

"That's fine," Bill Ryan said in his insipid drawl. "But don't take too long now. My philosophy is it's better to be weeks too early than a second too late."

* * *

She was back in her room.

Her room.

It was dreary and dark, though now she knew that a bright, hot sun was shining right outside. Everything about this room was wrong. She did not want to get used to it, or somehow be associated with it. She did not want to settle down in it. She did not want to become comfortable here.

Instead, she sat on the edge of the bed and waited. She had to be ready for the time when she would be rescued. Soon, this would all be over and she would be heading back home. Her mom would forgive her for running out that night. They would go out to dinner and pretend it never happened. They would laugh about things that happened when she was a little girl instead.

She had to remain strong—she would not cry again, she would not beg—she would just wait a day, or maybe two. Her mom would find a way to pull her out of here. Or maybe her grandfather on her dad's side would do it. He was a powerful man. She just had to wait, be patient, be strong, and stay ready to escape.

For a moment, the hall outside filled with men's voices. Deep voices, laughing voices, menacing voices—all just on the other side of that locked door. The gunmen, the guards from Honduras. Their sudden presence changed everything. All her thoughts transformed in an instant. She was not going to escape. She was not going to be rescued. A wave of helpless fear surged over her. Her heart pounded in her chest.

She couldn't stay living down here. Eventually these gunmen would decide that Darwin didn't want her, that she hadn't made the cut, that she wasn't worthy to live in another part of the house. She was down here, left out, forgotten.

Then they could have her.

She crept to the door and listened—she could not understand a single word they said. The voices brought back memories of the attack on the beach, then the darkness, waking up on the plane… waking up here in this room.

She had to get out of this room. She had to get out, into the rest of the house, the property, the sun. She'd had a small taste of it this morning, at breakfast on the patio with Mistress Elaine.

The place was amazing. They were at the top of a mountain, overlooking a wide blue ocean. Lush plants were all around them, with gigantic green leaves and flowers in red and blue and yellow. There were hummingbirds here the size of her hand. They drank nectar from feeders left out for them, and their wings made a loud whirring sound.

This was an island near Central America, close to Honduras. Darwin owned the island, and for some reason the country of Honduras gave him soldiers for his protection. Maybe Darwin and Honduras were allies. Maybe Darwin owned the soldiers now.

Darwin also owned her, apparently.

That couldn't be right. How could he own her? There were other girls here—she saw three of them hanging around sun tanning by the swimming pool—and Darwin owned them. That seemed possible, but not for her, not for Charlotte.

Charlotte, my name is Charlotte.

It was odd. The 21 thing was starting to creep in. She was beginning to have strange thoughts. Thoughts like: *21 needs to find a way out of here.*

They were doing this to her. They were making her think this way.

Darwin had told her he bought her from her parents, but that was definitely wrong. Her father was dead, and had been since she was young. She remembered him, so skinny, so pale, his eyes so sad when he saw her. Her father was like a bad dream to her now. She loved him, and she remembered a different version of him when she was very young, but he was fading. The healthy, happy dad, and the sick, dying dad, both were almost gone now. But either way, he couldn't have sold her to Darwin. He wasn't even alive.

And her mother would never sell her. Not in a million years. They'd had their problems, more recently because her mother never wanted her to go out, but nothing to the point where her mother would *sell* her.

Jeff.

Jeff would sell her. Her mom's boyfriend. He didn't like her. Or maybe he just didn't care about her. He didn't seem to pay attention at all. She had overheard him sometimes, though. He wanted to travel, to go away, to take vacations. But they were stuck because Charlotte was in school. Plus all the money for college was going to be a drain. Jeff didn't like that. Her mother said her grandfather would probably pay for her college, but Jeff didn't believe it.

Jeff would be happy to get rid of her. And if he got money for it? All the better. But how could he convince her mother to do it?

How could he?

21. Your number is 21.

It was crazy. She wasn't a number. She wasn't someone's slave. 21 was no one's slave.

Darwin had seemed almost nice. He told Charlotte she was perfect, an angel come to life. He might have been handsome once. He was old, but not old the way a lot of men got. He seemed like a young man with an old man's head attached at the top of the neck. He had white hair and blue eyes.

She knew what he wanted. She saw the way he looked at her. It was scary. She wasn't ready for anything like that.

He knew that, too. And he seemed okay with it.

But then he put her back down here in this dungeon. They were beating her down, that's what they were doing. She saw it. She wasn't stupid. She could do what Darwin wanted, be his happy slave, jump through hoops like a trained poodle, or she could live down here in the dark, surrounded by gunmen from Honduras. Gunmen she had to ask to let her out so she could go to the bathroom.

A lump welled up in her throat. She had promised herself she wouldn't cry again.

Don't cry. Don't cry. It's okay.

It wasn't going to work. It was NOT okay.

Suddenly, her heart was racing. She couldn't breathe. She gasped for air. Her hands and face went numb. She seemed frozen in place. This couldn't be real! It couldn't be real! It wasn't happening. She would not believe in it.

She was still wearing the plush white robe that Elaine had given her to wear. She wrapped the robe around her body, hugged her knees, and sat there trying to think. What should she do? She did not know.

She sobbed silently. In her mind, she howled in agony, like a wounded animal. She shrieked in despair. But in the real world, she did not utter a sound. She wanted to be quiet, so as not to bring attention to herself.

She had to stay strong. But deep down, she knew she was weak. She wanted to go to the door, and bang on it.

"Let me out! Let me into the sunlight!"

Darwin could take her. He could have her, whatever he wanted, if they would just let her out of this horrible place.

CHAPTER SEVENTEEN

6:45 p.m. Eastern Standard Time
Las Olas Boulevard
Fort Lauderdale, Florida

"The beautiful people are loose on the streets," Luke said.

"Beautiful is a word," Ed said.

Luke shrugged. "What's another word?"

Ed smiled. "Stupid."

Luke nearly laughed. That was something like the Ed that he knew.

Luke and Ed were among the early evening throngs in the fabulous shopper's paradise of Las Olas Boulevard, just as the sun began to set.

During the last thirty minutes, the street had begun to fill with glittering, well-dressed specimens of humanity, almost as if a nearby dam had burst, and instead of water, these hip and lovely people had gushed forth. The restaurants and sidewalk cafes were filling up. Car traffic on the street tightened and slowed.

Luke and Ed had flown down in the jet they had taken to Myrtle Beach. Trudy had couriered them both dossiers of the missing girl. Luke took the opportunity to look through it during the plane ride. He realized that up until now, he had known very little about her.

He looked at the photos first, of course. There were half a dozen of them, provided to the FBI by the girl's mother. One photo was of the girl and her mom. The mom was a young middle age, attractive but starting to get tired. The girl was wearing a blue and gold cheerleading uniform. She was very pretty, with straight blond hair, and wore a cheerleading uniform in most of the other photos as well. It seemed that she had been a cheerleader since about the age of eleven.

Luke glanced through the rest of the documents. Father deceased. Mother a lawyer. Charlotte was a decent student, not exceptional. A's and B's. They used to have a thing called "the gentleman's C." If you really belonged, you didn't want to get grades that were too good. Maybe this was the cheerleader's B-plus.

In addition to cheerleading, Charlotte spent two years on the dance squad, whatever that was. She had played lacrosse in junior high school, but apparently gave it up. She was on the student council her sophomore year in high school, and was on the activities committee. She made the morning announcements over the school intercom one day each week.

So she was a joiner. Her mother's testimony suggested she was a happy child and teen, and very popular among her peers. She was resilient, and had seemed to recover from both the divorce and her father's death quickly.

How did this happen? Why did it happen?

Why would someone target this particular girl?

The mother's boyfriend came up again. Jeff Zorn. The local cops had checked out his computers, his phones, and his cars. They had swept the cars for DNA and hair fibers. They had restored deleted files from the computers, and gone back through years of emails. They had subpoenaed years of phone calls and text messages.

Nothing. The man had barely mentioned the girl at all.

Zorn was supposedly a publicist, but he had very few, if any, actual clients. Yes, his father had been a Wall Streeter. Was he living off an inheritance? Or was he doing something else for money? The dossier didn't say.

"What do you think of this boyfriend?" Luke said to Ed on the plane. Ed was thumbing through his own dossier, which contained all the same files.

He shrugged. "I think it's one thing to surrender all these devices to the cops with no trouble. But they were going to take them anyway. And just because he gives up two phones, doesn't mean there isn't a third. Just because he gives up two computers, doesn't mean there isn't another one somewhere. It's fine, but it doesn't prove anything."

That's what it was. The guy was clean. He was too clean. He had handed everything over because he knew there was nothing incriminating to discover.

"I'd consider picking him up, shaking his tree a little."

Luke pointed at him. "Good idea."

"That's what I'm here for," Ed said. "I'm full of good ideas."

Luke called Trudy as soon as they were on the ground.

"If we can get a tail on the boyfriend, Jeff Zorn, I think we should do it."

There was a pause over the line. "The Wilmington PD talked to him for six hours," Trudy said.

"After we finish down here, Ed and I will bring him in for an hour, maybe two. I don't think we'll need any more than that."

"It's official FBI business now," Trudy said. "And he's not a convicted felon out on parole like Louis Clare. You can't treat him the same way."

"That's fine," Luke said. "We'll be gentle. I just want someone to keep an eye on him until we get back up there. See what he does, see where he goes, see who else is around when he gets there."

"All right," Trudy said. "I'll talk to Don."

Now, Luke gazed out at the glowing night. If anything, the crowds had gotten even thicker in the last ten minutes. The lights seemed to put a haze around everything.

A large man walked up the street. He was tall, nearly Ed's height, big shoulders, wearing a well-tailored sports jacket and slacks. He had dark hair closely cropped, and a three-day growth of beard and mustache. He seemed very fit, like a guy who had just given up playing tight end for a professional football team. His eyes were sharp, like an eagle's eyes, and dark.

He came right up to them as if he had them memorized.

"Gentlemen," he said. "I'm Special Agent Bowles."

Ed reached out to shake the man's hand. "Ed Newsam. You're our partner from the Bureau proper, eh?"

"Call me Henry," the man said as he shook Ed's hand. "Partner's a little strong, I think. I prefer the term babysitter."

Luke smiled. Just what they needed, a wiseass. He shook the man's hand. "Luke Stone. I guess I was expecting someone a little… older."

Henry Bowles shook his head. "Your reputation precedes you. Both of you. And to be honest, I'm the only one who would take this job. Guys with seniority in the Bureau don't like to stay out all night."

The three men stood in a rough triangle as the crowds passed around them. Luke and Ed eyed each other.

"And they don't like it when things get messy."

"How about you?" Ed said. "Do you like it?"

Bowles smiled. "I try not to let it come to that point."

There was a silence.

"Well… are you ready to say hello to our friend the human trafficker, Felix Cienfuegos?"

* * *

"You understand this guy is dangerous, right?"

Luke was talking to Bowles. They were sitting in a sedan half a block from the house. Until a moment ago, Bowles had been intending to walk up the front path and ring the doorbell.

Bowles was still wearing his jacket and slacks. Certainly, he must have his service gun on him. Ed and Luke were suited up with Kevlar, helmets, visors, batons, shotguns, flashbangs, and Tasers. Luke also had a Glock 17 pistol. Ed had a Heckler and Koch MP5 strapped across his chest. He had loaded thirty-round magazines for the gun, stuffed in various pockets. They had brought all this stuff on the plane with them. They were ready to go in hot. Luke didn't really see another way.

"This isn't a tumultuous entry," Bowles said. "We have tactical teams for things like that. There are only just the three of us."

Ed shook his head. "Three of us who are going to get our asses blown off if we just stop by and say hello."

Bowles shrugged. "We don't know if Cienfuegos lives here," he said. "We don't know if he's even in the country. We don't have accurate data about who lives here. We don't have a warrant for his arrest, or for anyone's arrest. We don't have evidence that anyone in that house committed a crime. We're gathering information about a crime that took place eight hundred miles from here. We're stopping by this house because a man on a video who rented a van might bear a passing resemblance to a person described by a convicted felon. The felon described this person during an interrogation which, if conducted by a different government, we might refer to as torture."

He was talking about the Louis Clare interview. Of course. The South Carolina cops had brought Clare in, and he had complained that someone worked him over a little bit. Bowles was privy to this fact. Bowles probably knew everything, not just about this case, but about Luke and Ed in general.

"We did nothing to hurt that man," Ed said.

Luke didn't say anything.

"Mock executions count as torture," Bowles said.

Ed shook his head. "Didn't happen."

"It was an extrajudicial arrest, by federal officers who invaded the interviewee's home, bagged and disoriented him, locked him in the trunk of a car, took him to an isolated location, dangled him above live alligators, threatened him with a silenced gun, left him tied to a chair for hours, explicitly and repeatedly threatened to murder him, slapped him, banged his head on the floor, choked him, and refused to identify themselves the entire time. What does that sound like to you?"

Ed looked at Luke.

Luke shrugged. "We let him smoke cigarettes. Considering the circumstances, I thought that was—"

"I read the report," Bowles said. "Let's leave the KGB stuff in the old Soviet Union where it belongs, shall we?"

"The guy is a human trafficker," Ed muttered under his breath.

"Former human trafficker," Bowles said. "Who has rights."

Ed sneered at Bowles. "That former human trafficker, who has rights, like the right to remain silent I suppose, told us the location of a warehouse where three dead children were found. If he had remained silent, he wouldn't have told us about that and those kids would still…"

Bowles shrugged. "Those kids were there a long time. They're dead. They aren't any less dead because you found them."

"All right," Luke said. He raised a hand. "Okay? Enough."

This guy was about as straight-laced and matter-of-fact and by-the-book as they came. This was who the FBI wanted looking over the SRT's shoulders? Okay. But there was going to have to be an accommodation to reality somewhere. Ed was passionate. Ed was big hearted. Ed would shred the rulebook to save lives, or even just to bring a dead child home. If they couldn't live with that, this wasn't going to work.

"Let's do this," Luke said. "At the very least, let me and Ed knock on the door. We'll do the good cop, bad cop."

Bowles shook his head. "We're not here to play games."

"It's just that I'd feel bad if you walked up there and got killed," Luke said. "I'm starting to take a shine to you."

Bowles gave a half smile. "Knock away. I'll hang back. When they open, I'll follow you in to question whoever we find. I happen to be fluent in Spanish."

"Sounds fair," Luke said. He looked at Ed. "You ready?"

"Born ready," Ed said.

Ed and Luke left the car and walked up to the house. They moved slowly, Luke soaking it in as they moved.

It was a typical Florida house, a low-slung one story place, maybe a little larger than most. There were palm trees on the property, and thick bushes. There were two cars in the driveway, a blue BMW and a black Acura. Both of the cars had small dents and scuffs. They were not new off the showroom floor. Behind the drawn blinds in one room of the house, there were flashes of light suggesting a large TV was on.

Luke and Ed went up onto the small stone front porch of the house. It was under a hard plastic awning.

Bowles was back behind them somewhere. It was a good place for him.

Luke knocked on the door, then stepped briskly to the left. Ed stepped to the right. Luke half expected a ten-year-old boy to answer, say his uncle wasn't home. Something along those lines. Even so, they were flanking the door now, on either side of it. It wasn't a good way to be if someone checked the peephole. But it was a good way to be in case someone came out. They'd have the jump on him.

It was also a good way to be in case…

BOOOM.

A gun blast ripped a wide hole through the wooden door. The hole was at chest and head level. It shredded the door like poorly made Swiss cheese—too much hole, not enough cheese. A shotgun did that. It would stop a large deer, or a large man.

Instantly, Luke had one of the M84 stun grenades in his hand. He pulled the pin, let the spoon go, and tossed the grenade deep into the hole where the door had just been. He covered his ears, jamming a finger into each earhole. He closed his eyes and turned away.

"Watch it!" he shouted. "Fire in the—"

BANG!

Inside the house, the ear-piercing sound came, with a blinding flash of light.

Half a second later, Ed jumped into the breach. He did not hesitate at all. He stepped in front of the door and stuck the snout of his MP5 through the hole.

DUH-DUH-DUH-DUH-DUH-DUH.

The sound was loud. LOUD.

"Got him," he said. "Got the shooter."

He raised one giant foot and delivered a monster kick to what remained of the door. The hinges held. The lock held. The door itself came apart. He kicked it again. Now the hole was huge, gaping. He turned sideways, put his shoulder to the shards of wood, and bulled his way through it.

Luke, pistol out now, was one second behind him. He stepped through into the living room. The TV was playing. It took up one entire wall. A Mexican variety show was on, complete with crazed, balding, late-middle-aged male host, and the young female dancers in tight gowns, shaking their ample bodies everywhere.

A dead man lay on his side on the dirty gray carpet. The carpet might have been white once. The man's body was twisted, his arms splayed out above him. A pump shotgun lay on the floor behind him.

The carpet near his head was red. The pool of blood was spreading like a halo.

Ed moved up the hallway, Luke three steps behind him. Another man popped out of a room to their right. He had a gun, something big. Luke barely had time to see it. Ed opened up with his MP5.

DUH-DUH-DUH-DUH-DUH.

The man's head snapped back, his body jerked, and he went straight down.

Ed was a killing machine.

Now they moved through the house, one room at a time, closets. The place was barely decorated or furnished. There were narrow beds or mattresses in the bedrooms, piles of clothes on the floor, more clothes hanging in the closets. A few toiletry items in the bathroom. Cologne. Hair style goop.

Like every drug and safe house before it, the place was spare, utilitarian. These people were all business, and didn't bother much with personal effects.

Luke and Ed stepped over the corpse on their way back down the hall. They came into the living room. The TV was a riot of colors and images, but the sound was all the way down. The first body lay on the living room floor, the rug becoming saturated with blood beneath it.

They had entered the place maybe two minutes ago.

"That was it?" Ed said. "Are either of these guys…"

Luke put his hand up. STOP. He listened. He thought he heard a sound in the kitchen. He crept in there, light on his feet like a cat. There was a dingy white pantry door, which almost seemed to be trembling.

Luke stepped to the side of it and whipped it open.

A man was there. He was dark, short, with black hair. The man was young, barely more than a kid. His eyes said this was not what he wanted. He hadn't signed up for sudden gunfights. But he did have a gun in his hand.

Luke put his own gun to the man's temple.

"*Policia*. Drop it."

The man dropped the gun.

"*Tirate al suelo!* On the floor. NOW!"

Hands raised, the man came out of the pantry and slowly went to the peeling linoleum floor. Luke pulled the man's wrists back, took a zip tie from the loop of them on his own belt, and cuffed him. The guy gave him no resistance.

"You speak English?"

"*Sí. Un poco.* Little."

"Is there anyone else in the house?"

The man shook his head. "No. *Tres hombres.* Three men. *No más.*"

"Felix Ramirez Cienfuegos," Luke said.

The guy turned his head a little, as if to get a better look at the person asking him dumb questions. He gestured with his head across the living room at the man with the shotgun, the dead man who had blown away the front door and gotten cut down by Ed a second later.

"There."

"That's Cienfuegos?"

"*Sí.* It's him."

Luke and Ed looked at each other. The primary person of interest was dead. They had killed him. Actually, Ed had killed him.

"I threw the flashbang to stun the guy," Luke said.

Ed shook his head. "No. No way. He fired on us."

"The kid in Newark nearly killed you. You didn't shoot him."

"Different circumstances."

Luke nodded. "We didn't need information from that kid."

Ed shrugged. "Let it go, man."

Okay. Okay, Luke would let it go. But he tucked it away in the back of his mind. It was something to think about, not now, but soon. He looked at the guy on the floor.

"Ortiz?" he said. "El Tigre?"

The young man looked at him strangely now. Luke could almost read his eyes. *They know about El Tigre.* El Tigre was a phantom, a legend, a ghost. You had to be careful answering questions about someone like that.

"*Se fue,*" the guy said.

He left.

"He no live here now."

"Where did he go?"

"Jupiter, maybe." The way he said it, the word sounded like *Yoopiter.* "I don't know."

Ed moved toward the dead man on the floor, the one who was supposedly Cienfuegos. Luke got up, went over, and converged on the dead man from a different angle. The man was sideways, nearly face down, and Ed toed him to turn him over just a tiny bit. Ed had shot him the face several times. The man's head was half demolished, stove in like someone strong had taken a steel pipe to it.

"That look like the guy in the video to you?" Ed said.

Luke shook his head. "No. The guy in the video had a face. This one doesn't."

"Oh my," someone said. "A bloodbath. I wish I could say I was surprised."

Luke glanced up and Bowles was standing in the doorway to the outside. As Luke watched, Bowles stepped through the gaping hole, pushing some of the remaining wood shards away with his big shoulders. He looked down at the dead guy on the living room floor, then glanced at the other dead guy in the hallway.

He smiled. Carnage didn't upset him, Luke noticed. Give him a few points for that. "Would you say it's a little hard to question people when you kill everyone you meet?"

"You're welcome," Luke said.

Bowles raised an eyebrow, his smile fading into a smirk. "I'm welcome? For what?"

"If we'd done it your way, and you walked up here like a Mary Kay saleslady, you'd be dead now."

Bowles shrugged. "You don't know me very well."

"Anyway, there's still one left," Ed said.

Bowles went into the kitchen and stared at the man on the floor. He nodded, more to himself than anyone else. "He looks about seventeen. I'm sure he'll know all the secrets we want and have a lot to say about them."

CHAPTER EIGHTEEN

10:15 p.m. Eastern Standard Time
FBI Miami Division
Miramar, Florida

The man did have a lot to say.

They stood in an observation room, watching him through one-way glass. Speakers were mounted just above the glass. Four people were in the observation room—Luke, Ed, Bowles, and a young man who was a simultaneous translator from Spanish to English.

Through the window, the prisoner sat at a long wooden table. He wore the same T-shirt and jeans they had found him in. He took a long gulp of what appeared to be water. Then he leaned back, smoking a cigarette. There was a half-empty pack and a lighter on the table near his left hand. He seemed relaxed enough, maybe because he could smoke as much as he wanted.

"What's his name?" Luke said.

"No confirmation on that," the translator said. "He wasn't carrying identification. He says his name is Daniel Cruz. They're waiting for fingerprints to come back. Hopefully, he's been arrested somewhere, for something."

Two Hispanic men stood across the small room from the prisoner. They were sharp dressers, dark business suits, slicked back hair, expensive leather shoes. They looked more like young Wall Street types than FBI agents. They looked like they should have their own TV show.

One of the interrogators said something, too fast for Luke to understand. He heard the name Camilo Ortiz. He heard the phrase El Tigre. The prisoner started speaking.

"What do I get?" the translator said. From there, he began to translate both what the prisoner said, and what the questioners said.

"What do you want?"

"Freedom. I want to go home. I'm done in America."

"I have a hunch," Bowles said. "He isn't going home any time soon."

"Where is home?"
"El Salvador."
"What is your hometown?"
The young guy shrugged. "Where else? San Salvador."
"How old are you?"
"Twenty years. My twenty-first is next month."
"Have you done something we should know about? Something that makes it hard to give you your freedom?"
The man stared at them.
"You know what I did."
"No. We don't."
He took a deep drag on his cigarette, held it, and blew it out.
"They're killers, okay? The Tiger is a killer. These other men. Dangerous people. What you are asking from me is a lot. If I tell you anything, I will be marked for death. This is not so terrible, I guess. I am not afraid of death. But I want something in return."
"We will keep you safe," one of the interrogators said. "I can promise you that. You can get a new life. Maybe you can go home. We'll have to see."
"What about my family?"
"In El Salvador?"
"No. Here. I have a girl and a baby."
"If you cooperate, we can keep them with you. We have a program called Witness Protection. You will be safe. They will be safe."
The promise of safety seemed to be enough.
"The Tiger was with us, yeah. He was staying at the house."
"Well, at least now we know he exists," Ed said. "That's something."
"He is a bad person. He and Cienfuegos took a job up north. They went away, flew I think, came back the next day."
"Where did they go?"
"I don't know. North. Carolina, maybe. Virginia. They didn't tell me. And your friends killed Cienfuegos. So now we will never know."
"Where is the Tiger?"
"He left again. I don't know where he went. He and I are not friends. We don't talk that much."
"You know very little, it seems. If you know so little, why do you say he and Cienfuegos went to Carolina together?"
The man tapped the side of his head. "I listen. I hear things. You have to be careful in this line of work. People who are not careful die too soon. Listen more than you speak. That's my rule."

"What is this line of work?"

The man shook his head, took another drag of his smoke. "I don't know. If you don't know, then I also don't."

"You say the Tiger took a job up north. Who was he working for?"

The prisoner sighed.

"The man from Jupiter. The island of Jupiter. A very rich man. Very connected. He has powerful friends. How do you say it? He is untouchable."

"What is his name?"

"I don't know. You will know better than me."

"What were they doing for him? He was paying them to do something, so what was the job?"

The prisoner eyed the questioners very carefully. He seemed to be on a knife's edge about what he said next. Falling on either side of it had consequences. Those consequences were unpredictable.

The situation was far out in front of him. A look, possibly resignation, came over his face. He wanted out. To buy his way out, he had to say things he didn't want to say. He nodded. He had decided.

"The man likes girls. You know this, I am sure. Young. Teenage girls. He likes a certain kind. Special. Fresh. Clean. He brings them to his big house in Jupiter. Makes them his slaves."

The man indicated his wrists, making a motion like he was slapping steel handcuffs on them. It was a pretty good pantomime. Luke got it right away.

"Bingo," Ed said. He said it barely louder than a whisper.

"He gives them to his friends," the prisoner said.

They were close now, and they both knew it. Jupiter Island was right up the highway from here. Call in a TAC squad. It was still early. They could have the girl back tonight.

"Wait," Bowles said. "Stop the interview."

* * *

"What's the matter?" Luke said.

Bowles was walking down the hallway as if he was planning to leave.

Ed took several running steps and got in front of him.

"You don't just walk out like that, friend."

Bowles was big. Not as big as Ed. But not afraid of him, either. They stood toe to toe, face to face.

"You're about to make a big mistake," Bowles said. "If you think you can assault a fellow officer…"

Ed raised both hands, as if Bowles had pulled a gun on him.

"We just want to talk."

Bowles shook his head. "There's nothing to talk about. We've stumbled across an ongoing joint investigation between the FBI and other agencies and organizations, including, for starters, the Miami-Dade Police Department and the Palm Beach County Sheriff's Office. I happen to know a little bit about it. First and foremost, it's classified. As such, our investigation has to stop here until we get guidance from above. Hopefully, we haven't stepped on the existing investigation too badly."

He shook his head. "We hit that house. I knew we shouldn't have done that. Two guys are dead. And this guy…" He gestured back toward the interrogation room. He shook his head again and sighed. The air seemed to go out of his body, like a car tire that had just been sliced with a hunting knife.

"Who else is involved?" Luke said.

Bowles gave him the drop dead look. "That's classified, too. This is a national security issue, if you haven't guessed yet."

He started to walk again. Luke grabbed him by the arm.

"Stone…"

"Who else is involved?"

Bowles smiled. "I'd tell you, but then I'd have to kill you."

"Who is the man on Jupiter Island?"

"I'm sure you guys can figure that out on your own. You shouldn't bother, but you probably will anyway."

Bowles shook free of Luke's arm, then walked briskly toward the doors. He stopped just before he reached them, and turned around.

"The case stops here, guys. You don't have the clearance to move forward, and neither do I. You might as well just go back to whatever else you were doing before you came down."

With that, he pushed the door open and went out into the night.

CHAPTER NINETEEN

10:35 p.m. Eastern Standard Time
Cape Fear Memorial Bridge
Wilmington, North Carolina

"I knew it would come to this."

Jeff Zorn didn't even know he had spoken.

He had just pulled his beloved BMW Z3 to a stop in the right lane near the Wilmington side of the bridge. The top was down, so he put the hazard lights on, stood on his seat, and stepped out of the car across the passenger seat.

He climbed over the horizontal iron bars and onto a small walkway between the road and the vertical tower of the bridge. It was a vertical lift bridge, with a tower on either side that served as an elevator. The elevator lifted the roadway for large container ships to pass underneath.

It was also an old bridge, rusty from the salt in the sea air. He reached the base of the bridge tower, and found that he could easily climb the diagonal supports. He had spotted these diagonal supports weeks ago, and had been thinking of them ever since.

He moved along the iron rungs like a monkey. The rungs were more like mini-stairs, wide enough to accommodate a person's feet. They were caked with rust, and the paint on the silo around them was peeling. Bird droppings were everywhere.

Below him and to his right, probably ten feet down now, a car pulled up behind his. The car was your typical unmarked cop sedan, no style at all, hard to tell what color in this light. Blue, black, green, could be anything. Suddenly, the car was flashing bright lights, in the back, in the front, on the dashboard. A black man in a sports jacket got out of the car and dashed toward the tower.

Of course he did. The man had been following him. They'd been following Jeff for at least the past hour. Could be they'd been following him for days, and he just picked up on it. Sure. They were probably watching him the whole time.

"Hey, man!" the guy shouted. "Hey, Jeff!"

Jeff started moving faster. He climbed lightly upward, racing, moving so fast he quickly became dizzy and out of breath. His pace slowed, and then it changed. He crawled up the rungs, hands gripping each new metal railing, pulling himself along. He was moving at a snail's pace. The structure seemed to go on forever.

He looked down. The cop or whatever he was, agent, secret policeman, was following him.

"Don't come up here!" Jeff shouted. "Leave me alone."

"Jeff! Wait a minute! Let's talk."

Jeff reached the top of the support. He was on a small metal platform now. Above his head was a metal trapdoor, hanging down. Through that hole a ladder, bolted into the vertical support, went straight up to the top of the bridge.

The man climbed the diagonal supports behind him, zigzagging his way. He was coming along, moving slow. Why rush? They knew they had him. There was nowhere for Jeff to run.

He started up the ladder and climbed through the hole. It went up and up. The ladder was rusted and sharp, and ancient paint flaked from it. It was cocooned by a tunnel of sorts, which protected him from the wind. But he knew where it was going. All the way to the top of the bridge, high above the water… totally exposed.

He used to look at bridges and wonder who would ever do these jobs. He hated heights, and yet, tonight it didn't bother him. It didn't matter now. He had been out driving around, trying to think, trying to make sense of everything that had happened.

Joy was in shock over the loss of her daughter, practically catatonic. She had taken a leave of absence from work. She wasn't eating. She could barely get out of bed. It was terrible, and to be expected. And yet, somehow he hadn't expected it.

There was something wrong with him. He knew that. There had always been something wrong with him. It was like he had never become an adult. He couldn't think things out ahead of time. He couldn't imagine consequences for anything he did.

He'd had money problems. He came from a rich family, his dad was *the Jeffrey Zorn*, but Jeff wanted more. He wanted to add his own pile. And he liked risk, too much risk. He had an appetite for it.

Gambling. It didn't matter what. Sports. Boxing, football, basketball. Penny stocks. Casinos. Business investments. He was a light touch for friends who were opening bars or restaurants. He had backed a friend's independent rap music label. Those were his bigshot Manhattan days. What was wrong with him? He had squandered a fortune from his father's side, then another, smaller one from his mother's side. He was so deep in, it was unspeakable. He felt dirty all the time.

He was sick. He had a sickness.

Darwin King had carried him a long time. How had it started? A little bit here, a little bit there. The guy was a billionaire, or so people said. After a while, Jeff realized he didn't have any money of his own. It was all gone. The only money he had was the money Darwin fronted him.

He owed a lot. He couldn't keep track of it. The interest was high, much higher than a bank. He was afraid to ask how bad it had gotten. And he and Darwin weren't even really friends. They knew each other on the Upper East Side. They were in the same social circle, the same party scene. It was superficial at best. At worst, Darwin had knowingly trapped him.

Anyway, all that was gone now. Darwin left New York for Florida, and Jeff came down here to North Carolina. Then Darwin didn't even seem to live in the country anymore. Jeff thought maybe it was a new start. But Darwin's people were still around. And Jeff was still caught, like a fish on a hook. Owing Darwin King money was like owing money to the mob. There was no escape.

One day a man met him on a bench in a local park. Just two guys sitting, chatting quietly, at either end of the bench. If you watched them from afar, you probably wouldn't even notice they were together.

"You need to put up something of value," the man said. "His patience is gone. It can't go on like this anymore."

Jeff couldn't think of a single thing. The cars? Darwin wouldn't care about that. He probably had a hundred cars. The 1948 Hudson, his pride and joy, wasn't even all original. There were a bunch of modern replica parts in there which for any real collector would crater the value. Jeff didn't like to admit that, not even to himself, but it was true.

"I don't have anything," he'd said. "I mean I am just tapped out."

He fully expected the man to take his head right then and there, sitting on a bench in a public park in the middle of the day, and twist it off his shoulders. But it turned out the man already had something of value in mind.

"What about the girl?" he said.

It seemed crazy, like a joke. He had heard rumors about Darwin's proclivities, but he had never really taken them seriously. People talked, that was all.

"What girl?"

The man shook his head. He was a large man, and stern. His face was so blank, he almost didn't seem to have a face. There was no intelligence behind his eyes. Nothing meant anything to him. He could have just as easily said, "What about the couch?"

"You know what girl."

Jeff didn't say anything. He didn't even want to dignify it by responding. He remembered how he trembled slightly.

"He's seen pictures. He likes her. Also, she's connected. This will settle an old score that you don't know about and don't need to know about."

"She's not my girl," Jeff said, as if that was an answer.

"No, but you can help get her. Just make it go smoothly. It's not the easiest thing in the world sometimes."

Nor should it be.

But it turned out it was easy, almost too easy. It was nothing to track what Charlotte was up to, her little secret meetings with friends, her undercover communications, the times she snuck out of the house to go to parties with her friends.

Charlotte thought she was the coolest kid on Earth. She thought she knew everything. She was a spoiled brat, really. There was a lot she didn't know, about the world, about herself, and about others. For example, Jeff helped her get away with sneaking out a couple of times. She didn't know that. She didn't know he was watching her, and even worse, she didn't know that *they* were watching her.

The truth was she didn't know anything. She was oblivious, just a dizzy teenage kid.

To Jeff, it seemed like a strange dream. It couldn't be real. This was how he was going to get off the hook? By giving Joy's daughter away? When the big night came, he wasn't sure if it was actually happening or if it was just practice.

Then she was gone. Just gone. He spoke to the police, of course, the concerned boyfriend. Suspicion naturally fell on him, but it wasn't like he had attacked and beaten up the Hastings kid. He wasn't at the party. And there were no communications between him and the real kidnappers.

Everything was done on an anonymous, encrypted phone Darwin's people gave him. He never saw a bill. He didn't even know what network it used. On Friday afternoon, he took the battery out of the phone and dropped it in the river.

He'd been thinking of killing himself ever since. Yes, it seemed he had gotten away with it, but that didn't mean he deserved to live.

And as soon as he noticed these plainclothes types following him, he knew it was over. He hadn't gotten away with anything. It was just completely over. There was no sense pretending anymore. He couldn't go to jail. He couldn't face Joy. He couldn't face the media.

He was moving quickly again, as fast as he could, and the ladder shook as he climbed it. He did not want that cop to catch up to him. At the top of the ladder, he clambered out through yet another trap door.

He emerged onto a wide platform. It was high, much higher than it had seemed from the ground. The height was crazy, and the platform sloped gently downward from the center to the edge. One side of the platform looked out over the harbor and the distant islands, and the ocean, and maybe the whole world. It was dark that way.

On the other side of the platform was the city. He could see the lights of the buildings downtown. He imagined he could almost see people moving, hurrying along city streets, all the hustle and bustle. But that was a different city, not Wilmington, not North Carolina. That was New York. It was almost like he was hallucinating now, or having visions. It was like he could understand things, things he'd never understood or even thought of before.

He had been such a fool. Just a sorry clown who skimmed along the surface and never tried to understand anything. Now, too late, he saw that he could have been smarter about it all. His life could have been different.

He started to cry.

He walked toward the edge. It was an amazing view. More than amazing, it was magic. A strong wind blew, shaking the structure beneath his feet.

Behind him, the man clambered out onto the platform. Jeff turned and looked. He was a tall black man, fit, handsome, maybe mid-thirties. The guy had everything going for him. His sports jacket billowed around him. He had a gun in a leather shoulder holster. Everything about this guy was stylish. He was the triumph of style over substance.

"Jeff," the man gasped. "Let's just talk. You're not in trouble. We don't know anything right now. But there's nothing that's been done that can't be undone. I can tell you that much."

Jeff backed away. He took a step, then another step. He was just a few feet from the edge now. He glanced down behind him. There was nowhere left to go.

"I'm afraid you have no idea what you're talking about."

The man raised both hands. "Okay, maybe. Maybe I don't. Even so."

Jeff stepped backwards, right up to the edge, his back to the abyss.

"Look at it, Jeff. It's a long way down."

And it was. He glanced back and the water seemed far below, as if they were standing on top of a skyscraper rather than a bridge. He did a quick calculation: four stories back to the roadway, another five or six to the water after that. A ten-story fall. It would do the trick.

He raised his arms out to his sides.

"Jeff, don't do it. You're going to die."

Jeff nodded. He took a deep breath. He hoped that death was just a long darkness and nothing more.

"I know," he said, and let himself fall backwards.

CHAPTER TWENTY

11:15 p.m. Eastern Standard Time
Marriott Extended Stay Suites
Fort Lauderdale–Hollywood International Airport
Fort Lauderdale, Florida

"The man's name is Darwin King," Trudy said.

Luke looked at Ed. Ed shook his head.

"Never heard of him."

"I don't know," Luke said. "Might ring a bell, might not."

They were sitting in the generic living room of Luke's incredibly generic hotel suite. It was nice, in its way. Clean, spacious, with a good kitchen. Everything worked. But it had zero character or charm. It was a place for tired business people flying from Point A to Point B all week to lay their heads for a night or two.

There was something both alienating and comforting about it. If you were in San Francisco one day, and Kansas City the next, and Chicago the next, it might be reassuring to stay in hotel suites that were the same everywhere you went.

"Well," Trudy said. "Get ready, because he's a corker."

They were on another conference call with SRT Headquarters. Swann, Trudy, and Don were all still up and at the office. Luke might call that dedication, except it was nothing more or less than it should be. He and Ed were still on the job.

"Do tell," Ed said. Ed had killed two men tonight. It didn't seem like it had exorcised any of his demons. He looked both murderous and exhausted at the same time.

"Darwin King," Trudy said. "He's fifty-eight years old. Tall, handsome, a lifelong playboy. He comes from old money, and can trace his ancestry to both early Dutch traders who settled in New Amsterdam, as well as fanatical Puritans who settled Massachusetts and Rhode Island, both groups going back to the mid-1600s. He grew up in Greenwich, Connecticut, and on the Upper East Side of Manhattan."

"So he's one of the people who inherited this country," Luke said.

Trudy's disembodied voice came out of Ed's phone, which was sitting on the kitchen counter. "He seems to think so. He's believed to have a net worth in the range of one to two billion dollars. No one can be quite sure, because much of his income comes under the table, and is undeclared and untaxed."

"What does he do?" Ed said.

"His main business is arms deals. He has amassed an arsenal of old Cold War weaponry, mostly Soviet stuff, what we would consider obsolete. He sells it to Central African warlords, despotic regimes in Central America, and rebel militias just about anywhere and everywhere. He's thought to have kept the civil war in Liberia going years past its expiration date by dumping cheap weapons on any ragtag group that could rub a few dollars together. He's ruthless and utterly amoral."

"War is good for business," Swann said.

"If your business is war," Trudy said. "And his is that."

"You said it's his main business," Luke said. "What else does he do?"

"Oh, you name it. He owns a wide array of legitimate cash businesses, including restaurants, Laundromats, pool halls, and video arcades. He has almost certainly used them to launder money for South and Central American drug cartels. He is even considered something of a loan shark, since that's one of the best returns on money you can get. And that's the tip of it. There's probably a lot more that we don't know about. What we do know is he runs his businesses like a Mafia empire."

"How does he fit into this?" Ed said. "And why does stumbling upon him stop our investigation?"

"It's complicated," Trudy said. "He appears to have protection at the highest levels. There's possible intelligence agency involvement, though all information on him held by the CIA, NSA, and DEA is classified, if it exists. He has an enormous Rolodex. My sense is that his relationships with Third World dictators, Swiss and Cayman bankers, militias, cartels, oligarchs, foreign intelligence, and various other flotsam and jetsam make him useful. He lived in Manhattan for a long time, and his parties there were known as a who's who of politicians, celebrities, and sports figures. The tentacles of his businesses reach all over the world."

"Even so, what does that have—"

"Here it comes," Trudy said. "He has a large estate on Jupiter Island, Florida. His property is about twenty-five acres, with ocean frontage, gated and behind high walls. About five years ago, in response to several missing person complaints, the Palm Beach County Police Department opened an investigation into activities taking place at King's estate. Namely, teenage girls from around the city of West Palm Beach and neighboring areas had begun to disappear.

"In general, they were girls from troubled backgrounds, broken homes, foster care. In a couple of cases, they turned up again months later, and said they had been living on King's compound. The suggestion was that these girls were either enticed onto the compound, or were abducted and brought there. They became sex slaves for King and his friends, possibly including household names in the worlds of politics, international business, European aristocracy, filmmaking, and other fields. Some of the girls who disappeared never turned up again."

"How many?" Ed said.

"It's hard to say," Trudy said.

"Guess," Ed said, "if you don't mind."

Luke looked at Ed. Ed's eyes were tired, but also alert. He was hungry. He was on a hunt. He was going to fix something in the past, something that couldn't be fixed. He had risked his life earlier tonight stepping in front of a door that had just been blown apart by a shotgun. And he had killed the man they were hoping to interview.

He would do it, Luke knew. He would drive up to Jupiter Island right now, as soon as this phone call ended. Then he would scale the high walls of some billionaire's estate, and fight the man's bodyguards to the death.

Ed needed a break.

"Twenty-seven," Trudy said. "But not all of them could have been at King's house. There's also been known serial killer activity in South Florida over the past ten years. At least some of those girls may have been murder victims. Others may have simply run away, changed their names, fell off the radar. But some of them, certainly, appear to have ended up at King's house."

"Twenty-seven girls have disappeared?" Ed said. "Twenty-seven?"

"Yes," Trudy said.

"How is the investigation going now?" Luke said.

"It isn't," Trudy said.

"Why?"

Don's voice appeared. "You know why, son. Two police departments, the FBI, and at least one or two other agencies are on the case, but somehow the can keeps getting kicked down the road."

"Someone is squashing it," Luke said.

"Good boy," Don said.

Luke shook his head. "I'm not as dumb as I look."

"Who's there now?" Ed said. "At the estate?"

"Swann?" Don said.

"Yeah, uh, I've done two drone flyovers in the past hour. I took my time, got a look at all of it. It's quite a spread, like the Palace at Versailles. A main house, with two wings. Must be thirty or forty rooms. Beachfront, rolling lawns, a big inground swimming pool. Everything is lit up, but it seems as if no one is there. I didn't spot a single human being anywhere on the compound."

"It appears," Trudy said, "that King has left the country. He's known to have a private island in the Western Caribbean, called St. Simon's Saw, which is about forty miles off the coast of Honduras, near the border with Nicaragua. He has a close relationship with the Honduran ruling class and military. St. Simon's is also a quick flight to Grand Cayman, where he appears to do much of his banking."

"No one is at the Jupiter Island place?" Luke said.

"I didn't see anyone," Swann said. "But it doesn't mean there's no one there. If I had to guess, I'd say there are some maintenance people around."

Ed was quietly seething. "This man has stolen twenty-seven girls, he has an estate on Jupiter Island, and he has an entire island of his own?"

"No one claims he stole twenty-seven girls," Trudy said. "There are twenty-seven girls in that part of Florida who have gone missing in recent years."

"There's some intelligence chatter about him that I've come across," Swann said. "He's paranoid. He moved his entire household and entourage down to the island. He felt that even if the investigation was stalled, it was still too close to him. As a result, he decided to leave town, maybe for a while, possibly for good."

"So why don't we just go there," Ed said, "and get the girl back? And any other girls that happen to be there?"

"It would take a security clearance that we don't have," Don said. "The Bureau is watching us like a mother hen. If they, or some other agency, or someone in power, deliberately stopped an investigation into this man, then the odds of the Bureau sending us to Honduras…"

"Do we need them to send us?" Luke said.

"Yes," Don said. "This is why you're attached to Special Agent Bowles. Or, more accurately, why he's attached to you. He's supposed to oversee your work."

"Bowles seems to have lost interest in us."

"Oh, I think he'll be back."

"In the meantime…" Ed began.

"In the meantime, you guys should get some much deserved rest. Let me see if I can touch base with a couple of people, and get some clarity on this."

"By clarity, you mean…"

"I think you both know what I mean. Provided you're up for it."

"I am," Ed said.

"Good," Don said.

Don was going to go forward. He was not going to wait for clearance, or even ask for it. That was the takeaway Luke got. Don suspected where the blockage was, and he was going to go above it, or around it.

Luke didn't know how he felt about that. The Bureau had already crashed their party once. If they had done it once, they could do it again. It was as simple as that.

"How's the security situation there?" Luke said. "Find any bugs crawling around?"

"We swept this place from top to bottom," Swann said. "At least for the moment, we are clean as a whistle."

When they hung up, Ed looked at Luke. It was time for Luke to go back to his room, and go to sleep. He welcomed it. Ed's eyes were tired, and wired, all at the same time. He looked like he might never sleep again.

Luke was concerned about him. He was going to drive himself too hard. Then he was going to slip up. In a sense, he already had. He had killed Cienfuegos tonight. That was bad enough. The next time, he might get them both killed instead.

"Do you believe Swann?" Ed said. "Do you think that place is clean?"

Luke thought about it for one second. "Absolutely not. I think they're listening to everything we say."

CHAPTER TWENTY ONE

March 29, 2006
1:35 a.m. Eastern Standard Time
A white Lexus parked on the street
Georgetown, Washington, DC

"The mother's boyfriend killed himself tonight," Miles Richmond said. "Threw himself off a bridge."

Don Morris sat in darkness in the back seat, nearly shoulder to shoulder with Bill Ryan. Miles Richmond sat at the steering wheel. The three of them could be the world's oldest gangbangers, plotting the world's slowest drug deal.

In fact, Don was updating them on the status of the case. He wanted to put the idea out there, an SRT surgical strike on Darwin King's island. It was Richmond's idea to talk in his car, like a bunch of teenagers. He didn't want anyone to overhear them.

Don hadn't heard of this suicide until now. It could be that it would change things. It could be that it would change nothing.

"I'm sorry," he said.

Richmond shook his balding head. "Don't be."

"Why did he do it?" Bill said.

"No one knows for sure," Richmond said. "I have my suspicions, however. Joy isn't necessarily a bad mother, but I'm sorry to say that she makes bad choices. This guy Zorn was one of them. I wouldn't put it past him to have been involved in this somehow."

"Did Zorn know a man named Darwin King?" Don said.

Richmond's eyes laser focused on Don in the rearview mirror.

"Everyone of a certain ilk knows Darwin King," Richmond said. "I'm sure Zorn knew him. I'm sure that if you look, you'll have no trouble finding pictures of them partying together. Darwin King likes his parties."

His eyes didn't waver from Don's. "Why do you ask?"

"None of what I'm about to say is guaranteed," Don said. "But we've been tracking leads, and we've shaken the tree a bit. My people now believe that Darwin King took your granddaughter. He didn't personally do it, obviously."

"Obviously," Richmond said. "Darwin King isn't capable of doing anything himself."

Now Don eyed Richmond. "Do *you* know him?"

"As I indicated, everyone of a certain ilk knows him. I qualify, unfortunately."

"Do you have reason to believe that he might want to hurt you?"

The eyes still stared at Don. But now tears had begun streaming from them.

"I swear to God," Richmond said. He shook his head. "If he does anything to her…"

"Did you know this from the beginning?" Don said. "My men risked their lives to get this information. They killed two men. They found three dead children. If you already knew…"

Now Richmond shook his head violently. "Absolutely not. I had no idea. I had no reason to think it was him until this moment. But I do know him, and I know he's a terrible person. We've banged heads in the past. He was a client of mine at one time, to be frank. But he wants what he wants when he wants it, and if he doesn't get it, he decides he doesn't have to pay. Then he gets taken to court, where he loses. And even with judgments against him, he still doesn't pay. Instead, he demands back the money he paid upfront. He's notorious for this."

Richmond took a deep breath. "He thinks I stole from him, but the truth is, he stole from me. And now…" His voice trailed off.

"Now he's taken Charlotte?" Bill Ryan said.

Don nodded. "We think so, yes. We think he hired professional kidnappers, human traffickers, to take her. Two of those men, as I mentioned, are now dead."

Richmond nodded. "Good."

"We believe he took Charlotte to an island off the coast of Honduras."

Richmond's shoulders slumped. "Honduras?"

"Yes. It's outside United States jurisdiction, obviously. He's far beyond the reach of law enforcement, and he has protection from the Honduran military."

"I will pay anything," Richmond said.

Don raised a hand. "I have men that are willing to go there and attempt a rescue. It would be on the company dime. But you have to understand a few things. One is we don't know for a fact that he has her. It could be a mistake, so you shouldn't get your hopes up. Two, if we go there and he does have her, it's going to be a dangerous operation to get her back. She could be hurt during it. She could be killed. You need to know that before we do anything at all."

Richmond stared at Don in the rearview. His eyes were red, but he had stopped crying. That was good. Don got the sense that Richmond was trying to be strong.

"All right," he said. "I can accept that."

"There's one more thing," Don said. "I need to speak with my superiors. I'm going to feel them out. I may not get a green light from them, but if I don't, my instinct is to do this anyway. That means this will not be a sanctioned hostage rescue. It will not be a police action. It will be a clandestine special operation. It will be completely secret. If my agency is revealed to be behind it, or the covers of my men are blown, I'm going to be in deep doo-doo. I will need the help of influential people who can…"

"Consider it done," Richmond said. "If you can do this for me, whether it succeeds or fails, I will owe you my life. I will move heaven and earth for you and your people, now and in the future. With Bill Ryan, and God, as my witnesses, I promise you that."

Bill nodded. "I agree with Miles. I'm with you, Don. You will always have my protection and help, such as it is. I consider you a great friend, one of my best, but more than just a friend. I think of you as my ally."

Now Don nodded. Bill was prone to sappy emotional talk like this. That was fine. He had always been a loyal friend. Don had no reason to doubt him. Richmond was the weak link in this chain.

"Miles," he said. "Know that I'm going to go forward, based on this conversation. We may not talk again. This is me, telling you that I am moving on this."

"Good," Richmond said. "I want you to. I'm ready. I understand the risks."

"You need to keep quiet about it. You cannot tell a soul."

Richmond nodded. "Of course. Of course."

"Do not tell your wife. Do not tell your mistress. Do not tell anyone."

"Yes."

"And know that I might come calling on you one day. Maybe about this, maybe about something else."

"I welcome that, Don."

"Good," Don said.

"And Don?"

"Yes."

"When your guys find Darwin, if it's at all possible, ask them to kill him. For me."

Don's eyes and Richmond's eyes were locked together in the mirror. Don could feel Bill Ryan's eyes on both of them. This was one of the risks of associating with people outside the circle. They talked too much, and they said the wrong things.

Anyone with a tape of this conversation could easily cut it to make it sound like a murder for hire. But Richmond didn't even seem to notice his error.

"Okay?" he said.

CHAPTER TWENTY TWO

5:45 a.m. Central Standard Time (6:45 a.m. Eastern Standard Time)
La Sierra de San Simon (St. Simon's Saw)
Near Honduras
The Caribbean Sea

"Go away."

The seabirds were screeching and calling, letting him know that somewhere out there, the early sun was peeking over the horizon.

Here it was still dark.

And the bedside phone was ringing. Darwin King reached one hand to the table and picked it up. His first instinct was to immediately hang it up again. But that was the wrong instinct. If a call came this early, and it made it to his bedside, then someone thought it was important. He didn't get where he was by avoiding important calls.

He put the phone to his ear.

"What?"

"Sir, I'm very sorry to bother you at this—"

"Save it. What's going on?"

"There's a call from the United States."

"Okay. Put it through."

A pause came while the man put the call through. This far from civilization, the phones worked like they had in the past, when this place was still a hotel. There was a switchboard downstairs, in a room near the kitchen, and a person plugged lines into the switchboard, just like in movies from the 1950s and 1960s.

Darwin reached a hand behind him and touched the warm flesh of a young thing. The girl made the groan of someone who was comfortably asleep. It was nice. It was reassuring. There was something nostalgic and romantic about it.

There were two other girls besides this one in the bed with him. That's where the romance ended—three young girls in a gigantic bed.

He sat up at the side of the bed. He extended the antenna of the cordless phone, stood up, and padded nude to the balcony. He passed through the doors to the outside.

It was a different world out here. Cool but humid, white mists hanging across the dense trees as they descended down the side of the mountain. It was still dark, but light was entering the sky, as if someone was very slowly turning up a dimmer device. The fog was so thick, he couldn't see the ocean from here.

"Darwin?" a voice said. It was a man's voice.

"Yeah."

"I was told to call you."

Darwin nodded. "Okay."

"It's happening. The thing you were warned about."

This was what people like Bill Ryan didn't understand. Ryan was so self-centered, he somehow thought that he was the only one who had access to information, or that his access was the best, or was exclusive in some way. It wasn't.

The hint Ryan had given him was enough. Darwin King had his own ways of finding out more.

"When is it happening?"

"We don't know. We are on top of it, though, and we will find out."

"Do you know what form it will take?"

"Well, we don't expect a hundred vice cops to pull up at your house, if you get what I'm saying. Given the people involved, we can only guess it will be some kind of undercover thing. Like a black op. More than that, we don't know at this time."

Darwin didn't like that. It conjured to mind images of ninjas in black pajamas, moving unseen, creeping down darkened hallways with knives between their teeth.

"Is it about number 21?" he said.

"Yes."

Darwin ran a hand through his hair. He had a moment of weakness then. Nothing had happened yet. She had pledged herself to him, but he hadn't consummated their relationship. She was still downstairs in the Tombs, softening up, getting ready, *ripening*, as he liked to put it.

She was probably ready now, but he liked them all the way ready, completely malleable, no resistance at all. He liked to remake them, and their images of themselves, according to his vision. He was like a master painter in that way.

Give her back.

Maybe he had overstepped after all. Maybe he had underestimated Miles Richmond. It was just one girl. She was not harmed, other than a little bit of psychological shock and physical discomfort. She would get over that. He could give her back. If he did, this problem would go away, and these people would leave him alone.

But that wasn't him, was it?

He shook his head and smiled. No.

You didn't become Darwin King by backing down.

"What else?"

"As I understand it, there was some talk of terminating your lease."

"Terminating… my… lease."

"Yes. If you understand me."

Darwin nodded. "I do."

That settled it. People didn't talk about terminating Darwin King's lease. It didn't happen. They weren't going to kill him. They weren't even going to come close. It was a joke. He would increase security here on the island, as a precaution, and he would derail their efforts at the source. He would keep the girl and do anything and everything he wanted with her.

"Can we stop it?" he said. "Crush it, like an insect? Make them sorry they even considered it?"

"Yes, of course," the voice said. "We have someone very close to it already. But derailing it is one thing. Crushing it will cost extra."

Darwin wanted to be completely clear. "I'm talking about a total loss for them, and total victory for us. Completely one-sided. Devastating impact. Such that no one ever tries anything like this again."

"Yes, I understand."

"Good," Darwin said. "In that case, money is no concern at all. Spend whatever it takes. And keep me in the loop."

"Okay. We will."

Darwin hung up. He went inside the bedroom and looked at the enormous bed in the gathering light of dawn. The sheets were tangled and twisted. Live bodies were strewn this way and that, heads buried in masses of blond and brunette hair. It looked like some kind of abstract art piece. If he were an artist, he would put a canvas on an easel right now and paint it.

"Total victory," he whispered to himself.

That's what he would call it. That's what his life was. That's what his art would be. That's what every single painting he ever made would be called.

He decided he was in no hurry to start his day. He was in no mood to worry about black operators, spy versus spy. That would all take care of itself. And if past was prologue, it would take care of itself in his favor. Meanwhile, he had better things to do with his time.

He smiled and slid back into bed.

CHAPTER TWENTY THREE

8:25 a.m. Eastern Standard Time
Marriott Extended Stay Suites
Fort Lauderdale–Hollywood International Airport
Fort Lauderdale, Florida

"I could get used to this," Special Agent Henry Bowles said.

Luke looked at Ed. Ed shook his head.

The man wore blue jeans, and a plain black long sleeve T-shirt that hugged the muscles of his upper body. Bowles was jacked. He had a pair of leather sandals on his big feet. He wore a black baseball cap that said *Spy Kids* in white across the front. His face had the same three-day growth of beard it had the day before.

He looked like a male model. Specifically, he looked like a model doing a travel magazine shoot where he played a happy, healthy, prosperous dad on a Florida vacation with the family.

Bowles had a blue tray and was in line at the free breakfast buffet in the lobby of Ed and Luke's hotel. He had already put eggs, sausage, toast, and a glass of orange juice on his tray. He was about to pour himself some coffee.

"What are you doing here, Bowles?"

Bowles shrugged. "I came to talk, that's all."

"So talk."

He gestured at a round, empty table. "I came to talk over breakfast."

Hordes of tourists dressed in bright colors milled around the buffet. Three television sets were mounted on different walls, showing a morning talk show. A line of people were at the reception desk. Piles of luggage were near the front door. Every now and then, a small mass of people went out that door to catch the shuttle bus to the airport, which was roughly half a mile from here.

There was a steady buzz of conversation, TV chatter, phones ringing, and a low, pleasant tone sounding every time the front door slid open. It was a busy place, and not at all quiet. It was a good place to talk. They had a 9 a.m. call with SRT headquarters coming up. Maybe this little chat could inform that one in some way.

They sat at the table. Luke dug into his eggs.

"Let me ask you a question," Ed said to Bowles.

Bowles smiled. "Ask away."

"When you shave each morning, how far away do you stand from the razor? I mean, is the razor in the bathroom, and you're in the kitchen? Is the razor out on the front stoop, and you're in the backyard? I'm just trying to work this out in my head."

Luke laughed. He was in a good mood today, better than yesterday. He had slept like the dead last night. The bed was king-sized, and he had just spread out and sunk into it. He didn't even remember falling asleep. Now he felt refreshed, and a little lighter. He was seeing things with new eyes. Maybe having Bowles turn up again wasn't the worst thing in the world.

Bowles nodded. "Very funny. Very original. I hadn't heard that one before."

"Because it works better the closer you stand to it," Ed said.

They ate in silence for a long moment. Luke reflected that Bowles was the only person he'd ever seen pile his plate as high as Ed.

"How can we help you, Bowles?" Luke said.

Bowles didn't look up from his food. "I want in."

"In?" Ed said. "In to what?"

Bowles shrugged. "Whatever you guys are doing, or are about to do."

"What makes you think we're doing anything? We don't even know what we're doing. For all we know, we're about to get a call telling us to come home."

Bowles looked up now, and eyed them both.

"I don't believe that for one minute."

"What do you think we're doing?"

Bowles shoveled food into his mouth. He glanced around, as if he was checking when the next shuttle was leaving, or maybe whether his wife had come downstairs yet.

"Here's what I know. You guys have a reputation that precedes you. They didn't assign me to you because you color inside the lines. There is no doubt in my mind that you've figured out who the subject is in this case."

He looked from Ed, to Luke, and back to Ed. Then back to Luke again.

Luke shrugged. "Okay. If you like."

"And that means you know he's not here anymore."

Luke said nothing to this.

Bowles's eyes suddenly became fierce. He spoke quietly, but with an intensity he hadn't shown before. "Listen, do you think I like it? Do you think I like dirtbags like this guy, who think they're above the law, who think they can act with impunity? Do you think I like it that they're right most of the time?"

He shook his head and answered his own question. "I don't like it. Of course I don't. But what can I do? I'm one man, and I wasn't fortunate enough to join a mysterious rogue agency within an agency. We play it by the book around here, partner. And that means bad guys with clout walk away free."

He raised a finger. "But this one time, it doesn't have to be that way. I'm actually assigned to you guys. I have wide latitude to interpret what that means. And I know where the guy is. I know where he is right this minute."

"So do we," Ed said.

Bowles raised his hands. "So you guys went cowboy. I was along for the ride. What did I know? I got caught up in it, had to go with the flow. But then it worked out, a very bad guy went down, and all is forgiven. The people protecting him? There's nothing they can do. By the time they realize what's happening, it's too late. And they scurry away like mice. A few eggs were cracked, but a very nice omelet was made."

He dug into his food again.

"The guy is radioactive. If we get out ahead and take him down, no one will lift a finger. They can't. No one will even admit to knowing him. I'm very confident of that."

"This is how you really feel?" Luke said.

Bowles stared right at him.

"Yes. This is how I really feel. If you're planning something, I want in."

Ed shook his head. "Then what was that whole act last night at the headquarters?"

Bowles shrugged. "It was exactly what you say it was. An act. I had to do that. The walls have ears. We had all the information we needed from that kid. I figured at that point, you guys were going to move forward, regardless of anything more he might say. Things are sensitive. This case has been killed from on high again and again. Everyone witnessing that interview—and believe me, people were witnessing it—needed to think I shut it down. I did my job. The investigation hit a wall. It's over. Go home."

"Were you assigned to us to kill the investigation?" Luke said.

Bowles smiled and shook his head. "Why do you think? To help move the case along? I've been down here a long time. Things work a certain way. I wouldn't call it corrupt, but I wouldn't call it anything else, either."

"Do you have any experience with this kind of thing?" Ed said.

"I don't know what you know about me," Bowles said.

"Why don't you tell us?"

"I was 1st Special Forces, you probably know that. This was back in the nineties, before the Middle East wars started. I did covert missions, on loan to the DEA, breaking up cartel traffic. Mexico, El Salvador, Guatemala, Colombia. Night jumps, surveillance." He looked at them with meaning. "Interdiction."

Luke looked at Ed. Was Ed convinced? It was hard to say.

"More than that, I can't really tell you. But yes. Rest assured, I have experience. I can hold my own out there, and then some."

Luke glanced at his watch. They had five minutes before the phone call. There was a lot to talk about.

"We'll let you know," he said.

* * *

"Jeff Zorn is dead," Don Morris said.

His voice came out of Ed's telephone, sitting on the generic kitchen counter of his extended stay suite. The counter was also covered in papers. The papers came out of a leather briefcase. Downstairs, a man in lime green slacks and a yellow golf shirt had walked up to Luke near the elevators and said, "Sir, I think you forgot your case."

Luke had smacked himself in the forehead. "Oh yes, that's mine. Thank you. Wouldn't want to lose that thing. My whole life is in there."

Now, he and Ed stood over the counter, sipping coffee and staring down at the various pages.

"Tell me," Luke said.

"I requested a tail on him like you asked for last night," Trudy said. "The local FBI followed him leaving his house in a blue BMW Z3, the same car he previously surrendered to the police. At some point, he recognized the tail. He drove around seemingly at random for a while, then stopped the car on a bridge over the Cape Fear River. He climbed to the top of the bridge and threw himself off. The local agent followed him up there, tried to engage, but said Zorn wouldn't talk. They recovered the body downriver about six miles, near where the river dumps into the ocean, caught on an old Army Corps of Engineers retaining wall."

"What does that tell us?" Luke said.

"It tells us he was involved. Turns out Jeff Zorn and Darwin King are known associates. They used to party together when they both lived in New York City."

"Ah," Luke said. "Do we still think the girl is on the island?"

"We do," Don said. "I don't think this man's suicide changes anything, except now we know how King got access to the girl. So let's do it. Trudy, tell us about the island."

One of the pages on the kitchen counter was a large map of the island. Trudy Wellington took the handoff from Don, and started giving them the rundown.

"St. Simon's Saw," she said. "It's a private island about forty miles north of the Honduras coastline. It is basically a series of small, very steep hills or mountains rising out of the ocean. Hence the name. Early mariners thought the jagged peaks looked like a long saw, and named it for Saint Simon the Zealot, traditionally one of the twelve Apostles of Christ, thought to have been martyred by being sawed in half."

"Lovely," Luke said.

"Beautiful story," Trudy said. "It was a pretty common method of execution for many centuries. I could show you some nice woodcut images of people being sawed in half during the Middle Ages."

"No thanks."

Suit yourself," she said, and moved on. "There is a large stone house, Casa del Sol, or House of the Sun, at the top of the tallest mountain. The house was built in the 1890s by Mexican industrial baron Carlos San Patricio. The stone was brought to the island by boat, and was pulled up the mountainside by mules.

"Over the years, San Patricio had acquired vast tracts of land throughout Central America, including several islands off the coast. He was a devout Catholic, and repeated disease outbreaks in the region—cholera, typhoid, and smallpox, to name a few—led him to believe the world was ending. St. Simon's Saw was where he planned to wait for the resurrection of Christ."

"How long did he wait?" Ed said.

Trudy laughed. "He's still waiting."

Luke looked at a topographical map. The island was a misshapen thing, rounded to the west, with a long peninsula of what looked like beach at the bottom of some foothills stretching out to the east. The base of the island, basically an outer ring all the way around, was at sea level. The house appeared to sit at an elevation of 1,100 feet, the highest point on the island.

"Is that an airfield I see at the north end?" he said.

"Yes," Trudy said. "The island changed hands numerous times through the twentieth century. In the mid-1960s it was an exclusive resort of the emerging international jet set. The house became a hotel, with numerous smaller cabana houses both on the grounds of the house and down near the beach. People would fly in on private planes."

Luke picked up an old, full-color, three-panel brochure. *Visit fantastic St. Simon Island.* The cover was a photo of a rambling, whitewashed stone house, surrounded by dense green foliage. Inside the brochure, a beautiful woman in a one-piece bathing suit lounged by an inground swimming pool near lush gardens, the ocean visible in the distant background. Finally, there was an aerial photo, probably taken by helicopter, of a long, seemingly deserted white sand beach, with waves crashing.

"Didn't work, I gather," Luke said.

"It seems that it was up and down," Trudy said. "The resort changed hands and names several times. The ocean along the island's beaches can be rough. A handful of people drowned while vacationing there, which didn't help the place's reputation. That area also tends to get pummeled by hurricanes and tropical storms. The beachfront cabanas were repeatedly destroyed, and the whole beachfront accommodation idea was eventually abandoned."

"When did King buy it?" Ed said.

"It's not clear that he ever bought it," Trudy said. "I've researched it and haven't found a deed of sale, a quitclaim, any kind of transfer of ownership to him. It's officially owned by a shell company based in Grand Cayman, called Heritage Trust Royale, which may be affiliated in some way with an entity known as Royal Heritage Bank. The headquarters of both is the same post office box. The company has owned the island since 1979, when Darwin King would have been about thirty-two years old. It's possible he is Heritage Trust Royale, and he bought it as an investment when he was a young man. Whenever and however he came into possession of it, he seems to have started appearing there in the early 1990s. The place had fallen into disrepair by then, and he renovated it, returning to the idea of using it as a home, not a hotel."

"A place to escape the law?" Ed said.

"Indeed," Trudy said. "Darwin King prefers to live outside the lines. St. Simon's Saw isn't claimed by any country. In a technical sense, international law prevails there, but in reality no one is there to enforce it. Honduras is the country most nearby, but the government is utterly corrupt and King has close ties with several people in the government and the military. They do not interfere with him.

"On his own private island, to a large degree, he is the law. When he's in hot water in the United States, such as the ongoing investigation in Florida, he retreats to St. Simon's. He's thought to have been living there for the past six months, with occasional visits to Honduras, the Cayman Islands, and possibly, Colombia and Venezuela."

"Who's the woman with him?" Ed said.

"In the photos we sent?" Trudy said.

"Yes."

Ed was holding a photograph of a younger Darwin King and staring at it intently. In the photo, King was dressed in a nicely tailored black sports jacket, his hair only a bit gray, at some sort of cocktail party. On his arm was a thin, lovely short-haired brunette in a green dress, which matched her striking green eyes. They were both holding drinks. On the counter there was another photo of King with the same woman, this time on a boat. In that one, the woman was wearing a green windbreaker jacket.

"That's Elaine Sayles, fifty-one years old. An heiress to the old Sayles furrier fortune from the nineteenth and early twentieth century, long since diversified into cosmetics, high tech, defense, and real estate."

"Furs," Swann said.

"Yeah," Ed said. He had not taken his eyes off the photo. "Out of fashion."

"She grew up in New York, London, and Paris. She ran with a fast crowd when she was young, movie stars, musicians, artists. She did some magazine modeling, and appeared in low-budget avant-garde films. She took up with King sometime in the 1980s, and began to appear on his arm at charitable events, dinners, shows. Maybe she was his girlfriend in those days, maybe she wasn't. Now she's thought to be a procurer of sorts for him, bringing teenage girls into his orbit. She is also thought to play den mother and disciplinarian to the girls, keeping them organized and in line."

"She's a pimp," Ed said.

"If you like," Trudy said. "Either way, she is definitely a member of his household, and is his longtime friend and partner in crime."

The look in Ed's eyes was very, very dangerous. Luke flashed back to the way Ed looked when he was dealing with Louis Clare.

"You planning to kill somebody?" Luke said.

Big Ed shrugged. "I don't have any firm plans right now."

"In any event," Trudy said, "as far as we know, Darwin King is on St. Simon's Saw. Our best guess is that Charlotte Richmond is there as well, likely along with several other abducted or trafficked teenage girls, any number of household staff, a squad of personal bodyguards, and possibly a dozen or more rank and file Honduran soldiers. And also Elaine Sayles."

"Do we know any of this for a fact?" Luke said.

"Stone," Swann said, "I've been flying a gossamer drone, very light, up near eighty thousand feet, in that area since before dawn. Although I'm way up high, I have pretty good optics. There was thick fog around the island this morning, but it has mostly burned off. Skies are clear and I'm looking at it right now, almost in real time. I can see the whole island and the compound around the house in detail."

"Let's hear it," Luke said.

"There are troops present at both the house and the airfield, hard to say how many. There is a small modern jet and two military-style jeeps parked at the airfield. There is a checkpoint and guard station near the entrance to the house, along with a couple more jeeps, at least one of which may have a rear-mounted gun. Also, there is what looks like security fencing around the entire house compound. Inside the compound, there are four or five people at the pool. There are other people milling around, what I would guess are servants or bodyguards."

"Terrific," Luke said. Not only were there soldiers to fight, there were all kinds of civilians to get in the way. He stared down at the map.

"Would you say that's about a mile from the airfield to the house?"

"A mile and a half, closer to two," Swann said. "And bear in mind the road goes straight up the hillside."

"Okay."

"Here's the best part," Swann said. "Along that perimeter fencing, there's something moving, which I'm going to guess… Hold on, let me see if I can pull in a bit. Yeah, it looks like what you've got there is two fences, with a bit of a gap between them. And there are dogs in the gap."

"Dogs?" Luke said.

"Either that, or small ponies. Something on four legs. Bear cubs? I think probably dogs. Dobermans, Rottweilers, something along those lines. Four, five, I count at least six. Could be more."

"How about something friendly, like Labradoodles?" Luke said.

"Sure," Swann said. "If you prefer. It's a security dog run filled with friendly, happy dogs. Bring some chewy treats."

"And a Frisbee," Trudy said.

Luke sighed. "So what's the plan? We go there by airplane, ask for permission to land, hitchhike two miles up to the house, waltz right past all his people and his killer guard dogs, and arrest the man?"

It seemed far-fetched, at best.

"This is a rescue operation," Don Morris said. "Not an arrest. It's an extraction."

"An *extraction*?" Ed said.

"Yes," Don said. "We have one objective. Infiltrate, find, and extract the Richmond girl, and get her back out safely. Everything else is superfluous. You are not there to arrest Darwin King. You are not there to go to war against the Honduran army."

"What about the other girls?" Ed said.

"It's tricky," Don said. "We don't know how long those girls have been there. We don't know why they're there. We don't even know for sure who they are. Many people who are being trafficked don't know they're being trafficked, or have forgotten how they came to be in these situations. Many will take the side of the traffickers. It's going to be hot in there, and you do not want to waste time trying to drag people out who do not want to leave. If you encounter evidence of human trafficking, acquire it, and we'll go back in there with Black Hawks and squads of Delta. I will see to it myself."

Ed didn't answer.

Luke looked at him. Ed was taking a sip from his coffee mug, his eyes peering over the top. Those eyes said this was not an arrest, or an extraction. It was a hit. At least, that was how Luke read them.

This was beginning to seem impossible.

"Yeah, but how do we even get in there?" Luke said. "The island looks like dense jungle pretty much everywhere, and it's a steep hillside, so it would be hard to parachute in, especially at night. The airfield is doable, but they control it. Even if we do get in, how are we supposed to get back out again?"

"Right," Don said.

"Is that an answer to my question?"

"Do you remember a guy named Buzz MacDonald?" Don said.

Luke shook his head and smiled. What was this, some sort of nostalgia game? Of course he remembered him. Mike "Buzz" MacDonald was an old combat junkie from even before Don's generation, when special operations wasn't a term yet. He was still around Joint Special Operations Command when Luke was just coming on board Delta.

They used to call him Buzz Mac. Buzzsaw. Iron Mac. Big Mac. A bunch of nicknames. He was the ultimate cowboy, even more so than Don himself. Don could play along well enough that the brass trusted him with men under his command, and now with his own agency. Buzz MacDonald was out there on a limb, all by himself. The gossip was that Buzz had lived through more than a hundred missions.

"Yeah," Luke said. "I remember him."

"He's waiting to talk to us," Don said. "I believe he can get you men in there."

CHAPTER TWENTY FOUR

Morning
An Island Near Honduras
The Caribbean Sea

21 needs to get out of here.

It was the first thought on her mind as she slowly came awake. She knew it was daytime because the light had changed, from absolute darkness to a dim twilight. She also knew it because she was hungry, thirsty, and had to go to the bathroom. She was learning to tell time by her bodily urges.

21 better think of something.

Soon, a small, dark man in a green uniform would open the door and wordlessly walk her down the short hall to the grimy bathroom. After that, he would bring her breakfast on a tray, with water and tea. Or maybe, if she was lucky, Mistress Elaine would turn up and take her outside onto the bright, sunlit patio for breakfast.

She knew where she was now, more or less, and she had some sense of the time. Her orientation was much better than it had been. She still had no idea how long she had been gone from home, but it now seemed like she had been here just a few days.

Last night before she slept, in the pitch dark, she went over the day in her mind. She didn't think about Darwin or Elaine, per se. She did not want to think about them, or what they wanted from her.

She thought instead about the place.

It was an island near Honduras. She knew that. Near, but far. Not so close that you could swim there.

The house was very big, with lots of rooms. When they led her upstairs to see Darwin yesterday—it was yesterday, wasn't it?—she had lost track of where she was going.

There were men here, soldiers. They carried rifles. There were other men, as well, big white men in suit jackets with dangerous looks in their eyes. In fact, all the men here had dangerous looks in their eyes, from Darwin on down.

There was a fence around this property. She had noticed that. She had also noticed the looping razor wire at the top of it. The place was a fancy beautiful prison, and she was trapped inside.

There were telephones here. Darwin had one on his table. It was old, but it was definitely a working phone. She had been posing for him, showing him her body, and then one of the big men had come in and told Darwin there was a phone call. She noticed Darwin look at the phone. After she left, he was going to pick it up and talk on it.

People could call here, and that probably meant you could call out.

Call where?

Home, of course.

How?

She didn't know. Did you have to dial a certain number to get an outside line? Did you have to dial one followed by an area code? Was there a special code because you were out of the country? She didn't know any of these things.

And if she reached someone, what would she tell them?

"I'm on an island near Honduras." Would that be enough? Were there a lot of islands near Honduras? How far away was Honduras?

There was so much she didn't know.

She had seen a photo of the beach here. Elaine had told her that one day, when they trusted her, they might let her go off the property and down to the beach with the other girls. Could you swim away from here? Was there another island nearby that you could swim to? Charlotte was a good swimmer.

Charlotte. My name is Charlotte.

But she wasn't swim-across-the-English-Channel good. She wasn't Olympics good.

Also, what if there were sharks in the water?

That wasn't going to work.

Just then, the familiar sound of the bolts being pulled back came. Charlotte was still on her bed, with the robe still on, and face down under the threadbare blanket. She rolled over and pulled the robe tightly around her. She prepared to shield her eyes from the sudden onslaught of light about to come.

The door opened and the light streamed in. There were two figures in the doorway. One was a man, probably the same man who opened this door every morning. The other figure was a thin female—Mistress Elaine. Good. That was good. Charlotte did not like Elaine, and was afraid of her. But she would brave almost anything to get out of this room and into the sunlight again.

"There she is," Elaine said. Her voice was cold. "Sit up."

"Good morning," Charlotte said, moving to a sitting position. She was trying to sound cheerful, but not too cheerful. Every step, every word, every gesture, could be putting your foot down on a bomb.

"What's good about it?" Elaine said.

Charlotte was hesitant. "I don't know."

"If you don't know, then why did you say it?"

"I don't know."

"You don't know anything, do you?"

Charlotte didn't answer.

"Are you really that stupid?"

Elaine stepped into the room. Charlotte's eyes were already adjusting to the light, and she could see that Elaine was carrying a leather switch, the kind that she liked to hit Charlotte with. The man with the gun stepped in behind.

"Answer me, 21."

"I don't…"

"Is that all you can say? You don't know?"

Charlotte was stuck. There was no good way to answer these questions. Elaine was angry with her. Or maybe she was just acting angry to manipulate her. It was impossible to tell, but it seemed real.

"You're making his life very difficult, did you know that?"

"I…"

Elaine had the switch in her left hand. She stepped quickly across the room and slapped Charlotte across the face with her right hand. Hard. Instantly, Charlotte's cheek stung. She raised a hand to it. The skin was hot.

"Speak!" Elaine said. "Say something, you dumb slut."

How could she speak? What could she say? She had no idea what this person was talking about.

Elaine slapped her again. And again.

"They think they're coming to take you. Okay? But they're not. They're not going to make it here, and even if they do, they won't know where you are. Do you know why? Because you're going to be in this room. No one is going to find you down here, princess. No one. And anyone who tries is going to die."

She smacked Charlotte with the switch. It sliced across Charlotte's bare neck. The sting was such that every time she felt it, it seemed like it ripped open the skin there. It always felt like she would bleed. But instead it raised a welt, one which would go away in a few hours. Already Charlotte had realized why.

Elaine was not to damage the merchandise. Charlotte belonged to Darwin, not Elaine. Elaine's attacks were superficial. They hurt, but did no lasting harm.

Even that little bit of knowledge gave Charlotte power. The tears streamed down her face now, but the emotion didn't reach her heart. It was an act. Elaine couldn't hurt her. She wasn't allowed.

Elaine herself probably belonged to Darwin.

And someone was coming. Someone was coming here to rescue her.

She knew it!

"Don't get your hopes up, dummy. I see it in your eyes. But you might as well forget it. No one is going to save you."

Elaine turned to the man with her.

"Give her the bucket."

The man reached outside the door and came back with a white plastic bucket, like something chlorine for your pool would come in. He dropped it and kicked it into the room. It made a hollow sound as it slid across the floor.

"That's your bathroom break today, bitch."

They left the room and the door slammed shut. The bolts closed. Charlotte was in near total darkness again.

They hadn't left her food, or water. And they were going to make her pee in a bucket. That was too bad, but it also didn't matter.

Someone was coming. She needed to be ready for that.

CHAPTER TWENTY FIVE

10:30 a.m. Eastern Standard Time
Marriott Extended Stay Suites
Fort Lauderdale–Hollywood International Airport
Fort Lauderdale, Florida

"Greetings from Nicaragua," Buzz MacDonald said.

Luke looked at Ed and smiled. The guy was a character.

"Hi, Buzz," Luke said.

"Hello, Stone. Who else you got there for me?"

Luke introduced Ed. Introductions were made around the table at SRT headquarters. Formalities and niceties were exchanged.

"What are you doing in Nicaragua?" Luke said.

"What am I doing here? I live here. Beautiful beaches. Beautiful women to spend Uncle Sam's pension money on. And I'm a foot taller than everyone I meet. At least a foot. Big, long waves if you like to surf, and I do. And the fish jump into your boat. The real question is: what are you doing there?"

Now even Ed smiled.

"The commies don't bother you?" Luke said.

The United States had been fighting the communist Sandinistas in Nicaragua during Buzz's time. Whatever the government in Nicaragua called itself now, many of the middle-aged politicians in suits were just older versions of the young revolutionaries in fatigues from decades before, and with guns borrowed from Cuba.

"I like commies," Buzz said. "They scare the tourists away. If you drive just a little ways down the road from here, the college kids are turning friendly, welcoming Costa Rica into one big drunken wet T-shirt contest. No thanks. I'll take a stern communist and a little bit of vitamin deficiency any day. It gives the people soft bones."

Luke shook his head. But Buzz wasn't done yet. "Oh, I like to go swimmin', with bow-legged women," he half said, half sang.

"I think we should call this meeting to order," Don said.

"I think I'd like to second that," Luke said.

"I was ready an hour ago," Buzz said.

"Buzz and I talked early this morning," Don said. "Without going into a lot of preamble, Buzz knows the waters around St. Simon's Saw. Buzz?"

"I do," Buzz said. His tone switched instantly. Now he was all business.

"I've fished those waters quite a bit. There's a small island about ten clicks to the south and west of St. Simon's. The locals call it Isla de los Jabalies. There's been nobody out there in recent years. A little bit of raised terrain on the northeast side, but flat as a pancake across the rest of it. Grasslands primarily. Some mangroves to navigate, but on the island proper, the trees were mostly cut down ages ago. It's wide open. You guys can do a night drop in there easily. The Hondurans won't bother your airplane—they'll think it's a cartel run, if they even notice it. I'll already be there with a Zodiac, ready to go. The water can get big between islands, but nothing we can't handle. I'll ram it up on the beach on St. Simon's, below the house. There's a hiking trail that goes up the side of the mountain. I think your girl has done a little bit of research on all this."

"A hiking trail?" Luke said.

"Trudy?" Don said.

"I'm your girl," Trudy said. "Yes, it sounds like a plan that can work. Isla de los Jabalies, in Spanish, means Island of the Wild Pigs. In the mid-1800s, rich landowners from the mainland stocked the island with boars for hunting."

"Are there boars out there now?" Luke said.

Getting charged by a wild boar while tangled in a parachute didn't sound like the best way to start an operation.

"No. The impoverished peasants killed them all and ate them a hundred years ago. But the name stuck. The island has been inhabited, off and on, throughout history. In recent decades, the shanty towns that popped up tended to get knocked flat by hurricanes. Hurricane Mitch in 1998 seems to have rendered the place uninhabitable, at least for the time being."

"I can vouch for that," Buzz said. "There's no one out there. There had been a few tumbledown huts remaining, but a storm last year washed them all out to sea. The ocean came over the top and dumped a lot of salt on the ground. The only thing that'll grow right now is seagrass. Eventually, I imagine the people will start coming back, but they haven't yet. There's nothing for them."

"What about this hiking trail?" Luke said.

"It seems like the best way into the compound," Trudy said. "There are mentions of it in old hotel brochures. It was considered a challenging hike for adventurous visitors. It turned into another one of the island's misfortunes. Over the years, at least two people fell and died while attempting it."

"Sounds like a fun place," Mark Swann said. "I can't imagine why it went out of business."

"It's a series of switchbacks that cut up the steepest side of the mountain. There are spots where the trail itself ends, and there are simple iron rungs bolted into the cliff face. You go straight up those like a ladder. The first ladder you encounter is four stories high. There are two smaller ones after that. At the very top of the trail, it flattens out and then supposedly you have exceptional views back the way you just came, down to the water. In the old days, the trail would take you right onto the grounds of the house. Now, if my guess is right, it probably dead ends at the perimeter fence."

"And the dogs," Ed said.

"Yes."

"Swann, can you see this trail at all?" Luke said.

A moment passed as Swann fine-tuned the imagery from his drone.

"Yeah, I can see it. It's pretty overgrown, but it's still there. I can see a bit of the trail obscured by the trees and undergrowth, and maybe some of the old iron rungs, glinting in the sun. I'd say, if you were going to try going that way, I'd bring something for hacking down the forest on your path, and also some way to move up that cliff face, pitons that you can drive in, say, in case a rung or two is missing."

"And bring something to cut the fence," Trudy said.

"And treats for the dogs," Swann said.

Everybody was a comedian today. Some were better than others.

"Would you say that fence is electrified?" Luke said.

"I'd say it isn't," Trudy said. "This is an island, far from anywhere. It has to be self-sufficient. It is likely making its own electricity, using some combination of solar power, wind power, and gasoline-powered generators. Certainly, the hotel used to tout its solar and wind projects in its advertising brochures. And this is supposed to be an idyllic retreat for Darwin King, or at least give the impression that it is. Gasoline generators are loud. I'd say he likes to keep that kind of noise to a minimum. It ruins the effect. In other words, I doubt he would waste his very limited juice on an electrified fence. More likely the fencing is thick, sturdy metal, with small holes making it hard to climb, and something sharp at the top."

"And electricity running through it," Swann said.

Trudy laughed. "Right. Might as well assume the worst."

"Okay," Luke said. "We'll bring bacon chewies for the dogs, and one hundred percent pure rubber gloves to touch the fence while we cut it open. So let's assume all that goes fine and according to plan. How do we get back out?"

"You could go out the same way you came in," Trudy said.

"Hot," Ed said. "Very hot."

"Yeah," Luke said. "Figure we're going to be leaving in a hurry. We'll have a disoriented girl with us, who we can assume has zero climbing skills, and may be too terrified to do anything even if she did have some. It's going to be hard to go back that way. It gives us an element of surprise coming in, but going out? I don't know."

"Guys," Swann said. "There is a small parking lot on the property maybe fifty meters to the left of the front door of the house as you exit. It's in the shade of some trees, so I can't see all of it. But at this moment, there seems to be at least three large cars there, maybe SUVs. There might be a limousine. Looks like there might also be a sports car, like an old MG convertible."

"Darwin King is careful about security," Trudy said. "In fact, you might even say he's obsessed with it. He's an arms dealer, after all. So there's a good chance those SUVs are armored."

"Right," Swann said. "You could potentially take a car and ram the gates on your way out. There are also jeeps at the guardhouse. You might be able to take one of those. Make a run straight downhill to the airfield."

"Hot," Ed said again.

Luke nodded. "Very hot."

But he liked it. Come in by boat, out by plane. If they were stealthy on the grounds of the house, and hit hard, they might catch the whole place napping. Leaving the grounds wouldn't necessarily be a mad dash with guns blazing. If they got lucky, they might practically cruise out of there.

He and… Henry Bowles?

"Henry Bowles wants to come," he said.

"Who is Henry Bowles?" Buzz said.

Luke smiled. "He's just some guy who has taken an interest in our work."

"Bowles is an agent assigned to us by the Bureau proper," Don said. He sighed, just a bit. "How does he know about this?"

Luke shrugged. "They seem to know what we're doing before we do."

"Okay," Don said. "If he wants to go, okay. He may be an asset to you out there. But I would limit his knowledge of the plan, feeding him details only when he needs to know, and I would try to curtail any communications he might have with his superiors. Are we clear?"

Luke looked at Ed. Ed shook his head, but said nothing. Limit what? The SRT was a boat full of leaks at this point.

"Clear," Luke said.

"Once you're in the air, you have a decision to make," Don said. "If you're free and clear, you can head north and east, and come straight home. If you have any problems, there's an old airfield in Honduras, deep in the rainforest near the Nicaraguan border. In an airplane, you can be there very quickly. We'll make sure you have those coordinates."

"Who runs it?" Ed said.

"Friends of ours."

"We'll need a pilot on the ground with us," Luke said.

"I'll wrap around the island while you guys go up the trail," Buzz Mac said. "I can meet you at the plane. I know the airbase in Honduras. They used to call it Amistad, for friendship."

"You can fly a plane?" Luke said.

"Don't you know by now, Stone?" Buzz said. "I can do anything."

CHAPTER TWENTY SIX

12:45 p.m. Eastern Standard Time
Boulevard Burgers
Hollywood Beach Boardwalk
Hollywood, Florida

"In or out?" Luke said.

Henry Bowles stared at him across the table. They were sitting in the outdoor eating area of a popular joint down at the Hollywood waterfront. To Luke's left, a steady stream of joggers, roller bladers, shirtless weightlifters in tight shorts, bloated tourists and young girls in sexy bikinis went by on the wide stone walkway. The sun was high and hot. The ocean here was bluish-green.

Bowles was drinking a pint of beer with his burger and fries. This was probably to show he was as much of a cowboy as they were. Luke and Ed were drinking water. Bowles's facial hair was still perfectly set at three days.

"What's the operation?" he said.

"You know the operation," Ed said.

Bowles shook his head. "How does it work? What are the details? When do we go? How do we get in? Do we have someone inside already?"

"That's classified," Luke said. "Need to know. If you're not coming…"

Ed finished the sentence for him. "Then you don't need to know."

Bowles took a minute to think about it.

"All right," he said. "I'm in."

"You comfortable with a night jump?"

"Of course."

"Could be hot."

Bowles smiled. "I like it hot."

Luke nodded. He gazed out at all the people. A long-haired man was staggering by dressed as Jesus Christ, complete with a bloody crown of thorns around his head, and a heavy wooden cross on his back.

It was a literal freak show just a few feet from Luke's left elbow. This was a good spot for people watching.

He almost wished he could just sit here all day. Here in South Florida. For an instant, he flashed back to the brief conversation he'd had with Becca twenty minutes ago. He and Ed were going on a stakeout tonight. He would be out of touch until at least tomorrow. No big deal, and they wouldn't be in harm's way. They certainly weren't leaving the country or anything like that. Just people watching in Florida, basically.

He put his hand out to Bowles. "Let me see your phone a minute."

Bowles stared at him, but then handed his phone over. It was a black Nokia flip phone. Luke opened it. "Work phone?" he said. "Personal phone?"

Bowles shrugged. "I have no personal life. It's the only phone I carry."

Luke looked at it for a few seconds. Then he smashed it against the table. He hit it once and the flip top broke off. Now it was hanging by a wire. The screen was already cracked. Luke smashed it into the table again. And again.

He was mindful not to cut his hand. He dropped the phone on the ground and stomped on it with his shoe.

A group of ladies at a nearby table watched him in amazement.

He smiled at them. "Just been having a lot of trouble with this thing," he said. "It's always dropping calls."

He picked it up off the ground and slid the crushed remnants of it back across the table to Bowles.

"Sorry about that," he said. "We're leaving in an hour. We have all the gear you're going to need, so you're with us for the duration at this point. We'll give you the details on the plane, everything we know, and exactly how we're going to hit. There will be plenty of time to talk."

Bowles shook his head. He picked up the ruined phone.

"You didn't need to do that."

Luke shrugged. "I'll get you a new one when we get back. A nice shiny Motorola, courtesy of your friends at the Special Response Team. If you're in, you're all the way in. I can't have you getting cold feet and sneaking off, calling your superiors to tell them where we are or what we're doing. No mixed allegiances. You said yourself that the investigation into Darwin King has been stonewalled for years. There's a good chance that the Bureau is compromised on this."

"Better than good," Ed said. "I'd say close to a hundred percent."

Luke nodded. “The fewer people who know we’re coming, the better.”

“I wasn’t going to call anyone,” Bowles said.

“I believe you,” Ed said. He gave Bowles big doe eyes.

“Trust but verify,” Luke said. “A very smart man said that. Consider yourself verified.”

He pushed his seat away from the table.

“Now let’s go.”

CHAPTER TWENTY SEVEN

2:15 p.m. Central Standard Time (3:15 p.m. Eastern Standard Time)
La Sierra de San Simon (St. Simon's Saw)
Near Honduras
The Caribbean Sea

"This house is a palace," Darwin King said.

It was a strange thing to say, especially when he was by himself. But it was true. There were echoing stone floors, wide-open spaces, huge windows and doors. There was a magnificent southern exposure, looking out across the green hillsides to the open ocean far below. Today, it seemed like every window and door was thrown wide—curtains billowed on the ocean breezes.

He sat on his private terrace, gazing out at his domain. Far away, across the water, he watched the sky darken. What looked like a rain squall was coming across from the Honduran coast. Even the rain storms here were fantastic. Sheets of rain blowing sideways, chain lightning, earthshaking rumbles of thunder.

Why not? He had the best of everything else. Why not have the best storms?

Darwin had eaten lunch and was enjoying a glass of white wine. The glass decanter was stationed in a metal bowl filled with ice near his elbow. The wine gave him a pleasant buzz. He wished he could stop time right in this moment.

He was a king—no, a sultan—and this house was his palace. He had wealth beyond the imaginations of most people, all those dirty, grasping, toiling masses of humanity, just trying to make it from one week to the next. He had his harem girls, at his beck and call, and ready to carry out any whim. He had his rich and powerful friends and business associates.

It was incredible to be him.

But even so, doubts sometimes crept in. He hadn't been to his place on Jupiter Island in six months or more. The police investigation, no matter how many times it had been quashed, repeatedly reared its ugly head. When he left, it was beginning to make life uncomfortable for him. There were whisperings on the social scene. His parties were not as well attended as they had been in the past. A little time away, out of the country, seemed in order. Let things die down again. He thought he'd be back in a month, maybe two, but half a year later, here he was.

"I don't really miss it," he said.

And that was true, as far as it went. He was going to be fifty-nine years old. His appetite for parties was not what it once was. In other ways, his appetites were as healthy as they ever were. But having lots of people around him, sycophants, yes men, blood suckers, and hangers-on? People like Jeff Zorn, the degenerate gambler, pathetic little money borrower and late night bridge jumper? Darwin could live without people like that. It was hard to believe that he had once considered Jeff among his friends.

The only worthwhile thing Jeff had ever done, in his entire miserable life, was give 21 to Darwin. And even that came with drawbacks.

No. Darwin would take the isolation here over people like Jeff, or Miles Richmond, or Bill Ryan, or innumerable other parasites, knowing as he did that the situation would not last forever. Life went in seasons, and this season of life was sure to end.

The thing he didn't like was the feeling of being driven out. He left Florida voluntarily, but there was a certain amount of duress involved. They had been trying to get him. And now they wanted to come here and get him.

They. Them. Who even were these people?

Enemies.

Everyone had them. It was hard to reach such a point of absolute power that you had no enemies at all. But wouldn't that be grand? Imagine being so powerful that the moment someone even thought of crossing you, you simply ground them into dust?

It was something to strive for.

He suddenly realized that he didn't have to sit here, merely waiting to see what happened next. Would his people in the United States be able to stymie the attack before it happened? When was it supposed to happen? When would he find out?

He did not have to wait. He could take action himself. He could bring the fight to the enemy. It was a Eureka! moment.

It occurred to him that what he really had been doing was puzzling over the 21 problem in his subconscious. Give her back? Not a chance. Get rid of her some other way? When he was younger, it was possible he would have chosen that option. He had gotten rid of quite a few over the years. Some, you could pass down the line. There were places in this world, notably the Sunni Arab states of the Persian Gulf, where girls of the type Darwin preferred commanded top dollar, or even better, favored business arrangements.

Others… sometimes you just had to get rid of them. They were damaged goods. Psychological problems, mostly. Failure to thrive. Trauma from bad upbringings. Those ones had to go. The fun wore off.

He sighed. Bad memories tended to weigh heavily on him. He could go that route with 21, he supposed. The route of bad memories, of cutting his losses. But he didn't want to. He liked her, and they hadn't even had any fun yet. He couldn't just write her off as a dead loss. It wasn't her fault that these people were trying to rescue her. Not really. He should give her a chance before he took a step like that.

Today. Tonight. He would do it. He would give her that chance to redeem herself.

In the meantime, taking the fight to the enemy. Oh my. Oh yes.

That was the ticket.

He smiled and picked up the phone on the small table. It was the same phone that he kept in his living room. The base of it was hardwired to the house. It was on a long cord, and he could just carry it out here onto the terrace. It was a weirdly elegant thing to do. He loved it.

Cell phones were for modern jerks. Darwin King was a throwback to a simpler, classier, better time.

He put the handset to his ear and dialed zero.

A moment passed.

"Operator," said a voice.

"It's Darwin. Get me an outside line."

"Of course, sir."

He got the line, and dialed a number from memory. Darwin had a near photographic memory for numbers, figures, contractual amounts, details of all kinds. He was practically a savant.

He waited as the call traveled thousands of miles to a place right outside Washington, DC.

"Hello?" a voice said.

"Do you know who this is?" Darwin said.

"Of course I do."

Darwin smiled. "I have a project I'm working on."

"I might have heard something about it," the voice said.

"Yes?" Darwin said. "Do tell."

"Rumors, nothing more."

See? He hated that. People talking. Especially a person like this one. It was hard to know who anyone was. The government? The CIA? Someone worse? The players obscured their origins, and half the time, you weren't even quite sure who you were dealing with.

The thing to know was he had a project, it was his project, and they worked for him. That was the important thing to keep clear. And this man, on the other end of this line, had never made the mistake of seeing arrangements in any other way.

Darwin's money was good, and they had mutual friends in common.

"I need you to do something for me," Darwin said. "Right there in town. And I don't want to wait. I need it done tonight."

"We're always happy to help," the voice said. "You know that. What is the nature of this thing you would like me to do?"

"I have a headache," Darwin said. "Two of them, in fact."

He could almost hear the man smile over the phone.

"We are the best pain reliever there is."

CHAPTER TWENTY EIGHT

8:35 p.m. Eastern Standard Time
An underground parking garage
The offices of Richmond, Baker, Hancock and Pearl
K Street, Washington, DC

"Do you know who I am?"

The voice came from the back seat of the car. Miles Richmond froze at the sound of it. The tiny hairs on the backs of his hands, and on the back of his neck, stood straight up. He had just slid into the driver's seat of his white Lexus. He hadn't noticed anyone sitting back there, but the lights in this garage were dim, and he hadn't thought to look.

Miles was the last person to leave the office tonight, by a lot. He had been waiting for word about the rescue operation, word that had not come. And he had not been careful, that much was clear. He was alone, alone with this stranger, and they were sitting in a darkened car, deep in shadow, at the back of a parking lot.

"How did you get inside this car?"

"You're very stupid, you know that?" the man said. "People get in and out of this car anytime they want. This car is bugged, my friend. This car, the car before it. They've been listening to you talk for years. The only reason you're not in jail is they like you where you are."

Miles began to turn to look at the man squarely.

"Don't turn around. You can see me in the mirror."

The man spoke forcefully, and Miles found himself obeying that voice. He looked in the mirror instead.

The man was Hispanic, with a dark face, dark eyes, and dark hair. Everything about him was dark, save one thing. There was a long vertical scar down the left side of his face. That raised tissue stood out pale, nearly white, against the rest of the man's skin.

"I haven't committed a crime. There's no reason for anyone to put me in jail."

The man smiled and shook his head. He looked up at the sunroof of the car, as if he might find God there, and they might have a good laugh about how everyone denies everything. But God sees all.

“Do you know me?” the man said. His English was good, but he spoke it with a faint accent that suggested it wasn’t his first language.

Miles shook his head. “No. I’ve never seen you before.”

“You know of me, then?”

“What’s your name?”

“I have no name. They call me El Tigre. In English, the Tiger. The tiger is a solitary creature. Do you know this nickname?”

“No. I don’t know it.”

There was no mercy in those eyes. No compassion, no humanity. They were the hardest, coldest eyes Miles had ever looked into.

“I took your granddaughter. It was just, how you call it, a job. I do things like that for money. I gave her off to the people who paid me. I did not touch her, and she was in perfect health when she was with me. You should know that.”

“Okay,” Miles said. He could not seem to move now. His body was locked up. It occurred to him that the thing to do was open his door and burst out of the car, then run screaming through the garage. But he didn’t seem to have the muscle control to even try it. He couldn’t lift his hand to touch the door.

“She’s a beautiful girl,” the man said. “I took good care of her.”

Miles said nothing in response. He was stuck in place. He was stuck in time. He could not move forward from this moment into the next.

“Two of my friends were killed by the FBI. One was a very good friend. He was with me a long time. I don’t blame you for that, even though you sent the agents.”

“Thank you,” Miles said.

He gazed out through the windshield at the parking lot in front of him. It was a bleak, forbidding place, a subterranean nightmare of a place. There was no one here. There were no cars here. Just dismal yellow light, bare steel pillars, and an empty concrete lot. It was hideous. He almost couldn’t believe that he had been parking down here for so many years.

To makes matters worse, everyone parked down here—all the employees, the partners, the clients, the guests. Miles Richmond strived for excellence in everything he did. But look at this garage. What kind of impression did this place make?

“I don’t come here because my friends got killed,” the man said. “When people get killed in my line of work, you can say they lived a dangerous life, and it was their time. The bill came due, that’s all. I always think that way. It’s for the best. You didn’t kill them, and revenge is a bad idea. I take revenge on you, someone takes revenge on me, someone else takes revenge on your wife and kids, on and on. It's not worth it."

Miles was losing the thread of this conversation. The man was talking around in circles, talking without coming to the point.

"Do you know why I am here, if not for revenge?"

Miles shook his head. "No."

"I came because someone paid me to come. This is another job. You need to understand that as well. There's nothing personal. It's just business. I know almost nothing about you, for sure not enough to hate you. You're just some guy who is on the wrong side. And it's okay because you're old. You would have died soon anyway."

Miles finally understood. Despite the fear, despite the terror that would see him turn to stone and never say another word, he found his voice.

"You don't have to do it," he said.

"Yes, I do."

Miles felt something pressing against the back of his head then. He glanced in the rearview, and could just make out the reflection of a gun. It was a handgun with a long silencer at the end, and the man, The Tiger, was holding it to Darwin's head.

The Tiger's eyes showed no obvious emotion. He wasn't angry. He wasn't worried. He wasn't sorry. "*Adios*, Miles Richmond."

"Wait. You don't have to do this. We can work something—"

"Darwin King says *hola*."

Miles saw the gunshot that killed him. He watched it in the rearview mirror. It happened in an instant, but time seemed to slow to a crawl, if only for that instant. A lick of flame appeared at the end of the barrel of the gun. Something traveled from that hole, an energy more than something physically seen.

Miles felt it enter his head.

CHAPTER TWENTY NINE

9:15 p.m. Eastern Standard Time
Lincoln Memorial Reflecting Pool
The National Mall
Washington, DC

"Beautiful."

William Theodore Ryan, Minority Leader of the United States House of Representatives, had just left work for the evening. The night was chilly, and he wore a long wool coat over his suit.

Inside his coat, there was a shoulder holster he wore when he left the Capitol each night. Guns were not allowed in the House chamber, and he respected that tradition. But once he left the chamber, he was permitted to carry a concealed weapon, and he chose to do so.

The gun he typically carried was small, a Beretta Nano—what they called a pocket pistol. Macho types that Bill had known over the years might say it was a "lady gun." But it was a nice solid gun, heavier than it looked, loaded with eight rounds in the magazine, and very accurate for its type. No external safety—no fiddling around. Just pull it out and shoot bad guys.

As he sometimes did, he had walked here to the Reflecting Pool, lit up in the evening, stood here below the base of the Lincoln Memorial, and gazed across at the Washington Monument.

He enjoyed coming here. He enjoyed the anonymity of it. It was night, a handful of people out strolling or jogging or simply taking in the sights. No one recognized him. They were in their own bubbles, and so was he, soaking in the grandeur of American history.

There was a lot to admire about this spot. For one, the design of the park, the genius, the sheer epic scale of it, and how it led you to contemplate the place in history of the country's two greatest presidents.

For another, the men themselves. Not ordinary men, certainly. Everything about them was gigantic, larger than life. Physically, they were just bigger than other men of their times. Washington was broad-shouldered, and thought to stand six foot two or six foot three, in a time when a more normal height for a man was five foot six or five foot seven. He was so imposing that people were hesitant to approach him from behind.

Lincoln was even larger, perhaps six foot five, and as a young man, known for juggling axes and other feats of strength. One of the earliest photographs in existence was a distant shot of Lincoln just before delivering the Gettysburg Address, standing head and shoulders above the men around him.

Washington likely died of pneumonia, from being out in a cold rain all day. Lincoln, of course, was shot in the head. So not ordinary men, but mortals nonetheless. Their greatness, and their permanent place in history, lay in how they responded to crisis. How they stepped up to face the dangers and the opportunities of a challenging moment.

This was a place where Bill Ryan allowed his imagination to run wild. He pictured himself in the august company of these two men, not as their underling, but as their equal. The United States was in crisis again. A president had been kidnapped and murdered. His own vice president had been implicated in the murder and forced to step down, though no link had been proven.

The new president was seventy-four years old. He had also been kidnapped, this time in a hijacking of Air Force One by Muslim extremists, and taken to Somalia. He had only survived by the skin of his teeth, and through the efforts of an extraordinary group of American soldiers. There was very little chance that he would run for office again. His hand-picked successor, the current vice president, was a weak man, and compromised in every way.

The time was coming once again for a strong man to step up and claim his rightful place in history.

Bill Ryan was that strong man.

Removing that weak vice president, Thomas Hayes, from the equation before he got the chance to ascend to the presidency and bring ruin upon everyone, was of paramount importance. Darwin King held the key to removing Hayes.

Ryan didn't like dealing with Darwin King. That was an understatement. His disdain for the man was as large as the big sky of Montana. Darwin was what many people in this town (and New York, and London, and any other capitals of finance and government you cared to mention) seemed to think of as a necessary evil.

Darwin reveled in getting his hands dirty. He was the go-between, the man who was happy to make deals with the worst people on the planet. Why wouldn't he? For all his privileged upbringing, he was one of them.

Sometimes, the United States needed to deal with the worst people. But they couldn't be seen doing it. They couldn't be seen passing weapon systems, as obsolete as they might be, to warlords in the diamond mining regions of central Africa, despots who disappeared thousands of their own citizens across the Americas, and mafias of all kinds.

How could the United States provide automatic rifles and security fencing to Afghan militias using slave labor to harvest the opium crops? How could the United States airdrop guns and grenades to Al-Qaeda-aligned Islamic militias working to undermine the government in Syria? How could the United States provide technical assistance and support to the left-leaning Haitian government controlling Port-au-Prince during the daylight, while arming the right wing death squads terrorizing the countryside at night, *at the same time*?

The easy answer was: they couldn't.

That was where Darwin King came in. He would do the dirty work. He would roll in the dirt, and get it all over himself.

The smell, the stench of Darwin King, was unreal.

And in the process of rolling in the dirt, he was allowed to become vastly wealthy. And he was allowed to make friends with the famous, and the infamous, and the powerful. And he was allowed to indulge his most deranged, most sinful proclivities. People were supposed to turn a blind eye to all this, but Bill Ryan could not.

The man was an animal.

An animal that was no longer taking Ryan's calls.

That was a problem.

Bill Ryan *needed* Darwin King. But apparently, Darwin King felt he no longer needed Bill Ryan. He was wrong about that. Darwin had retreated to his island far away, but no man was an island. Darwin had overstepped this time, badly, and Ryan was going to take him to school. Darwin only existed, only thrived as he did, because people like Bill Ryan gave it the green light. There were other men just like Darwin in this world, who would be all too happy to take his place.

Darwin needed to be reminded who he worked for.

He would survive the coming shakeout, in all likelihood. He would keep his place, and his wealth, and his connections. But he would be chastened. He would…

Suddenly, there was a man about fifty feet away to the left, who had fallen. He was writhing on the ground, having some sort of seizure. People turned to look, but stayed away. Now others moved toward him.

From Ryan's right, a jogger approached, moving fast. He wore dark blue shorts and a red hooded sweatshirt. You could not see his face.

The jogger was a blur, coming straight toward him.

A strong hand grabbed Ryan from behind, around his throat. Before he knew it, he was on the ground himself, on his back. The two men were on top of him, punching him, beating him in the face.

Somewhere nearby, a woman screamed.

"Help him! Help that man!"

One of the men smacked Ryan's head against the pavement.

He was dazed by the impact. The man did it again. He had Ryan by the hair now, and was repeatedly banging his head on the ground.

Ryan reached inside his overcoat. He could hear his own breathing, loud, harsh, fast. The attackers hardly made a sound. They didn't say a word.

A big fist connected with his face.

A foot kicked him in the stomach.

He was going to pass out.

His hand found the holster, his fingers undid the snap, and now he had the gun. He rolled over onto his stomach. One of the men kicked him in the ribs, very hard. A man punched him in the back of the head.

He rolled over, onto his back again, pointed the gun at the sky, and fired.

BANG!

It was loud this close to his ears.

Another person screamed.

The men jumped back. They reminded him of scuttling crabs. The second man wore jeans and a windbreaker jacket. He had a wool hat on his head, and he was wearing sunglasses. This was the first Bill had seen him.

He was small, but his body was thick and muscular.

Ryan aimed for his center mass.

BANG!

Missed. The man had darted quickly to his right. Like a crab.

Ryan aimed again, but now the man was running away. Ryan turned to shoot the jogger, but that man was running too. He was already in the distance.

The man who had the seizure was gone.

Onlookers were milling around Bill Ryan, but keeping their distance. He aimed one more shot, straight up into the night sky, and fired.

BANG!

Another woman, poor over-alerted mouse, made a startled yip. The last shot was just to keep any more attackers at bay.

Overhead, the stars gazed down at Bill Ryan, distant, impassive, and uninterested.

He had been beaten like a dog in the street. It wasn't a mugging. It also wasn't an assassination, and thank God for that. They had come so fast, they would have easily killed him, had that been their intention. It was just an old-fashioned beatdown.

Bill Ryan hadn't gotten to where he was by not reading the signs. This was a message. Who would send him such a message at this moment?

He could not speak. He was breathing too heavily. But his lips moved.

"Darwin," he would have said.

He rolled over onto all fours again, and vomited his late dinner onto the ground.

"Sir, are you okay?" someone behind him said.

He shook his head. He didn't feel okay. His ears were ringing from the gunshots. His head was floating, unmoored. He wiped his mouth with the back of his hand. The hand came away with blood on it.

He found his voice. It was somewhere between a croak and a gasp.

"Please call nine-one-one," he said.

CHAPTER THIRTY

8:35 p.m. Central Standard Time (9:35 p.m. Eastern Standard Time)
The skies approaching Isla de los Jabalies
Near St. Simon's Saw
The Caribbean Sea

"Gentlemen," a female voice said from the cockpit. "We are ten minutes to the target area. Prepare to disembark."

Here comes the bad news.

They had been flying all afternoon and evening. They had switched planes at a remote airfield in Jamaica. From there, they had taken this junker of a jump plane, an old Beechcraft. They had been under radio silence ever since.

The plane was small. On the outside, it was so weather-beaten it looked like it had taken ground fire in a war. Not a recent war. World War Two.

On the inside? Well…

They sat on heavy crates in the lurid darkness of the cargo hold—ten feet high, maybe twenty feet across. The plane itself bounced and bucked. The plane was not fully sealed, wind was coming in from somewhere, and you practically had to shout to be heard over the engine noise.

Ed Newsam had dozed for a while curled up on the floor. While he was asleep, Luke had made an executive decision. He had been on the fence about it all day. If he really thought about it, he'd been on the fence since Ed rushed into the house in Fort Lauderdale and killed Felix Cienfuegos. Or maybe since they had found the dead child in the box truck.

But Luke wasn't on the fence any longer. He'd made up his mind, and he knew it was right. Ed wasn't coming on this mission. He wasn't coming on the jump. He wasn't coming to Darwin King's house.

Luke was the ranking officer. Luke and Ed played it like they were partners, and they were. But Luke was also Ed's supervisor.

The timing was bad. Luke knew that. He'd made Ed come all this way. But events had moved quickly, and Luke hadn't been entirely sure before. He needed to let it all sink in. Also, if he had made the decision earlier, Ed would have appealed to Don. Luke would have had to tell Don, in no uncertain terms, that Ed was not on point. Luke didn't want to go there.

No. This was for the best.

Ed and Henry Bowles rested on the long bench along one wall of the plane. Ed still seemed asleep, but Luke knew he was awake. In a moment, he was going to start checking his gear. Luke wanted to talk to him before then.

Luke was cold. He was always cold before a jump. He checked the altimeter on his wrist. They were flying at about 11,000 feet. This was a good altitude. Outside the jump door's window, it was full-on dark. Away on the western horizon, there was a glow of light. That could be the last of the sunlight far away, or maybe some ground lights in Honduras.

He stood and stepped over in front of Ed. Ed's face, like those of both Luke and Bowles, was painted with black and dark green camouflage.

Ed leaned back on the bench, resting against the wall. His eyes were closed.

"Ed."

He gave Ed's leg a light kick.

Ed's eyes opened.

Ed had an MP5 submachine gun belted to one side of him. He had a stack of loaded magazines for the gun, stuffed in various pockets of his jumpsuit. There were handguns mounted to his waist, and tiny .25 caliber pocket pistols taped to each one of his calves. Ed was strapped with guns, just how he liked it.

Luke sat down, a few feet away and just across from Ed. In a moment, he would have to go and strap his own jump pack on. For now, he made a triangle with Ed and Bowles, in a spot where both of them could hear him.

He hated to do this. But it was too late. There was no turning back.

Luke looked at Bowles, then looked at Ed. He paused for a moment. Not bringing Ed gave him second thoughts about this whole mission. Going with Bowles gave him second thoughts.

Ed was watching him. It was almost as if he was waiting for this.

"I got bad news."

Ed raised an eyebrow. "What's that?"

Now Bowles's eyes opened. With his face painted, his eyes opening were like two albino frogs appearing out of the mud.

"It's just me and Bowles this trip, man. I'm sorry."

Ed shook his head and smiled. "What's that supposed to mean?"

"You're not coming. You've been off your feed. You have a baby on the way, you're distracted, you've been taking chances I don't agree with. I don't want to get hurt out there, and I don't want to see you get hurt. You're on the bench."

Ed's eyes flashed anger. "Stone."

"It's my decision to make, man. You know that. I've been thinking about this all day. You're a game time scratch. That's the deal."

Ed shook his head. "I'm overruling. I'm coming anyway. You're going to need me, you'll be sorry you decided this, and it'll be too late to change it by then. So I'm just going to come, and we'll forget we had this conversation."

"Sorry," Luke said. "You can't do that."

Now Ed really looked at him. Ed's big right hand curled into a gloved fist.

"What are you going to do? Forbid me from jumping? How will you stop me?"

"I anticipated this," Luke said. "I already stopped you."

"What?"

Bowles was staring at Luke intently now. He hadn't said a word since he opened his eyes.

"I cut your chutes while you were sleeping. Primary and secondary, so you wouldn't be tempted to…"

Without warning, Ed was up and across the space at him. His right came fast and hard. Luke's arm was up, blocking it and knocking it away. But Ed's left came around in a hook. Luke tried to slip it, but there was nowhere to move.

Ed's big left hand caught Luke across the jaw.

Luke's head turned hard with the impact. He let his entire body go with the momentum of the punch, then spun around and away. It rung his bell, but an instant later, he knew he was still in the fight. He looked and Ed was right there, following him. Luke bounced back, out of reach. Ed was immensely strong, but Luke was faster.

Except there was nowhere to move in this plane. It was too cramped. And Ed was too big. He could cut off any escape routes.

"Guys!" Bowles shouted. "Guys!"

Luke didn't even look at him. Neither did Ed.

Ed moved in.

Luke took another step back, his hands up.

"You better watch it, big man. I promise you're gonna lose."

Luke had no idea how to back up that statement.

Ed shook his head. "No."

"I'll fire your ass."

Ed stopped. His shoulders slumped. "Is that really how you think you're going to play this? You're going to sideline me for no reason, and take this punk with you instead?"

He gestured backwards at Bowles.

"Then you're gonna fire me because of a decision YOU made? That's how it's going to work?"

Luke thought about it, but only for a second. "No. You're right. I'm not going to fire you. Take your best shot." He supposed he owed Ed that much. And you never knew. Luke might surprise him. He'd surprised a few guys Ed's size before.

"Let's do this."

Ed nodded. "Good. Because I'll tell you, if I'm fired I have no reason not to kill you."

Ed circled in. It was close. There was no room.

Luke watched those hands.

"Hey! Dummies!"

It was Bowles. Luke ignored him. Ed did the same.

"Stop or I'll shoot."

This time Luke did look at him. Bowles was in a two-handed shooter crouch, gun in hand. Now Ed turned to look.

"We're supposed to jump in a few minutes," Bowles said.

"What are you going to do?" Ed said. "Shoot us?"

Bowles didn't waver. He held the gun pointed at Ed's body mass. "No. I'm going to put you both on report, and get you suspended from your jobs. We work for the same agency, you idiots. I'm above you. Technically, this isn't even your mission. It's mine. And you're both jeopardizing it with your schoolyard behavior."

Ed turned to look at Luke. His eyes were on fire. "This won't stand. It's wrong. I need redress."

Luke shrugged. "We can do it another time. I need to get ready."

Ed looked at Bowles again. He hadn't put the gun away yet.

"Satisfied?"

Bowles shook his head. "They told me you were both crazy," he said. "But they didn't tell me you were this crazy."

Ed shook his head. "Said the man who pulled a gun on his co-workers, while inside an airplane."

He looked at Luke again. "It's a bad move. I'm telling you. Rethink it."

"What's done is done," Luke said. "I want you alive, happy, and healthy for your many descendants."

"Even if you're dead," Ed said.

Now Luke nodded. "Even if I'm dead."

Ed turned his and gave Luke his broad back. "It's dumb," he said over his shoulder. "Bush league. You'll never live it down."

"It's crazy," Bowles said again, holstering his gun.

Luke stopped and looked at them both. "Call it whatever you want. As long as everyone realizes it's my decision to make."

"If that was true, you wouldn't have sabotaged my chute," Ed said.

Luke didn't have an answer for that. But there was no time to argue. Now Luke and Bowles moved quickly, checking and gathering gear.

Luke looked at Bowles. "You know this already, but once we're out, no lights, no sound. Keep your eyes open. It's going to be dark out there. Got it?"

Bowles nodded. "Got it."

"Isla de Jabalies should be directly below us, so it's a straight shot. Buzz Mac will be sheltering in the southwest corner of the island, away from any prying eyes on St. Simon's. He said there's a small strip of pebbly beach there. If we lose each other, make for that southwest corner."

Bowles nodded again. His helmet was on. His pack was on. He was strapping guns to his jumpsuit. "Got it, Dad."

"We're at about eleven thousand feet," Luke said. He eyed Bowles closely, a new suspicion darting through his mind like a furtive rabbit. "You've done this before, right, Bowles? Night jump, rendezvous, clandestine extraction? Possible hostile encounter?"

Bowles raised an eyebrow. "1st Special Forces, Stone. Remember?"

"Does that answer my question?" Luke said. "You were ROTC at Yale before that. For all I know, they had you inventorying cans of chow."

"Knitting sweaters for grieving widows," Ed said.

"You're out of it, Newsam," Bowles said.

Ed shook his head. "I got my eye on your chute, man. Could be you've never done a night jump before. Wouldn't surprise me at all if you were a desk jock, or some kind of towel boy."

Bowles looked at Luke, seriously this time.

"I've done it. I've done everything, more than you will ever know. I have no hesitancy about this mission at all."

He went to the jump door and pulled it open.

At that moment, a buzzer sounded and a green light came on above the closed door to the cockpit.

"Gentlemen," the pilot said over the intercom. "It's go time."

Luke watched as Bowles stood at the open door. He seemed about to jump, then turned and looked back. He stared at Ed.

"Hey, Newsam!" he shouted. "Who's the towel boy tonight?"

Then he dove out and was gone.

Luke shook his head as he went to the door. He looked at Ed.

"Sorry about that. The guy's an idiot. I'll make it up to you."

Ed said nothing. The look in his eyes had changed. There was less anger than a minute ago, and more pain. Luke had hurt the man's feelings. That was somehow worse than the anger.

Now Luke was near the edge. The wind was in his face. Below him, there was nothing but darkness. Above him, he could see stars and wisps of cloud. He could see a last sliver of sunlight fading far to the west.

Not for the first time, he realized how amazing this moment was. If only it could last a little bit longer.

The plane hit a stretch of turbulence. It bucked and shuddered around him.

Luke dove out into the void.

CHAPTER THIRTY ONE

8:45 p.m. Central Standard Time (9:45 p.m. Eastern Standard Time)
La Sierra de San Simon (St. Simon's Saw)
Near Honduras
The Caribbean Sea

"You are my beautiful girl."

Darwin soaked in the sight of her. They had washed her hair, curled it, and woven flowers into it. The effect was understated, these small yellow and white flowers that grew wild here on the grounds, against her clean blonde hair.

She was wearing makeup, and a long, sheer nightgown that came almost down to her bare feet. Her fingernails and toenails were done in a French manicure. Elaine had outdone herself preparing the girl. She was an angel, a vision.

Elaine had been against this. She'd been furious with the girl, and didn't want to send her up. She said the girl wasn't ready. She said the girl hadn't bought in, and probably never would. Elaine said all these things, but Darwin overruled. He didn't do it often, but when he did, it stuck.

Darwin was the boss here, and Elaine knew that. In the end, she had transformed 21 into a work of art. A masterpiece.

He could see through the fabric of the girl's nightgown and follow the outline of her young body. It did not make him want to ravage her. That would come later. Tonight, her beauty made him feel love for her, a love so pure and unadulterated that he didn't want to ruin it. She was so innocent and he didn't want to touch that, he wanted it to be exactly what it was.

The tension of her innocence, poised on a knife's edge, right before her fall into decadence, was exquisite.

She stood on the stone tiles, eyes cast down. She was too shy to look at him. He loved that about her. Some girls came in here, and they were already bold. They were already experienced. They would look him in the eye, almost ready to challenge him. Sometimes girls like that didn't last.

But this… this 21… she was everything he wanted.

All around the room, and in fact, this entire apartment, candles were lit. The lights were all out, and there were perhaps a hundred white candles, candles on every flat surface, their tiny flames dancing in the warm breezes that came in from the outside.

There was a new bottle of red wine in an elegant glass decanter. He had been drinking all afternoon, and he didn't see any reason to stop now. He had won, or he was going to. Miles Richmond had reached out to Bill Ryan, and they thought they were going to take the girl back. Now Miles was dead, and Bill… well, Darwin supposed he'd see how Bill was doing at a later time. Hopefully, Bill was beginning to see the error of his ways. He had tried to send a commando team to what? Kill Darwin King? And how far had that gotten him?

It had put him in the hospital.

It was one thing to do away with Miles Richmond, of course. The man was a cockroach. His death would barely make the evening news. It was quite another to assassinate the Minority Leader of the House of Representatives. You didn't do that lightly. You sent a message first.

Message received.

The girl was standing there, still as a statue. She was ethereal, almost like a ghost. That was good. Darwin King gave her a physical essence. He granted her substance, reality itself. He could take it away if he wanted.

Her grandfather was dead now. He had been murdered in the garage below his offices. Terrible shame, but these things happened.

And her mother's boyfriend… Zorn. Not really a stepfather, Darwin supposed. He was also dead, by his own hand. He was a weak man, no one had ever supposed anything different about him, and now he was gone.

Her mother? Under sedation, apparently. Couldn't cope with the loss of her daughter. Now her boyfriend… my, my, my. Darwin could take care of the mother, too, if he so desired. He could pull the plug on her at any point. Who would blame her for committing suicide at this point? Who would suspect anything different if she just disappeared, then washed up on a beach somewhere?

Darwin was a god. He could take everything away from a person. And this girl knew nothing about how much he had already taken.

She thought he had taken her freedom. In fact he'd made her freer than she had ever been. A person with no attachments had complete freedom. Her attachments were gone. She was untethered, adrift, like a spaceman who lost contact with his ship and was now floating away into deep space.

"Come here, 21," he said.

He sat down in the plush white armchair that was behind him. He sank into it, so that when she walked to him, they were nearly the same height.

He reached and put his strong arms around her. He pulled her close. He wanted to smell her, and he did. There was the slightest sent of lavender and vanilla. She smelled like a confection, a light dessert.

She stiffened in his embrace.

"You don't have to worry," he said. "You don't have to be afraid of me. I never want you to be afraid of me, because I'm going to take care of you, and love you, and keep you safe. Nothing bad will ever happen to you again. Because I am going to be so good to you."

He pulled away for a moment and looked into her pretty blue eyes. "I love you, honey. You know that, don't you?"

The girl seemed frozen, unable to move. She looked down again, focusing somewhere on his shirt.

"I don't know anything anymore," she said in a small voice.

"That's the beauty of it," Darwin said. "That's the perfection right there. You don't have to know anything when you're with me. You just have to know the one thing, the only thing that's important. That I love you, and you love me. That this relationship is about love. That we love each other and we take care of each other."

He looked into her eyes again, and saw that she was silently crying, the tears sliding down her face. He caught one with a thick finger. Then he put it on his tongue.

"Your tears are so salty," he said. "But why are you crying?"

Her face broke up into a grimace, a mask of anguish, like the face of a small child. When she spoke, her voice was deep and husky, like the sound was caught in her throat. But it also made her voice sound more like that of a woman. Womanhood was coming.

"I want to go home," she said.

Darwin shook his head. "Angel, you are home."

Her mouth was quivering. "I'm not. I'm not home."

"That other place was never your home," he said. "This was always your home."

She stood there, his hands on her arms, her body shaking. He found it disturbing, the way she was acting. She was not adapting. She was not appreciating.

This island was breathtaking. She could have a life here like none other. Total luxury, an existence that others could only envy. Instead, she was still crying and whining about a life that was gone.

It was the kind of thing that could make him lose his temper. These girls could be brats sometimes. It was Elaine's job to discipline these tendencies out of them. This was nothing that Darwin wanted to deal with.

The girl shook her head. "I want my mother."

"I think you need to learn to appreciate what you have. Instead, you're reverting to these childish—"

"I want my MOTHER!"

Before he knew what he was doing, Darwin's right hand reached out and grabbed a chunk of the girl's hair near the scalp. He got a nice, tight grip, and pulled her to the ground by her hair. In a second, she was on her knees.

"You don't have a mother," he said.

He put his face close to hers. He had loved her moments ago, he remembered that, but now he was seething with hatred for her. This happened sometimes. When he was drunk, he could get very angry. It was important that he not do anything rash. He didn't want to ruin this opportunity. He didn't want this girl to fail.

She could end up leaving the island, and not in a good way. Not in a going home to mother way.

"Listen to me," he said. "You need to grow up. That life you think you remember is over. This is your life now. And if you don't start appreciating me, and what I'm doing for you here…"

He pushed her head away from him. Now she was on her knees, curled in a ball, weeping abjectly.

"I don't know what I'm going to do with you."

She just kept on crying.

"Boo-hoo," he said. "Boo-hoo."

He picked up the telephone and pressed the button.

"Yes," a voice said.

"It's Darwin. I need another couple of girls. There's something wrong with the one that I have here. It seems like she might be defective."

He thought about who he wanted. He wanted ones that were completely obedient, loyal, girls who had learned their place, who had adapted to life here. He wanted girls who were residents of paradise, girls who owed their very lives and well-being to him, and who damn well knew it. Girls who would show this one what it was all about.

"Send me number 11, and number 17. Thanks."

He hung up. He looked down at 21. It disgusted him, the way she was.

"I'm going to show you what we do here," he said. "Tonight, you're going to watch, and then you're going to participate. My patience is through. So now I'm going to show you what's expected of you."

CHAPTER THIRTY TWO

9:05 p.m. Central Standard Time (10:05 p.m. Eastern Standard Time)
Isla de los Jabalies
Near St. Simon's Saw
The Caribbean Sea

The sea grasses were man high.

Luke could see how this island might once have been a good place to hunt boar. But good was a relative term. The grass was so deep you would never see a boar until it was right on top of you.

He checked his compass and hiked through the grass to the rendezvous point. The island was an inexorable down slope in that direction.

It was quiet, hardly any sound except the wind rustling the grass, and the crash of waves on the pebble beach ahead. As the water retreated into the ocean, it made a sound across the rocks like fingers scraping across bones.

He came out onto the beach, and there were two figures to his left in the darkness. They stood near a large inflatable motorboat, its engine up. As he came closer, Luke saw the white hair gleaming in the night. MacDonald was smaller than Luke remembered. Bowles was here already. He had landed first and hadn't bothered to wait for Luke. Bowles seemed to tower over Buzz. The man was shrinking. Old people did that.

"Buzz Mac," Luke said.

MacDonald turned to look at him. Buzz Mac was indeed shorter than either Luke or Bowles. He had a full head of hair on his head, all of it completely white. He had a white goatee on his face. He wore a dark T-shirt and cargo pants. In the dim light, Luke could tell that he was deeply tanned.

"Luke Stone," Buzz Mac said. "How long has it been?"

"I'd say about seven years," Luke said. "Maybe eight."

Mac nodded. "You were a baby then."

"So were you," Luke said.

"Hardly a baby," Mac said. He stuck a hand out to Luke and Luke took it. Buzz's grip was firm and strong.

"I brought you a present, Stone. I wanted to repay you for the ring."

"The ring?" Bowles said.

Buzz nodded. "Yeah. I was sixty-five when they finally pushed me out of the Army. I never wanted to leave. I was having too much fun. Don Morris was the one who drew the short straw and finally had the talk with me. I could tell that dreaded it, and hated every second of it."

"What did he tell you?" Luke said.

"He said, 'Mac. You're a sinking ship, and you're dragging everybody else down with you. Put your retirement papers in so you can have a graceful exit.' It was kind of him to tell me, to be honest. No one wants to be the guy who pooped his pants, and everybody knows but him. I sure didn't."

"If you were sixty-five when he pushed you out, that would make you…"

Buzz nodded. "That's right, seventy-two going on sixteen."

He looked at Bowles. "Anyway, Stone, Don Morris, a bunch of guys who were around chipped in and bought me a ring. I wear it every day. I don't know if I can even take it off at this point. I call it my Super Bowl ring."

"We called it your wedding ring," Luke said.

"I was never married to the Army. She was my mistress, but not my wife. Anyway, it's a doorknocker."

Buzz held up his right hand, and good as his word, he was wearing it, even here. Luke remembered the ring well. It had a large stone made out to resemble the black, gold, and white star of the US Army. A group of small glittering diamonds circled the star. Around the perimeter were the words *Be All You Can Be*. Looking at it again, it was actually pretty nice.

"You could render someone unconscious with this thing. I try never to smack myself in the forehead."

"So what did you get me?" Luke said.

Buzz smiled. "It's in the boat. I thought you might need it tonight."

The three of them went over to the Zodiac and Buzz pulled a rifle carry case up onto the gunwale. He undid the latches and opened it. Inside was a gun and a number of accessories, all snug in their own compartments.

"M24 sniper rifle. Bolt action. Comes with telescopic sight, bipod, sound suppressor and flash suppressor, all here in the carry case. The case can be double-strapped to your back for when you go up the cliffs.

Plus I loaded up a couple of five round box magazines for you." He looked back at Luke, a mischievous glint in his eye. "You ever used one of these before?"

Luke nodded. That was going to be a hell of a thing to carry up a cliff face. Even so, it was probably a good idea to have it along. "Maybe. But Buzz, that gun costs a lot more than I chipped in for your ring."

"Yeah, well… call it interest."

"It's been quite a reunion so far," Bowles said.

Buzz nodded. "It has. Did I tell you about the time Stone and I went on an operation together? It was our only one. My days were numbered at that point."

"You never told me about anything," Bowles said. "I just met you."

"That's right," Buzz said. "So I'll tell you now. Stone was a big kid with wide eyes. Scared half to death."

"I was 75th Rangers before that, Buzz," Luke said. "I was handpicked by Don Morris. I'd already seen combat in…"

Buzz raised a hand. "It's my story. Let me tell it."

Luke shook his head and smiled.

Buzz went on. "So they gave me bright eyes here, and we did a critical mission. An eleven-year-old boy was dying of cancer, and his last wish was to ride with the special operations guys." He sighed.

"Sweet kid. Aaron something. Very skinny. His mom was having a heart attack about the whole thing, but we promised her he'd make it. We met him at Camp Lejeune, the training grounds the Marines have in North Carolina. We did an easy jump at dawn, the kid tandemed with Stone. We touched down, rendezvoused with a Stryker armored vehicle. Ran it through the swamps they have out there, water and mud splashing everywhere, the kid riding up top, helmet, goggles, he looked like a pipsqueak tank commander. We took him to a shooting gallery out in the woods. Kid fired a bunch of guns, finished with a Jeep-mounted M30, a thousand rounds in a minute or so."

"We had him stab a fighting dummy," Luke said.

Buzz nodded. "That's right. The kid was so tired by then, he could barely lift his arms. But he stabbed the stuffing out of that thing. He wanted to kill it. I didn't know whether to laugh or cry. And that was it. It wasn't even eleven a.m. I hope it was enough."

"I think it was," Luke said.

"It had to be," Buzz said. "The kid died a month later."

He paused and took a deep breath. "Kids, man. It's hard sometimes. His mom sent me a letter. I was out on the street pretty much right after that. My last mission."

He shook his head. He seemed to stare into the black distance for a moment.

"You boys ready?" he said finally. "This little girl isn't going to rescue herself."

* * *

The surface of the water was shrouded in fog.

The Zodiac rode the big swells. Up and down, up and down, ten feet high, the boat coming up over the top, then plunging into the valleys between them. Each time they crested, Luke could see the glow of the Darwin King's compound floating high in the sky, creeping closer.

"It's coming up," Buzz said.

It was one of the few things he had said since they climbed aboard. He was at the stern, working the engine and the tiller. Now he started talking.

"I'm going to run this up on the beach. Be ready for anything. If somehow they know we're coming, this could be a short trip."

Luke and Bowles were at the bow, either side, along the gunwales. Both of them had their MP5s out, straps over one shoulder, snouts poking forward.

"If it drops that way, you guys rip them up hard, I'll back this thing up and out, and then you fall back to me. I'll be five feet off the beach. Just drop in and we're out the way we came. Don't give up on it, though. When I turn around, I want you facing backwards, laying down suppressing fire the whole way. But don't shoot me."

Buzz was calm. His voice exuded authority. A hundred missions? Hell.

"Got me?" he said.

"Roger that," Bowles said.

"Roger," Luke said.

They approached the shoreline of the island. It was a sandy strip lined with palm trees. Luke was on red alert. Even in the night, from some distance out and through wisps of white fog, his eyes were so sharp he could see the beach etched in tiny detail. If anyone was there, they were back in the dunes.

For a second, he glanced up at the millions of stars in the dark sweep of sky above them. The boat skimmed the smaller waves closer to shore, and for a moment, with the sea breeze blowing past and the sensation of dark speed, he caught himself feeling good. It was the first time in a while.

Here we go.

The boat crested a breaker, sliding down the face in white foam. Luke and Bowles leaned back simultaneously. For an instant, it felt like the boat might flip over forward, then it dropped into the wash, caught the energy unleashed from the broken wave, and burst out ahead of it.

"Ride 'em cowboy," Bowles said quietly.

"Get ready for impact," Buzz said.

They hit the beach and slid forward onto it. Luke and Bowles were out instantly on either side, kneeling, taking firing positions. Luke scanned the tree line and the dunes. Shadows moved as the trees swayed in the warm breeze.

Nothing. It was a quiet night. A long moment passed.

"Best case scenario," Buzz said.

Luke looked at him. He was standing in the boat, a very fit old man with a black matte pistol in his hand. The gun gave no reflection. He had pulled the engine up and forward so it was off the sand and rocks.

Already, Buzz began to unload gear from the boat. Luke went to the boat and pulled his gear out. They were here, and unchallenged. It was real. Now it was time to climb the mountain. Bowles got his pack. Luke strapped the sniper rifle case onto his back. It was heavy.

"I'll see you boys on the other side," Buzz said. "I'll be laid up in some bushes, waiting for you. No sense taking the plane until you get there."

He looked at them. "Make it brief, will you?"

Luke gestured at the boat. "What about this?"

Buzz shrugged. "Normally I'd scuttle it, but I'm gonna tie it up to a palm tree instead. You never know. If we can't get the plane, we might find ourselves looking for another way out. If something happens to me, don't forget this thing is here."

"See you over there," Luke said.

He and Bowles headed single file up into the dunes, Luke in the lead. Large crabs skittered and darted around them, clicking and rattling their claws as they plunged into dark holes in the sand. The men crouched low and moved quickly through the high grasses. Luke scanned ahead of him, looking for soldiers hiding in the grass.

More nothing.

They passed through the trees, and in another moment, came upon the trail. It was old and disused, but still obvious. It was like a tunnel, snaking to the left through dense underbrush. The mountains were over that way, towering high above the beach.

They moved without speaking. The trail wound ever upward. After a few moments, they reached a set of steep, rough-hewn steps. The breeze had died. It was a humid night, and the air was jungle dense back here in the bushes.

They climbed the steps, which plateaued maybe three stories higher, and then they picked up the trail again. There were spots where the trail was broken or washed out, and fell away to the ocean, now several stories below. It was easy enough to take large steps across these gaps.

They moved in darkness, depending on starlight and the acuity of their eyes. A little higher, and the trail dead-ended at the cliff face. Rusty iron rungs were bolted into the stone, and went straight up into the darkness above their heads.

This was the first ladder, and the longest one.

Luke grabbed the first rung.

"Wait a minute," Bowles said, his voice just above a whisper.

Luke looked at him.

Bowles was patting his vest and the pockets of his black cargo pants. He looked at Stone, his eyes wide with what? Embarrassment?

"I'm missing three magazines for my gun. They must have fallen out in the boat."

"What?" Luke said. His voice was more like a hiss than a whisper. He couldn't contain his exasperation. "I thought you said you've done this before. How did you—"

"I don't know," Bowles said. "They must have fallen out. I need those magazines."

"No kidding," Luke said. "Didn't you do a gear check on the beach?"

He tried to picture Bowles back on the beach, but he couldn't see it. Luke was former Delta. You checked your own gear in Delta. There was never any need to babysit anyone. That was true in Delta, and just as true on the Special Response Team.

"I'll go back," Bowles said. "I'll run. I'll see if they're in the boat, and I'll run right back here. Maybe Buzz is still there, and he has them." Bowles gazed up the cliff face. "I'll meet you at the top of the ladder. All right?"

Luke shook his head. What else was he going to do? Leaving Ed behind for this clown was suddenly starting to smell like a bad move.

Luke had been spoiled by people like Ed, and by Swann, and Trudy, and even by Kevin Murphy. Ed had been a little twitchy recently, but he was a consummate pro. He would never do something like this. It wasn't even possible.

"When I reach the top of this cliff, I'll wait ten minutes," Luke said. "I'll scope out the trail ahead of us a bit. But I'm not going to hang around all night. We have a job to do, and we don't want to do it in the daylight."

Bowles nodded. "Understood. I'll be right behind you."

He turned and headed back down the trail, moving fast. In a few seconds, he was already gone.

Luke sighed and turned back to the ladder. He started to climb, his hands moving along the iron. He took it slowly at first, not trusting the strength of the rungs. He tested each one, pulling on it hard, trying to press it down. Five rungs up, and a rung was missing. It wasn't bad. He reached past it to the next higher one and pulled hard on that one. It was bolted securely. He yanked himself across the gap.

"Bowles," he said. He could picture Bowles falling off this thing, breaking his back, and not dying. Then Luke would have to carry him over his shoulders, up the ladder, up the rest of the trail, then rescue the girl with Bowles the giant albatross around his neck.

Up and up the ladder went. Luke scaled it quickly now, trusting the rungs a little better than before, each test a quick grab and pull now. He broke into a sweat. Between his pack and the gun case he was carrying some weight, but it was okay. The straight vertical climb was cooler and in a sense easier than the rugged, overgrown hike. The higher he went, the less heavy the air.

The dizzying fall dropped away behind him. He saw it from his peripheral vision, but he did not turn and look down.

He tuned the height out and focused on his climbing instead—hands and boots on the iron rungs, one step at a time, his own breath in his ears, his heart thumping, the gear weighing him down, the night wind blowing around him.

After what seemed a long time, but by his watch was only five minutes, he reached the top of the ladder and pulled himself up and onto the cliff. He lay for a moment on solid rock, breathing heavily. He took his pack and gun case off and rolled onto his back. He watched white clouds skid across the dark sky, as he let his breathing subside.

"Bowles," he said to the sky. "Let's go."

* * *

"What happened, Bowles? Did you forget something?"

Bowles moved out of the thick bushes and onto the sand. Large crabs ran in front of him toward the sea. The water shimmered, waves washing in.

The old duffer had dragged the Zodiac up the beach and away from the tide. He had tied it to a palm tree right at the edge of the sand. Now he was sitting on the gunwale, facing back toward the ocean and drinking from a canteen.

Bowles came closer and saw that Buzz Mac was drenched in sweat. It was a hot, humid night, and Buzz was an old man, after all. He was a tough bird, Bowles would give him credit for that. Most guys his age wouldn't dream of coming on an operation like this. He was probably saving up some energy before making the hike across the island to the airfield.

Well, he needn't worry about that.

"Some people will forget their own heads if it's not attached," Buzz said. He gestured behind him. "I left the magazines you dropped for you. They're in the boat."

"Thanks," Bowles said. He stepped over the gunwale. Buzz's broad back was to him now. Buzz took another long gulp from his canteen. Beyond him, Bowles saw the white foam of the breaking waves. It was a pretty night.

"I knew Stone didn't drop them. The guy's a machine. I imagine he had an aneurysm when you told him you had to go back."

"Yeah," Bowles said. He slid the six-inch serrated hunting knife from its sheath at his side. It didn't make a sound. "He did."

Buzz nodded. "He should. This isn't the rookie leagues, kid."

In one move, Bowles stepped up, grabbed Buzz around the mouth with one hand, then ripped the knife across his throat with the other. It took less than a second, and he cut very deep with the knife, severing the major blood vessels there.

Buzz tried to scream, or make some sound, but it was already too late.

"Mmmmm!"

Bowles renewed his iron grip on Buzz's mouth. It was important that this happen silently. Stone was up the mountain now, but sound traveled.

Blood jetted from Buzz's neck. It looked black in the dark night. He bucked and jerked for another few seconds, Bowles's hand clamped tight around his mouth. After a moment, the blood pressure sank away as the heart slowed. Now the blood just flowed out, pouring down the man's chest.

Bowles pushed him forward onto the beach. The body sprawled there in the sand. Bowles breathed heavily, his chest heaving. His arms trembled the tiniest amount. It had been an effort, but not much of one, to kill Buzz. The man barely put up any resistance at all. He was too old, too weak. And Bowles himself was still young, and still strong.

Bowles thought of other times when he had killed men in close quarters like this, times when he exhausted himself, when he lay side by side with his defeated foe and retched on the ground. When his entire body shook, his teeth chattered, and he thought he might have a heart attack afterwards. Nothing like that had happened here.

Bowles stared down at the corpse of Buzz MacDonald. He felt nothing about the man. Well, not nothing, but almost. He felt that Buzz was foolish for coming out here. The guy was playing cops and robbers long after he should have stopped. He'd lost his edge long ago. And now he was dead.

The American hero. The legendary grand old man, the man who was doing special operations a generation before the idea existed.

Bowles shook his head and sighed. He really should leave Buzz here for the crabs, but it wouldn't do. Buzz needed to disappear for a little while. He grabbed Buzz by the arms and dragged him down to the water, leaving a bloody trough of disturbed sand in his wake. He waded out to his thighs and let Buzz go, then pushed him in deeper. Buzz began to move with the waves. His body seemed boneless, like a jellyfish. He turned over and over as he moved with the tide.

"Idiot," Bowles said. "Goodbye."

These guys, the Special Response Team. What was it? A bunch of overrated cowboys, bluffing and half-assing their way to oblivion. What was Buzz even doing here? He came out as a favor for an old friend? He came out because he was bored? What in the world? Did they offer him any money to die like this?

Bowles was getting paid to be here, that much was certain. Yes, he was getting his salary as an FBI agent, assigned to be out here babysitting a mission that was already going very wrong. And yes, he was getting his per diem payment as a CIA informer infiltrating and working undercover as an FBI agent.

But he was getting a lot more money than that, wasn't he?

Yes, he was. He was getting paid as a freelancer to destroy the mission. This one job would deliver him, in cash, close to what Stone probably got all year in salary.

He shook his head again. These people, Luke Stone and his rabble, didn't understand where the real money was, and where the real power lay. They were on the wrong side. Bowles supposed they thought they were working for America. But there was no America, not really, not in the way someone like Luke Stone thought of it.

There were the rulers, and there were the governed. There were the helpless, hopeless, powerless masses, and there were the people who ran the show. The trick was to figure out who was who, and work for the right ones.

That's what Henry Bowles really did for a living.

Buzz Mac was about ten feet out in the water now, drifting down the beach. Maybe he would drift out to sea. Maybe he would wash up somewhere further down. Maybe a bull shark would come and eat him. Bowles supposed it wouldn't matter in the end.

He walked up the beach to the Zodiac. He still had his knife out. He plunged it into the boat, driving it through the tough fabric, putting his weight on it to force it through. Then he ripped backward several inches and pulled the knife out. He went around to the other side and did the same thing over there. The boat was deflating fast. In a little while, it would be as flat as a ruptured tire.

Bowles looked up at the mountain. Somewhere up there, Luke Stone was waiting for him, hoping to complete the mission, save the girl, make America proud. It wasn't going to happen.

"No way out, Stone," Bowles said.

CHAPTER THIRTY THREE

9:25 p.m. Central Standard Time (10:25 p.m. Eastern Standard Time)
The skies near St. Simon's Saw
The Caribbean Sea

"Stone!"

Ed Newsam punched the wall of the plane one last time. The plane was so old, he almost felt he could punch a hole in it.

It had taken him this long to calm down. For the first several minutes, he had imagined going out the jump door anyway, finding Stone in the dark sky, grabbing him tight around the middle, and forcing him to pull the cord with the man he rejected attached to him.

Ed shook his head and took another deep breath. That stuff only worked in the movies. All he'd do was kill them both. If he was lucky. If he was unlucky, he wouldn't even find Stone out there, and he would just plummet all by himself at terminal velocity into the turf.

Whew! He'd seen a couple of guys go like that during his time in the military. One guy, the chute malfunctioned. The other, the guy just didn't open it for some reason. No one would ever know why. The first guy bounced about four stories into the air. The second guy, the ground was soft bottom land, watery, mud. He just went right into it and became embedded.

Neither option looked good.

Ed got up from the bench, crossed the plane, and pulled the jump door closed. He wasn't going out there, and he knew it.

He knew something else, too. Stone was right. Not about keeping him off the mission. And certainly not about tampering with his parachute. That was an amateur play, strictly bush league. Ed would let him know that.

But he was right that Ed was off his feed. This job had gotten to him. It was like being stabbed in the heart, finding that kid in the ice chest. He'd become unhinged. In fact, sitting here reflecting on it, he realized that he barely remembered what had happened since then.

Okay. But Stone should have pulled him aside and talked to him about…

He shook his head again. Who was he kidding? That would never have worked. Ed knew himself better than that. A good talking to, huh? "You're putting yourself and others at risk. You need to snap out of it. You've got a child on the way."

From Stone, of all people?

Luke Stone, who never met impossible odds he didn't like? Luke Stone, who had no personal hobbies other than being shot, blown up, stabbed, and dropped from the sky? Luke Stone, who spent the night before his own baby was born in a firefight with Islamic extremist militants on a cold mountaintop in northern Iraq?

Yeah, a conversation with Luke Stone wouldn't have done much. If anything, Ed would have dug in deeper.

But this? Being stuck here on the plane after Stone had jumped out with Bowles was a wake-up call of the first order.

Stone hadn't done that lightly. And now he was on the ground with a makeshift team that included their FBI minder Bowles, whose special ops record he didn't choose to share except in the vaguest terms possible, and Buzz MacDonald, who was so old that he needed to lubricate his joints with 10W-40 just to move.

Ed didn't like it. If it went wrong, it was going to get ugly down there. Those guys would never make it out of there on their own. Stone, maybe. The other two?

Ed got up, went to the cockpit door, and knocked on it. He heard it unlock on the other side and open an inch. He pulled it open the rest of the way.

They were sitting side by side in the small cockpit, the dark night everywhere through the windshield ahead of them. On the right was Rachel, the brawny, fiery redhead. She was a mixed martial artist in her spare time, and Ed reflected that a couple of years ago, he wouldn't have minded grappling a few rounds with her. On the left was Jacob, the tall, bespectacled glass of water who never seemed to have much to say. Elite soldier or not, as body types went, Jacob was closer to Mark Swann than to Luke Stone. Jacob was like Swann with a sense of discipline, but without the sense of humor.

These two were military pilots from the Night Stalkers, the160th Special Operations Aviation Regiment, who had graduated to working with the SRT.

"Hi, Ed," Rachel said. "We heard you rattling around back there. Why didn't you jump? Is everything okay?"

"Stone pulled me at the last second," Ed said. "Long story."

She nodded. "Ah. One of those."

"One of those," Ed said. "Exactly. Listen, refresh my memory here. What are your orders now?"

"We're headed back to the airfield in Jamaica," Rachel said. "The SRT plane is waiting there. After we land, we're done. Our day is over. I was thinking it might be nice to call in sick and stay a couple of days, but sourpuss here…"

"Any chance we can stick around here instead?" Ed said.

"Here?" Jacob said. "Where's here?"

Ed shrugged. "Here. In the sky. Near the objective."

Jacob shook his head. "We're pretty far from the objective at this point. You've been beating the walls back there for a while. Anyway, we don't really want to hang around. We're flying a bit of a junker, and anybody who's watching probably thinks we're a drug plane. If we loiter in these skies long enough, we're liable to get some attention, and not the kind we want. Also, there's the fuel issue. We don't have an infinite amount."

Ed nodded. "What about the airfield in Honduras called Amistad?"

The pilots looked at each other.

"It's supposed to be a last resort," Rachel said. "If we go there, we have to announce ourselves. If we announce ourselves, people will want to know what we're doing there. We are civilian aviation. That close to Darwin King's island, someone is going to know something's up. We could blow the cover off the mission. We're only supposed to use that place in an emergency. Those are our orders."

She turned about halfway around and looked up at Ed.

"Is there an emergency?"

"Let's just say I'm concerned," Ed said. "I'd like to be a little closer to the action than Jamaica."

Now Jacob shrugged. "I suppose we could go there. If someone asks, we could say we had an engine problem. If anyone asks more than that, we could say the mission is classified, and then shut our mouths. They're used to that."

"What if they were tracking us?" Rachel said. "What if they saw us come from Jamaica, do a pass near Darwin King's island, turn back for Jamaica, then turn around again? That hardly looks like engine trouble."

Jacob nodded. "Right. It looks fishy."

"We could end up blowing the cover," Rachel said again.

"How about if we just fly around in circles for a while?" Ed said.

“Did I mention the fuel issue?” Jacob said.

CHAPTER THIRTY FOUR

9:45 p.m. Central Standard Time (10:45 p.m. Eastern Standard Time)
La Sierra de San Simon (St. Simon's Saw)
Near Honduras
The Caribbean Sea

A thick hand appeared at the top of the cliff.

Luke sat leaning against the far wall, watching it. It moved around like a spider, looking for something to grip. It didn't find anything.

"The last rung is missing," Luke said. "You just have to press yourself up."

It was true. Luke had inspected the edge while he waited. There had once been a rung bolted at the very top of the cliff face, standing upright, which gave climbers something to grab. It was a good idea. At one time, you could hold that rung and practically step onto the top of the cliff. Not anymore. The bolts were still there in the rock, but the rung itself had broken off.

Bowles's head appeared over the top of the cliff.

"Did you get the magazines?" Luke said.

Bowles heaved himself up and over. He rolled onto the plateau and lay for a minute on the ground. He breathed heavily. His MP5 was strapped across his chest. Various guns, knives, and explosives were strapped to his legs, his waist, and were hanging from his vest. His cargo pants seemed to be wet up to the thighs. That was odd. Buzz had grounded the boat on the beach. They hadn't set foot in the water.

"Yeah," Bowles said. "I got them. They were in the boat, just like I thought."

"Was Buzz still there?"

Bowles nodded. "Yeah, he was there. He was resting for a few minutes, drinking some water."

Luke could picture it. It was a hot night. Buzz was old. The hike was at least a few miles around the base of the mountain. He'd probably have to force his way through thick undergrowth.

He shook his head. Buzz was crazy. If Luke was still trying to do this stuff in his seventies, he hoped someone would be kind enough to handcuff him to a radiator.

"Did he leave after you got there?"

Bowles pushed himself up into a cross-legged sitting position. "He's gone."

Luke nodded. "Okay. Take a minute and get your head together. We're already about halfway up, by my estimate. You can see that it's brighter up here. That's light from the house and the grounds, right above our heads. This is where it gets serious."

"Serious," Bowles said. "I know."

Now he pushed himself to his feet. He took a long, deep inhale, and let it out. Then he had a pistol in his hand.

"Sorry, Stone. Not sorry."

He pointed the gun.

For a long moment, too long, Luke didn't believe his own eyes. "What are you doing, Bowles?"

"You guys are stupid, you know that?" Bowles said. "You've been blundering around, and never, not for one second, did you realize what you were dealing with. Now the mission is over, and it's all been a waste. What did any of this accomplish, do you mind my asking?"

"You had a gun on us in the plane," Luke said. "If you wanted to kill us, why didn't you just do it then?"

Bowles shrugged. "And tell the pilots what?"

A terrible idea occurred to Luke.

"Did you kill Buzz? Is that why you went back down there?"

Bowles nodded, almost as an afterthought. He reached with his fingers into a small pocket on the front of his vest. He pulled something out and tossed it at Luke. It hit Luke's chest, bounced off and landed on the ground in front of him.

It was Buzz Mac's right ring finger. The doorknocker US Army ring was there, right above the bloody edge where Bowles had cut the finger off.

"There's his precious ring. Of course I killed him. Just like I'm going to kill—"

Luke launched himself across the ground. He was at Bowles's legs in a split second. Before Bowles could fire a shot, he gripped him behind the knees and lifted Bowles's feet off the ground. Bowles fell backward, landing on his back on the cliff. His gun slid away toward the cliff's edge.

Luke slithered on top of him, but Bowles was strong. He pushed Luke off and scrabbled backwards and away on his hands and feet.

He was going for the gun.

Luke couldn't let that happen.

He jumped up, took two steps, leapt, and landed on Bowles. Bowles reached at his waist for something, a knife in a sheath, but Luke locked up his arm with his own. They wrestled on the ground, arms and legs grasping and clawing. There was no sound but their heavy breathing.

Bowles was strong. *Strong.* Luke reached to Bowles's waist and pulled the knife. Bowles knocked it out of Luke's hand. It flew away off the cliff.

They fought on, rolling on the loose dirt and rock. Bowles punched Luke in the side of the head. Luke's ear started ringing. He slipped behind Bowles and pushed his face again the ground. Bowles spun and rolled over. Luke continued the spin and now he was on top. They were face to face, very close to the edge. Bowles grunted like a pig.

"Huh! Hnh!"

The sound was barely more than a croak.

Luke covered Bowles's mouth with the blade of his hand. No one could know they were here. More than anything, this had to be quiet.

Bowles bit down on Luke's hand. Hard.

Luke's first urge was to pull his hand away, but he drove it in deeper instead. He pushed Bowles's head backwards against the ground with it, exposing the throat. Bowles's hands reached for Luke's face. Luke slapped those hands away. He punched Bowles in the Adam's apple.

"Guuh!" Bowles said. It was a sound that was barely a sound.

Luke reared back and hit him again in the same place. And again. And again.

Four punches to the windpipe, and Bowles stopped fighting. He just lay there, making strangling noises. Luke rolled over and lay next to him on the ground at the edge of the cliff.

Luke stared straight up at the sky. His heart was pumping. His brain was thudding. He took a moment to compose himself. Skidding clouds flew by over his head, just as they had done before. But now they seemed malevolent, like something from a horror movie. He glanced at Bowles.

"If you're going to kill somebody," Luke said. He could barely get the words out. "You should just do it. Don't talk about it."

It was too late for advice. Bowles's eyes were wide open. His breathing was rapid, shallow and high-pitched, like steam escaping from a ruptured pipe. His hands grasped at his own throat, trying to do the impossible, which was reopen a crushed breathing passage.

Luke waited while his own breathing and heartbeat slowed down. He listened to the wind rushing along the cliff face. He felt the throb of pain where Bowles had bitten his hand. If he thought about, it seemed he could feel where the bite marks were swelling with blood.

A whole series of assumptions came crashing apart. Bowles had been assigned to them, yes. It had seemed that the Bureau had wanted to rein them in. And maybe that's all it was at first. Run the case into the ground, block it, make it go away. But now it was more than that. Bowles had tried to kill him.

This entire mission was a disaster. And Luke had turned this part of it, this incursion onto the island, into an even worse disaster. He had called off Ed and sent him packing, when Ed was the exact person he needed right now. Luke was here by himself, faced with infiltrating a compound full of soldiers and bodyguards.

Bowles had killed Buzz MacDonald.

Luke had a moment then. It was a moment of despair so profound he might never be able to describe it to another human being. It was more than disappointment. It was heartbreak. This cipher, this zero, this corrupt cop currently suffering through his last breaths, *had killed THE Buzz MacDonald.*

It made Luke so angry that he wished Bowles could heal, just so he could kill him again. He kneeled over Bowles and looked at him.

Bowles lay on his back, rasping, gasping, eyes staring up at Luke.

"Who were you working for?" Luke said.

Bowles was choking. He was barely getting any air at all. He would never be able to answer any questions now, or ever.

Luke went cold in a way he did not remember going before. He reached down and unclipped the strap holding Bowles's MP5. He took the gun away. He reached in various pockets of Bowles's vest, and pants. He took the three extra magazines for the gun. He took three grenades off of Bowles's vest. He laid them all aside.

The merciful thing would be to simply kill Bowles now. He couldn't be trusted, and there was nowhere to get him emergency medical attention anyway. His throat was crushed. Maybe Darwin King had a doctor working here, but Luke doubted he was a trauma surgeon.

Bowles's pistol was along the cliff's edge. Luke went over and picked it up. It was a Ruger P90. Might as well take that, too.

He looked at Bowles again. The man had stopped moving. His eyes were wide open and staring.

Luke took a deep breath, and then exhaled all the way. It was like the air going out of a tire. He kneeled down next to Bowles again, and pushed the man's heavy body to the very edge of the cliff. Then he rolled it over the edge. Seconds later, he heard it crash into the trees and underbrush four stories below. If he hadn't been quite dead before, that had finished the job.

Luke shook his head. He steeled himself. It was going to be a hard night. He felt something settling over him, a feeling of anger, but even more than anger. It was a feeling of murderous rage. These people, Darwin King and whoever was protecting him, thought they could act with impunity, steal children, do whatever they wanted, kill whoever they wanted. But they couldn't.

He looked over the edge. In the darkness, he fancied he could just make out Bowles's body down there, limbs spread at strange, broken angles. Like a matchstick man whose little wooden arms and legs had been snapped.

"Goodbye, Bowles," Luke said.

* * *

There was nothing to do but go forward.

Luke moved higher through an enormous boulder field. The stones formed a winding stairway. Someone had put effort into this, in the days when this was a hotel. It had all been for nothing.

Ahead, the trail meandered up a steep switchback. He followed it. He climbed another ladder of iron rungs, and a few minutes later, another one. He did not stop. He did not think. He moved quickly, in a kind of a daze.

He was strapped now with two MPs, six extra ammunition magazines, the sniper rifle case, Bowles's pistol and his own, knives, and grenades. He was like a mule, the things he was carrying, but he barely noticed.

Soon, the trail leveled off and he walked through some dense forest, before one final climb to the summit. Just in front of him was a steep drop-off, a dozen stories down a sheer cliff. The spot offered a commanding view of the shimmering water disappearing into the dark distance. Buzz was dead. Bowles was dead. No one was left but Luke.

He turned and the mansion was *right there.* Many of the rooms were lit up, as were the grounds surrounding it.

It was still a bit above him, but not by much. Now he got low to the ground, and moved in a crouch. He needed to go quickly. He was in a vulnerable place. Though he was dressed all in black, to the right kind of eyes, he should be easy enough to spot.

The fence was just ahead of him. He crept closer. He stared up at it—two stories high, looping razor wire at the top. There was another fence ten meters beyond the first one. The space in between was the dog run.

He looked both ways—no dogs here at the moment. He dropped his backpack on the ground, dug through it, and pulled out the heavy wire cutters. He crouched at the bottom of the fence and touched it with one finger. Nothing. It was not electrified. Give Trudy credit. She had guessed correctly.

He started at the very bottom, and began to cut away the fence. He cut the metal loops easily, with a little bit of pressure—Snip! Snip! Snip! Even so, it was going to take a while to cut a hole that he could fit through, enter the dog run, and then cut another one through the other fence.

A few more snips, and the first hole was open. It was just enough space for Luke to slither through. He took out his pistol and threaded the silencer to the barrel. He bent back the fence, pulled it as far as it would go, and ducked under.

His pack snagged on a jagged edge for a few seconds, but he pulled it free. He dragged the rifle case in behind him. He had so much stuff, he was like the Joads driving across country to California.

He placed the silenced pistol on the ground and kneeled by the next fence. From the corner of his eye, he caught a movement. He looked to his right. A large black dog with a massive head and jaws trotted toward him along the narrow gap between fences. It growled deep in its throat.

He watched it come. It was an adult male Doberman, ears pinned back.

There was another one behind the first.

"Don't come here," Luke said.

He heard a sound behind him, a breath, a heavy pant—he turned, and here came another one the other way.

Three adult male Dobermans, all converging at once. They were coming.

He grabbed the gun and bounced to his feet. Instantly, he assumed a shooting position—it was a deep squat, arms out, two-handed shooter's grip.

The first dog was the biggest and most aggressive. He came straight on without hesitation. He didn't bark. He approached in a loping run, and then launched himself from about five feet away.

Everything slowed down.

Luke fired.

CLACK!

The gun made that sound that silenced guns made. To Luke, it always sounded like someone punching a typewriter key.

The dog's massive head snapped sideways, its entire body following, carried by its own momentum. It crashed into the fence and fell to the ground. It landed on its back, and did not move.

The next dog came.

CLACK!

It rolled over, its paws scrabbling at the dirt, a high whine in its throat. It dragged itself to his feet and began to stumble away. Luke shot it again, to end its misery.

CLACK!

The last dog was there. It stared at Luke, and Luke stared back. He looked deep into its eyes. There was a spark there, of intelligence, but also an uncertainty. The dog wasn't sure if it wanted a piece of Luke anymore.

"Don't do it," Luke said. "Go home."

The dog turned away, whined, then trotted off down the dog run.

"Good dog."

Luke looked at the dead dogs. One of them had its teeth bared as it had died. It was brutal to look upon. This was a brutal job. Now he had killed two dogs. They'd made him do it. Who used dogs like this? Who put dogs at risk like this?

Bad people, that's who.

That surge of anger, of rage, went through Luke again. He had to stay calm. He had to stay poised, and in control. Angry people slipped up, made mistakes, and died in situations like this. In the end, he had benched Ed for being angry. That's what it was. Anger would get you killed.

And yet, anger was driving him now. He raced along with it, surfing a wave of anger. He was angry at them, at Darwin King, at Henry Bowles, at whoever and whatever they were. He was angry at the world, the violence of it, the injustice, the unfairness. And he was angry at himself.

He went to the fence, kneeled, picked up the wire cutters, and got back to work. In a few moments, he had cut a hole in the second fence.

He squeezed through it, and now he was inside the compound.

CHAPTER THIRTY FIVE

11:05 p.m. Eastern Standard Time
The Headquarters of the FBI Special Response Team
McLean, Virginia

"Tell me," Don Morris said.

The entire building was darkened, except for this conference room, Don's office, Trudy's office, and the strange dense warren of wooden shelves, laptop computers, desktop computers, standalone hard drives, wiring, electronic equipment, and empty soda cans that Mark Swann called his office. The overhead lights weren't on in there, but the machinery gave the place an eerie glow.

Swann was good at his job. Don wouldn't normally let an office like that stand. In this case, he was prepared to make an exception.

The three of them—Don, Trudy, and Swann—sat in various corners of the room. It was late, and he was sure these kids wanted to go home, but Don needed to see this through. They had been flying blind until moments ago, no idea what was going on out there, on the ground or in the sky.

"We got a message from the jump plane," Swann said.

"Okay."

"It was sent in the code we've been using, and it took me a few minutes to decipher it. It reads *Big man did not go. Boss held him back. Proceeding to destination 2.*"

Don sighed. "What does that mean?"

Swann shrugged. "Well, Ed is the big man. The boss is Stone. It sounds like Stone told Ed not to jump with them. Why he would do that is beyond me. Destination 2 is Airbase Amistad in Honduras. For some reason, Ed is still on the plane and the plane itself isn't going back to Jamaica. It's going to Honduras instead."

"I know that much, Swann. I mean, what is the reasoning behind it?"

He looked at Trudy.

Now she shrugged. Her eyes were tired behind her red glasses.

"Stone always has his reasons. He goes by instinct. You know that. It sounds like he kept Ed on the plane, and told them to go to Honduras in case he needed backup. Why he would go with Henry Bowles and not Ed is anybody's guess."

"And that's all we've heard?" Don said.

"That's all we've heard," Swann said. "And that message just came through a few moments ago. So that means to me that nothing has happened yet."

"Do you still have the drone in the air?"

Swann shook his head. "I returned it several hours ago. Its night optics aren't great, so we weren't going to see much. Anyway, it's better that we don't have it."

"Why's that?" Don said.

Swann looked at Don, then to Trudy, and back again. It was a rare moment when Swann could almost be thought to have a steely gaze.

"This needs to stay in this room," he said.

Don suppressed a smile. Trudy said nothing.

"I was talking to a friend of mine," Swann said. "Not really a friend. A guy I know. As you're both aware, the SRT seems to have sprung a leak somewhere. I've been wracking my brains, trying to figure out where it is. We've been sweeping these offices like crazy. We use codes and encryptions. We're keeping information tight, on a need to know basis. So where's the leak?"

Don had been beginning to wonder if Swann himself wasn't the leak. "Okay," he said. "And did you find an answer?"

Swann nodded. "Maybe. Maybe one answer. Maybe there are more than one, but this might be an important one."

"So give it."

"ECHELON," Swann said. "It's a monster computer application they have at the National Security Agency. The Patriot Act authorized its existence, but I know NSA had earlier versions of it going back to the mid-1990s, and possibly before. Those were unauthorized. The newest iteration is the most advanced and comprehensive data monitoring program ever invented."

"I've heard of it," Trudy said. "It can intercept messages."

"It can intercept every digital communication sent in the United States," Swann said. "And communications are all digital now. Phone calls have gone digital. Emails, texts, satellite communications. It vacuums all of them up and collects them."

"Okay, but what good is it?" Trudy said. "No one can monitor all of those messages. It would take thousands of people, working in three shifts, twenty-four hours a day…"

Swann shook his head. "That isn't the point of it. That isn't their intention. The program gets tripped by keywords. Any keyword they want can flag a communication for further investigation. Bomb. Assassinate. Al-Qaeda. Whatever keyword interests you. That narrows down who to listen to."

"I don't know what kind of emails you write," Trudy said. "But I don't generally use those words."

"It doesn't matter," Swann said. "They can also just pick and choose people to hone in on. My acquaintance suggested to me that the SRT has been flagged for close monitoring the past three months, maybe longer."

"Our communications are encrypted," Don said. "Are they not?"

Swann shrugged. "Yes and no. The encryption package we have was developed for us by the Bureau. Can a rogue outside party figure out what we're saying? Absolutely not. Can NSA data scientists unravel standard FBI encryption? Of course they can. Or maybe NSA just reroutes our communications to FBI headquarters, where they have the decryption keys."

He looked at Don closely. "They gave us the encryption. You see what I'm saying? You said that was okay at the time we started. We work for them. We use their resources. They own this building. Of course we'll use their encryption methods. It would seem a little odd if we didn't."

"So you're saying…"

Swann nodded. "Yes. They never needed to bug this place. They can listen to us whenever they want. They know what we're doing almost before we do."

He paused.

"And they probably know Ed is going to Honduras."

CHAPTER THIRTY SIX

10:15 p.m. Central Standard Time (11:15 p.m. Eastern Standard Time)
La Sierra de San Simon (St. Simon's Saw)
Near Honduras
The Caribbean Sea

"So much for night vision gear," Luke whispered.

The place was lit up like a wedding was going on.

He was holed up, lying on his stomach, the sniper rifle on its bipod, in dense foliage at the edge of the compound, watching the house. With the black face paint on, and the dark clothing he was wearing, he was confident that no one could see him. But he couldn't stay in here forever.

The house was massive. There was a main house, and then wings heading off to the right and left. There were three floors, and there must be dozens of rooms. Some windows were lit up, and some were not. An area on the third floor, on the left, western wing, had dim, flickering lights, as though it was lit by candles. That might be something, and it might not.

There was no way to search a house this big, not by himself, not with a dozen guys. He was going to have to take a hostage, preferably someone who knew where the girl was kept, and have that person lead him there.

But he needed to make it across the compound to the house first.

To his far left was the inground pool area. A blue light from the bottom of the pool shone, causing an eerie glow. There didn't appear to be anyone over there.

Closer, to his right, was an outbuilding, probably left over from the hotel days. Maybe it had bathrooms, or changing rooms, or some kind of snack bar. Three men dressed in drab green military uniforms were posted near the doorway to this building. They were smoking cigarettes and chatting in low voices. They had rifles slung over their shoulders. Hondurans.

Directly across from Luke, maybe a hundred meters out, was an open rear door to the house itself. It was at the top of about six wide stone stairs. Two more men stood in that doorway. These men were larger, broad-shouldered, in civilian clothes. Luke guessed that they were private bodyguards, Americans in all likelihood, former military, maybe men like himself.

The outbuilding was much closer. The men were on this side of it, standing in a little bit of shadow, shielded from the doorway to the house. The angle suggested that it was possible to take those guys without alerting the ones over by the house.

That meant killing three men in cold blood, men in the Honduran military, who were assigned to this task, and might not know anything about Darwin King. Young men with families, perhaps. It would be easier to kill private contractors.

"They know," Luke whispered to himself. "They know what goes on here. They witness it every day. They work for the bad guy. They're bad guys. It's that simple."

After everything that had happened, there wasn't much mercy left. He didn't need to remind himself of the girls who had been kidnapped. He didn't need to remind himself of Buzz MacDonald dead. He just needed to flash back to the child's corpse in an overlarge ice chest. Yes, that case was unrelated to this. He knew that. He knew it rationally. But it was about impunity. This impunity in front of him was the same as that impunity behind him. Stealing people, children, treating them like objects to be used or discarded.

That's what he was dealing with.

Moving slowly, carefully, he pointed the sniper rifle in that direction. Its long snout, with the massive sound suppressor attached, poked through the bushes. The three men stood together. Smoke rose between them. One said something, and the other two laughed. Luke could just hear their low voices from here, but nothing of what was said.

He put one of the men in the circle. The man's face seemed inches away, close enough that Luke could see the black stubble on his face. The man put the cigarette to his mouth.

This would have to go quick. It was a bolt action rifle, so he had to manually expel each spent cartridge. Luke practiced changing the aim on the rifle, moving it from man to man.

He put the first man back in the circle.

Chung!

Bingo. Luke ejected the spent cartridge and moved the gun.

The next face looked down in horror at what had just happened.

Chung!

Luke changed the aim one last time. The third man was crouched, his gun at the ready, staring out into the night, looking for where the shots had come from.

Chung!

Three men were now on the ground in a pile over there. None of them had made a sound, other than the rustling they made as they sank to the dirt.

Luke checked the door to the house. The two big men were there, impassive as before. They hadn't moved. Okay. Now he was in business.

He left the gun in place, went back into the bushes, and wrapped around toward the outbuilding. He darted out across open land to the building. The three dead men were piled near the doorway. Luke glanced in. It was just a big open space, maybe a dining hall or a dancehall or a bar at one time.

Luke took two grenades, put them both on timers for three minutes, and tossed them inside. Then he crossed back to the copse of jungle again.

He checked the timer on his watch. Two minutes had already passed.

He went to the sniper rifle. The timing needed to be good, not necessarily perfect, but close to it.

Thirty seconds left.

Twenty.

He put one of the men at the doorway to the house in the circle of the telescopic sight. He was a tall guy in a black T-shirt, broad chest, big shoulders, close-cropped blond hair, a holstered gun at his shoulder. Hard, mean-spirited eyes.

Ten seconds.

Chung!

Dead.

He tried to put the sight on the second man, but that guy was already gone, disappeared. Luke looked over the top of the telescope, but he didn't see him. The guy had training. The moment his buddy got hit, he…

BOOOM!

There was a flash of light and an eruption of sound, like an earthquake. The first grenade went off, taking out the far wall of the outbuilding. An instant later…

BOOOM!

The second one went off, deep inside the building.

Luke was running now, staying low, the burning outbuilding to his right, the pool grounds to his left. His breathing was loud in his ears. He came at the doorway from an angle. The guard who had ditched was still gone.

There was shouting to his right side. People were moving toward the outbuilding from the other side of it. He could just see them from the corner of his eye. Something inside that building had really caught fire. There was a tinkling as glass windows shattered and flames licked outward.

He reached the doors to the house and darted up the steps, two at a time. His pistols were out, one in each hand, his and Bowles's, two MP5s strapped across his chest, more grenades hanging from his vest.

He burst through the wide double doorway.

Here was the man who had ducked. A big guy in a Hawaiian shirt. He was moving down the wide hallway toward Luke. He was part of a group of three, two big guys, flanking a woman in a green dress between them.

They had guns. He had guns.

Luke aimed both his guns. The men aimed at him.

BANG! BANG! BANG!

BANG!

They all fired at once.

Luke shot them both in the face. One of their shots missed entirely.

The other hit Luke in the left shoulder. It knocked him around sideways. The gun went flying out of his left hand.

He heard himself grunt from the impact.

He looked down at the injury. His vest was ripped apart there. It was bloody. A chunk of meat had been taken out. It looked red and raw. He couldn't tell how bad it was. He couldn't tell if the bone had been hit.

It didn't hurt, but that was the adrenaline talking.

There was nothing he could do about it. There was no time. The fight was on. He had to do everything now, own this place, sow chaos, destroy opposition, press his advantage before he lost it. Injuries would have to wait.

The woman stood there, between the corpses of the two men who had been with her a moment ago. She hadn't moved, but she didn't seem fazed in the least. She didn't even glance down at the dead men. Her eyes were hard and cold.

Luke walked toward her.

She gestured at his shoulder.

"You're shot. You better get that looked at. We wouldn't want you to bleed to death."

The woman's eyes were a startling shade of green. They went with the dress she was wearing. She was not tall. She was thin, and very pretty, middle-aged, maybe fifty. She stared at Luke with those eyes. Something about them made her seem as if she wasn't real. A different race, a different species.

"They told me there was an explosion in the cabana. I thought I'd better come down here and check it out myself."

Luke put his remaining pistol to her forehead. It was Bowles's gun.

Her eyes never wavered. "You'll never get out of here alive."

"Elaine Sayles, I presume," Luke said.

She nodded. "Of course. And you are?"

Luke shook his head. "No. I'm here for Charlotte Richmond. You're going to take me to her. You start now, or you're dead in two seconds. I won't even count them."

"Surely you wouldn't shoot a woman," she said. "Look at me. I'm unarmed."

"I don't care," Luke said. "If you're here, you're complicit. It's open season on complicit people."

She hesitated.

Luke jabbed her forehead with the pistol. She winced at that.

"Last chance," Luke said. "I'm out of time, and so are you."

Something had changed in her eyes. She believed him.

"Follow me," she said.

* * *

"Stay behind me, sir," the bodyguard said.

There was a security area on the first floor, the closest thing this home had to a panic room. It was a suite of rooms, with double-paned bulletproof glass, concrete reinforced walls, reinforced ceilings, its own dedicated generator, food and water to last several weeks, and satellite communications.

The entrance to the area was sealed by an old bank vault door. Once closed, it was next to impossible to open or breach. The area was fireproof, bombproof, and was rated to withstand a Category 5 hurricane. There was one door to the outside of the house, which led to the parking lot and the small fleet of armored, four-wheel-drive SUVs. That door, double steel, flush with the outside walls, could not be opened from out there, and provided a last escape hatch, should all else fail.

The problem, which Darwin had not considered until this moment, was that the security area was two floors below his private apartment. Getting there in a crisis… well, he was discovering how fraught that was. A hurricane was one thing, but this was an invasion.

A group of seven came down the stairs from the private apartment, and moved along the wide hallway on the second floor. There was Darwin himself, the tallest person in the group. There were the three girls, 11, 17, and 21. And there were three big, stern-faced bodyguards. The men were doing their jobs.

Two men walked in front, at either side of the hallway, guns out and pointed down. The third man walked in the middle of the hall. Darwin walked directly behind his broad back, the girls following along behind him. He hadn't gotten the chance to show 21 the error of her ways tonight, but that was beside the point now.

She had brought this upon him, whether she meant to or not. These people, whoever they were, were attacking because of her.

They would be beaten back, and once they were…

BANG! BANG!

The lead man on the right, and the one on the left, both fell to the floor. Darwin saw a cloud, a spritz of blood, exit the back of the man on the left's bald head before he fell. The girls behind him screamed. The man in front of Darwin froze into a crouch, his gun pointed up the hallway in front of them.

The men on the floor were not moving at all. Pools of blood were forming around their heads.

"Darwin!" a female voice screamed. Darwin recognized that voice instantly.

He squatted behind the last remaining bodyguard in the group, his hand on the man's back.

At the far end of the hall, two people appeared. One of the people was Elaine. She wore the shimmering green dress that he liked so much. There was a man behind her. He held a gun pointed at her head, and stayed low to keep Elaine's body in front of him. He was hard to see back there. He was using Elaine as a shield.

"Can you kill that man?" Darwin said to the bodyguard.

"Only if I shoot Elaine first."

The man over there was big. He wore all black. His face was painted black and dark green. He wore a black cap. It was impossible to say anything about him. He was close to Elaine, one gloved hand around her throat, the gun to her head with the other hand.

"Darwin," Elaine said. It sounded like she had a lump in her throat. Darwin had never heard her sound like that before.

"Shut up!" the man said.

Darwin found himself unable to speak. He crouched there, behind his bodyguard, his voice failing him. He should take charge here. He should…

"Sir, what do you want to do?" the bodyguard said. "Should I take the shot?"

What was he asking? Should he kill Elaine so that he could kill this other man? Was he insane? Darwin and Elaine had been together for more than twenty years. But Darwin couldn't speak. He couldn't answer the question.

If the bodyguard killed Elaine, and then killed the intruder, Darwin would be safe, for the moment. Maybe he could just shoot Elaine and get her out of the way, but not kill her. It was impossible to discuss that possibility in this moment, though. There should be a policy, but there wasn't one. This had never been anticipated. He would leave it up to this man, this hired help, to set the new policy for himself.

"Charlotte Richmond!" the intruder called. "Come here, Charlotte. Your mother sent me to get you."

Darwin heard 21 gasp behind him. Darwin glanced back at her. Her eyes were huge. She was still wearing the sheer nightgown. Even in this extreme moment, she looked beautiful.

"Come to me," the man said. "It's all right. Come to me, Charlotte."

Darwin wanted to keep her. He wouldn't let them take her. He reached out and grasped her around her thin wrist.

She tried to pull away, but he held her tight.

"Bite him!" the man said. "Just bite him."

"21," Darwin said. "Don't you listen."

The girl bent over and put her mouth to Darwin's hand. He felt the stinging pain as she dug her teeth into his flesh. He pulled her closer, but still she bit, tearing into him. He didn't dare come out from behind the bodyguard. For a brief moment, he and the girl were in a tug of war, he pulling her small body closer and closer, while she ripped his hand apart with her teeth.

She kicked at him with her bare feet. He was low, and she kicked at his legs, and at his sides.

The pain in his hand became too much. He let go. The back of his hand was bleeding. He was going to have an imprint of her mouth in his flesh.

"You bitch!" he shouted at her. "You little—"

"My name is Charlotte," she said.

She turned and ran up the hall to the man.

"Stand behind me," Darwin heard the man say. Everything, every word, every sound, echoed in this wide hallway.

The man still had the gun to Elaine's head. "That's all I want," he shouted. "The girl is all I came for. I'm alive, you're alive. Cool?"

Darwin suddenly realized that the man wasn't even talking to him. He was talking to the last gunman here.

The guard gestured at the two corpses on the floor. "What about them?"

"They're not your problem, are they? Your problem is you."

"There are thirty men on these grounds. You'll never get out of here alive."

"That's not your problem either," the man said.

A long second passed, and then the bodyguard stood tall. He raised his hands and holstered his gun. Darwin was still crouched behind him. Darwin glanced back again. The two remaining girls were here, sweet girls, loyal girls, 11 and 17. They could be blonde twins. They were behind him, hugging each other and crying.

Darwin looked down the hallway. The intruder, Elaine, and 21 were all gone.

"I want that man dead," Darwin said.

The bodyguard shrugged. He was staring down at the two dead men.

"Kill him yourself," he said.

* * *

"You have the keys to one of these things?"

The three of them, Luke, the girl, and the woman Elaine, moved quickly across the parking lot toward the line of SUVs.

The girl was barefoot, but she seemed to be managing. Her nightdress was basically see-through. Luke was going to have to find her some clothes. And if they made it through this, probably some kind of rubber room to hang around inside of for a while.

The house loomed behind them, and behind that, the flames of the burning outbuilding cast an orange glow against the dark sky. The explosions, and the fire, had bought him some time, but probably not much.

"No," the woman said. "I don't drive them."

Luke was through messing around. He was finished. His patience was just… gone. He had left two captive girls behind. Who knew how many more were here on these grounds, and in the house?

He might have ended it by killing Darwin King, but he couldn't get a clear shot. The bodyguard did exactly what he was paid to do—put his own body in the way of harm. Luke had already lost track of how many he had killed since Henry Bowles, just to get here. Six men, anyway. Maybe eight. Two dogs. Buzz Mac was dead. And now Luke was walking away—make that running away—from the whole thing. It was a mess. This job had been FUBAR from the beginning, and it had never gotten any better.

Luke's gun was pressed against the woman's head as they walked. He jabbed her again, to remind her it was there.

He shrugged. "If you can't get me into one of those cars, and get it started, I have no reason to keep you alive."

The woman sighed. She could have been exasperated by an incompetent maid.

"There are no keys. It's keyless entry. I know the code. There's a microchip inside a plastic fob sitting in a slot where they used to put the ashtray. We just leave the fobs in the cars. The motor recognizes the presence of the chip. Once you're inside the car, you can start it by pressing a button on the dashboard."

Luke nodded. "Good. Then that's what we'll do."

He went to the first car in the line. He turned and looked back at the house. There was movement in the shadows. Men were massing near the guardhouse. The tall metal gates were closed. It was going to be hot getting out of here, if it wasn't hot already.

"Mister…" Charlotte said.

He turned. She was staring up at him with big blues eyes. She gestured behind her. Men had appeared, coming from the other direction. They were shadows themselves, moving around the far end of the house.

"Get down!" he shouted.

Charlotte and Elaine dropped to the ground.

THUNK. THUNK. THUNK.

They were shooting. That was a bad sign. Luke had hostages. He supposed they didn't care anymore. He crouched down and unstrapped one of the MP5s from around his shoulder. He stepped on one of Elaine's wrists.

"Don't even think about running."

He stepped to the edge of the car, turned the corner, and opened with the gun.

DUH-DUH-DUH-DUH-DUH.

It was LOUD.

Charlotte and Elaine both screamed. The girl put fingers in her ears. He wasn't trying to hit anything. He couldn't see anyone.

Luke reached down and pulled Elaine to her feet.

"Now. Open the car. Let's go."

Elaine bent to the task, her fingers shaking. On the driver's door, there was a dimly lit numeric pad where the key slot normally would be. She began pressing buttons. "I don't know if I can—"

"There's no time," Luke said. "Get it right. If I'm going to die here, so are you."

A beep sounded, and the door unlocked. Luke pulled it open.

"Get in," he said to Elaine.

"Am I driving?"

Luke shook his head. "No. Slide all the way across."

He looked at the girl. "Charlotte, get in the back and sit right behind the front passenger seat. Okay?"

The girl nodded and got in.

THUNK. THUNK. THUNK. THUNK. THUNK.

Bullets chewed into armor.

Luke slid in behind the wheel.

"Shouldn't I drive?" Elaine said. "And you hold a gun to my head? Isn't that how we're supposed to do it?"

"No," Luke said. "You're not a good enough driver."

"How do you know that?"

Luke smiled. "I just know."

He took Bowles's pistol out of his belt. He checked the chamber. Empty. He ejected the magazine and let it drop out to the floor on his left. He turned to the girl.

"Charlotte, this is a gun. It's ready to fire. It's a little bit heavy, so use two hands."

The girl tentatively took the gun in her small hands.

"Put your finger on the trigger, but don't press it. Yep. Just like that. I want you to hold the gun to the back of Elaine's head, okay? If she tries anything, just shoot her."

The girl nodded. "Okay."

"Good. Let's go."

"You can't do that," Elaine said, apparently unaware that the gun was empty. "You can't give a gun to a child."

Luke found the big starter button and pressed it. The engine roared to life and he put the car in gear. "I just did."

Suddenly he got a better idea. He put his foot on the brake. He reached in his vest pockets and came out with a pair of hard plastic zip ties. He looked at Elaine.

"Turn and face the window."

For once, she did what he said without argument.

"Hands behind your back."

She gave him her hands and he zip-tied her wrists together.

"Good. I like you better this way."

She turned and faced front again. Her arms were pinned behind her back and against the seat. "It's very uncomfortable sitting this way."

Luke shrugged. "Life. It gets uncomfortable sometimes."

He let his foot slowly off the brake. The car rolled slowly out of the line. The headlights had come on automatically, so it was going to be clear to any interested parties which car they were in. He tapped the gas. The car felt heavy, a little sluggish. That was good. Armor was heavy.

The gate was straight ahead. There were men in the shadows on either side of it. Somewhere behind the house, the fire was dying down. He had gotten a little luck so far, now he needed some more.

He stomped on the gas.

The car took off, pushing through the drag caused by the weight of the armor. It accelerated, as its big engine kicked in. Now they were tearing, moving fast, racing by under the dense canopy of trees above them. It was like being in a tunnel. The house was behind them.

Here came the black steel gate. The guardhouse was to the right.

Men were crouched.

Luke saw the flashes of their guns.

Rounds hit the car, all over. DUM. DUM. DUM. DUM. The passenger side windows cracked and spiderwebbed. Charlotte shrieked now. Elaine groaned. The windshield smashed, but did not break. The armor was good. The armor was holding.

A man fired from the darkness on Luke's side, a rocket of some kind. It skimmed the roof and went over. Were they crazy?

The gate loomed ahead, coming fast.

Men were running, diving out of the way.

"Hold on!" Luke shouted.

The gate was RIGHT THERE. It looked solid as hell.

Please please please please...

BAM!

The sound was huge, impossible, heavy metal CRUNCH at high speed. The impact jarred his shoulders, wrenched his entire body. His hands slipped and his head nearly hit the steering wheel. Everyone was screaming. Bullets ripped up the sides of the car.

He sat up. Sparks were flying all over the outside of the car. There was a sound like SCREEEEEE.... They were through, but they were dragging part of the gate.

"It's steep here!" Elaine screamed. "The road is steep!"

The road went straight down. It was like driving off a cliff. The car caught air. There was a long second where Luke's butt and legs came off the seat. His stomach was in his mouth.

"Aaaahhhhhh..."

The car hit the road and bounced. He swerved, trying to regain control. He tapped the brake. The car skidded, fishtailing left... right... left... it was going to roll. The road was nearly vertical. If they went over at this speed...

The car straightened out.

Luke didn't even slow down. Now they tore downhill at incredible speed. They were out.

He looked at Elaine. Her head had hit the dashboard. Blood ran down the right side of her face.

"Thanks for the tip," he said.

She shook her head. "The hill ends abruptly."

Luke slammed on the brakes. The car skidded the last thirty yards, and hit the spot where the hill ended and the level road began. The impact of it was nearly like a car crash itself. The car slid to a stop.

Steam rose from the grille, mixing with the steamy night air here at sea level.

"I think that's the steepest hill I've ever driven on," Luke said.

"Congratulations," Elaine said.

Luke pressed the gas again and the car lurched forward. It was a good car, and it had done its job, but it wasn't going to last much longer. A couple more hits and those passenger side windows were going to come down. The windshield was wrecked. He could barely see through it.

It didn't matter. There was nothing to see. There was only one road on the island, Luke knew, and it would take him straight to the airfield.

After that? He was just going to have to get lucky again. There was a plane there, and maybe there was a pilot. If not, he was going to hold Elaine Sayles at gunpoint until they brought him one.

It wasn't a great plan, and the other team didn't seem to care that much about Elaine's safety, but…

He didn't know. He had come this far. All he could do was keep going, keep pushing, and try to catch one more break.

CHAPTER THIRTY SEVEN

10:29 p.m. Central Standard Time (11:29 p.m. Eastern Standard Time)
The airfield
La Sierra de San Simon (St. Simon's Saw)
Near Honduras
The Caribbean Sea

"Oh hell. What's next?"

The pilot's name was Warren Cross. He had the plane parked at the end of the runway, engines already running. He could be in the sky in no time.

He had been relaxing in the passenger cabin, thumbing through a copy of *Conde Nast Traveler*, when he heard the first explosion. A moment later, alarms started blaring.

Cross had been working for Darwin King for the past eighteen months, and somehow he had always known it would come to this. Bombs going off, alarms shrieking, guns popping, people screaming over the radio in a mix of English and Spanish. It had only been a matter of time.

Cross had mostly stopped going up to the house months ago. Why go up there and see things he didn't want to see? Why witness events that might find him in a court of law one day? Instead, when he was on the island, he stayed down here at the airfield. There was an old building with bathrooms and showers. Troops came and went, and some of the guys brought him food down from the house. He slept on the plane.

It was a lot of waiting around, but it was better this way. He was happiest when Darwin sent him somewhere on an errand, which happened frequently. Sometimes he went to Tegucigalpa, sometimes to Kingston, sometimes to Grand Cayman or even Miami. That was the best part of the job—being gone from here.

Suddenly, there was shooting right outside the plane. Cross didn't like shooting. He'd seen too much of it doing corkscrew landings at Baghdad Airport during the war. He was thirty-six years old now, and away from that kind of action. He had hoped to stay away from it forever, but now here it was again.

He went to one of the windows. Out there, in the dark by the gate, Honduran soldiers were firing at something that was coming. Something was tearing up the roadway, a car of some kind, a shadow, sparks shooting around it, headlights out. It was coming straight at the gate. The men scattered and…

BOOM!

The car plowed right through the fencing, dragging a chunk of it into the parking lot. Cross just stared. It was one of the black SUVs from the house.

It came crunching and limping across the tarmac to the plane. A man in black jumped out of it, turned, and started firing back at the soldiers. The angry blat of automatic fire ripped open the night. It was close, and it was LOUD.

Now three people ran across the short distance to the passenger door. Two of them were female. One was Elaine Sayles. One was an anonymous teenage girl, of the kind Darwin King liked to collect.

No one had given Cross any orders. He was just here in the airplane. He flew the plane. That was it. He was innocent of any crimes. He hadn't done anything.

Someone started banging on the door. Against his better judgment, Cross opened it.

The three people came bursting in. Elaine's face was a bloody mess. Cross didn't mind that. He thought of Elaine as evil incarnate. If people could be evil, Elaine was one of those people. She might even be more evil than Darwin King. Could that be possible, that someone was more evil than Darwin?

God! Cross should have quit this job a long time ago. He should have quit after the first week. But the money was too good. And now it was too late to quit.

The man in black pulled the door closed behind him. He had one machine gun in his hands, another draped across his chest. His face was painted black and dark green. His left shoulder was torn apart and bleeding, but he didn't seem to notice. His eyes were hard and flat. Cross had seen the eyes before in war zones.

Murderer's eyes.

The man pointed his gun at Cross's head.

Cross raised his hands. "It's cool, man. I'm just the pilot. I didn't do anything to anybody. This plane is gassed and ready. I will take you anywhere you want to go. Just don't shoot me."

The gunman's demeanor didn't change at all. He gestured with his head. "Give your clothes to the girl. Then let's get out of here."

Cross glanced at the teenager. She looked about twelve. She was wearing some kind of see-through whatever. Of course she was. She had no shoes on. Her eyes were wide and staring. This was why Cross didn't go up to the house anymore.

Cross was about eight inches taller than the girl, and he outweighed her by probably seventy or eighty pounds. He was wearing a blue short-sleeved shirt over a wife-beater T-shirt. He was wearing madras pants over boxer briefs.

"Man, my clothes aren't going to fit that girl."

The gunman shook his head. His eyes were wild now. "We have no time. I'm not going to argue with you. We're on the run, in case you haven't noticed, and she's not dressed for running. We'll roll up the pants, and put your belt as tight as it will go. Okay? Now do it, ten seconds or less, before I decide to fly the plane myself."

Cross sighed, pulled his shirt off, and tossed it to the girl.

"Go!" the gunman shouted. "Let's go!"

* * *

The cockpit door was open during takeoff.

Luke hung back from the doorway, out of sight of the guns on the ground. For some reason, no one fired a shot. Luke took that as a good sign. This was Darwin King's private airplane. He probably didn't want to see it get hurt.

He probably thought that once the girl escaped and was safely in the United States, he could have his plane back. He probably could. King had always gotten away with everything before now. Why wouldn't he get away with this?

Luke felt the rush of acceleration as the plane taxied down the runway. The nose went up, the wheels left the ground, and then they were away. The pilot climbed steeply into the black sky, then banked to the left, headed north.

Luke looked at the pilot. He nearly laughed. The guy was wearing a white sleeveless T-shirt and bright red boxer briefs. That, and deck shoes with no socks.

Luke took a deep breath and slowly exhaled. They were out.

That wasn't so bad.

"What's your name?" Luke said to the pilot.

"I don't know if I want to answer that."

Luke smiled. Fair enough.

"Where'd you learn to fly?"

"Eight years, United States Air Force."

Luke nodded. "Good man."

"Where am I flying this thing?"

Luke shook his head. He hadn't thought that far ahead. They could rendezvous with the SRT plane in Jamaica, he supposed. If things looked clear, maybe they could take this thing all the way back to the States.

"I don't know. Jamaica? How's that sound?"

"You mind telling me what's going on? It's not every day I get hijacked."

Luke nodded. There was no reason to hide anything from this guy. "My name is Luke Stone. I'm an agent with the FBI Special Response Team. The girl with me was kidnapped. What you just witnessed…"

"She was not kidnapped," said a voice behind him. "She was there voluntarily. You're the one doing the kidnapping."

Luke looked back. Elaine Sayles was in one of the leather recliner seats, arms still behind her back. Her face was red and raw.

"You're bleeding on the furniture," Luke said.

The girl Charlotte smiled. She was seated well behind and away from Elaine. She was swimming in the pilot's shirt, but the pants looked okay, rolled way up and cinched tight around her waist. It was good to see her smile. Maybe she was the resilient type. She would need to be. This was going to be a lot to process.

"FBI, huh?" Elaine said. "After this fiasco, I promise you'll be out of a job."

Luke nodded. As the adrenaline was wearing off, his shoulder was starting to throb. Pretty soon it was going to be a sharper pain, maybe even agony. He wasn't looking forward to that.

"I hope you're right," he said. "This job is for the birds."

"You'll be in prison the rest of your life. I saw you murder four men in cold blood."

"Elaine," Luke said. "If you can behave, I will cut your wrist ties. If you can't behave, I'm going to consider you a risk to self and others, and leave you just the way you are. It's your choice."

"Stone," the pilot called. The change in his voice was palpable.

Luke went back to the doorway. "What's up?"

"We got bogeys on radar, man. They just came off the mainland of Honduras, moving fast. We're right on their nose."

Luke's shoulders slumped. "Can we outrun them?"

The pilot shook his head. "Not on your life. They are howling."

"What did you think would happen?" Elaine shouted. "Did you think you could just attack someone's home, kidnap people, and nothing would happen to you?"

"I'm the FBI, you idiot."

"I don't care who you think you are."

The pilot glanced back at Luke. Luke saw it then, in the man's eyes, all over his face: fear. The guy was afraid. He learned to fly in the Air Force. That didn't mean he was a combat pilot.

"Got any bright ideas, Stone? We'll never make Jamaica, I can tell you that."

Luke patted his cargo pants. "I have another destination. It's a small airfield in Honduras."

"Darwin owns Honduras. That's no good."

Luke found the page and pulled it out. The paper was protected by some lightweight laminate. He handed it to the pilot.

"This has the coordinates. It's a tiny place, a speck on the map. It's classified, run by American intelligence."

"Darwin owns American intelligence!"

Luke shook his head. "No one owns American intelligence. It's too big. Too many factions. These people are friendlies, as far as that goes. We just need to get there."

The man looked at the sheet. "Okay. Okay, it's close. Changing heading. We are going to…"

He glanced at the radar. The air seemed to go out of him.

"Two more bogeys, closer, coming from the east. Seven miles and closing fast. I don't even know where they came from. They must have been patrolling out over the water. We're cooked, man. We are not going to make it."

"Steady," Luke said.

"Two behind us, two coming in from the east. We are cooked."

Luke shrugged. "They can escort us to the airfield if they want."

"I doubt it," the pilot said.

"Why's that?"

"One of them just fired a missile. It's coming from our right. Six miles." He turned back to Luke again. He looked like he was almost about to cry. "Better go buckle up. This is going to be awkward."

Luke felt something in the pit of his stomach. It wasn't despair. Call it disappointment. A deep, bitter, dark disappointment.

"Can you evade it?"

"I'm going to try."

Luke went back into the passenger cabin. Suddenly, before he could get to a seat, the plane lurched to the left. It banked hard and Luke tumbled to the floor. He landed on his wounded shoulder. A searing pain went through it, so much that he nearly passed out. He gritted his teeth.

The plane was shuddering, it was banking so hard. The pilot whipped it around the other way, leveling, then banking hard to the right. Luke rolled over the other direction. Elaine, wrists tied behind her back, fell out of her chair. Now she was on the floor, five or six feet from Luke.

"Heat seeking!" the pilot shouted. "I can't shake it!"

"Charlotte!" Luke shouted. "Put your seatbelt on!"

The pilot went into a steep climb. Luke was pressed to the floor. He crawled like a worm to a seat and yanked himself up into it.

He clipped his belt. At that second, the plane went into a steep drop, nose down. It was so sudden that Elaine flew off the floor and into the air. She screamed as she was thrown against the wall. Behind Luke, Charlotte also screamed.

"Here it comes!" the pilot shouted.

The plane banked hard to the left again.

Ga-BOOOOM.

An explosion rocked the plane. Bright light was everywhere at once, flashing through the windows. Luke was thrown forward, against his seatbelt. His head whipped around. For a second, he thought the plane had broken apart.

The cabin lights were knocked out, and everything went dark. Weak green lights lit up along the floor. A red EXIT sign came on over the door.

The turbulence was incredible. Was the pilot even alive?

"Pilot!" Luke shouted.

"Mayday!" the pilot screamed. "We have Mayday!"

"Where are we?"

"Land coming! We are over the beach. Losing altitude."

"Are we hit?"

"I don't know. We're losing fuel. We lost an engine. Something's—"

The plane lurched, dropping altitude.

"Oh God."

Luke unbuckled, stood, and stumbled to the cockpit door. The plane bucked and bounced. He shouldn't be standing, but someone needed to steady this pilot.

"How far to the airfield?" Luke said.

The pilot checked his instruments. "Uh... thirty... thirty-five miles."

"Can you keep it up that long?"

"No. We're right above the treetops now."

Luke looked out through the cockpit window. It was impossible to see out there. The plane started to shudder again. It rode some turbulence.

Instruments started to blink off. The entire panel was going dark.

"Go sit down," the pilot said. His voice had changed again. It sounded resigned. "I'll hold it up as long as I can."

"Can I help you?"

The pilot shook his head. "There's nothing you can do."

Luke nodded. "Okay. Good luck."

"Good luck to you."

Luke worked his way back through the plane, swaying from side to side. Elaine was on the floor, twisted at an odd angle. She was not moving. The plane lurched again, dropped altitude. Luke was off his feet for a second.

He went all the way to the back, as far as he could go. Charlotte was this far back, and he sat down beside her. The back of the plane was the safest place to be.

The plane lurched and dropped again. It went up hard on its left side.

The pilot screamed, a howl, no words.

Luke looked at Charlotte. The girl was crying. He reached and took her hand.

"It's okay," he told her. The words meant nothing. It was obviously not okay. It was anything but okay.

He closed his eyes and sat back. An image of Becca and Gunner appeared before him. The plane bucked and shuddered. There was a loud BANG as it hit something. Then another BANG. And another.

The pilot screamed again. The plane's nose was up, way up.

They dropped. Then everything changed. They were moving fast, the plane rattling, shaking. Luke couldn't move at all. There was sound everywhere, the sound of metal ripping metal. It was LOUD, so LOUD he couldn't hear the pilot screaming.

The girl squeezed his hand.

He turned to look but she wasn't there. Luke could not see. All around him was total darkness.

They dropped through… something. The plane was falling apart. They were still moving. Luke was thrown forward. It was so violent, his face hit his knees.

Everything went black.

CHAPTER THIRTY EIGHT

10:40 p.m. Central Standard Time (11:40 p.m. Eastern Standard Time)
Airbase Amistad
Rio Platano Biosphere Reserve
Honduras

"Lock those coordinates," Ed Newsam said.

He was standing inside a corrugated aluminum shack in what amounted to a fenced in, glorified clearing in the middle of a vast wilderness, ten clicks north of Nicaragua.

There was a man who sat inside this shack, monitoring an array of electronic equipment while smoking cigarettes. He took the smokes back to back. He had a lit one in his hand right now, and there was a pile of dead ones in a tin tray at his elbow.

He had a pile of newspapers and magazines at his other elbow. *Forbes, Fortune, Kiplinger's, The Wall Street Journal.* Apparently, he was managing his stock portfolio while listening to the chatter from communists in Nicaragua and drug traffickers everywhere else.

The man said he worked for the "State Department." He said it just like that. He put little crow's feet around the words with his fingers. He wore civilian clothes. He had on a loose-fitting, button-down white shirt, a pair of khaki shorts, and sandals. His feet were big, almost grotesquely so. He was a little overweight and wore glasses. His glasses kept fogging up. It was steamy around here.

The man hadn't bothered to introduce himself. Either that, or he had made a point of not doing it. It was hard to say.

Until a moment ago, he had been showing them the radar position of a small jet plane that had left Darwin King's island. He had also been showing them the radar positions of fighter jets converging on the plane.

There appeared to have been an attack. Now the first plane was gone, off radar, and the fighter jets were moving to the south at full speed.

"I need to get in there," Ed said.

He looked back at Rachel and Jacob. They said nothing. Ed already knew what they were thinking. There was an old Black Hawk helicopter outside. If it could still take off, they could certainly fly it.

"That's a hairy place to get into," the man said. "This whole area is hairy. Steep hills. Dense jungle. Illegal logging operations. You'll find a bunch of clear cuts and burns out there. You can see them from the air. Insects… Jesus. They're as big as your hand. The worst bugs I've ever seen. They give me nightmares. Hostile locals. Cocaine smugglers. The national police. The military. It's hard to say who the worst of the bunch are. Suffice to say, if you run into anyone out there, it's someone bad."

"Buddy," Ed said. "Look at me a second, will you?"

The guy had almost not even glanced at Ed the entire time he'd been here. They had landed twenty-five minutes ago, a mysterious beat up plane appearing out of nowhere, and Ed Newsam had climbed out of it, strapped with guns. The guy barely noticed. That's how jaded he was. He'd been out here too long.

Now he did look at Ed. His eyes went from the top of Ed's head, down to his feet, and back up again.

He nodded. "Okay. You're as bad as they are. Is that what you're saying?"

"I am worse than they will ever be."

The man shook his head. "Somehow I doubt that."

Ed gestured at the door. "I need that chopper out there."

The man shrugged. "If you can fly it, take it. It's a piece of junk. And we're in between pilots right now."

"We'll fly it," Rachel said.

"Okay, but don't hurt it. Junk or not, I'm going to need a helicopter, if only to say I have one. There's a line of rain squalls coming across the country from the west. You should know that. When it rains here, it really rains, you know what I'm saying?"

"I need some men," Ed said. He was pressed for time, and this guy was talking way too much. "Men who have done helicopter drops into combat zones before."

The man turned all the way around in his chair and faced Ed. Ed normally sensed the way he intimidated people, and sometimes he used that to his advantage. He didn't intimidate this man at all.

"Absolutely not," the man said.

"Our people were aboard that airplane," Ed said. "You've got soldiers out there. I need some."

It was true. There were four guard towers along the perimeter fencing. They were manned, two armed men to a tower. There was a cluster of Quonset huts set back from the runway, about a quarter mile from here. There were almost certainly more soldiers, currently off duty, in there.

The man shook his head. "This is a listening station. It's not a combat post. We don't get attacked because the Hondurans, and the Nicaraguans, know better than to attack the United States. You know what kind of soldiers I get here? Since the wars started in Iraq and Afghanistan, I get National Guardsmen. The guys I have now are from Vermont. They're an armory unit from Burlington. *They man an armory.* In Vermont. They also have a motor pool. None of them have seen combat, except one guy who is forty and was in Desert Storm fifteen years ago. He has high cholesterol. It runs in his family. He had a stent put in last August. Half of the kids don't even believe in war, they're just in this for the college tuition."

Ed stared at him.

"Their orders are to hold the line around this patch of mud. Their orders don't include jumping out of a helicopter at the site of a plane crash on a wet hillside in a Central American jungle in the middle of the night, potentially under enemy fire. Sorry, Charlie. I'm a civilian and I don't have the power to modify their orders. Frankly, even if I could, I wouldn't be all that interested in putting them in harm's way."

He took a drag from his cigarette, then seemed to wave Ed, and Rachel, and Jacob, away. "But take the chopper, by all means."

He exhaled a long stream of smoke.

"Just don't hurt it, okay?"

CHAPTER THIRTY NINE

10:50 p.m. Central Standard Time (11:50 p.m. Eastern Standard Time)
La Sierra de San Simon (St. Simon's Saw)
Near Honduras
The Caribbean Sea

"I want them found," Darwin King said. "Now. Tonight."

He sat on his private terrace, a strong vodka tonic in one hand, the telephone in the other. He stared down at the guttering remains of the cabana, which once housed the old hotel bar. A crew was out there, watering down what was left of it. Acrid smoke was still rising into the sky.

Honduran soldiers were everywhere, sweeping the property to see if there were any more intruders. They'd found two dead dogs in the dog run. They'd found a body washed up on the beach, along with a small inflatable motorboat.

Now they were everywhere. *Now* they were finding things. Where were they an hour ago? They were supposed to have been on high alert.

"Mr. King, our pilots describe the plane as breaking apart on impact," a deep male voice on the phone said. The voice spoke English slowly and formally, carefully enunciating every syllable. It was the voice of someone who grew up speaking Spanish, then learned to speak English through years of schooling. It was also the voice of someone who thought it important to communicate clearly.

"Do you understand?" the voice said. "The plane is in pieces in the deep wilderness. I believe your… people… are dead now."

"I don't care what you believe," Darwin said. "If they're dead, I want to know that for a fact."

"My friend, the plane went down in an isolated region. There are mountains. The terrain is steep. The jungle is dense and forbidding. It is a difficult area to reach, it is raining there right now, it often rains, and the visibility is not good. It will be very difficult to send anyone there before daylight."

"General…" Darwin began. He did not want to hear anything from this man except agreement.

"Darwin, please be reasonable."

Reasonable. That was a word that made alarms shriek in Darwin King's mind. You did not become Darwin King by being reasonable. And you did not respond to a violent invasion, arson, murder, kidnapping, and theft by being reasonable.

In his mind, Darwin could still see his dead bodyguards, bleeding out on the stone tiles of the second floor hallway. It was an affront so large, so impossible, that he almost couldn't absorb the magnitude of it.

"General, shut up! Just shut up. Okay? I don't feel like I need to remind you who our mutual friends are. I don't feel like I need to remind you of the things I know about you, about your brother, about the things you've both done. I don't feel like I need to remind you of my reach, but I will. I will reach right into your home, if I want. I will destroy you, sir. I will destroy you in every possible way. I will take everything away from you. Your position. Your family. Your very life. Do you understand me?"

"Darwin," the man said, but the voice was smaller now, less in command than a moment ago.

"Do you understand me?" Darwin said again. "Do you even know who you're dealing with?"

"Yes. I do. Of course."

"Then put your men in helicopters, or airplanes, or jeeps, or however you do it. I don't care. And send them up to the site of that plane crash. Someone very important to me was on that plane. Elaine Sayles was on that plane. You know Elaine."

"Yes, I do, and I regret your loss."

"It isn't a loss yet! It isn't a loss because you're going to send men up there right this minute. And you're going to go up there with them and personally oversee this mission. Elaine might still be alive, and if she is, you're going to find her and help her and rescue her."

Darwin paused and took a breath. Elaine. She had been with him for so long, it was like there had never been a time when they weren't together. She was his kindred spirit. No one in this world understood him as completely as Elaine. The idea that she might be gone… It hurt. It was going to take a lot to get in touch with and process that loss.

But the anger... The anger was easy to process.

"The man who took her, I want him too. I want him dead. And I want his head, here, delivered to me, on a plate."

This was good. This was right. These were the correct instructions. Medieval people knew more than modern people about the way to do things, the way to fix things. The way to make this right was to have that man's head. Not figuratively, not as a metaphor for something else, but to have his actual, physical head here, cut off so Darwin could look upon his agonized face.

"Do you still understand?"

"Yes. Yes I do. And if the girl is there, and alive?"

Darwin shook his head. The girl was what had caused all this. Taking that girl had set these events in motion. Zorn. If Jeff Zorn hadn't owed him all that money, none of this would have happened.

"Darwin?" the voice said.

"Just kill her," Darwin said. "Get rid of the body. I never want to see her again."

"Yes," the voice said.

"Keep me informed of your progress," Darwin said.

"Of course."

Darwin hung up. He took a sip of his drink, then another. He stared out at the night for a long moment. Even the night was wrong. Usually, the lights on the grounds here were muted, and he could see the stars, and maybe the moon, and the way it played on the water far below.

Now there were bright lights on all over the property. Spotlights were constantly sweeping the dense foliage at the edge of the grounds. He could not see the stars, or the sea. It was awful.

He picked up the phone again. He took a deep breath. There were people in the real government, the American government, who he was never supposed to call. These were people who were too high up now, old friends who'd had to distance themselves. The vice president was one such person, but there were others.

Darwin knew what they thought of him. He wasn't a fool. They thought he was the dirty one, the sick one, the untouchable. They stayed away because he was the monster in the closet. But if that's what he was, what did that make them?

He was their past, and they knew it. He was the things they could not hide from themselves. He was what they saw when they looked in the mirror.

There were channels set up for him to communicate through. It was indirect, it was frustrating, but it worked. When he needed help, there was help available. There had to be. Sometimes, Darwin King was a crisis that had to be contained. He knew that about himself as well.

He called the operator and got an outside line. He dialed a number and waited while the call traveled.

A voice picked up, a man's voice. Had he been asleep?

"Hello."

"Do you know who this is?" Darwin said.

"Of course I know who it is. The phone tells me who it is. What can I do for you at this time of night?"

Darwin thought about it for several seconds. This call could be premature. Everyone on that plane might be dead. But then again, they might not. There were loose ends out there, and they might very well need to be snipped off.

No. It was the right time to make the call.

"I may have a problem," he said.

CHAPTER FORTY

Time Unknown
Location Unknown
Honduras

She was alive.

Charlotte opened her eyes. It was dark here, so dark that for a moment, there was no difference between having her eyes open or closed. She could not see details, but certain differences began to emerge.

Ahead and to her right, sparks began to shoot out of something. The colors were dazzling, in red and orange and yellow and blue, and when she blinked, they left swirling imprints on her retinas.

The sparks made a sizzling sound, like bacon and eggs cooking, which mixed with a light drumming sound happening above her head. It was a pattering, like someone tapping their fingers on a thick table. Within that sound, she heard another, the sound of water dripping somewhere. The two sounds came together to create an image in her mind. It was raining outside.

And that meant she was inside. She was inside the crashed airplane. She started, her body jolted by the memory of it.

A white light appeared, beyond where the sparks were shooting. The light swept around, moving from place to place on the floor. It was a flashlight, which meant there was a person attached to it.

"Hello?" she said.

"Charlotte?" a male voice said.

"Yes."

She was definitely Charlotte, if there had ever been any question.

The white light came closer, and a man materialized behind it. He was the man from before, the tall man who had rescued her.

"Luke?" she said.

"Yes. I'm Special Agent Luke Stone. I work for the FBI Special Response Team. There isn't going to be a quiz. I'm just reminding you so you know you're in good hands. Okay?"

"Okay."

"Are you hurt?" he said.

She shook her head gently. "I don't think so. I'm not sure. My head hurts a little, I guess. But other than that, I don't feel any pain."

She could barely see him behind the light. He seemed to be sweeping her body with it. "Good," he said. "But if you feel any pain, if anything sore gets worse, you have to tell me right away. Okay?"

She nodded. "Okay."

He held something out to her. "Take these."

She took them and held them up to the light. They were a pair of pretty green shoes, flats, almost like sneakers. Good for walking, probably. She remembered that her own feet were bare.

"Try those on," Luke said. "You'll probably need to undo your seat belt."

She looked at the shoes again. Green like the shoes Elaine had been wearing. Elaine wore green a lot. Charlotte had never seen Elaine wear anything but green.

"These are Elaine's shoes."

"Yes."

"Is Elaine…"

"Dead?" He nodded. "Yeah. She won't need the shoes anymore."

Charlotte didn't say anything. Her first instinct was: Good. That was good. But things were more complicated than that. Charlotte didn't wish anybody dead, not even someone as cruel as Elaine. The amount of people who had suddenly started dying was hard to accept.

They're dying because of me.

"It looks like she died in the crash," Luke said. "She didn't have a seatbelt on and got thrown around. They're not kidding when they tell you to wear your seatbelt."

"She was handcuffed," Charlotte said. "She couldn't fasten a seatbelt."

He had handcuffed her.

He nodded again. "I know. That happens. Play stupid games, win stupid prizes. Elaine played a lot of stupid games in her life. We're not going to worry about it right now."

"The pilot…" Charlotte said.

She could just picture him. He had given her his clothes. Well, Luke had made him, but he seemed cheerful enough about it. He had been flying the plane in his underwear.

"He's gone," Luke said. "The cockpit is totally gone, and he was in it. The plane came apart. We're lucky to be alive. Try those shoes on, will you? There are people coming up the hill toward us, and I don't think they're friendly. We need to get moving."

She reached down and slid a shoe on her right foot. She yanked it all the way on. It fit okay, a little bit snug.

"Where are we going to go?" she said.

"That's a good question," Luke said. "Anywhere but here."

* * *

"I don't see anything yet," Ed said.

He sat by the bay door, scanning the ground with binoculars. The chopper had a spotlight controlled by Rachel, and it moved to and fro in the darkness. It reminded Ed of a light flashing on a dark ocean.

It was raining now. The dense trees were swaying in the winds driving the rain. Downhill, well to their east, trucks had assembled in a clearing of some kind. More were rumbling up a zigzagging roadway over there. He could see their headlights breaking through the mists. Closer, smaller lights, probably flashlights held by men, were making their way up the hillside.

Troops were on the ground, and on the move, looking for the plane.

The chopper passed over an area where there were no trees. The ground was suddenly barren, chopped apart, the line between the jungle and the empty area straight enough to draw with a ruler.

"Clear cut below us," Jacob said. "Make a note of that. It could be a good place for an extraction point."

After less than a minute, they left the area behind and passed over dense jungle again. The chopper moved downhill, toward where the lights were coming uphill. It banked left, sweeping the treetops with its spotlight. Several moments went by, the light skimming the deep darkness.

"The troops down there are attempting radio contact," Rachel said. She was listening to something coming through her helmet speaker. "They are warning us in Spanish to identify ourselves or leave the area immediately. This is a restricted government area. If we do not identify ourselves, we will be shot down."

"Terrific," Ed said. "Ask them if they know a good restaur… Wait. I got something."

It was there. Something was right there, below them.

"Right under us. Put the light there."

It was the plane, or what was left of it. It was wrecked, and spread out over a wide area. His breath caught in his throat. It looked bad.

Trees were knocked over, sideways, broken apart, in a long line. After that, there was a depression, a gash in the earth, that seemed to lead into the forest.

"That has to be it."

"That's it," Rachel said. "That's a plane crash."

Ed was already up and moving. "I'm going in."

He dropped the rope over the side.

"Ed," Jacob said. "It's pretty dense down there. You drop through that canopy, you have no idea what you're going to hit."

Ed didn't have space in his mind for debate. He decided to keep it simple.

"I'm going," he said.

"We can drop you back at the clear-cut. At least you'll be able to see what's about to kill you."

"No time," Ed said. "I'd have to hike back over here. We don't have all night."

To their left, a light flashed in the distance. It came from the ground. Ed knew what it was instantly, without thought.

"Rocket," he said. "Incoming."

"I see it," Jacob said. His voice was completely calm. "Hold on. Taking evasive action."

The chopper banked hard now, to the right. Ed went to the floor, his fingers gripping the metal slats. From the corner of his eye, he saw the rocket zip past. It was a dumb weapon, no brain. Some guy threw the launcher up on his shoulder, took his best shot. And missed. Somewhere in the distance, the rocket exploded, the sound muffled by the rain and the distance.

The chopper leveled out again.

It came down the hillside, stopped, and hovered.

"We don't have a lot of time to hang around here," Jacob said.

"In other words," Rachel said. "If you're gonna go…"

"I'm gone," Ed said. He jumped up, checked his weapons, his water, his gear. He grabbed the heavy rope.

"Remember the clear-cut," Jacob said. "West and a little bit south."

"Got it. Thanks for the ride."

He didn't hesitate. Fast roping was not like jumping from a plane. Jumping from a plane, there was always that moment, that split second when… Jumping from a chopper was like over the falls, here we go.

He dropped through the darkness.

He crashed through the upper canopy. The branches were thick, sharp. He was tangled, they tore at him, ripped him. He plunged down through it, sliding along. His face was scratched. He turned his head away.

In the distance another missile launched. He saw the light flash through the trees. It was the only thing he could see.

That chopper needed to go. Whether he was on this rope or not, they were going to start moving.

He let go of the rope. The drop was sudden. His guts rose into his throat. He fell through the dark, hoping that it…

Boom. He hit the ground and rolled. Ten feet, he guessed. That last drop was only about ten feet. He lay on the ground.

The rope was gone, yanked upward and out of the forest. The helicopter zoomed away, its rotor chop disappearing into the distance. Somewhere over there, the rocket exploded.

Ed lay another few seconds, listening.

The chopper was out there somewhere, moving away. It was still up.

Ed climbed to his feet. He didn't take a break. He didn't stop to think. He just started moving down the hill. The embankment was steep, and the ground was soft. He was slipping and sliding, grabbing tree trunks to anchor himself. Below him, the flashlights were moving uphill. He could just see them now, their glow against the sky.

If the plane was where he thought it was, he and those lights were going to converge on it around the same time.

He started moving faster, plunging blindly downhill.

* * *

"Trouble coming," Luke said.

He was speaking to himself. He stood at the ragged, gaping hole where the cockpit had been, peering out into the darkness.

A helicopter had just passed overhead. A couple of rockets had been fired. Was it a firefight? He couldn't see enough of what had happened to tell. The chopper was well off in the distance now.

The lights in the forest below them were moving closer.

He had his MP5. He had four magazines. He had a couple of grenades left. A couple of knives. But he was one man. It wasn't enough. Not nearly enough. His shoulder was in bad shape. Soon he wouldn't be able to lift his left arm. And he could barely walk.

It seemed that he had done something to his ankle in the crash. He probably sprained it. It wasn't the level of pain he associated with a broken bone. But it was swelling, and it hurt a lot. It was hard to put weight on it.

He still had his pack. He should dig out a painkiller, but there was no time. They had to move. If they could put some real estate between themselves and those guys coming up the hill, he would stop and take a painkiller then. The men were looking for this plane, not any specific people. Once he and the girl were away from the plane a decent distance, they would be a lot harder to find.

He sighed. It was going to be a long, wet night out there, and the morning wasn't guaranteed to be any better.

"We need to go now," he said to Charlotte. She was standing behind him. He could feel her presence there.

"What if they're coming to rescue us?" she said.

He shook his head. "That would be nice. But in my experience, no one really comes to the rescue. You kind of have to do it on your own."

"You came to rescue me, didn't you?"

He looked back at her.

She looked at him. Then she looked past him. Suddenly she screamed.

There was something behind him. Luke turned, but it was going to be too late. He seemed to be moving in slow motion.

Oh no. Not like this.

A man was looming there, outside the plane, just a few feet away. A large black man in dark clothes. He was holding a machine gun.

"Stone," the man said. "I didn't even see you there. I nearly walked right into you. I'd say you blend in with the darkness pretty good."

Ed?

"Ed," he said. The sound came out almost like a gasp.

Ed nodded. "Who else? I dropped in here to rescue you guys. But we have to go. There are some soldiers coming up the hill. The first ones are almost here. We don't know what they want, but I don't want to stick around and find out."

Ed peered inside the plane.

"Where is everybody else? Buzz Mac?"

Luke shook his head. "Dead."

Ed made a sound. "Ah. That hurts. Bowles?"

"Also dead. He killed Buzz, then I killed him."

Ed looked at him. "He did what?"

"It's a long story, man."

Ed nodded. "We'll worry about it later. How are you guys? We have a bit of a hike ahead of us to the extraction point."

"The girl seems okay. I got shot in the shoulder. Did something to my ankle. It's hard to walk. I don't know. I'm not saying leave me behind, but…"

Ed looked past him.

"Are you Charlotte?"

"Yes."

Ed smiled. "It's a pleasure to meet you, darling. If you haven't noticed, a bunch of grown men are fighting over you."

Suddenly, voices were RIGHT THERE, down the hill, just below them. Flashlights moved in the near distance. Something had changed, something in the mists that had been muffling those voices shifted, and now they were here.

The soldiers were close.

Ed stepped inside the plane and leaned against the wall. He looked out into the darkness at the approaching lights.

"I'm going to lay down some covering fire," he said, very quietly. The gentle, almost sing-songy way he said it suggested he was speaking to the girl, not to Luke.

"And when I start shooting, you run straight out of here and across those woods, away from me. Get as far away from me as you can. Just run straight ahead, as straight as you can go. Don't worry about me. I will catch up."

Ed was already pointing the gun downhill.

"Are you ready?"

"Yes," Charlotte said. Her voice was barely above a whisper.

"I'm going to run, too," Luke said. "My ankle is bad."

Ed nodded. "On the count of three. Okay? One… Two…"

He crouched low in the ragged hole, making himself a smaller target.

"Three."

* * *

They were running through the jungle, staying low, moving fast.

Charlotte was holding hands with Luke Stone, who was running faster than her, pulling her along. He was grunting as he ran. Her own breaths were loud gasps. Her throat was raw from breathing so hard.

She slipped in the mud, fell, and slid along as he dragged her. She found her feet, one step, two step, and then was up and running again, right alongside him.

The big black man was behind them somewhere. Ed. His name was Ed. She couldn't turn to look. But she heard bursts of gunfire and flashes of light back there. The gunfire was very loud, angry blats, like farts. Her shoulders hunched every time it happened.

"Big gun! Get down! Get down!"

Luke pulled her to the ground. He dove and she fell after him, sliding through mud. Machine gun fire came from off to their left. The shots went flying just over their heads. She thought she could feel the wind from them. She didn't know if that was real.

Luke was crawling like a worm now. He dragged her behind him. She started crawling like he was, her face and belly pressed to the wet ground. Luke started moving faster and faster. Now she was crawling faster than she ever had in her life, faster than she ever thought was possible.

Her breaths came like: "Huh, huh, huh, huh, huh."

It was raining, and they were crawling through the rain. Above their heads, the wind was blowing, and the trees were swaying.

BOOOM!

A huge explosion erupted behind them. The noise was so loud, it was impossible. She screamed and covered her ears. Light turned night into day, for a long second, like a giant flashbulb popping. Images of trees, like people reaching to the skies, were imprinted on her eyes.

"Wait… Wait…"

BOOOM!

Another explosion.

Somewhere, men were screaming now.

Then Ed was there, crawling alongside them in the dark.

"That'll keep 'em for a minute," he said. "Let's go."

Luke yanked her to her feet. They were up and running again. She was stumbling along behind him now, gasping for breath, barreling through the darkness, the lights from the explosions still in her eyes.

Luke was limping as he ran. Every step he took, his body lurched to the left. He was running like a monster from a movie, or from a nightmare.

Ed was just ahead of them. He seemed to be screaming into his chest.

"Do you have my location? Beacon is on! Repeat: Infrared beacon is on. Approaching clear-cut, south and west of the crash site. Bringing out survivors. Need immediate extraction. Do you have my location?"

A voice crackled.

"Uh… roger that, Ed. We see you. Your location is very hot at this moment. They are right behind you."

"I'm in my location! I know how hot it is. Just get us out of here."

"Roger. Coming in. First pass is suppressing fire. Second pass is extraction. Cluster your people in a bunch around that infrared signal, and eat dirt for about sixty seconds. We'll try to miss you."

"Roger that," Ed said.

He leapt over the top of a ridge of dirt and disappeared on the other side. Charlotte and Luke were five steps behind him. They scrambled over the same ridge. It was a steep embankment. They fell and slid down to the bottom.

Ed was there, on his side.

"Wait here," he said. "Stay down."

Charlotte looked up. She could hear the sound of a helicopter approaching. A dark shadow was in the sky, moving fast, coming toward them. On the other side of the ridge, guns started firing. A missile went up, like a Fourth of July firework. Then another one went up.

A machine gun on board the helicopter started firing. The shots lit up the night, printing on her eyes again. They flew like Roman candles above her head, dozens of them.

The sound was metallic. DUH-DUH-DUH-DUH-DUH-DUH.

The helicopter whizzed by, right over them.

"Up!" Ed said. "Up! Let's go."

* * *

Luke lay in the ditch.

The girl was trying to pull him to his feet. They were a team now, he supposed. But getting to this point had hurt his ankle. A lot.

"You go. You can run faster than me. Stay with Ed."

Her eyes were wide and horrified. "What are you going to do?"

"I'm coming. Don't worry. I'm not going to stay here."

He shooed her away.

"Run!"

She gave him a last look, then was gone in the night. He worked his way to his feet, and bounced a bit on his good leg. He took a deep breath. Then he was running, in a crouch. Each step was pain. He kept going. If he made it, he was going to pay for this.

He reached the wide open clear cut and started across. This was the most dangerous part. He was a sitting duck out here.

It was hard to see his feet. He stumbled over a cut log. He lost his balance and fell. He scraped himself against cut and ruined wood.

"Unh-ah!"

He lay there for a few seconds, breathing deeply. The rain poured down on him.

He could hear the chopper. It had circled around and was coming in again, a dark shadow against the night.

Behind him, the shooting started again. Maybe he should just crawl the rest of the way. The chopper was coming down, dead ahead. Then he was up and running for it. He didn't remember climbing to his feet. He ran and ran, groaning with every step.

"Ah, ah, ah, ah…"

Gun shots fired from somewhere.

Please don't let them hit me!

The chopper was down. No, it was three or four feet above the ground. The ground was uneven, soaked, littered with junk. There was nowhere to land. The bay door was open. Bullets whined all around.

THUNK. THUNK. THUNK.

They were hitting the skin of the chopper.

He screamed.

He slid inside the door head first, like stealing home base.

The girl was here, and Ed was here, both on the floor. Ed was strapping the girl to the metal slats.

"Go!" Ed screamed. "All in! Go!"

The chopper lifted off.

Gunfire ripped into the side of it. A rocket flew, whistled, glanced off the metal.

BANG!

Then they were up and out, banking hard, zooming.

Luke lay there breathing, just breathing.

The gunfire was increasingly far away, nothing up here but rain and wind. Luke gripped the floor. The chopper was still banked. To his left, the dark jungle passed, well below them now.

After a long moment, the chopper leveled out.

"Welcome aboard," a female voice said. Rachel.

Ed lurched to his feet and pulled the bay door closed. He slumped in one of the seats and looked down at Luke, where he was still sprawled on the floor. It had been quite a night so far. Luke thought he might spend the rest of it right where he was.

"Hot," Ed said. "That was hot."

Luke nodded. He could hardly speak. "Hot."

Ed shook his head. "I said you were gonna want me with you. Right? When you left me behind on the plane, I said that?"

Luke didn't answer.

Ed turned to the girl now. Her name was Charlotte. That was her name. Maybe she would give an objective ruling on the situation.

"I told him, but did he listen?"

She looked at Luke, lying across from her. Luke looked back at her. She tried to suppress a sheepish smile, but couldn't. For a split second, her smile brought him a surge of images, memories, feelings. The images passed so fast he couldn't catch them all. High school football games. Backyard barbecues. A summer day on a lake somewhere.

In just that instant, she was a normal kid, an all-American girl. After everything that had happened, would she ever be a normal kid again?

"I doubt it," she said.

CHAPTER FORTY ONE

March 30, 2006
3:05 a.m. Eastern Standard Time
Dark Waters International, LLC
Boca Raton, Florida

Lie down with dogs, get up with fleas.

They called the man Max.

Max Impact. Max Resistance. Max Pressure.

It wasn't his name, or anything close to his name. Although he was American born and bred, his real last name was Zivojinovic, a Yugoslavian brick wall of a name that most Americans had trouble biting off and chewing on.

Nobody cared what his real name was. He didn't even care.

He was a brute, larger than the vast majority of men. And he was smarter, too. At least he thought so. His sense was that the urge people had to put him in charge of things was not because of his size, but because of his brains. He was a plumber, in a sense, and they had called him here because a pipe had sprung a leak.

"Here" was a nondescript brick building in a suburban office park, the headquarters of the private security contractor Dark Waters International. The logo on the building simply read DWI. It could be an insurance company.

He was sitting in an undecorated conference room, several people around the table with him. He recognized a few of them. One was a retired four-star general, down here in Florida most of the year because he liked to play golf. Another was an active duty major assigned to Central Command in Tampa. Tampa was four hours away by car. How the man had arrived here at something like a moment's notice was outside of Max's responsibility. Everyone in the room was dressed in civilian clothes.

There was a pot of lukewarm coffee on a narrow table along one wall. There were also sugar packets and a container of that fake powdered creamer that everyone hated, but people continued to insist on buying. There was a pile of napkins. There was a small coffee spill on the table, which no one had bothered to deploy the napkins against.

The coffee was swill. Max had already drunk two cups of it since he got here.

There was a black rectangular speakerphone device at the center of the conference table. Everyone stared at it. Max couldn't tell if they were staring in disbelief, or if they were staring at something anyone could have seen coming a mile away.

A voice squawked out of the box. "They left the country," it said.

Max had no trouble placing the voice. It was a man named Darwin King, a man who had become so well placed over the years that he had decided he was allowed to do anything he pleased.

He was a necessary evil, or maybe he was a friend, or maybe you owed him a favor, or maybe he had something on you. Whichever it was, and that depended on the individual, everyone had turned a blind eye to what he was doing. Worse than a blind eye, people had covered for him. They'd been doing it for so long, that what had once been damage control had long ago become policy.

"And who are they again?" a youthful middle-aged man at the table said. He was wearing a light blue dress shirt with the letters DWI over the left breast. He was awake, he was alert. He was clean shaven. His hair was perfect.

Max recognized the man, but he didn't care to search his own mental databanks to get the man's name or his position. He could very well be the CEO of Dark Waters International. One of these guys definitely was.

"I don't know who they are," Darwin said. "That isn't clear. Assassins, CIA agents, I have no idea. But they attacked my property here. They killed four of my personal bodyguards, as well as several Honduran military personnel who were assigned by that government to protect me. They kidnapped two of my guests, and also my pilot. They stole my airplane and crashed it into the jungle."

"And you think they're American operatives?"

"I KNOW they're American operatives," Darwin said.

Max nearly laughed. Darwin sounded drunk. He sounded overwrought and dramatic. He should be in a play on Broadway.

"I met one of them. He spoke English, like an American. The survivors of the plane crash met at least one other operative, were picked up by a helicopter, and went to a secret American airbase in the Rio Platano reserve, near the border with Nicaragua."

The major from CentCom raised a hand as if to say STOP. "Let's be clear," he said. "There is no American airbase in the area you describe."

"Whatever it is, whatever you want to call it, they went there. And from there they went to Jamaica. They left Jamaica in a private jet registered to an American company called Apex Digital Management. We know this is a front company for an American intelligence agency, but we don't know which one. They are flying on a heading that will bring them to the Washington, DC, area later tonight."

There was a long pause.

"There's a girl on the plane," Darwin said.

Max shook his head and smiled. Now they had arrived at the meat of the issue.

"She was reported missing about a week ago from North Carolina. I believe there's been a police investigation. She was with me. The lobbyist Miles Richmond was her grandfather."

Max eyed the speakerphone closely. They had gotten him out of bed for this. Miles Richmond was a name familiar to him. Last Max knew, Miles was an old duffer who was also alive and well.

"You say he *was* her grandfather?"

The retired general looked over at Max. "Miles Richmond was murdered earlier tonight."

Max smiled. "I guess someone's been having themselves a day, huh?"

"There's a lot here," Darwin said. "If I go down on this, they're going to want things from me. Not everyone in that room may know the scope of what's going on. But suffice to say there's a lot at stake, a lot that is jeopardized by this situation."

"A lot that you've jeopardized," Max said.

"A lot that I've made possible," the Darwin King voice squawked.

Max knew all about it. It was Max's job to know about things. There was a rebel group operating in the Darien Gap of Panama. The Darien was a lawless jungle, out of reach of the Panamanian government. For years, the rebels had allowed drug mules from Colombia to pass through their territory. Recently, for reasons not entirely clear, they had stopped doing that, and had refused to negotiate further.

So now they'd been labeled a terrorist organization. They had to go. A force of elite American soldiers from Joint Special Operations Command were going to go in there and clear them out. People in this very room stood to make money from this, a lot of money. Darwin had negotiated the terms of the payments with the cartels, and Colombian officials, and Panamanian officials. Drugs were big business. There was plenty of money for everyone.

And of course, it was important that the flow from South America, up through Central America into Mexico, and finally to the United States, remain impeded. That was practically a natural law. We had alphabet soup agencies whose mandate was to stop the flow. Meanwhile, we had other alphabet soup agencies who quietly guaranteed its safe passage. It was fun and games. No one knew what anyone else was doing.

No. That wasn't quite true. Some did. Max did.

He looked around the room at the faces gathered there. Max was done speaking to Darwin. Darwin was now beside the point. He was the child who had done the bad thing, and now it was up to the adults to fix it.

"What are we doing to mitigate?" Max said.

A man nodded. He was a sandy-haired, youngish guy in an open-throated dress shirt. He was unshaven, a bit bleary-eyed. Maybe they had gotten him out of bed, too.

"We're tracking the plane. We've got Navy fighters on patrol that are shadowing it. We haven't made contact yet, and they're ignoring our presence, but we assume they know we're there."

"Do we have any grounds to intercept the flight?" Max said.

"Plenty. They left an unregistered airfield in Honduras. They didn't submit a flight plan to the Honduran authorities. They changed planes in Jamaica at another unregistered airfield. They are not communicating with United States air traffic control. They appear to intend to unlawfully enter American airspace, and proceed to an unknown destination."

"Drug plane," Max said.

The man shrugged. "Could be. Drugs or other contraband. Human trafficking, in this case."

"Can we divert it?" Max said.

"Of course. What choice do they have? They can go where we instruct, or they can get shot down. The Navy pilots don't know any better. They're just doing their jobs. There's a mystery plane in the air that left Central America."

"Then I think that's what we do," Max said. He looked at the retired general. The general had a flattop haircut and hard eyes. He clearly kept himself fit. He looked irritated. This thing had probably messed with his 7 a.m. tee off.

"Divert it," the general said. "Somewhere we reliably control."

"Then what?" Max said.

"Max, you run the show," the general said. "We trust you implicitly. Take the girl back. Capture the agents, whoever they are. If they surrender without a fight, lock them up somewhere until they agree none of this ever happened. We'll bring some people in to talk to them. They'll understand. National security. That sort of thing. If we have to smooth out some rough waters later, we will. Could be an agency budgetary issue. Could be a couple of citations for bravery are in order. I don't know. Whatever it is, I'm sure it's fine."

"I'll need men and equipment," Max said. "I'll need an airport without much scrutiny, preferably one not that far from here. And I'll need a detention facility."

The man with the DWI shirt looked at him earnestly, eagerly. "This is Dark Waters," he said with pride. "I can get you all that stuff. We have all the men you need, highly trained combat vets, no nonsense, at a moment's notice. We have our own airport. We have armored vehicles, including a prisoner transport vehicle. We have a detention facility in Dania, unmarked, very secure, state of the art."

The man was making a sales pitch, as if any of that was necessary.

Max nodded. He had long ago given up wondering why private companies had all these things. The world had changed, and was continuing to do so. You could either change with it, or let it run you over.

But the man wasn't done with his pitch. "We already have existing blanket non-disclosure agreements with agencies represented in this room. We are, quite literally, the most capable and the most discreet security organization in South Florida, and we are available."

"Good," Max said. "You're hired. Just make sure everybody does what I tell them." He looked at the retired general. In the past few minutes, it had become clear that the general was the one in charge here. That hadn't been clear before, at least not to Max.

"What if they fight?"

The general shook his head. "Bring overwhelming force. They won't fight."

"What if they do?"

The general waved his hand, as if dismissing the entire idea.

"Just get rid of them."

CHAPTER FORTY TWO

4:35 a.m. Eastern Standard Time
Big Cypress International Airport (Abandoned)
Florida Everglades

"Should be just a few minutes now," the driver said.

Max took a drag on his cigar and nodded. The smoke wafted slowly into the air. He was tired. Four cups of coffee hadn't really put a dent in it. In the old days, he would have taken something a little stronger.

"Good," he said.

He gazed out at the darkness of the steamy deep Southern night. It must be close to a hundred percent humidity. This was not a quiet spot, not by a long shot. Somewhere nearby, there must be about a billion tiny frogs, peeping and cheeping.

An entire motorcade was parked here, in a line. There were fifteen vehicles, mostly armored SUVs, but also a couple of Jeeps, and one armored truck. All were black, with no markings of any kind. The guy from Dark Waters had put this all together very quickly, as if he'd had the whole thing on standby. Then he handed the team over to Max, no questions asked.

The guy was hungry. Max liked that.

The armored truck was a sort of paddy wagon, once used by the U.S. Marshals Service to transport prisoners. Apparently, it had been purchased by Dark Waters at auction, re-armored and retrofitted with the latest radar, GPS, and cloaking technology. It was still used to hold prisoners, but not your typical bank robbers or other felons.

The vehicles sat in the weeds along the edge of a gigantic, pitted and broken concrete runway at an old airport deep in the heart of the Everglades. The runway was two miles long. The entire airport was this runway and an empty control tower that squatted in the darkness about half a mile away. The runway and control tower were all that had ever existed.

They were going to have the old supersonic Concorde SST fly in here once upon a time. The plane was too loud to fly in and out of Miami, with the sonic boom from breaking the sound barrier, so they built this place out here in the swamp. Then the Concorde had a couple of high-profile disasters, and they decided to scrap the whole thing. So now this place just sat here. And Dark Waters had bought it, too.

Dark Waters International owned an airport.

It was a perfect place for an interdiction. It was a perfect place to take personnel into custody. It was a perfect place for a disappearance. If it came to that, it wasn't even a bad place for a shootout. The company owned hundreds of acres around here, and it was all closed to outsiders.

Max smiled.

If the police came here from Miami, or anywhere to the east, they'd have to find someone to remove the concrete barriers on the roadway and open the gate for them. This time of night? Good luck.

It was very unlikely the cops knew about the back entrance, across gravel roads, coming from the west. And it was very unlikely they'd come from that direction. Not much but vast wetlands, alligators, and Burmese pythons out that way.

Max sat up front in the shotgun seat of the lead vehicle, a Jeep. The driver was a crew-cut, stone-faced storm trooper type. Max liked no-nonsense types like this. The guy was certainly ex-military. He had probably seen combat. If Dark Waters had hired him, he'd probably been up to his neck in it at one time or another. Whatever happened out here, he probably wouldn't lose much sleep over it.

The driver had a laptop wedged between him and the steering wheel. The laptop itself was steel-plated, armored, and sealed inside of hard, pressurized, watertight plastic. You could drop that laptop to the bottom of a swimming pool. You could run it over with your car. You could throw it against a wall.

Max approved of the laptop. He liked things that were hard to break.

In the glow of the computer, the driver was watching a blinking light against a dark background. The blinking light had just moved inside a concentric circle at the center of the screen.

"It's coming in," he said.

"We sure that's the one?"

The driver nodded. "Its identifier is Apex Digital Management. That's it. That's our target."

Max picked up the communications radio handset from the dashboard and depressed the TALK button. The vehicles were on their own, closed and encrypted network channel. The radio would talk to every man on this mission, coming straight out of the stereo speakers.

"Listen up," he said. "This is Max. As you know, I am your commanding officer tonight. The plane is coming. Mission is green light. Here's your refresher course for slow learners. As soon as the plane is down and stopped, B team takes up positions blocking its further forward movement, with all guns trained on the cockpit. C team takes up positions blocking rearward movement, guns trained on tires, wings, and rear of the fuselage. Wait for my signal, and listen carefully. We are trying to avoid a bloodbath. A bloodbath is bad optics. We are also trying to avoid a circular firing squad. Remember that. The most likely order you will receive is to take out the tires."

He paused to let that sink in.

"A team, you're with me. We go in the door to the passenger compartment. Follow my lead. Bloodbath directive still applies, especially because I'm going to be standing in front of you. But also because we want the girl intact, if at all possible. We take her first, remove her to Car Number Four, rear seat, two men with her at all times. All other prisoners are cuffed, bagged, and removed to the wagon, but only after the girl is secure."

He took his finger off the TALK button.

"That seem clear?" he said to the driver.

The guy shrugged. "It's clear enough to me."

Max depressed the button again.

"We don't want a fight," he said. "But if they want one, we give it to them. First priority is the girl. Everything else is secondary. We've got about thirty guys out here tonight. As far as we know, they've got two men plus the pilots. Okay? It's a mismatch. So we go fast, hard, professional. We're going to close them out early. We won't give them an inch of wiggle room."

He put the radio back on the dash. Now, he could hear the engine of a jet plane approaching. In another moment, he saw the lights of the plane descending out of the sky. It came down, moving along the massive runway.

"Roll it," Max said, and the driver put the Jeep in gear. Now they were racing across the cracked concrete, a long line of vehicles, all of them moving fast.

The plane was just ahead, parked, waiting, its lights blinking in the deep darkness. It was sleek, a dark color, blue or black, with no obvious markings. The pilots had stopped it after taxiing a short distance. They had probably noticed that the runway was akin to the surface of the moon.

The Jeep pulled up about thirty yards from the passenger door. Max jumped onto the tarmac, pulling the pistol from his belt holster. To his left, black SUVs circled in front of the plane, facing it, taking a three-car wedge formation, blocking it from the front. Doors opened, and gunmen took positions behind them. To his right, more SUVs and another Jeep did the same. The paddy wagon was here in his group.

Men in black, helmeted, visors down, weapons out, ran to the passenger door. If a fight was coming, it was coming right now.

Max walked to the plane. He took his time. The men boarded the plane in seconds. The door was already open and the passenger stairs were down. Max jogged up the steps, ready for anything. He ducked through the low doorway.

The interior of the plane was set up like a living room, with plush leather chairs, something similar to a sofa, and a low coffee table mounted to the floor. A large, broad-shouldered black man sat on the sofa with a print copy of *The Wall Street Journal.* The pages were all over the place.

The man was as big as Max, or even bigger. He had a closely cropped beard. He wore a plain black, long-sleeved shirt, blue jeans, and a black baseball hat with SRT in white letters on it. Despite his sheer size, he didn't seem to have an ounce of fat on his body. He seemed relaxed, as if he'd had a pleasant flight.

He looked at Max. "Hi. Can I help you?"

"Who are you?" Max said.

The man shrugged. There were four Dark Waters troopers on here now, all with guns trained on him. It didn't seem to bother him at all.

"I'm Luther Sykes," he said. "Apex Digital Management. This is my plane. I think a better question would be, who are you?"

"Is anyone else here?" Max said.

"Just me and the pilot," the man said.

Max's back was to the door of the cockpit. There was another door behind the black man. Max gestured at it with his gun. "What's that door?"

The man shook his head and raised his eyebrows. "That? That's the bathroom. Uh, I left kind of a big one in there earlier. The water pressure on these planes leaves something to be desired, if you know what I mean. And I had a big salad for dinner. I don't think I'd go in there if I were you."

One of the men went over and kicked the door in. He looked back at Max.

"Nothing."

The door to the cockpit opened. A woman came out. She had flaming red hair.

"This plane is government property," the woman said. "It's owned and operated by the FBI Special Response Team."

Max gestured at the black man with his head. "He said he owns it."

"I told you who we are," the woman said. "And you are?" Her eyes were intense, angry.

"Never mind who we are."

"I want you to know something," she said. "It's an act of sedition for private entities to interfere with United States government business. I'd to see some identification."

Max shook his head. He would have smiled, but things were too serious for that. The girl didn't seem to be here. There was no fight, but there was also no girl. How could that be? They were going to have to take this plane apart, from top to bottom. They were going to have to take these two in and make them talk.

And that raised issues, a lot of issues.

"Lady…" Max began.

"We've radioed Washington, DC, as well as the Miami FBI field office," the black man said. He said it mildly and matter-of-factly, as if he didn't care one way or the other. He was just sharing information.

"We're expecting backup units to arrive any minute."

How? That was the question Max wanted to ask. There was no way in here. If the backup units were coming from the Miami office, they had a long drive ahead of them.

Just then, the plane itself started to shake. From outside came the heavy WHUMP WHUMP WHUMP of helicopter rotors.

"Oh," the woman said. She smiled. "That must be them now."

She went to the doorway and looked out. "Huh. Imagine that. They sent AH-64 Apache gunships. I forgot to mention we also have friends at Joint Special Operations Command."

She looked at Max. Max didn't like the confidence in her eyes.

"I think I'd have your guys drop their weapons, if I were you. Have you ever seen what one of those things can do to people on the ground? It isn't pretty."

Now her smile was ear to ear. "And there are three of them up there."

CHAPTER FORTY THREE

6:25 a.m. Eastern Standard Time
A Safe House
Annieville, South Carolina

"Are those really alligators?" the girl named Charlotte said.

Luke smiled, thinking of the time when Ed Newsam had said the same thing… when? Monday night. It was now Thursday morning. Monday could have been a month ago. Luke had been through the wringer since then. He was tired.

He glanced out the window. In the first weak light of day, a bunch of the gators were nestled in the mud on the far bank of the creek. If you didn't know any better, you might mistake them for logs that had washed up.

He nodded. "Yeah. They really are."

"Scary," Charlotte said.

Luke shook his head. The kid had been abducted and taken prisoner. She had been flown to another country. There were people out there who would kill her to protect the man who had done it. They had shot down an airplane and tried to murder her in the jungle. Yet alligators were the scary ones.

He had brought her here because it was all he could think of. He was out of gas. His shoulder was in serious pain, and although Ed had cleaned it out and bandaged it at the airbase in Honduras, it seemed like it might be infected. He was running a fever. And at this point, he could barely put any weight on his ankle at all.

Maybe he should have brought the girl to Washington. He didn't know. He didn't know who to trust at this point. Clearly, the SRT had been infiltrated by someone. Either a mole was working inside the organization, or the headquarters was infected with listening devices. Bowles was regular FBI, and had been sent to destroy the mission. He had nearly succeeded.

But he didn't, and they had gotten the girl out after all.

Jacob had flown them in the junker plane. He and Charlotte had simply stayed on the plane when they switched in Jamaica. Ed and

Rachel had made a big show of moving gear from one plane to the other, a lot of activity, in case anyone was watching. Jacob had hugged the ocean the entire way here to avoid radar. Luke hadn't told Jacob anything about where he was going or what his intentions were.

He just said, "Tell them where you dropped me off."

Now they were here. Luke looked at the girl. She was sitting on the same chair Louis Clare had once sat upon. She was wearing jeans and a gray sweatshirt a female National Guardsman had given her in Honduras. She was still wearing Elaine's green sneakers. The sneakers were utterly mud caked, and were now mostly brown and black, with a little bit of green showing underneath. The girl didn't seem to notice.

The barren kitchen surrounded her. There was nothing to eat. There was terrible stale coffee, and that was it.

Charlotte had slept on the plane, but she still looked exhausted. She seemed like she could barely keep her eyes open. She was a pretty girl, and smart. A survivor, maybe. She had survived this long.

Luke wanted to do the right thing for her, but he didn't know what that was.

At this moment, the right thing seemed to be waiting here to see who showed up. If they wanted to kill her, Luke would kill them first. If they wanted to help her, Luke would hand her over to them.

She was watching him, more than he was watching her. He was watching the windows and the doors, but he sensed her eyes on him.

"Thank you," she said quietly.

He glanced at her. She was staring at him.

"For saving me."

He shrugged. "It was my pleasure."

"Was it? Was it really a pleasure?"

"I don't know what it was, to be honest. I guess a lot of people died."

It was true. Luke hadn't tried to keep count, but there was a pile of corpses. Luke had killed a bunch of them on the island. Then there were the dogs, the pilot, Elaine, Buzz Mac. There was no telling how many men were killed in the jungle fight.

Now the girl began to cry. It wasn't much. Just a few tears running down her cheeks. "All because I went to a party."

Luke shook his head. "You shouldn't have done that, but that's not why it happened. It happened because some people are bad. That's not your fault."

She started to cry even harder. She put her face in her hands. Her body began to tremble.

He couldn't comfort her. He had no idea what kind of help this kid was going to need, but he wasn't it, not right now. He was spent. He didn't even know how much longer he was going to be able to stay awake. He almost couldn't keep his eyes open anymore.

He looked at the instant coffee packets again. He grunted. They were going to have to do. Brutal, stale, supermarket brand instant coffee. He practically needed to inject it straight into his veins.

Oh boy.

It occurred to him that Trudy had never gotten him the Dexedrine he asked for.

* * *

The man went by the name El Tigre.

It was a good name for a man like him. In the wild, the tiger was a professional killer. He hunted alone, at twilight, when the shadows made it hard to see. He moved under cover, camouflaged until it was too late for the other animals to save themselves.

El Tigre liked these associations.

He moved up the backwoods dirt road now, walking silently. He had left his car about a quarter mile back, pulled into a turnaround. There were no houses on this road, just one rundown shack on a creek, at the end.

But the road was not quiet, and that was good. Early morning birds called to each other. Somewhere, a woodpecker was hammering on a tree. Frogs called and insects buzzed in the swamps and in the overhead trees. In some trees there were so many insects, and they were so loud, it sounded like electricity was being generated.

All of these things were good. The sounds covered his movements.

The shack was just up ahead. He could see it now. It was an old wooden place with a rusted metal roof, no foundation, just raised up on stilts with a little space underneath. It looked like it didn't know which way to fall. There was a car parked in front of it, some generic sedan, like a rental car.

They had sent him there. Yes, he knew it was Darwin King who had sent him, but El Tigre never worked directly for Darwin. There was always a go-between, or more than one. They had flown him down from Washington, DC, landing just an hour ago. Private airstrip, no one around. An empty car waiting with a gun in the glove compartment.

This gun.

This silencer.

These bullets.

All just waiting for him.

The girl might be here, the same girl he had stolen just last week. Someone had stolen her back. Now the job was different.

"What would you like me to do?" he had said.

"You know what to do," the customer had said. Not Darwin King, because never Darwin King. The middleman. The arranger.

He shook his head. "No. I like it to be clear. I like you to say it."

"Eliminate her."

"Eliminate?"

The man nodded. "Yes."

"And then?" El Tigre said.

"There are alligators there."

El Tigre nodded. "Ah."

"If she's there, you might find a man with her."

"Okay," El Tigre said.

"Eliminate him too."

Now, in the dim light of morning, he moved toward the house. The gun was out, in his right hand, the silencer already mounted. He moved cautiously, taking careful steps, completely silent. He went up the stairs to the porch, stepping gingerly, testing each board first.

The house was quiet. The car outside said someone was here. The silence said otherwise.

Maybe they were asleep.

He moved along the porch and came to the door. He glanced inside. The door opened to a threadbare kitchen. From here, he could see a small refrigerator, a table and a chair. He put his hand on the doorknob and very slowly, he turned it. It was unlocked.

That was lucky. Very good fortune.

He took a deep breath and pushed it slowly open. He went through the doorway, careful not to make the slightest sound. Even his breathing was silent. Now he was inside. He could see the rest of the kitchen now. It took a second to absorb the scene.

There was a pot of water on the stove, and the water was boiling. There was a mug with some kind of tea bag, or coffee bag in it. There were a handful of sugar packets.

Someone was definitely here, had in fact been in this kitchen only a…

A gun was at his head, behind him.

"Move at all and I'll kill you," a male voice said.

El Tigre did not move.

"Now drop that gun."

He did as he was told. The gun made a loud thunk when it hit the kitchen floor.

Without warning, the man hit him in the back of the head. The impact was vicious, nauseating. Instantly, El Tigre knew what it was.

He'd been hit with a gun. A pistol whipping was coming.

The man hit him again.

And again.

Each blow was a blast of pain and blinding light. His legs became weak. He reached to grip something to hold himself up, but there was nothing.

He was hit again. His vision went black.

When he opened his eyes, he was on his back, looking up. His first thought was that he was dizzy and might vomit. His second thought was:

My gun!

He had dropped it here on the floor somewhere. It might still…

The man appeared, standing over him. There was no sense looking for the gun because the man was holding it. The man was tall, and broad, and had short blond hair. His eyes said he was very, very tired. His eyes also said he had killed before, and wouldn't mind doing it again.

"That's quite a scar on your face," the man said. "Tell me something. Does anyone ever call you El Tigre?"

CHAPTER FORTY FOUR

12:25 p.m. Eastern Standard Time
The Long Trail Tavern
Providence, Rhode Island

"Don't you guys have anything better to do?"

Eddie Alvarez was putting up pint glasses above the bar. He had worked here so long, even he couldn't remember when he started. Two regulars had just come in and sat down at the far end of the bar.

The Long Trail didn't serve food, other than little bags of potato chips, potato skins, and hot fries. There was no trail nearby. Technically, the place didn't open until two o'clock. The owner, Steve, didn't like people coming in much before then.

Steve didn't want to admit what everyone else already knew, which was that the Long Trail was a place where alcoholics came to drink cheap alcohol. That would make Steve complicit in people drinking themselves to death, and since he had gotten rich owning this dump, he wanted to be above reproach.

Steve would say, "I don't want a bunch of drunks coming in here at twelve-oh-one because they think that qualifies as waiting until lunch."

So Eddie didn't let people in at 12:01. But that was as far as it went.

He sighed. Customers were already here, so he turned on the TV behind the bar. He clicked around until he found a cable news station. In a little while, there would be a baseball game from somewhere. There always was.

A pretty, middle-aged woman with dark hair, some impossible to decipher mixed race, was reading the news. If Eddie looked closely, he felt that he would be able to spot the area under her chin where she'd had a bit of a tuck, or the way her skin seemed artificially smoothed out under her eyes, where there would normally be crow's feet, or the area on either side of her mouth.

He shook his head. What did it matter?

"Today, multiple federal agencies, and the United States Army Special Forces, in partnership with the Honduran Air Force and Navy, staged an early morning raid on an island off the coast of Honduras owned by mysterious billionaire Darwin King. King was present on the island, and was arrested in connection with human trafficking allegations stemming from numerous abduction cases in Florida, North Carolina, and New York City. He was also wanted in connection with the murder of the lobbyist Miles Richmond, who was found shot and killed in the underground parking lot of his firm in Washington, DC. At least half a dozen minors were rescued from Darwin King's island during the operation. Their names and genders are being protected for their safety.

"The Honduran president, Salvador Ruiz-Campo, issued a statement denying any previous knowledge of King's presence in Honduras. His spokesman said the government of Honduras was shocked to discover that an international criminal like King was living just off their coast, and the Honduran military was proud to play a role in his apprehension. He went on to say that all foreign nationals would now be subject to increased scrutiny, to determine if any other illegal activities were being carried out in Honduran territory. More as this case unfolds."

The woman stared directly into the TV screen. Eddie had seen that look before, about a million times. She was scanning the teleprompter, preparing herself for where the next story was going.

"In other news, United States House of Representatives Minority Leader William Ryan was released from the hospital this morning after being admitted overnight for observation. Ryan was the victim of a violent mugging attempt last night near the Lincoln Memorial. Gun rights activists are holding Ryan up as an example of the benefits of carrying a concealed weapon for self-defense. Some have begun to refer to him as 'Billy the Kid.' Ryan fired warning shots at his attackers, which led them to flee the scene. Gun control proponents are calling for an investigation into whether Ryan has ever carried a gun into House chambers. Upon leaving the hospital, Ryan joked to reporters that he would be back at work in a couple of days, and ready to settle some scores."

Eddie Alvarez smiled at that. He carried a gun, on nights when he worked the late shift. He gazed out the window for a moment, at the early afternoon. There were a few old scores he wouldn't mind settling himself.

Of course, a big-time politician would have an easier time doing that than he would. Those people could get away with murder.

CHAPTER FORTY FIVE

April 7, 2006
2:10 a.m. Eastern Daylight Time
United States Federal Detention Center
Atlanta, Georgia

"Guard!" Darwin King shouted. "Guard!"

It was late at night, and he was alone as always. They had put him in the most dismal dungeon, in the worst, oldest, most dysfunctional part of an aging decrepit prison left over from the nineteenth century.

He had to get out of here. It was cold. Moisture formed on the walls from condensation. Sometimes late at night, like now, the condensation formed a thin sheen of ice. There was a problem with his toilet. Water leaked from under it, making a tiny river across the stone floor.

He looked at it now. The metal toilet. It had a water faucet at the top of it, an odd combination. Everything else was made of stone, and in a fixed location. A narrow stone desk extended from the cinderblock wall, with a rounded stone stool like a small peg coming out of the floor in front of it.

Like the desk, the bed was narrow and made of stone. A thin mattress covered it and there was one green blanket made of wool serge, or some equally itchy material. There was a narrow window in the far wall, framed in green, perhaps two feet tall and six inches wide. It was always dark outside that window, except for a sickly yellow light that streamed into the cell from a nearby sodium arc lamp mounted on the outside wall. There was no way to cover the window.

They had put him here to punish him, to drive him insane. And it was working. There was no way a man accustomed to the finer things in life, not just to comfort but to opulence and splendor, should be forced to endure this.

"Guard!" he screamed.

Worst of all, he was the only one here. As far as he could tell, there were no other prisoners on this hall, and possibly none on this floor of the building. He might be the only prisoner in this entire falling down, disgrace of a wing. This place should be condemned. In a sense, it already was. Everybody was gone, except for him and the two guards that were always on duty.

They were supposed to be responsive. They were supposed to come when he called. At the very least, they were supposed to check on him once in a while to see if he was still alive.

He had to get out of here. He had to go anywhere but here. It was claustrophobic. It was terrifying.

His lawyers had asked for $20 million bail. It seemed a reasonable request. Who would run away leaving that much money on the table? Denied. No bail. Darwin King was deemed too much of a flight risk.

Privately, he had offered them everything he knew, if they would just get him out of here. Just put him in a modern facility where there were some people around. Was that so hard?

He had offered them gold. Who had done what, where all the bodies were buried. He had been around a long time, and he had amassed a tremendous amount of dirt on a lot of powerful people. If he started to talk…

And that was just it, wasn't it?

Powerful people didn't want him to talk, did they?

"GUARD!" he shrieked now.

Where were the damn guards?

* * *

The man was a ghost.

He wore the uniform of the federal prison system. He had a gun he didn't need. He had a nightstick—not sure whether he would need that. Probably not. He had a flashlight, keys, and codes. He had pepper spray and a Taser. He wore big black shoes that were comfortable for walking, and that wouldn't slip on hard surfaces.

The funniest part? The patch on his left breast said Brown.

It was a name that was not a name, for someone who had long ago disappeared. He wore a flat top haircut. He was big and strong, and had sharp features. He kept himself very fit. Like a laser beam, he liked to think of it. Like a rocket ship.

Once, he had a name. As time passed, his name had changed. At this point, he'd gone by enough names that he couldn't remember them all. This latest was his favorite, and he planned to keep it for a while. Brown. He introduced himself that way, if such niceties were necessary. Mr. Brown. He liked it. It made him think of dead things. Dead leaves in wintertime, especially. Burned out buildings with the people still inside.

They had let him right through security as if he worked here. They had waved as if they knew him. The real guards were gone. They had taken a powder. The man had no idea where they had gone, or what they knew. He had no idea what their cover story was going to be. It didn't matter. For now, they weren't here.

The cameras down here were off. That was what was promised, and he believed it. When someone told him the cameras would be off, invariably they were. Just another mystery for the newspapers and the blue ribbon investigation panels to puzzle out. Why were the cameras off? For Brown, the important point was they said the cameras would be off, and so they were off.

Who were *they*? Even he wasn't sure anymore. At one time, he had been a Navy SEAL, highly trained, highly in demand. Later, he had been on loan to the Joint Special Operations Command, and even later, the CIA. Now? Who knew? He was working for *them*. And *they* were paying him.

They were the people who contacted him, gave him his instructions, and gave him his money. The money, and it was good money, always came in cash. That's how he wanted it, and that's how it came. In this case, it was in a large canvas Adidas bag, like a professional basketball player might be seen entering the bowels of the stadium carrying over his shoulder. The bag had been in the trunk of a car parked in the lot of a busy suburban mall.

Tricky, that. The key to the car had come in the mail, no return address. A real key that you put into a slot, not one of those fancy modern clickers. You never knew what might happen when you slipped a key into a lock and turned it.

So he'd had Mr. Clean do that instead. And it worked like a charm. The car didn't explode. The bag was in the trunk. The money was in the bag. And Mr. Clean was here with him now.

Mr. Clean was also wearing the uniform of a federal corrections officer. Clean was a young guy from a similar background to Brown. Former SEAL, big, good worker, very tough, no fear. Also smart, and good with new technology.

Right now, the technology Clean was carrying was a sheet from the prison laundry. Clean had that name because he suffered from early onset male pattern baldness. Not a good look, so he shaved his head instead. He resembled the cartoon muscle man from the old cleaning product TV commercials more or less perfectly.

Brown glanced at Clean now. Clean was wearing black leather driving gloves. That was good. He looked at the name on Clean's left breast. *Jones.* It would have been funnier if it said *Clean.*

Footfalls echoed on the stone floor as the two men passed the closed, windowless steel doors of empty cells. Each cell door had a narrow opening near the bottom, like a mail slot, through which the guards could shove meals to the prisoners. But there were no prisoners. There didn't seem to be anyone down here.

"This place is the pits," Mr. Clean said.

Brown nodded. "Yeah." It was like being in a tunnel deep beneath the surface of the Earth. There was an old joke that Brown liked.

"Did they put him in jail? No. They put him *under* the jail." This place was that joke come to life.

Somewhere on this hallway, just up ahead, a man was screaming. It sounded like agony. It went on and on, no sign of ending, becoming increasingly loud and desperate in tone as they approached it.

"Guard! Guard! GUARD!"

Brown and Clean walked a bit further and came to a stop in front of a door, one among many. Clean slid a large key into the lock. The tumblers echoed in the deep stillness. The door was on some kind of slider—rollers, in all likelihood. As the door slid away, a tiny, dismal cell was revealed.

The prisoner stood in an orange jumpsuit, facing them. He was tall and had white hair, peppered with a bit of brown or black. He had a big jaw. A person would say he was very handsome, could have probably been a model in magazines when he was younger. Marlboro man, that kind of thing.

He could use a shave, though, and his eyes seemed deep set and hollowed out. There were dark rings beneath them. The poor man hadn't been sleeping well. In these surroundings, who could blame him?

"Hello, Darwin," Brown said. "How are you tonight? Are you ready?"

"You're not my normal guards," Darwin King said.

Brown shook his head. "No."

Darwin's eyes flitted to the sheet in Mr. Clean's hands. Those eyes then came back to Brown's. Darwin looked like he was about to cry. His chest heaved as if he couldn't get a full breath. Brown didn't feel anything about this at all.

"Who are you?"

"Isn't it obvious? We're the cleaning crew."

"I have money," Darwin said. "A lot of money. I can get it to you."

Brown shook his head sadly. “We’ve already been paid. The people who paid us frown on double-dipping. I think you probably understand.”

Clean moved into the cell with the sheet.

Darwin King’s body tensed as if he was getting ready to resist.

Brown nearly laughed.

“You can make this hard or easy,” Clean said. “On yourself. Whatever you decide, you won’t move the needle for us an inch in either direction.”

Darwin King’s eyes were wide.

“If I were you,” Mr. Brown said to those big frightened deer eyes, “I think I’d just try to relax. I’m not going to say that it won’t hurt. It will. But look at the bright side.”

He glanced around at Darwin King’s dreary surroundings. The man, once so rich, so prominent, so high-flying, was living in a medieval dungeon.

“This will all be over soon.”

CHAPTER FORTY SIX

4:05 a.m. Eastern Daylight Time
Pine Valley
Wilmington, North Carolina

Charlotte woke with a start.

It was dark in her room, the darkest time of night. She had been dreaming, something horrible, but she couldn't remember what it was.

She sat up in bed. Okay. Okay. It wasn't that bad, the darkness. The door was open, and there was a light on in the hallway. She hadn't slept with a light on since she was a little girl. Now she couldn't sleep without one. She could barely sleep at all.

Everything was different now. *Everything.*

They had given her a physical exam that was more intrusive than being kidnapped. She didn't like to think about that, and could mostly block it out of her memory.

They would ask her a million questions over and over, and then a new person would come in, and ask her the same questions again. Sometimes they did her the favor of phrasing the questions a little bit differently, just to keep things interesting. Or maybe it was to catch her lying. Who knew why they did what they did?

It went like this:

Yes, she had been attacked on the beach with Rob Haskins.

Yes, they were drunk at the time.

No, she had no idea who attacked them.

Yes, she had gone to an island where Darwin King lived. Yes, she had been taken there by airplane, against her will. Yes, they had drugged her during the trip. She couldn't remember much of it.

Yes, that was a photo of Darwin.

Yes, a woman named Elaine was there. Yes, that was a photo of her.

Yes, Darwin and Elaine held her captive on the island, inside an old mansion. No, she was not free to leave. They kept her locked in a dark room most of the time.

Yes, there were men with guns there. Wherever she went in the house, at least one man with a gun escorted her. Most of the men were foreigners and did not seem to speak English.

No, no one raped her. No, no one had sex with her.

No, she had never had sex before, not with Rob Haskins, not with Darwin King, not with anyone.

Yes, she had seen several people get killed. She wasn't sure how many.

Yes, the FBI agent named Luke Stone had rescued her. Yes, he had killed several people. Yes, that was a photo of him.

No, her mother's boyfriend Jeff had never touched her. Jeff had lived with them for a long time, but had barely even interacted with her, and showed no interest in her at all.

Yes, she knew that Jeff was dead. Yes, she knew he had killed himself. No, she had no idea why.

Yes, she knew her grandfather was dead.

That last one always hit her so hard, it ended whatever interview they were having. She couldn't answer that one without breaking down. Then she couldn't answer another one. She didn't want to answer another question, ever again.

She sat now, staring straight ahead in the dim light. Her bedroom was here, with all the things she used to like. There was a Britney Spears poster on one wall. *Oops, I did it again.* There was a David Beckham poster opposite Britney. He was wearing small blue shorts and no shirt and was kicking a soccer ball. She used to think how the two of them would make a nice couple.

There was a brown teddy bear on the bed with her that she'd had for a long time. Her father had given it to her to remember him by. She was careful with that teddy bear, and always kept it safe and perfect.

Her cheerleading uniform was still hanging on the closet door, right where she'd left it. Her computer was on her small desk in the corner. She had Hoggard High School pens and pencils. She had a Hello Kitty notepad. The desk was neat, everything lined up, the way she liked to keep things.

Jeff is dead. Pop Pop is dead.

Her bedroom was meaningless. It might as well be empty.

All those other people were dead, too. Elaine, who was so cruel to her for no reason, was dead. The pilot who had flown the plane was dead. Those bodyguards who came upstairs when the shooting started were dead. Soldiers in the jungle were dead. Other men who she had heard mentioned were dead.

All of these people were dead because of her. She had snuck out of the house, like she did sometimes, and all of the people had died.

She couldn't have known that was going to happen.

She was seeing a therapist every day. It was a woman therapist, who was older, and who wore glasses. Her name was Dr. Patricia Kelly. Charlotte would go into her office. Her mom would sit out in the waiting room

"You can call me Pat if you want," the therapist would say.

Charlotte didn't want to call her anything. She was nice, but she asked strange questions, too.

Was Charlotte feeling guilty? She didn't know.

Did she want to go back to school? No, she never, ever wanted to go back to school.

Why didn't she want to go to school? Because the kids there would think differently about her. They would think something bad happened to her. They would think it was her fault. They would believe all kinds of rumors.

Did it matter what the other kids thought? What kind of question was this? Of course it mattered. Did it matter if the world stopped turning?

Did she feel like she might be happier right now if she stayed in a hospital for a little while? Not really a hospital, just a place where people could watch her carefully and make sure she was safe and okay. No. She didn't feel like she would be happier in a loony bin, but thanks for offering.

Did she ever think about Darwin King? No. She never thought about him. She knew he was being held in prison, but that was it. She wasn't interested in him, and didn't care what happened to him at all.

That part was a lie. She just said it because she thought that was what the woman wanted to hear. The truth was Charlotte thought about Darwin all the time. It was strange, but she almost hoped that he would get free somehow, that the judge would find him not guilty, or that he would escape.

She pictured him in her mind. It was almost like he was in the room with her.

He was old, but he was also handsome in his way. He had probably been very handsome when he was younger. He was tall. He had blue eyes that she would never forget.

He had stolen her, but he had not hurt her. He could have, but he didn't. He didn't let anyone else hurt her, either.

He lived in a beautiful house, in a beautiful place.

He had chosen her to be there.

He had told her that she was beautiful.

He had told her that he loved her.

It confused her, the feelings she had about this. Yesterday, or maybe the day before (she was losing track of time), she had looked up a question on the internet.

Can you fall in love with the man who kidnapped you?

It turned out there was a condition some people got when they were kidnapped. They came to identify with the kidnappers. For some vulnerable people, young people, it could happen right away. They could come to believe that the kidnappers were in the right, and it was the rest of the world who was wrong. The condition even had a name.

"Stockholm syndrome," she said out loud.

It was okay, though. The feeling often went away over time, all by itself. She didn't have to do anything except recognize what it was. She could do that. She was a survivor, after all. She had survived her parents' divorce, and she had survived her father's death. Darwin King would rot in jail, and she would survive this, all of it.

"Did you say something, hon?" a voice said. "I thought I heard you call out."

Charlotte looked up.

Her mom was in the doorway. Her body blocked out some of the light from the hall. Her hair was tousled. Her eyes were puffy, as though she had been crying. Her shadow reached deep into the bedroom. Her mom wasn't sleeping these days, either.

God, she had missed her mother so much.

She had a flashback to when she was young, a little girl. She had loved her mother so much, so intensely, that it was impossible to describe the feeling. That feeling had faded over time, but she remembered it now.

As Charlotte watched, her mom came across the room and climbed onto the bed with her. Her mom hugged her, and they lay down together. Within a minute, she felt her mom's body shaking as she cried silently, her face in the pillow.

Charlotte hugged her mom even tighter. She felt a lump well up in her throat, but she would not cry. She had to be strong for both of them, she and her mother, and she would be strong.

"I said it's good to be home, Mom."

CHAPTER FORTY SEVEN

6:05 a.m. Eastern Daylight Time
Fairfax County, Virginia
Suburbs of Washington, DC

"What is this nightmare world?"

Luke and Megan Rose Abbott, the missing girl from his childhood, were sitting on the floor, facing each other. They were in a bright white room. The room was stark, nothing in it. The floor was carpeted in white. The walls were white. There were no doors or windows. The light was coming from somewhere, but it was impossible to say where. She watched him closely, but didn't answer.

"What is this nightmare world?" he said again.

Somewhere nearby, a siren began to howl.

Megan's eyes were blue, pale blue, bluer than any eyes had ever been since the dawn of time. They were also sad eyes.

"You're a good man," she said. "And a brave man. That's enough. It has to be."

"Okay," he almost said, but before he could speak, she began to evaporate in front of his eyes.

"I'm going to go now," she said. Soon, she was like a soft mist on a lake at dawn. Then she was gone.

The siren grew louder and louder.

Luke snapped awake.

The baby was crying.

Next to him on the table, in the dark of their bedroom, was a digital clock. He glanced at its red numbers.

6:07.

He took a deep breath. He couldn't fall asleep last night. There was too much on his mind. He had dozed off for an hour, maybe an hour and a half. It hadn't done him much good. If anything, it had made things worse. The clocks had changed last weekend. Spring ahead, so he'd lost another hour. That hadn't helped any, either. Luke had been stumbling around, half-awake, like a zombie, since he came back from Honduras.

A tuft of Rebecca's hair poked out from under the blankets. Soft blue light filtered into the room from a night light in the bathroom. Her voice came from under the covers, thick with sleep.

"Can you get Gunner? I got him last time."

That was true. Truer words were never spoken. She got him last time.

He nodded. "Yeah."

It was fair. It was normal. Becca was under the impression that Luke had gotten hurt when he and Ed wrestled a gun away and subdued a suspect while they were in Florida. That could happen to a normal husband who happened to work for the FBI. If she suspected anything more, she wasn't saying.

Luke stood and padded slowly across to the crib. Gunner was down in there, wide awake, his eyes the size of silver dollars, his mouth turned down, his face a grimace of anguish, existential horror, hunger, every bad thing. Terrible. Just terrible.

Luke picked him up, mostly using his right arm. His left shoulder was healing, coming along nicely according to the doctor, but Luke still wasn't getting much use out of it. The range of motion was not good. Lifting heavy stuff was out.

But he could use the hand. That part still worked. He ran that free hand over the kid's bottom. Nothing there. The diaper didn't need to be changed. Thank the Lord for small miracles.

"Bottles are in the fridge," Becca said. "Use the oldest one first."

Luke nodded. "Yep." She had it all organized, under control. The bottles were labeled with white surgical tape. Date and time. Use the oldest ones first. There was a system in place, it was simple and easy to follow. Even a butterfingers like Luke Stone could handle it.

He carried Gunner in one arm out of the bedroom and down the hall to the kitchen. He moved slowly, walking gingerly on his wrapped ankle. It was healing too, but it was taking its sweet time.

The kid knew what was coming and had already let up on the crying, if only just a little. Luke opened the fridge. Top shelf, there was a bottle right there, the first soldier in line. *4/12. 3:45 p.m.* Getting old. The one behind it was 7:15 p.m.

Luke glanced across the open counter and into the darkened dining room. The table was cluttered with plates and bowls left over from dinner. There was an empty bottle of beer where Luke had been sitting. You couldn't control everything. Sometimes even the best systems failed.

He went into the living room, bottle in hand, baby on his arm. He was ready for action. He plopped down on the couch.

He gave Gunner the bottle. The boy made a new face. He did something you'd almost say was shaking his head.

"Cold, huh? I know, but it's the best you're going to get right now."

Gunner realized that. He drank.

Luke glanced around at the house. They could have a great life here. It was a beautiful home, modern, with floor to ceiling windows, like something out of an architectural magazine. It was like a glass box.

God, it was nice. Between this place, and the cabin out on the Eastern Shore, could you really ask for a nicer lifestyle?

He could never afford this place on his salary. He knew that. Becca's family money had bought the house. In fact, her parents had simply given it to them. It said a lot, a lot he'd prefer not to think about.

What was he doing? What was he exposing himself to, and why?

He thought of Buzz MacDonald again. The man was dead. A seventy-two-year-old man had been murdered, possibly because Luke had made a bad decision. If Ed had been with them on that island, maybe Bowles…

"You can't know that," Don Morris had told him. "You can't know how it would have played out. You thought Ed was on a hair trigger, you thought he was putting his and your lives at risk. Maybe you were right, did you ever think of that? Maybe if Newsam was with you, you're both dead now. You got the girl out, the other girls got rescued, and Darwin King is where he belongs. That's what matters."

Don must have seen that Luke was not convinced.

"Here's the other thing. Buzz Mac died doing what he wanted to do. They had to kick him out of special operations because he was too old, and he didn't want to leave. The guy lived on the edge. That's where he wanted to be, riding that edge with guys like you, guys less than half his age. As much as it hurts, this was long overdue. He should have died thirty years ago."

Okay. Okay. Maybe Luke could buy that.

Maybe.

He didn't want to think about it anymore. He picked up the TV remote control, hit the green button. The big flat-screen TV came on across the room, the sound on low. It was the news. Wasn't it always?

Words across the bottom of the screen, in capital letters:

DARWIN KING DIES IN JAIL.

"Now for breaking news," the reporter said. He was a square-jawed, blond-haired man of indeterminate age. "Billionaire Darwin King was found dead of an apparent suicide in his cell at a federal holding facility in Atlanta this morning. He was discovered by a guard making a routine welfare check at approximately four a.m. local time. Initial reports indicate that he used a bed sheet to hang himself. King was under arrest in connection with multiple sex trafficking cases, and the murder of a lobbyist in Washington, DC. His death raises more questions than it answers, and even at this early hour, some lawmakers are calling for a congressional inquiry."

Luke shut it off. It was too much.

The world was too much. Maybe death was a punishment. Or maybe the real punishment would have been a long prison sentence. It was possible that Darwin King had walked off scot-free again. Luke couldn't decide. He was too tired.

He glanced at Gunner. The boy had annihilated the bottle of milk and was already sound asleep. That was a good way to be.

Luke lay back on the couch, the boy on his chest. He closed his eyes and allowed himself to drift.

The phone rang.

He looked at it. It was his cell phone. He had left it in here, on the coffee table, so it wouldn't disturb anyone's sleep. The ringer was off, but the vibrate mode was on. It made an annoying buzzing sound as it skittered slowly across the table.

He picked it up. Why not?

"Hello?"

"Luke? It's Ed Newsam. Did I wake you?"

Luke shook his head and answered honestly. "No.

"Good, man. That's good."

Things were still tense. They had promised each other they would work out the differences between them, but it hadn't happened yet. It was going to be a process. Luke didn't know when it would happen. He was on medical leave, recovering from his injuries. Meanwhile Don had given Ed some personal time off, to get his head together, and because…

The baby was coming.

"Ed…" Luke said.

Ed's voice was shaking. "Yeah, man. I wanted to tell you. It just happened thirty minutes ago. I was going to wait until a decent hour, but…"

Luke was silent for a long beat. He didn't say a word.

"It's a girl. A healthy baby girl."

CHAPTER FORTY EIGHT

7:45 a.m. Eastern Standard Time
Lincoln Memorial Reflecting Pool
The National Mall
Washington, DC

"I come here a lot," Bill Ryan said.

Don Morris walked on the gigantic mall between the Lincoln Memorial and the Washington Monument with his former classmate and longtime… friend? Don supposed he would call Bill a friend.

They had drifted apart for many years, to be sure. Don had been off fighting America's wars, and Bill had been here, doing that cloak-and-dagger thing that these politicians did. Now that Don was in DC, he found himself pulled more and more into their orbit. If the Special Response Team was Don's baby, and it was, then politics was how he kept that little baby alive.

It was a chilly morning, and people moved quickly to and fro in long coats, on their way to work.

Don glanced at Bill. Bill's face was healing. There was little evidence of the bruises left from the savage beating he had taken here less than ten days ago. It was clear that he was using makeup to cover up some of the damage, but Bill had already been back to work for the past week. He was a tough customer.

"I wanted to meet you here, Don, in this place. Because I want you to feel what I'm feeling, and know what's in my heart. These are the two greatest Americans. Both men were in a fight for the soul, for the very existence, of this country."

Bill's eyes searched Don's.

"And so are we."

That was nice, but Don wasn't ready for that kind of talk just yet.

"I appreciate that," he said. "But I have more practical issues in front of me. Miles Richmond is dead. This mission was done as a favor to him, and he made a promise to me before he died, one that he can no longer keep. The mission was a success, but a lot of people died. A good friend of mine died. And now I'm exposed rather badly."

Bill nodded. "I understand all that. I'm also very sorry for the loss of your friend."

"Buzz MacDonald was a credit to this country," Don said.

"I know," Bill said. "And I want you to know this. You don't need a promise from Miles Richmond, or anyone else, to continue doing the important work that you've been doing. You don't need another person's promise to feel protected. That's because you have me."

He put his right hand over his heart as they walked. It was sappy, but that was okay. Bill Ryan had a tendency toward making sappy overtures. He'd been making them since the day Don met him when they were eighteen-year-old knobs at the Citadel. What made it okay was he meant every word he said.

"I swear," Bill said. "With God as my witness, while I'm alive and have any influence in this town, you have nothing to worry about."

"There are vipers everywhere," Don said.

He could try to articulate just how offensive it was to him that *they* had tried to derail this mission to protect a corrupt billionaire. That *they* were eavesdropping on his agency's communications. That *they* had sent assassins, to kill Buzz Mac, to kill Miles Richmond, and even to try to kill Luke Stone. But it would take too long, and be too complicated, to describe the depths of his revulsion.

"It's a snake pit," he said simply.

Bill nodded, more emphatically this time. "I know it. Don't you think I know it? And we're going to change that. I want you with me, Don. That's what I'm saying here. You and I are allies in the battle. I brought you here to stand between these two great presidents, so we could renew our love for, and our faith in, this country."

He stopped. Don did the same. Ahead of them, the massive spire of the Washington Monument pointed into the pale blue sky of morning.

Bill shook his head, as if ashamed. "This town… this government… it reminds me of an open sewer sometimes."

"I feel that," Don said.

"There are actual degenerates in positions of power and influence," Bill said. "This is how someone like Darwin King could thrive for as long as he did. The degenerates would sooner see good men die than lose an ounce of their own privilege. I believe that it's a disgrace before God. I believe that we can never reach greatness as a people again until these tendencies are hunted down, choked, and stamped out for good."

Don nodded. "Agreed."

This little walk was beginning to take on the passion of a church meeting. He imagined that Bill would have preferred to hear him say "Amen."

"You know," Bill said, "for years I comforted myself by saying that one day a real rain would fall, a hard rain, and wash these streets clean. But it didn't happen. And I asked why. Why does the rain never come? And only recently did the answer occur to me. Only recently did I finally understand why I've been waiting in vain so long."

Don looked into Bill's eyes. Everything in their environment, the early morning, the people hurrying to their offices, faded deep into the background.

"And why's that?" Don said.

Bill Ryan pointed at Don, then back to himself.

"Because waiting is the wrong answer. We can't wait for something outside of ourselves. You and I, and men like us… we are the rain."

NOW AVAILABLE!

PRIMARY DUTY
(The Forging of Luke Stone—Book #6)

"One of the best thrillers I have read this year."
--Books and Movie Reviews (re Any Means Necessary)

In PRIMARY DUTY (The Forging of Luke Stone—Book #6), a ground-breaking action thriller by #1 bestseller Jack Mars, a Supreme Court Justice is taken hostage by a terrorist organization. With a consequential decision before the court, the death of this swing Justice could change the political landscape for decades.

Getting him back, against the backdrop of a massive marvel of engineering, would be mission impossible—a mission that only elite Delta Force veteran Luke Stone, 29, and the FBI's Special Response Team, may be crazy enough to take on.

In this action-packed military thriller, filled with shocking twists and turns, the stakes as high as can be, Luke and his team may be up for their most challenging mission yet.

PRIMARY DUTY is a standalone, un-putdownable military thriller, a wild action ride that will leave you turning pages late into the night. The precursor to the #1 bestselling LUKE STONE THRILLER SERIES, this series takes us back to how it all began, a riveting series by bestseller Jack Mars, dubbed "one of the best thriller authors" out there.

"Thriller writing at its best."
--Midwest Book Review (re *Any Means Necessary*)

Also available is Jack Mars' #1 bestselling LUKE STONE THRILLER series (7 books), which begins with Any Means Necessary (Book #1), a free download with over 800 five star reviews!

Jack Mars

Jack Mars is the USA Today bestselling author of the LUKE STONE thriller series, which includes seven books. He is also the author of the new FORGING OF LUKE STONE prequel series, comprising six books; and of the AGENT ZERO spy thriller series, comprising twelve books.

Jack loves to hear from you, so please feel free to visit www.Jackmarsauthor.com to join the email list, receive a free book, receive free giveaways, connect on Facebook and Twitter, and stay in touch!

BOOKS BY JACK MARS

LUKE STONE THRILLER SERIES
ANY MEANS NECESSARY (Book #1)
OATH OF OFFICE (Book #2)
SITUATION ROOM (Book #3)
OPPOSE ANY FOE (Book #4)
PRESIDENT ELECT (Book #5)
OUR SACRED HONOR (Book #6)
HOUSE DIVIDED (Book #7)

FORGING OF LUKE STONE PREQUEL SERIES
PRIMARY TARGET (Book #1)
PRIMARY COMMAND (Book #2)
PRIMARY THREAT (Book #3)
PRIMARY GLORY (Book #4)
PRIMARY VALOR (Book #5)
PRIMARY DUTY (Book #6)

AN AGENT ZERO SPY THRILLER SERIES
AGENT ZERO (Book #1)
TARGET ZERO (Book #2)
HUNTING ZERO (Book #3)
TRAPPING ZERO (Book #4)
FILE ZERO (Book #5)
RECALL ZERO (Book #6)
ASSASSIN ZERO (Book #7)
DECOY ZERO (Book #8)
CHASING ZERO (Book #9)
VENGEANCE ZERO (Book #10)
ZERO ZERO (Book #11)
ABSOLUTE ZERO (Book #12)

Made in the USA
Monee, IL
31 August 2022